SLEEPER BEACH

ALSO BY NICK HARKAWAY

FICTION

Gnomon

Tigerman

Angelmaker

The Gone-Away World

Titanium Noir

Karla's Choice

AS AIDAN TRUHEN

The Price You Pay

Seven Demons

NON-FICTION

The Blind Giant: Being Human in a Digital World

SLEEPER BEACH

NICK HARKAWAY

corsair

To Heather

CORSAIR

First published in Great Britain in 2025 by Corsair

1 3 5 7 9 10 8 6 4 2

Copyright © Nick Harkaway, 2025

The moral right of the author has been asserted.

All characters and events in this publication, other than those clearly in the public domain, are fictitious and any resemblance to real persons, living or dead, is purely coincidental.

All rights reserved.
No part of this publication may be reproduced, stored in a retrieval system, or transmitted, in any form or by any means, without the prior permission in writing of the publisher, nor be otherwise circulated in any form of binding or cover other than that in which it is published and without a similar condition including this condition being imposed on the subsequent purchaser.

A CIP catalogue record for this book
is available from the British Library.

HB ISBN: 978-1-4721-5889-5
TPB ISBN: 978-1-4721-5890-1

Typeset in Utopia by M Rules
Printed and bound in Great Britain by
Clays Ltd, Elcograf S.p.A.

Papers used by Corsair are from well-managed forests
and other responsible sources.

Corsair
An imprint of
Little, Brown Book Group
Carmelite House
50 Victoria Embankment
London EC4Y 0DZ

The authorised representative
in the EEA is
Hachette Ireland
8 Castlecourt Centre
Dublin 15, D15 XTP3, Ireland
(email: info@hbgi.ie)

An Hachette UK Company
www.hachette.co.uk

www.littlebrown.co.uk

'Men make their own history, but they do not make it as they please; they do not make it under self-selected circumstances, but under circumstances existing already, given and transmitted from the past.'

From *The Eighteenth Brumaire of Louis Bonaparte*
—Karl Marx, 1852

1

"Big guy," the lifeguard says, like he's discovered fire. I tell him my name. When you have a name you're more than just a big guy.
"Oh, right, sure. From the city."

Every beach between Venice and Bondi they have lifeguards that look like the ones on TV, but here on the East Shore there's a different way of doing things. The Shore is different altogether, like an old man left alone too long. The pretty people of Chersenesos mostly spend their summer along the north side of the lake or they go to the Atlantic islands. The sand at the Shore is grey with volcano glass and sharp under your feet. Real people come here, in station wagons and flatbeds, and they stay in the little places, the rooming houses and bed and breakfasts all along the dunes, mixing with the ordinary business of a few final fishermen and the big industrial plants outside town. You have to go twenty kilometres inland before you find a farm, and even that is sheep and goats, because the grass is as grey and dusty as everything else. The whole place smells like wet concrete all year round. Athena says it's something in the soil.

"This way," the lifeguard says.

"What's your name?"

"Simmonds," he says. "Dan Simmonds. Born here." Some time ago, looks like, but everyone looks too old to me now.

"I was born in Laedecker," I say.

That's an hour away to the north.

"Oh, yeah?" Dan Simmonds looks back at me along the line of his shoulder. It's round and slouched, with no definition, not even under the fat. Likely he doesn't have a lot of call to get in the water and save people—he's more the binoculars type. The kids from the town do the heavy lifting, and Dan Simmonds' job is to keep them paying attention to the sea and not the pretty tourists, and to raise the red flag when there's too much plastic on the current for swimming.

"Never been up to Laedecker," Dan Simmonds says. "Hear it's modern." The way most people would say "horrible".

Doesn't matter. I was lying anyway.

Simmonds picks his way over the sand like a fat heron, then stops and leans down to a glitter of something between two clumps of seagrass. Not wearing gloves. Picks it up anyway.

"Is that evidence?"

"Naw," Simmonds says. He holds it up: a perfect lump of polished obsidian the size of a quail's egg. "Souvenir," he says, passing it to me. "They got glass like that in Laedecker?"

Of course they do. From here north for five hundred kilometres it's all this way: grey and desolate and pretty like the far side of the moon.

"Not like this," I tell him, holding it up like I just took it out of my pocket. "Man I met once gave me this piece of rock. In a place called Shearwater. Okay town. Seemed like an okay guy."

Simmonds grins. "You got city polish, son."

"How you figure?"

"Never spoke to anyone from Laedecker worth a damn."

Like Laedecker is a foreign land.

"Body's over there," Simmonds says, pointing.

He leads me over a rise and I see the sea laid out from one side of the world to the other. It's early morning, cool air lapping at the land, the sun low out to the east. If I look up or down the strand, I can see the twilight still hanging around like last night's partygoers, too full of regret to call it a night.

When you live in Othrys, you live in a little cup of mountains all about the black lake, deep and cold three kilometres to the bottom, but everything is contained. Tappeny Bridge and Chersenesos and all the worlds in between fit in a few square miles of land along the fresh water.

The Shore has a wider outlook. It's the scale of the planet, the limitations of human vision. On a calm day you're looking at the curvature of the earth as you turn your head to take it in. Hazy salt air and midnight waves, and a pale white sun high up in a washed-out blue sky. Even the sand comes alive, all those sharp edges glittering, whispering, as the sea turns them over against each other. In a few thousand years it'll be soft here.

I start to ask myself if there'll be anyone to appreciate it, and then remember who I am. If there is, it might be me.

"Mind your feet," Simmonds says. "Between here and the water."

I ask him what to watch out for. I figure maybe large pieces of obsidian, or some kind of snake.

"Naw," he says. "Sleepers."

"What do you mean, Sleepers?"

Simmonds waves his hand. I look again at the dunes, and I realise there are dozens.

The whole beach from the high-tide mark to the water is covered in old white plastic sunbeds. I guess someone bought a whole load and just donated them: cracked and jelly legged, they slump towards the grey sand. Lying on each one is a human figure no better off: wrapped in a white blanket, the unfinished emergency kind that's just as good as what you buy in a store and costs nothing at all. Old, young, men, women, all of them are lying on their sunbeds and staring at the sky and the sea.

"Sleepers," Simmonds says again. "Don't interfere."

"Interfere with what?"

"They come here to die," Simmonds replies. "A couple more every month. Just walk on the beach and sit down and wait. Some of 'em eat, some don't. Some get up and go home again. Some die, some just . . . stay here. Eat, sleep and stare."

"Why?"

Simmonds shrugs. "Cos of people like you, I guess." He gives me that look again, along the line of his round shoulder. "You are a Titan, ain't you?"

"Involuntary," I tell him, and he peers at me as if I've turned into a dog.

"Weirdest fucking thing to say," he murmurs. "Well, come on, then, Mr Involuntary."

We walk between the sunbeds.

The crime scene is just a dead woman, wet but not floating. The corpse wears jeans and a T-shirt, some kind of new-wave running shoe. The district coroner wears gum boots and a business suit. Her steel hair has a red artificial streak in it over the forehead, like she's a skater kid. Three piercings in each ear, some kind of ink not quite low enough on the neck to be hidden by the starched collar. Even rebels get old and get jobs. The dead woman looks like she was too nice for any of that. Cookies and cream, but still dead on the beach.

"Fallon," the coroner says. For a moment I think she's swearing, but then I realise it's her name.

"Sounder," I say, and she nods: sure, like there are two seven-foot detectives from Othrys. She takes off one glove and bags it and we shake hands. I've been practising for four years. I get the pressure perfect. She takes her hand back and looks at it for signs of wear and tear. Then we both glove up again.

Simmonds drifts away, job done. I wave at him, but he doesn't see.

"What have we got?" I ask Fallon, because there's a form, a way things are done. You follow the form so you don't throw up or cry. You don't want to throw up or cry because both of those things would be bad form. She leans down to the dead woman.

"Name in the clutch is Ailsa Lloyd. Realtor. Died . . ." she sighs.

"What?"

"I feel ridiculous," Fallon says.

"You're doing fine."

She stands up. "I was ready for tall."

"I am tall."

"You also look, like, sixteen years old."

I look twenty. At twenty I looked younger. I carry a little bit of fat in the jaw and cheeks.

"I have resting babyface," I tell her. "I'm forty-one."

"Sure, you say that and it says that in your file. I feel like I should tell you to look away."

"I'm not good at that."

"Do you want an ice cream before we start?"

I get down on my knees by Ailsa Lloyd and do Fallon's job. I look into her eyes and breath in through my nose, smelling the dead girl, the sea and the black sand, that underlying tang of brine and sulfur that never goes away here.

"Odour is mostly seawater, something else, maybe perfume. Vanillin. Not much sign of decomposition, but there might not be if she was in black water for a while. She doesn't look compressed, but I'm not sure how I'd tell if she had been. Crushed organs, maybe." Sometimes people try to hide bodies in the deep part of Othrys. The ones that go down to the bottom come back up like they've been hit with a bat all over at the same time.

Fallon nods in spite of herself. I pick up Ailsa Lloyd's hand and look at the nails. There's something blue under them: paint or clay, mixed in with some brown that's probably blood, usable trace if we're very lucky, more likely garbled now by seawater. "Damage to the knuckles and fingertips. She was probably in a fight, and she went out swinging, but it could be there's something else. Trying to open something, untie something. No ligature marks on the wrists or around the neck so she wasn't restrained, unless it was done while she was unconscious and didn't chafe. Even then I'd expect to see the bruising at this point so I'm going with no. Although there's a mark here from a bracelet. Chain links and something stubby . . . charms? Or bells. She wore it a lot." I get right down into the sand and try to peer up under her shirt. There's something huge, a bruise around her lower back like from a giant's arm. Probably an impact, though I wonder, standing on the shore, whether something grabbed her in the water. Maybe this was an animal attack, like you read about in old books: a squid stole her out of a boat. I don't say that to Fallon because I don't want to sound like a child: *Greatest Animal Stories Ever Told*. "I'm going to guess cause of death was drowning. Figure you'll find a couple of broken ribs, but that's not enough by itself. And I'm going to guess within the last nine hours, but she only washed up here within the last six."

Fallon frowns. "Where you getting that?"

"So the rest of it makes sense to you?"

"It's not obviously wrong. Give."

I get up on my feet. It always feels like it takes a long time now. I step back so I can look at Fallon without looming over her. The knee I put in the sand is wet, fabric clinging to my skin. Athena made me a gift five years ago, after I woke up: a new wardrobe for my new body, suits in a linen mix for the summer and mostly wool for winter, made specially for my line of work. Among other things, they don't wrinkle, and they won't stain just because I kneel in some sand. They're a little fine for who I used to be, and I'm not sure yet what the new me looks like, but I promised I'd wear them whenever I was working, so I do. In a few years they'll look as old as the suits that don't fit me any more, and by then maybe I'll have an idea of whether I want them to.

I brush the sand away and straighten up. "You don't care any more that I have babyface?"

"You really are as annoying as everyone says, aren't you?"

"I am."

"Come on, give." But maybe now it's one pro to another, just a little bit.

I look down at Ailsa Lloyd's perfect dead skin. "You got here five hours ago, maybe a bit more. That's when someone called me. It wasn't long before that she washed up."

"How you figure?"

I move my foot without looking and hear the crunch. Fallon winces.

"Crabs," I say.

We stand there a while with dead Ailsa Lloyd, listening to the sounds of the beach. Seagulls. Waves turning the glass in little rolls. Somewhere out on the water, a dredger boat, huge and slow. A suspect, I suppose, though I don't buy it. If someone on a dredger wanted someone to disappear, I'm pretty sure they'd get it done. If I wanted to disappear someone, here, I'm pretty sure that's who I'd call.

Under the noise of the faraway engine there's something else, like a wire brush on stone: all the Sleepers breathing, eyes wide and empty as they stare out to sea.

"I'll have the boys come and take her away," Fallon says. "You want to be there when I do the cutting?"

"No. What time?"

"I'll be in Dansen's at five thirty for coffee. Walk back across the road at five minutes to six. First incision ten minutes after."

"See you at five thirty."

"It's good coffee."

"I doubt it's good enough."

She sighs. "Name one that is."

That's as near as we get to goodbye. I turn and walk between the Sleepers, up the beach to the road.

The town of Shearwater is like a dusty precious stone set in a concrete ring. All around the beach and the promenade there are still a few boutiques, for the pretty people and the students who drift by in the summer; for the local well-to-do—the owners of big fishing boats and family farms, the makers of artisanal local apple juice. Further inland are the cheap offices: the sprawling engine rooms of a dozen firms whose Chersenesos presences are single floors in the expensive towers, photogenic partners in windowed studios leaning on the telepresent others in these run-down and half-converted golden age casinos, lettered window glass replaced with the wired kind, and frontages still studded with the iron rods that once held neon signs. Along the promenade you can still see the ghosts of expensive labels on the boarded retail lots. Every hundred feet or so there are men and women with blankets covered in hats and sunglasses, or cycle carts of water, ice cream and hot dogs. Not enough custom for as many of them as there are: maybe competition gets violent. Maybe Ailsa Lloyd got caught in a hot dog drive-by.

If this place was still what it was there'd be a steeper class of idlers, cozeners and thieves wearing their best clothes and talking in loud voices about that party at Erskine Hill—the wine, the dancing, the scandal. Talking Monet and Klee on the walls at our place in Chersenesos, but of course simply everyone knows Martha likes the Dutch Masters and modern Bauhaus, and a wink and a smile and a friendly evening: bright angler-fish lures to roll tourists and fresh-faced kids into clip joints, rigged backroom games, rash romantic marriages culminating in humiliating October pay-offs. There'd be models and wannabes tumbling in and out of these stores, bags stuffed with ridiculous fashions, instead of steel shutters on all the vacant spaces and stencils peeling off the glass. Halfway down, between a pharmacy, with its green cross blinking in the early light, and a bookmaker shoehorned into what I'm pretty sure used to be a nail salon, there's a line of broken windows, building bricks lying inside on the floor amid the boxes of new fittings for some last-ditch effort at commercial life.

There'd be hope and greed mingled on this street, back in the old days.

Instead, it's morning, before the day really gets going, and there's just down-and-outs and fishermen, not always easy to pick apart because to be honest there's a sliding scale now. This decade hasn't been kind to Shearwater, nor the one before. Most of the fishermen have no boat to go to, because even the fish don't come here any more. They're sitting on the flaked white wooden benches facing a sea that never cared. Some of them have the greyed-out middle age of muscle and weather, that looks ancient when you're fifty-five. Others are young, in their twenties and just now realising this isn't going to be their world.

Young fishermen don't look the part. They're fit and fresh-faced and they wear clothes that layer well, don't soak up water. You'd take them for hikers or boot camp fitness coaches, except all of them have fast-release catches on their shoes and something weighty in one pocket that works to cut a longline or a net if it drags you in and down. You only have seconds before you go too deep to come back up.

As I walk by, two of them get up and start moving towards me. One is young, red hair cut close to the scalp, beard grown to the same length. The other's older, harder, low-grade ink on his knuckles: FISH FOOD. I adjust slightly to give them room, and so do they. No sense changing lanes again, they want to talk, probably throw me a scare. The other thing about being the big guy: a certain kind of passer-by just has to try his luck. So I make like this whole thing was my idea.

"Morning, gentlemen. My name's Cal Sounder. Figure you've heard there's been a murder."

Figure they haven't, because even rumour takes a while to get out of bed.

"A what?"

"A murder. There's a woman dead on the south beach by the foot of the promenade. Killed. Not a Sleeper. Just a civilian trying to get by like anyone else. Now, if a body washed ashore there, on the beach by all of those white loungers, who's the best person to tell me where it went in the water?"

They're still catching up. This conversation was supposed to run along a different track.

"Bill Tracey," says the younger one. "He might know." His friend rolls his eyes.

"Where'd I find him?"

"Boathouse, most likely. *Evermore*'s in dry dock."

"Point me the way?" There's cash in my hand now, not offered but implicate. "I'm way out of my home range, gentlemen, and I could use advice."

The older one shakes his head. "*Evermore*'s in the Mahalo

boathouse. That's on the other side of the Sleeper beach. South. Whatever. But you can find your own way."

"Thank you kindly."

I go to step past them and they watch me. There's not quite enough room to get by.

"Gentlemen?"

"Mister?"

"Do we have more we need to discuss right now?"

The older one shakes his head.

"I don't know that I believe there's a dead woman, fella. I think maybe you're having a joke with me and my friend here. Not the kind of joke I like."

The other bench-sitters are starting to pay attention. Pretty soon we'll have an audience and this'll go bad. Pride and hurt on the line: city boy with the temerity to walk in their street when they've got no jobs unless one of the captains comes by today with a berth. Unless they go inland to the factory. Unless they pick fruit or clean floors, and those are no jobs for a fisherman. And here I am, in their way. City boy.

Big city boy.

I make like he said something funny, then like I'm telling my story and it's a good one. Like this is all going just lovely. The audience on the benches loses interest a little, but not much. Through the smile:

"Tell you, boys, to this point we've made conversation even if we haven't made friends. You've refrained from being rude about my clothes and my babyface, and I've shown you some respect in your own town. Offered you some honest work that you chose not to take. Now, that's your right, I'm not holding a grudge and nor should you. That respect, that's a solid win on both sides. But I figure you, sir—I'm going to call you Mr Fish—you have a clasp knife in that pocket and, you—Mr Food—that's for sure a cordcutter in the back of your jeans, and those things are giving you a mistaken sense of purpose and invulnerability. I got to tell you your minds are in the wrong place. You don't want to be thinking about what's in your pockets. You want to be very concentrated about what's in mine. I'd be a damn fool to imagine I could beat you at fishing or navigating or piloting, now, wouldn't I? A damn fool. But there's a voice in your heads suggesting you have a chance to match me in my own professional competences. Ask yourselves how wrong that would be, positions reversed. And then when you're done thinking, let's pass by one another and keep all that respect we got."

Count to five. One. Two. Older man has his hand in his pocket now. Touching that clasp knife. But that's all he's doing. Three. He's just reassuring himself that he could make an issue, if he wanted to. I can see shame in him, but I don't know if it's because he almost started something or because he's now backing off. Hold the moment. Four. Five.

And then it's gone, that possibility of blood on flagstones, and we're just three guys walking different directions, sharing the day on the dirty street.

Welcome to Shearwater. It used to be nice here.

The rooming house is called Celia's. Celia's what? Hope? Hobby? Alimony? No further information given, and Celia is absent but present, her style everywhere, her family knick-knacks on all the tables. In the hallway there's a picture of someone posing with the original Erskines, Zac and Martha: a narrow white guy and a broad black woman, holding hands, and off to one side a too-cheery dark-haired extra making smiley face for the camera. Is it Celia or her however-many-times grandmother? Shearwater's roots are Portuguese and Angolan; its original name is Zagueiro, which the second and third waves of migration from flooded northern cities mistook for something to do with água. *I'm on a trip in West Africa*, says Celia's handwritten note, pinned to a board. *Please enjoy the house.* I can't help but wonder how old it is. Has she been back this century? If she even really exists at all.

Celia's surrogate is called Miles, but he's almost as invisible as she is. Grey as the waterline, he shows me to my room and then vanishes, butler style, into the back stairs.

The main rooms look right out over the sound to the little automated lighthouse that doesn't need to be there any more: a fat, short tower painted in red and white candy stripes, topped with a pair of parabolic mirrors the size of coffee tables floating on a bed of two-hundred-year-old mercury. It has a horn, too, controlled from a weather station half the country away, so sometimes on bright days when the air is clear and clean the low note moans across the bay and all the kids on kiteboards dodging clumps of plastic in the water cheer and wave.

My room is on the top floor, with pretty wooden beams in an A-frame over my head and a modern wall made of electro glass so I can be private when I want, or open up to the night and the sea. It's nice but not sophisticated or expensive. The water whispers in the tank under the eaves, and I hear the food is awful. Athena offered me a beach house, but I wanted to be in the ordinary flow of Shearwater, to trip over the same paving stones and curse the same poor civic planning as any other tourist. They say you're never more than two metres from a rat anywhere in the human world. The Tonfamecasca property portfolio is the same: for all I know we own Celia's. More likely we own the bank which holds the note for half the town. The other half is the Erskine family, old money from before T7 changed the landscape of economic power. An old man becomes a teenager again, wounds heal and skin gets taut. Scars are swallowed up. I read in an old book Athena gave me that wanting to lose the lines on your face means you haven't learned their lessons. I wonder what the author would make of the Titans, getting younger and bigger and richer with every dose. I wonder what she'd make of me.

Although I hear the Erskine family value their earned, lived wisdom when they buy their new youth. Their matriarch, anyway, must be as old as Stefan himself. I'd call them competitors, but no one competes with Stefan Tonfamecasca for the same reason that the Tonfamecasca company never has to advertise. There are comparable fortunes: the people who own the Internet, the energy people, the agri people. But Tonfamecasca owns post-mortality.

All the queens and kings of silicon, all the emperors of wheat and wind and waves: all of them, in the end, come knocking at Stefan's enormous door. Erskine is mining, plastic reclamation and carbon capture, plus whatever they can make from those processes. Billionaires in a stable state, neither expanding nor contracting. Athena finds them interesting. Athena finds all permanence and circularity interesting.

I open my suitcase and carry three outfits to the closet. I put my sponge bag on the tray under the mirror, a pair of smart shoes in a cubby at what for most people is knee height. You can hardly call it unpacking. I lie down on the bed. It's a superking, which means that if I lie diagonally, it's just large enough that I don't feel like someone's going to cut off my feet while I'm sleeping. The springs creak under me, paying their way. Just enough support that I don't feel like I'm in a hammock. Not enough that I want to stay here too long. I lie down for a while and think about nothing, and I miss the little window in my apartment that shows me the sky. The electro-glass wall is huge and perfectly angled, and all along the A-frame where you can't see there are little purple lights to draw the bugs in and suck them away to some incinerator deep down in the lower floors. Perfect convenience, but cold and hard as bone.

After a while, out on the water, the lighthouse wakes up: a long, dismal noise like learning to play an instrument no one wants to hear.

Walking down the main street in high day feels somewhere between roasting and haunted. Shearwater is mottled by decline, little retail islands still high and fine and cute, dressed stone and Deco steel storefronts, starbursts in bronze or nickel cut into the roads at each intersection. It has a town centre someone took pains over a longish while back, and even though there's grime now, and black obsidian dust in the cracks, you can't see the real decay unless you look for it: the lights that don't work, so many broken windows, boarded and left alone. The patches in everything.

At the turning, the beeper for the crosswalk screams a single continuous note that sounds like a seabird finding its nest full of half-eaten eggs. People turn to look at me because no one local ever uses it, and then they keep looking because people do. I have resting babyface and I'm seven feet tall. They look at me until I'm all the way over, and around the corner, and then the world starts again.

Dansen's, opposite the coroner's office, used to be a beach bar until the tide changed. It's empty now, at the wrong end of the shore. The Sleepers have taken over the beach in front of it, wandering back and forth at the edge of the water, empty-eyed and weird like cave fish. The deck is still there, faded sun umbrellas and a freezer chest for ice cream. The pictures on the side of the chest are as old as I am, bleached white at the corners, names I used to look out for: Kraken came in three colours for grape, lime and blueberry; MisterRacer was stripes of peach and apple; Lucky 7 was vanilla on the inside and some weird frozen shell with a random number printed on it, and if you got a seven they sent you a prize, though I never did. Oyster, RocketDog, ShimSham, Maid Marion, Ghost Eyes. All the old familiar flavours, except almost none of them exist any more, and when I look in the chest there's just a single box of ices, too covered in frost to see the brand, and the rest is full of frozen lobsters. Imported, because there used to be a factory at Laedecker, and the ones here are full of chrome.

"Hi," Fallon says, across a cup of something dark and unappealing. "I've done the scans."

Autopsies start with x-rays and CT scans; things you can do before you break what can't be put back. People get hung up on the cutting so much they forget there's a lot you can tell by just looking.

"I'll have one of those, only less so," I tell the waiter, and he laughs.

"There you go, with that boyish charm," Fallon says, "I just want to reach over and pinch your little cheeks."

"You're just pissed off because you don't like doing autopsies on nice people."

"How do you know she was nice?"

"Because you're pissed off."

"Well, that's great."

Fallon drinks. I wonder if it's just coffee, or if there's white liquor in it. I wouldn't take alcohol before cutting a murder victim if I was in her shoes—but if I was in her shoes, I wouldn't be able to stand my job.

"So what's in the scans?"

"Nothing. Childhood fracture, left arm. Spiral pattern. Fell off a swing, maybe."

"Or maybe not."

"Statistically, it's the swing. But yeah, maybe not."

Fallon's eyes are set deep in her face. Twenty years ago, she would have looked brittle. Now there's a kind of beauty, a strength of bone and time. Exactly the kind of thing T7 would take from her, not that anyone will give Fallon a dose. No Titan would ever notice her except me, and I'm not running around with that kind of power in my pocket.

I say: "Did you meet her?"

"Me?"

"It's a small town. Mutual interests, maybe. That would make it hard."

"I never met her."

"But you know someone who did."

"Like you said, it's a small town."

"And they say she was nice."

"They do."

"You mind I ask who?"

She slides a handwritten paper across the table. I put it in my wallet next to a couple of small bills and a picture of Athena long ago, and the waiter brings me something like black lava in a steel cup. Fallon says we need to go across the road. The waiter says she can bring the cups back another time.

We walk together, like we're friends, and I look down towards the sea and the white sun loungers. Figure Fallon is a doctor.

"What's wrong with them?"

She scowls. "What does it look like?"

"It looks like the beach furniture of the damned, but that's not what it is. Why doesn't someone fix it?"

"They're not an 'it'."

"If you don't want to talk about them I'll ask someone else."

"They have spontaneous dysphoric and psychogenic cognitive atrophy. Okay? Is that better?"

"It sounds like words put together to sound like a thing."

"Well, then, they're dying of no one gives a shit."

She takes me through the neat little cottage-style door and down into the Shearwater mortuary.

The cutting station is all steel and ceramic tiles and high Kelvin lighting. At least the bulbs are the modern kind, not the weird old lamps Musgrave the city pathologist has in Chersenesos, which emit green and purple tints to counterfeit daylight white, and make even the living look like corpses. Ailsa Lloyd is pale and pretty on the slab, laid out by some nameless flunky so that she seems as if she's sunbathing.

Fallon reaches out to offer me a paste to go under my nose, but I wave it away. Every medical examiner has their own favourite: menthol; cajput, cinnamon and clove; cedar and camphor. This one smells like thyme, and I wonder if she ever eats lamb that way any more. The idea is to overwhelm the scent of the corpse, especially if you're dealing with decomposition, and if we were then I'd take it, but Ailsa Lloyd isn't that far gone, and sometimes there are answers in the odours of the dead. I won't shut my eyes when Fallon begins to cut; why would I block my nose?

She shrugs and turns back to the body on the bench, attending to detail. Her eyes and her fingers investigate, walking like butterflies over the dead flesh, scraping the blue funk out from under the nails and straight to the hopper of a chromatograph, lifting the maybe-blood into another sampler destined for a different machine. In Othrys, there's a central lab right by Musgrave's office and all the other stations send their little slides and vials. Here the machine is a smaller model, slower and older, but this isn't a bulk operation. Fallon takes the sample and slides it into a black box, and a moment later the terminal chirps.

"Paint," she says, like that's helpful. I wait for a moment, and she adds, "Waterproof seal paint." Which is better—but here, not much. We'll get a brand name later, if we're lucky.

The door opens and two men come in, uniform cops from across the way. The first one is Dijkstra. The second is called Keenan. I looked them up when I knew I was coming here. Officer Keenan has strong hands and sharp little eyes set in a round face. Spectacles, mid-grade; watch, mid-grade; shoes, top of the range for an actual working stiff. He likes walking holidays and line dancing. It takes all sorts to make a world.

"You must be Sounder," Keenan says.

"Yes, sir. Thank you for making room for a private consultant."

Out the corner of my eye, I can see Fallon staring at me. It's really not so absolutely shocking that I know how to be nice.

"Didn't have much choice, now did we, Mr Sounder?"

"Nope. But that doesn't mean I shouldn't thank you. Manners don't cost me anything."

The other cop snorts. "Didn't think Titans worried much about cost." Dijkstra: angrier, but not at me. Dijkstra, J. S. is angry when he wakes up in the morning. That's why his marriage is four years in the tank and he can't catch a break in a bucket.

"Well, sure, and the rumour is that I am kind of an asshole, but that doesn't mean I have to be the same kind as all the others."

Keenan can't quite stop himself from laughing, but only once, and it isn't the kind of sound that feels out of place in this room.

"This is Dijkstra," Keenan says, just remembering his manners. "I'm Keenan. Captain Iverson'd be here, but he's up at the house."

Like there's only one, so that would be Bail Erskine's house, the big old mansion that looks down on the whole of Shearwater.

"I greatly look forward to not making your job any harder than it has to be," I tell them both. "I probably will piss you off a time or two, but I aim it should be in the course of doing my job, not because I'm just annoying to have around."

Keenan takes my hand and lets it go. It barely counts as a handshake.

"Believe it when I see," Dijkstra replies, and when he shakes my hand he does test the grip. I let him grind the bones a little, and he quits, happy.

"If you're ready," Fallon says, and we all stand in line like schoolkids so she can open up a dead woman and show us things we never wanted to see. She pulls back the sheet and I make sure to get another first impression before she starts: mid-twenties, strong but pretty face. High forehead now that someone has brushed back her hair and combed it out for trace. Out of nowhere, I think of children's parties and babysitters, yellow ice cream and jelly. A mark from a watch on the right wrist rather than the left. Dimple on the littlest finger of one hand: Ailsa wore a signet ring. A small tattoo, unexpected, over her heart: a black bird on the wing. Keenan sighs once and looks away.

"You going to cut through the ink?" he says.

Fallon cocks her head. "Seems a shame. I'll try not to."

The last favour anyone can do for Ailsa Lloyd.

An hour later it's over and I'm standing outside watching Keenan and Dijkstra walk away, and we all know we're stuck with each other. It really doesn't matter if they never call me, but if they ever do I will take that call and listen to what they have to say, be it tomorrow or next year or some impossibly distant day in the future, because once you have stood with someone by a steel table and seen the dead interior of what should be a person held up and weighed and bagged, they can always call. It's not the same for Fallon and she knows it: the person doing the cutting doesn't get to join the team, so she has her own, even more tight and for ever than ours.

When I took off the plastic baggie shoes they make you wear, there was spatter on them. I folded them away and wondered as I always do if I should give them a decent burial rather than putting them in the contaminated equipment box for incineration. Now I'm walking down the street feeling my feet not slip the way they did inside the cutting room, with the baggie shoes and the brushed steel floor. Solid ground and contact, not sterile, and welcome back in the world.

Four kids go past me on scooters laughing, and a woman in a business suit runs for a cab. The cab is Olde Worlde, that's the actual brand, with a horn that makes a cheerful honk. The woman is embarrassed but she evidently needs to be somewhere. Her face as the cab pulls away is harried and drawn.

I keep walking, listening to the street. Orientation is part of the job: learn the place where it happened, see what everyone sees. Not the unusual but the given, the assumptions that are too obvious to mention.

People think investigation is like what Fallon does, because that's how it is in the movies. They think that you gather facts and put them together like the pieces of a broken picture and when you're done, even if you don't have all the pieces, you can still see the face of what happened. Sometimes, I suppose, you can do it that way, but mostly the world is an endless shingle of the pieces of nine billion puzzles falling from the sky and sliding one over another until they drift like snow. If you could get far enough away, perhaps you'd be able to see a single face that would tell you what it all means.

I'm not sure I ever want to get that far back. I think that journey is the one Stefan is on, further and further from the surface, knowing more and more and less and less as you travel until finally you've become something so vast it's impossible to distinguish you from the sky.

Instead, you can find out about a thing by sitting in the place where it happened, walking and listening and seeing, until the space gets smaller and smaller around you and in the end there's just you and what was done, so close to one another that you know it by touch before ever you can speak its name.

So that's what I do. I walk, and I look around at a holiday town grown old.

I walk down to the part of the beach where the Sleepers aren't and sit with my back against a low wall, and from there, looking out at the sea where Ailsa Lloyd died, I call the office. The phone answers on the second ring.

"Cal Sounder Investigations," says Taormina Denton.

Five years ago, I got in a fight with two Titan wannabes named Mac and Mini Denton, and afterwards it turned out that Mac Denton was a coercive asshole and Mini was actually not a bad person. I hooked her up with a friend who specialises in little people fighting much bigger people, and after she kicked Mac out she was looking for a job about the same time that I needed an assistant.

"Hey, Sporty Jasmine."

I was heavily anaesthetised the second time we met, and Mini was wearing a very particular perfume. They haven't even sold it now for half a decade, which is why the name is more hilarious every time I use it.

"Always funny, Cal. How's the Shore?"

"You ever go to your grandma's house and realise she was really broken down and sad?"

"No. She's a terrifying old woman who eats beige food and does distance walking. What did the coroner say?"

"Murder by drowning."

"That's horrible."

I wonder if it's more horrible than any other way. Is murder incremental? And if it is, does that mean it can be done in parts, hollowing someone out until the corpse stops walking?

Until the person just lies down and sleeps their life away?

Mini Denton taps on her phone, sharp shellac nails against the mouthpiece. "Hey, Cal? You there? You want the jacket now?"

"Highlights."

Deep breath. "Ailsa Lloyd, twenty-six, not married. Apartment in West Bridge which she shares with a trainee music therapist named Tilly. Not shares like romance, shares like they found each other in the small ads looking for a halfway decent place to live. Works for Deerborn Real Estate, has done for two years. They're a buyer's agent. You know what that is?"

"Very rich people use them to save money buying very expensive things."

"And to get those things before other very rich people do."

"She on the clock down here?"

"Apparently so."

"Do we know who for?"

"Jove Media. But we do not know why, or what exactly they wanted to buy."

I wonder if it's the whole town, or just a summer house the size of an airfield.

"Go make nice at Deerborn. Then do friends and family."

"Boyfriend girlfriend, watercooler, Uncle Freddie with the inappropriate eyeline. Gotcha."

"You get any sign of Uncle Freddie, call Chief Gratton and find out whether he or she does more than look."

"Statistically, it's he."

"Statistically I'm not a Titan and Mac put your body in a barrel full of lye. You're not wrong, but check anyway."

She laughs, free and sharp. "He wishes. Sleep tight, boss."

She doesn't know I have a meeting at midnight. I don't tell Mini everything. Not yet. It's a habit of mine to hold things back, even from people I trust. It's how I know I can trust them.

When you call my office out of hours you get a service. The service offers you three options: call back in daylight, leave a message, or use the flare line. That's flare like when you're a ship in trouble, when you don't have time for the ordinary rhythm of life. When you're about to be arrested; when you're scared and you can't call the cops; when you just flat out don't know what else to do. Calling the flare line is supposed to mean paying for the premium tier, but most people who can pay for the premium tier don't need the flare line. Most times I just get woken up and all I can do—all they want me to do—is listen to the worst stories you've ever heard; to problems that don't yield to my kind of solutions, problems with mean banks or hurtful words or the missed opportunities that make up what we call the world. For every big break there's a thousand that didn't fly.

A little after five a.m. this morning, the flare line rang. Athena made a little noise and turned over. A strand of hair was in the corner of her mouth and I scooped it out, then slipped away into the living room. There's a fake fur throw on one of the couches that I leave there so I can take calls without getting cold.

"Sounder."

"I need you, Mr Sounder. Shearwater, as soon as you can."

"Who is this?"

"If you open your banking window, you'll find a retainer already paid and an escrow note with a daily fee and bonus structure exceeding your most inflated rate. You want the beach south of the town. Ask for Fallon."

A woman's voice, deep, cultured, serious. No hurry, no panic, just haste. I opened the banking window, but I didn't need the confirmation.

"All right," I said. "I'll be there. You want to tell me anything else?"

"I'll meet you later. Further up the strand, where the old hotel used to be."

"Why there?"

A pause. "Do you know Shearwater?"

"No. But you do. Why there?"

Laughter, like stones in a brook. "I like you already, Mr Sounder. See you at midnight."

She cut the call, and I went to the guest room for the go kit I keep there, next to the one Athena has made up, her long coat folded neatly on top, the second-chance armour panels slotted into place.

Somehow, when the TV crews come through to show the world the life of Stefan Tonfamecasca's favoured child, they always stop at the walk-in closet and the dozens of shoes. If they asked about the coat, they'd have to consider why someone might have beef, and they don't want to do that out loud.

Figure the "old hotel" means the Grand Erskine, the husk north of town with what used to be private access to the water and an arm of shingle sweeping out into the bay, perfect for late-afternoon sun. Now it's all shadows and soft sounds in the summer night: laughter between the vines growing up the old facade, in the scars of fire and rain.

Shearwater was one time *the* place to go. The Erskines were rich and beautiful, and the burg was what they call unspoiled: a fishing town with character, gourmet food and spas. There was a private rail line direct from Othrys Union to the Shearwater Marina station, and in early July the road to the Grand Erskine Hotel had so many limousines on it you'd think it was the most expensive funeral cortège in the world. Then the tides changed, the plastic came in and the imported yellow sand washed away. Something something Atlantic thermocline, and now between Reykjavik and the Gulf of St Lawrence there's a valley in the ocean floor that's pale honey like Hanimaadhoo, three thousand metres deep. The Grand Erskine burned down one winter and they never bothered to build it up again. The hulk sits quiet along the north beach, a fine and picturesque ruin where Chersenesos photographers do underwear shoots and local kids get stoned and have sex. It's a little too early in the night for that, I suppose, but there's a party starting somewhere, brash and stupid and fun. Someone's running lights off a high-capacity battery, flashing white and purple and gold.

I find a date palm leaning the right way and sit down under it, my back against the trunk. After a little while, a boat ticks in and a dozen kids get out. I call them kids but they're in their twenties, perfect and real. One of them stumbles, and the others tease him for it. They make their way across the beach to the hotel, not seeing me because they're not looking. There's a pecking order, the way there always is, a tall handsome boy in the middle of the pack is in charge: every romantic lead in every teen movie ever, dark hair with curls and a deep beach tan. He's playing chivalrous to a pretty brunette in a dress that qualifies on a technicality. When they get to the low wall between the beach and the Grand Erskine, she makes him lift her over and holds on, shoulders and chest pressing. Then she gives him a high-voltage smile and breaks away.

When the hell did I get so old?

And how do I look younger than them?

I'm still sitting there a half hour later when the sound system blows out and the lights flicker and die, and suddenly the whole beach is quiet. The party kids are silent with surprise, and just for a while I can hear another sound drifting along the shore. A shuffle and scrape, and an endless shared sigh: the sound of the Sleepers almost a kilometre away.

I wonder if they ever have sex. Do people waiting to die have sex? Yes, obviously. But do people who have chosen this kind of dying, who lay down each night and wait each day for death—does that kind of person still have sex? If you had sex on the regular, might that not lead to life, again? Does anyone ever get up and walk away from those sunbeds, just back into the daytime world?

The kids are back, torches in hand as they work on the lights. The boy from the boat is out front, fussing with the battery, re-starting everything. The girl is with him, giving instructions, and it's pissing him off. I can hear them arguing: she's right and he's wrong. They need to reset the board first, then the trip, and finally turn all the gear back on. He doesn't listen, and when the lights come up there's a pop, that rich funky sound of media equipment overloading, then shutting down.

"Torrance," the girl says clearly, into the silence. "You're an asshole." Like it's not news to either of them.

Torrance glares at her.

"Fuck you."

"Oh, definitely never again."

I figure he'll call her names and walk away. For a kid like Torrance there's always another fish, even or especially in a town like this one. Instead, he gets quiet and comes back towards her, hands by his sides like he wants to talk this out, even apologise. Maybe he does, but I'm not sure. I stand up and start walking, just fast enough that I can slow down to a kind of amble when I get to where they are.

"Oh," I say, like I'm embarrassed. "Hi."

Torrance stares at me. "Who the fuck are you?"

"I'm Cal."

"Well, get lost, Cal."

"Actually, I kind of am lost. Hey, what's your name?"

"If you don't know, you really don't need to."

"Oh, okay. But could you tell me how to get to the Grand Erskine Hotel?"

The girl laughs. It's not unkind.

Torrance glares at me, then at her. A minute ago he had a bunch of obvious imperatives: deal with me, fix things with the girl, fix the lights, be the hero, get laid. Now I'm a wandering idiot and he's lost his rhythm. He stares a minute longer.

"It's right there in front of you, guy." He rolls his eyes. "Hey, Ashley?"

Ashley sighs. "Yes, Torrance?"

He flips her the bird with both hands, low at the waist, and wanders off.

Ashley rolls her eyes. "Asshole," she says again. Then she looks over at me, careful. "Was that a rescue?"

"I just happened by."

"Sure. So who are you, Cal?"

"Support staff," I say. "Summer job. If you call out the switches, I'll reset the board, and you can have the whole thing up and running."

She steps away, over to the rest of the gear, and doesn't turn her back. Smart kid. She walks me through the shutdown, and when the lights come back up this time, they stay that way.

"Hey, Ashley. You happen to know a woman named Ailsa Lloyd?"

"Another woman when I'm standing right here?"

"I don't think fixing a lighting board makes us that close."

"Sure, I met her a few times."

"What was she like?"

A moment's thought. "Elsewhere."

"Distracted?"

"Sort of. That thing where someone's not in the room, even when they are. So, who are you, seriously?"

"Cal. Seriously."

"Support staff Cal. Looks like a basketball player but with those eyes that go all the way to the horizon. I'm used to men looking through my clothes. Not so much through me, though."

"Does that make me elsewhere, too?"

"Maybe."

"I'll try to be more predictable."

"You do that." She grins. "That's some terrible bullshit, Cal. You're just wandering around in the dark to help out at an illegal beach party. Do better, my man."

"I go where I get paid."

"How old are you?"

"Older than you."

"You have babyface."

"I do."

She reaches out for my hand. "Ashley."

"So I gather."

We shake, and I hear a tinkling sound and look down at her wrists. She's wearing bracelets, loose—quite a few.

"So . . . Cal Babyface, you wanna be my new date?"

I can smell coconut and white musk. She has to tilt her face to look at mine.

"I have a thing."

"But if you didn't?"

"Well, Ashley, if I didn't have to be where I'm going, I'd have to be someplace else. But if you mean are you all kinds of gorgeous in that dress you are very nearly wearing, then the answer is yes.

And if there is a smart kid in your group who knows what a job is and makes you feel good about yourself, I would go ask that one to be your date."

"Mom? Is that you?"

"Have a great night, Ashley."

"Hey Cal?"

"Ashley."

"What if the lights go out again? What if I need more support?"

I give her my card. It just says my name and number. She flicks it with her thumbnail.

"This is a nice card."

"I guess."

"Petherbridge satin, there hundred and forty gsm."

"The woman knows her paper stock."

"Beats the dress all to hell, right?"

It does not, in any way at all.

"Gift from a client," I tell her. "That's the last one. Then I'm back to reading out my number so you can send me a message."

She grins. "Thanks for your help, Cal."

"You're welcome, Ashley."

Black satin and beach shoes laced to mid-calf. She walks away, carefully careless, and part of me can't stop watching. I'm a new Titan, which makes me, libidinously, about nineteen or twenty years old. I see sex everywhere the way a paranoid sees cameras. I see sex in table legs and clouds, in the leather seats of expensive automobiles and the smooth lines of copper bathtubs. I see sex everywhere because it is, but if it's everywhere, it's not evenly distributed, and Ashley walking back to the Grand Erskine with my card held high between her long, strong fingers is a high-density phenomenon.

I wait until she's gone inside, then drift away up the beach to the water. It's midnight in two minutes, and I find the place where the bright light of the party casts the blackest shadow on the black shingle and I can disappear. I lean down and pick up a handful of glass pebbles and throw them one by one into the water. Maybe I'll hit a fish. *Splash.*

Torrance absolutely is an asshole.
I throw another one. *Splash.*
Splash.
Splash.
And then nothing, like my fifth pebble just goes away somewhere. A wave rolls in out of synch with the others, like there's another boat coming, a big one, and then the little chunk of sea-polished glass lands with a thunk in the wet seaweed at the tideline in front of me. A ghost of a chuckle, like stones in a brook, and a shape too big to be what it is.

"Hello, Mr Sounder. I'm Martha Erskine."

It takes me a while to make her out in the water. In the dark she looks momsy, fifty-five and domestic. That sort of serious yes-young-man-you-will-still-tidy-your-room-when-you-come-home-from-college face. Not old, not young, and very broad. A living face, full of acquired smarts and uncommon sense. The face in the picture with Celia's great-aunt. But big.

Really big.

"I'm your client," Martha Erskine says. "You could at least offer me a towel."

"I don't have one."

"And I'm not getting out of the water. I so rarely do, any more. But it's the form of the thing, you know. And I know you do know. Athena says you're ever so gentlemanly."

"I thought late-stage Titans couldn't swim."

"But I like to swim, Mr Sounder. Why else would I live by the sea?"

"Would you like me to get you a towel?"

"No, dear. And they don't make one big enough for me, anyway."

Truth. She must be sitting in the water. The shelf goes out shallow for a hundred metres beyond the waterline, and Martha's body is all submerged, moonlight picking out the ripples at her neck.

As big as Stefan, maybe bigger, but the voice is different. Maybe it's because we're outside, and it's coming over the sea, but it's not painful to hear.

I don't ask how old she is. A gentleman doesn't, and I really don't want to annoy her. Martha Erskine is a four-dose Titan, or—if she was petite to begin with—even five. And that makes her far and away the oldest Erskine alive, the actual matriarch of that whole family. That means she personally owns . . . oh, just about everything worth having for a hundred miles up and down the East Shore.

"What can I do for you, Ms Erskine?"

"Martha."

"What can I do for you Martha? I'm Cal."

"I know you are, Mr Sounder."

All right, then. I wait for her to answer the question.

"You can find out who killed Ailsa Lloyd, of course."

"Why?"

"You can find that out too."

"I mean why do you care?"

"It's not enough that she's a nice dead girl on my beach?"

"It's not."

"It is."

"No, it's not. You have a hundred guys for that."

"Ohhhh, well. Those. Corporate men. And women. I don't know if you've noticed, Mr Sounder, but within a structure like the Erskine Company people tend to lose initiative and individual thinking. Consensus takes over. I don't need consensus, I need answers."

"You asked already."

"I did."

"Who?"

"Bail's people. That's Bail Erskine, of course, CEO in this generation. My . . . oooohhh, great-great-something. Grandson. Nephew. One of those. A sensible boy, but quite driven. Getting a little silly now he's turned seventy. Time for him to join the T7 ranks, but he's holding out for a few years of natural age. Don't ask me why. Authenticity of experience, he says. Young people nonsense."

"So what do Bail's people say?"

Her face flickers. It's hard to play poker when you're that big. For a moment she's looking at the Grand Erskine Hotel.

"You just saw their answer on this beach, Mr Sounder."

The pretty kids and their boat. The boy with that absolute certainty of ownership, his hand on Ashley's waist.

"Torrance?"

She nods. "Torrance James Erskine, of course."

He didn't seem like a kid with a fresh murder on his conscience, but maybe he doesn't have one.

"And why would Torrance kill Ailsa Lloyd?"

"A very easy story for me to swallow. You might almost think that was its most salient feature. Pretty entitled boy meets pretty poor girl and they strike up a summer of love. Fornication at the drive-in, lust among the dunes. Dancing and sweat and passion, the scent of sun lotion and the rasp of denim coming off. This season's dirty novel—but then, as these things will, it goes wrong. Perhaps she wants it to be something more than temporary. Perhaps he does. Perhaps they have a drunken fight. Does he knock her down and panic? Or is it something more benign? Maybe she drowns while they're making love in the surf. Or more monstrous: perhaps he holds her down while the waves roll over her face, just to watch and know how it feels. But you can see it, can't you? A traditional cautionary tale of wealth and beauty among the young, the kind of thing that makes for excellent true crime drama, if the lawyers can be pacified. *A Season in Shearwater*, after the watershed so they can show some skin. Well. Let it be. All the great families have ghost stories. The marriages we get unmade. The unsuitable suitors we run off. The girls who die. Boys, too, of course, and more often than you might think. As I said: a human tragedy of money and power, common as a sunrise. Not worth my notice at all."

She waits for me to say something, clever eyes on mine.

"You think they're covering something up."

"I wonder if they might be."

"Hiding it from you."

"From me."

"From *you*?"

"From *me*," she says, and there it is: the fury. A Titan who thinks she's getting the runaround from the ephemera.

I'm a little over forty and I look maybe twenty. I'm already out of step with all but a few thousand human beings, and my offset is only a couple of decades. My face says college kid, but most of the people I was at college with have kids of their own now, and they've found their level, their track, their ceiling. They've watched their parents get old and maybe die, and they've begun to name the decade in which they'll likely do the same. They're fathers and mothers who say the words "when my mother passed" and hear the echo in their own selves. Their planning horizon for careers and retirements is visible from where they stand. They don't have time to reinvent themselves, choose a new life and live it. In a few more decades they'll be gone, and I won't. Maybe I'll be old, but the chances are I'll get another dose. Most of us do, unless we choose otherwise.

Most of *us*.

Now imagine your offset is measured in lifetimes. Three lifetimes. Four. You've watched that process of die-off happen not just to the people you knew when you were actually young, but to their kids. You lost touch with the families of those people when it got as far as grandchildren, because by then the relationships were attenuated to the point of meaningless. And then that generation got old and died around you too, and nothing changed.

Baseline humans are temporary. They're energetic, angry, entitled and then—then they're gone. Blink and miss it.

And the idea that someone like that would think that whatever they're concerned about warranted deceiving Martha Erskine? It's . . . absurd. Offensive and absurd.

Martha's offset is more than two hundred years. Ten times mine, and even I get irritated sometimes when people are giving me the runaround. Like: how can you possibly think you have leisure for this bullshit?

I wait until the coals burn down in that huge, soft face.

"What makes you think it's a lie?"

"That very banality, Mr Sounder. That obviousness, squalid and regrettable. The waste of young life. You want it not to be true, so you believe it all the harder. Swallow your medicine. A sad moment in passing, a payoff to her family, a brief scandal, gone in a few years. Throw the boy to the lions if you can get away with it, *pour encourager les autres*, but his mother is a huge pain in the ass, so you probably won't. Whatever. A short, uncomfortable while and then it's done. An answer to my question that is complete and knowable; that has no consequences worth worrying about."

"You couldn't have known all this when you called me. It's too fast."

"And yet here we are."

Figure Erskine Security had the call from the local cops. Is that standard, if there's a bright young thing on a slab? Maybe. Figure they were on the ball: went out, had a look. It's damn fast. Maybe just enough time, if they already knew who she was. Or if they already knew what had happened.

"You said your people were slack."

"I said they were prone to consensus. I didn't say they were inefficient."

True, but.

"There's something else."

"There is."

"And you're not going to tell me."

"I am not."

"Because . . . it's a test?"

"Oh, no. You're obviously not a fool, so you'll make the connection if it's there."

"But you want me to make it so I don't necessarily make it your way."

She smiles, impossibly wide teeth. Orca smile, here in the midnight sea, and just a little scary.

"*That* was a test," she says, like a magician with a rabbit.

"How did I score?"

"You're doing fine, Mr Sounder. Now, go on, get back to your hotel. Sleep, the way you young ones do."

"You don't?" I hadn't heard that.

She smiles again, eyes looking through me into that place only four-dose Titans can see, the deep black water of life and years. This time it's more than just a little scary.

"Perhaps I'm sleeping now," Martha Erskine says.

She turns slowly in the water and pushes off. It takes a long, long while for her body to reach its full stretch, and then the glide lasts for ever. I see her shoulders briefly break the surface, huge and round and strong. There's a faint sound of waves on the shingle, that laugh again, and then the huge head actually submerges, vanishing into the midnight sea. I keep watching, waiting for her to sound, but she never does.

2

The next morning is bright, and even before nine it's getting hot. Too hot for a suit, so I put on a T-shirt and carry a jacket in case I need to impress anyone with how professional I am. The bed at Celia's is less comfortable than I thought: too soft and too empty without Athena in it. I go to breakfast on the roof, sit under a shade made of bamboo. With the sun on it, Shearwater smells of damp rising from stone, and when the wind blows from the inland side, something else, something sweet and just a little bit cloying. Fruit trees too far gone. Honeysuckle at the end. Maple sugar. It makes the food taste bland and the coffee bitter, leaves you feeling a whisper of nausea in the pit of your stomach at the idea of anything salty. I manage a bowl of cereal, generic and soft.

Miles the surrogate is standing by the buffet in case I want to order eggs. Turns out I'm the only guest at Celia's this week. It feels like living in a house haunted by a ghostly butler.

"Hey, Miles?"

"Mr Sounder—milk? A tisane?"

"What's that smell?"

He sniffs lightly, then opens his mouth to appreciate the full flavour.

"Toast, sir."

There's brioche toast in the basket beside him.

"Not the toast. Sweet, coming from the west."

His lips make a disappointed shape. "Oh. That's the Erskine Company food plant. They make high-quality synthetic flavourings for the international market. The scent can be a little intense."

"The Erskines own that?"

"The Erskine Company is the main employer in Shearwater."

And anything they don't own is strictly Mom and Pop. "People okay with that?"

"The Erskines personally are very well liked in Shearwater. The company is quite hands-on, quite involved in the community. Recently there's been some dickering over pay, but"—he shrugs—"isn't that how it goes with industry?"

"I guess it does."

"But they do what they can to maintain the social fabric of the town. When the summers … slowed down, after the sand went, the market traders couldn't break even. Bail Erskine set up a grocery store so people could buy food without going out of town. You can rent a pitch inside. Some of the farms do. I buy eggs there, for the hotel."

But not for himself, because it's expensive. The Erskine percentage on top of cost.

"The town generally is not at its best. You already know that. Terrible thing. But Captain Iverson can't field enough patrol officers, so the company helps out. People feel safer if they see a uniform."

A regular corporate paradise. A big city like Othrys, even Stefan can't control directly. He controls the space around him, and the lives of others in a web, but there's always someone, however ridiculous, who's willing to take him on. The Marxist brothers in their little saloon bar; a crook with arms even longer than Stefan's; a few journalistic idealists. Occasionally me. Othrys can't be owned or even ruled, it can only be bent into the shapes he wants. But a place like Shearwater, now, with only a few cops and not enough people living there to make a whole district? That's a place you can own from the high-water mark all the way to the ghost of the Lipscombe glacier: shore, town and farms beyond, all dancing to one tune. Of course, it helps when the top cop is almost family.

The police station is small and discreet, because back in the day you certainly would not have wanted to imply the need for a serious cop presence, not with all the shiny, glittering people bringing their jewels and their fine clothes to lounge on imported sand. But on the other hand, you would want a visible symbol of order, someone like us keeping us safe. Someone who understands that there's no harm in the frivolities of the well-to-do, no need to search us for cocaine, to ask us to quiet down the party. A big, solid guy who inspires the right kind of confidence and the right kind of limits.

The desk sergeant signs me in and gives me a sticker to go on my jacket—Visitor/Consultant: Shearwater Police—so that no one arrests me for being a stranger behind the glass partition.

I walk in and I see him right away, behind his desk, and it's like looking in a mirror that shows your insecurities. Shearwater's captain of police is as a big as I am, craggy and experienced in the face. His name is Timothy Iverson, and he is one hundred and seven years old.

He sees me, too, and gets up from his desk. Keenan and Dijkstra watch from the far side of the room, cop-curious: *Here's a tense moment, I wonder how it'll go.*

Iverson is only called Iverson because his grandmother never married Don Erskine. Family drama: noted scion of the clan dumped by a civilian, and her six months pregnant at the time. It cost her immortality, in the end, but apparently she never regretted the choice. Does that make him Martha's great-grandson? Titan family trees only get more complex over time, and more and more the generations are measured not by date of birth or line of descent but by date and number of doses. Iverson, like me, is a promising up-and-comer.

He has his grandmother's jaw and cheekbones, high Scandinavian genes that come from embedded money, older than the Titans and spread out small enough among so many descendants that you could almost miss how much of it there is. Middle class and yet nothing like.

The Erskine lines are there too, hints and aspects in the jaw, in the shape of the eyes and maybe some Sápmi ancestors, even further back—but it's almost impossible to connect him with Martha as she is now. It doesn't feel right, trying to tie someone like me to what Martha has become, her finger outstretched like god's in Michelangelo's chapel, not blessing humankind but just barely still in touch with it as she drifts away to something new.

Considered for himself, though, Iverson looks the way Titans do in magazines and TV shows, expensive teeth and eyes that seem profound because they're set a little deep in the skull, salt and pepper hair cut long like a Danish architect. Fair's fair, he's older than I am by almost seven decades, going on three of them since his first dose. He knows what he is and how to be it. He didn't get his T7 after a fight he lost that he should have seen coming.

"Sounder," he says, sticking out his hand.

"Pretty sure that's my line, Captain Iverson."

We shake. His grip is brief, solid and dry. Like me, Iverson doesn't care to show off. Unlike me, he obviously doesn't have to concentrate any more to get the pressure right.

"Welcome to Shearwater. You mind if I call you Cal?"

"I'd be grateful. I don't want to screw up so bad we get to 'Sounder'."

The grin is uplifting, like sunshine. I swear to god, this guy keeps the peace by force of niceness. You get lawmen that way, rarely, in small towns: part friend, part priest, part educator, but all the same all cop. Figure he can cool a barfight just by making a little disappointed noise.

"Well, that's a relief, Cal. I got no desire whatsoever to get in a pissing contest with a man who spends his days sassing Stefan Tonfamecasca."

"I only do that when he's wrong."

Iverson laughs. "Until you came along, I gather he never was. Call me Tim. I hear you're staying at Celia's. Good place."

Figure a man like Iverson hears most everything, one way and another.

"Thank you for letting me sit in on the autopsy."

Iverson winces. "How was it?"

"Reasonably horrible. Ordinary."

Another wince. Iverson lived a whole lifetime before he got his first dose. A cop lifetime, punctuated with slabs and corpses and the appalling everyday of other people at their worst. "I should have been there, but I find those harder and harder every year. Especially the young ones. Such a fucking waste."

I think of the Sleepers, waiting to die on the beach. My eyes flick away towards the sea, and Iverson doesn't miss it. He waves his hand as if rejecting the foreshore entire.

"That is a whole other world of shit I cannot understand. But we are what we are. Of course we don't get it."

"I haven't forgotten what it was like before. I wouldn't have understood it then, either."

He looks at me. "You sure about that?"

I am, but I'm not sure I'm right.

He takes my non-answer as good enough. "Did you learn anything in the cutting room?"

"Fallon's good at her job."

"She is."

"Ailsa Lloyd was murdered."

"Yes. I guess that was inevitable. How?"

"Fallon thinks she was choked unconscious, then thrown off of a boat with the anchor."

"While she was still alive?" His lips twist in a kind of nausea. "Jesus."

"Maybe the killer didn't know. She would have been pretty far gone."

"Or maybe he did and he's a fucking psychopath."

But not a serial. There's nothing repeatable about this that I can see, no trophy and no triumph in it. Just a murder and a hasty disposal. Panic. Amateurism.

Youth.

Iverson shrugs like a man putting on a heavy coat. "So, you're gonna be around a while? Looking into that?" He's nodding to let me know that's okay by him.

I nod back.

"But only that, right? Nothing else?"

"Such as?"

"Strikers. There's some bad feeling at the plants right now. Wages and such."

"Not my line at all."

"People from out of town tend to expect me to side with the Erskines on that sort of thing. Comes as a surprise when I say I think the plant boys have a point."

"Likely it does."

"And I figure people tend to make certain assumptions about you and the Tonfamecascas which ain't necessarily so."

"Wouldn't be unheard of."

He grins. "You already been to see the company boys?"

By which I guess he means Erskine Security.

"Nope."

"You going there next?"

"Nope."

Iverson looks at me. "You been to see Bail?"

"Figure we'll meet when we meet."

"Oh, he is not going to love that."

"I'll be sure and apologise."

Iverson snorts. "Shit. I had it you were playing nice, but you just don't think I'm in your weight category."

I make like I have no idea what he means.

"Okay, Cal, the way I see it, you run your own hunt. If we keep meeting up, fine, we're on the same track. If we don't, then we're on different ones and that's even better. You get something that wants resources you don't have, call me. If you think you're getting close, call me. If you run into something that's too big for you—and I realise even as I say those words that you have no idea what they mean—call me. I don't want a messy showdown in the main square or some upscale drawing room, but more than that I do not want to be in the position of explaining to Athena Tonfamecasca how I came to let her boyfriend get himself killed here on the Shore. I don't know the lady but I'm gonna guess she'd be vexed at me and that's not displeasure I'd be wanting any part of. So let's all be grown-ups."

"Okay."

"And I'll give you anything I get that's hard for me to touch." Like it's an afterthought, which it's not. I look him in the eye.

"Hey, Tim?"

"Cal?"

"Let's not spoil this with undeclared bullshit."

He raises his hands, palms out: surrender, conciliation, peace.

"All right, I'm declaring my bullshit."

"You want me to play the rude boy from out of town so you don't get in trouble with the gentry."

"Persistent, rather than rude, I guess. You don't know the local proprieties, the gossip, and you don't care. You're a new Titan, they're always a little frisky."

"You're making me sound like something of an asshole."

"Think you can work with that?"

"I'm familiar with it. I don't love it."

"I do have to live here, Cal." I feel like I'm in the principal's office. I wonder whether to drop Torrance Erskine's name. Iverson will know it's being said. He'll have an opinion. But I won't know what it's worth until I've done some digging, and if I let him tell me how it goes here, I'll just be following his track.

"Fine. Persistent."

He smiles. Athena's going to laugh at me when I get run out of town.

"I suppose you better have a look," the manager says, which is nicer than "go fuck yourself" but shares something in the delivery.

Ailsa Lloyd was staying at a place named the Caffrey, which turns out to be a tiny rooming house on the western edge of town as far from the ocean as you can go and still call it Shearwater. Drive another twenty minutes and you're in Ringko, the beginning of the vast in-between that goes all the way to Tammik Town on the far coast: a thousand kilometres of rice, geothermal and ribbon towns feeding the coastal cities and Othrys, storing people for later use.

The Caffrey is functional, but tired and old and not very executive at all. I wonder if Deerborn Real Estate insists on sending its employees to budget accommodation even when they're expected to impress the very rich, or whether Ailsa Lloyd was economising on her expenses, checking out of somewhere flush to stay here and pocket the difference.

The manager wears a badge that says her name is Sandra Ku. Sandra doesn't love having me there. She hovers like I'm going to steal something, like there's anything there to steal except soap. The room is brown with nicotine inflections that I think are supposed to be cappuccino or caramel. It has a woven wallpaper and a wood laminate desk. I sit down in Ailsa Lloyd's chair and feel uncomfortable, my knees too high, the chair too slight under me.

I open the main drawer and find a bible and the local paper. The bible's cheap, the binding smells of bile and the pages are coming out. The newspaper is called the *Shearwater Mercury*. I wonder if whoever started it appreciated the irony when the tide started dropping heavy metals on the shore a decade gone and they had to close the beaches for a year. Figure probably not. The front page is the strike action: five guys and four women holding cardboard signs and making determined faces. They look serious but just as tired as the Caffrey. The headline, like however many thousand before, says A Living Wage! Bare bones: the Erskine Company isn't known locally for its generosity right now, whatever Miles has to say about it.

I open the smaller drawer and there's a white plastic card, blank like a hotel keycard. There's a slot in the long edge for a lanyard that the Caffrey entry cards don't have. I keep a dust brush in my coat pocket now, from an executive spy shop that sells forensic tools styled by Dior and Hermès, but this is from their backroom range. It's not pretty, it's just really good. I lift the card by the edges and test it, one surface and then the other, but there are no prints. Someone wiped it down after using it, but there, inside the lanyard slot: a tiny fleck of blue paint, like a sailor waving on a raft. Blue paint under Ailsa Lloyd's nails, blue paint on the card. I put it in my pocket, then close my eyes and try to imagine I'm smaller, and lighter, and a twenty-six-year-old woman working on a pitch I really care about. I might get paint under my nails. I wouldn't let it stay there. Would I scratch it out with the corner of a keycard? Would I use the slot? It doesn't seem like that would work.

I run my hands along the sides of the desk. A power cable has fallen halfway down the back.

"Yours?"

Sandra shakes her head. So where's the terminal? Bottom of the ocean, maybe. I could get Martha Erskine to go look.

I asked her the wrong question, I realise now. Ailsa Lloyd wasn't murdered on Martha's beach, she was murdered in Martha's ocean. Is that like her parlour? Does she have some kind of executive raft or undersea chalet? Does she live in a boathouse? On a boat? And if she does, who else lives there? Because those people would have been out on the water the night Ailsa Lloyd died, looking outwards because that's their job. Might have seen something, heard something. Might have killed her. For that matter, technically, Martha is a suspect too.

A little shiver down my spine remembering those huge eyes, briefly looking into Titan elsewhere, the mind behind them briefly different.

Perhaps I'm sleeping now.

Is that what she wants me to find out? Whether the reason Erskine Security is so keen to put Torrance in the frame is that they want the ball to stop rolling before it reaches Martha?

But not everything happens at scale just because the world has Titans in it, and I should know better than to dance before the music starts. I need to do the job, and let the history speak for itself.

I push the chair all the way over to one side, get down on my hands and knees and search the carpet by touch. Soft brown squares, like the skins of teddy bears. I don't find anything, and Sandra Ku's opinion of me does not get higher.

I get up and go over to the bed, a queen-size pushed up under the window, neat little nightstand covered in traveller's junk: train ticket, pocket change, a small bottle of alcohol disinfectant for the hands. I sniff at it: acid pear drop tang. There's something else, though, faint and sickly. I pull back the bedspread and there it is again, sweet and wrong. I smelled it on the body on the beach, and over breakfast, and here it is too: synthetic vanillin. It's made by feeding plastics to a particular bacterium. Junk in, flavour out, and much easier than growing orchids to harvest the beans. Someone still grows orchids, of course, but that's for Chersenesos pastry shops, not tourist ice creams on the black sand.

Out of the window you can actually see the plant, the big chimneys and the front gate, little figures standing in a crowd: labour making its voice heard, but it's a noisy room and even shouting doesn't get you much.

I lean down to the sheet and inhale. Sandra Ku says, "Oh, Christ, I'm calling the cops." I smell body odour, not old, and the vanillin again, harsher and more insistent. Back in the day, there was a spy service that kept samples of sweat and cloth in ceramic jars. You'd think it'd fade, but it turns out you can retain an accurate record of the way someone smells for years—or a few days, in the sheets of their bed. Ailsa Lloyd smelled like summer sweat, sunscreen and dessert. I check the nightstand, the inside of the pillow and the quilt: no bracelet, no broken links. Ocean floor again, unless the killer has it in their wallet now, for auld lang syne.

"How far is the food plant?"

Sandra isn't stupid, she just doesn't know my job. The question makes the connection in her head and she puts down the phone. "Five minutes by car. Ten, maybe." Grudging approval now. "You think she was killed at the plant?"

"She was drowned in the sea. But she went to the plant."

"Oh."

"Is it the kind of place people get killed?"

Sandra's eyes flick away. "No."

"But there's trouble."

"Sure. Trouble." What kind of trouble she doesn't let on, excepting it's the kind she doesn't want.

"When did you last see her? You remember?"

Sandra thinks about it, which is good. Every night can get to be pretty much the same from the front desk.

"Day before yesterday, maybe eight o'clock. She was going out."

"You sure?"

"Yeah, I noticed her clothes. Good clothes but not sexy."

"Work clothes."

"No, in the daytime she wore work clothes. Sometimes a suit, sometimes proper work, like a cleaner. But the day before yesterday, the evening, she was just ordinary. An ordinary woman."

"Jeans and T-shirt. Running shoes. She have a coat?"

"Not that night. Like she was in a hurry."

"But she normally had a coat."

"Sailing jacket. A red one. It gets cool when the wind blows."

"But mostly when she went out you figured it was a party?"

"Oh, hell yes. Right up to here and down to here." Hands high on the thigh, low on her chest. She shakes her head.

"She went out a lot?"

"Plenty."

"She take the bus?"

"Not always. When she did she had on a long coat. Other times she took a car."

"Nice car or shitty car?" Because in Shearwater there's no middle ground.

"Taxi, but the good kind."

"You get the name of the firm? They call ahead?"

"They'd never call, but I'd see them through the window. Mostly Highwater Cars. The one with the green and white checks."

"Day before yesterday?"

"Like I told you. Nice clothes but not party clothes. Maybe say they were wholesome. And no taxi."

So either she took the bus, she walked, or someone came for her and she or they didn't want Sandra to know.

"Thank you, Sandra." And then because she wanted to call the cops when she thought I was a pervert: "I'll try to do right by her, if I can."

On the porch I give her money. Sandra doesn't want to take it, but she wants the things it can buy that she needs and cannot afford. I tell her it's how this works, that good information is priced in, that it has value and the client pays. The money disappears into her pocket.

"Have a nice day," she says, not entirely ironic, and then I'm in the street.

The masthead on the *Shearwater Mercury* gives an address along the Laedecker Road. The newspaper is another fragment, a piece of my crash course in the Shearwater reality. I can't become a local in a day, but I can start to see the shape of local life. It's not even so much what they tell me as how: how they feel, where their eyes rest. Pen or pencil or stylus; brogues or boots or sneakers; fresh paint, bare brick or concrete; aged skin and chipped nails or SPF and mani pedi. Ailsa Lloyd didn't just die here; for however long, she lived here, and that means everything talks, if you just listen to what it has to say.

First reality: the public bus seemingly comes on a biannual basis if at all, but there's a steady stream of bored delivery drivers making short runs up and down the coast, and one of them picks me up when I wave a hand with a bill folded in under my thumb.

"I don't imagine you have trouble finding a journalist willing to talk to you, Mr Sounder," Jeanine Baskar says, in her office at the *Shearwater Mercury*. I don't have any idea how old she is: something between thirty-one and sixty, made indeterminate by late nights, caffeine and callisthenics. "Or women generally. Look at that adorable face on a man with real experience. And those shoulders. It's a disgrace."

"I'm not always welcome when I come asking questions. People tend to want it the other way around."

She shrugs. "Maybe in Othrys. Here, I take whatever I can get. You may have noticed we're no longer the first option for the summer party circuit. Why are you in town?"

"I thought you were happy not asking questions." She doesn't look it.

"But happier when I do. Come on, it'll take me all of ten minutes to find out. Less, if I just make up a sexy rumour." Which she will, if she wants to; if I don't play a little. But I knew that coming in.

"The woman on the beach."

"There's a lot of women on the beaches along this coast, Mr Sounder, even now."

"This one's dead."

"Oh, that woman. Such a shame."

"You know anything about her?"

"I guess she was a bad swimmer. If she'd been skinny-dipping, I could do something with that."

"She was killed."

Now she does look happy. "You brought me a present. How nice. Was she murdered?"

"Fallon says probably. You could ask her for more."

"Oh, Fallon. She won't talk to me. And Iverson's no better, all pious just because I published a picture of him punching out some felon one time. Unduly sensationalist, he says. Dignity of the office, he says. It was a great picture. I even captioned it nicely: 'the strong arm of the law'. The picture boys wanted to go with 'kapow!' Have you met him?"

"This morning."

"He says if I print a proper paper, he'll treat me proper too. The nerve."

"He struck me as a man of his word."

"I'm sure he did. So, come on, how can I help you? We could share juicy morsels, if you like."

There's something in her eye that says maybe we're not talking about news. "Maybe."

Another shrug, jerky and all shoulders, like a spider jonesing for a cigarette. "All right, then. Why are you in my office?"

"Gossip."

"Any gossip in particular?"

"What have you got?"

"Well, there's the Sleepers. Are they a cult? A mass suicide on our shores? A bizarre scheme by nefarious persons to depress real estate values and make a killing?"

"Are they?"

"Not that I know of, worse luck. I think they're what they look like. Human discards. Casualties of the real."

"What about the Erskines?" Just another question. I don't want her to know that's why I'm here.

"Well, they're not your Chersenesos type at all. Very stuffy. Martha swims, Bail works and Dixie's a kind of permanent soccer mom. If she wasn't a Titan she'd be a tragedy. Iverson's got a thing for her, not that he'll ever see the inside of her boudoir. She has higher aspirations, though if you asked her I doubt she could tell you what they were."

"I don't think you like them very much."

"I'm hardly on the guest list. We nod at one another at galas and school fêtes. They cut ribbons and wave at the little people. We actually are little, of course. Hilarious."

"I saw the picket line at the plant. How angry is it?"

"Oh, our great industrial action. How many were there? Six people? Four? And Rudi Basu, of course"—she glances at the desk calendar—"no, it's one of his office days. Well. It's a real strike, Mr Sounder, after a proper vote and everything. Rudi's a proper union man. The mills grind slowly, or however it goes. And he's right. Production is down and Bail hates it. Rudi keeps just enough going that the plant pays for itself, no danger of layoffs, but that's all. I hate it almost as much as Bail does, for the opposite reason—so damn sensible—but they're probably doing it right."

"What about sex?"

"Be still my beating heart. Was that a general question or more of an invitation?"

"The Erskines."

"Do they fraternise with the proles? Oh, Bail used to. Quite the wild man. There wasn't a bar he wouldn't fight in, tail he wouldn't chase. But he's all sober and pontifical now. Boring as hell. Why do you care about all that?"

"Getting the lay of the land."

"Even if that's about the landlords getting laid? I'm sorry. Once a headline writer, always a headline writer."

"It wasn't bad."

"It wasn't usable, I know that."

"I heard there was a tearaway kid."

"What, Torrance? Hardly. Sure, he's promiscuous, but he's barely twenty-five, and even so he's not what you'd call a hellraiser. A few windows and some noise ordinances shattered. Public indecency from time to time. He likes to screw on the beach—away from Martha, of course, and from the Sleepers. It's something of a trophy for the out-of-town girls, god knows why. If they took twenty minutes to talk to the locals they'd find it's hardly a rarity to get Torrance on his back. All of which does nothing for me. There's only so many times I can put his skinny ass on the third page with sand all over it and a black bar across his junk. Anyway, he's taking a company job. In a few months, Torrance will be a little clone of Bail: prim and upright and ever so forgetful about all the bikini rodeos and forgiven misdemeanours. He'll marry some young money and get divorced when it turns out Martha has no intention of giving him a second life to do better with. If my successor is fortunate, he'll drive a fast car over a cliff somewhere and make one decent headline before he fades out of the world."

"You don't care for the Erskines much."

"I don't."

"I heard they were popular in this town."

"You're staying at Celia's, aren't you?"

"Does it show?"

"You've been talking to Miles. He's one of those people. The doing-fines. The oblivious, happy service class."

And now, just for a second, I see something more in her face than what she's shown me, more than what she wants me to see. The jaded seeker after sensation slips aside and there's anger, deep and old and sharp like broken glass in soil. I let her run.

"They owe us more," she says. "They've taken this town and now it's theirs but they don't have anything to do with it. They're supposed to bring the glamour, the possibility. The roulette wheel. Well, where is it? Where are the parties, the movie stars? Or if you like, where's the jobs and the scholarships? The infrastructure? Where's the school for the smart kids to work management? The fancy restaurants buying from the local smallholders and longliners? Where's the hospital? God Almighty, what about an addiction clinic? But no. There's just houses you can't afford and empty lots for chain boutiques who don't want to be here any more, and on the beach there's dying people and a burned-out hotel. We don't even get scandals on Olympus. We get fiscal prudence from billionaires, a gradualist union man and eviction notices from banks. So no, Mr Sounder, I don't care for them at all. I wish Torrance was a little monster I could hang out to dry. I wish he'd hurt someone so I can ruin him and make all the rest of them have a bad, bad day. I wish I could bring Dixie Erskine to my office on her pumiced knees and make her kiss my ass." She shrugs. "Was that what you wanted to know?"

Another piece in the mosaic. But no, it wasn't.

For a miracle, there's a bus heading back to the Erskine food plant, and I ride up by the driver and get another glimpse of the Caffrey, two streets down and a hard left turn by the sad little scrap of land they're still calling a park.

Looking out the other window I can see the stacks leaking steam and sickly vanillin into the blue Shearwater sky. I get off and walk the rest of the way.

Some time back someone put some effort into designing Shearwater to be pretty, and I guess its wrecks are pretty still. There's what ought to be a middle-class neighbourhood between here and there, with self-conscious byways for standalone houses and European terraces, overgrown and dilapidated now so that the front doors need painting and the yards are weedy and cracked with rubble rockeries, and where once you figure Uncle Bill had his telescope or his pigeon loft there's now just flat roofs and washing hanging on an old plastic cord between rusted electrical boxes. Old men and old women sit out on striped canvas deck chairs, but they don't play chess or wave and they aren't taking tea. Instead, they're looking at form sheets or working their way through a stack of scratch cards. From the upper windows, kids look down who ought to be in school—and maybe they are, just not today. I look for needles and don't find any, but that just means the city still sends guys round to sweep them up in this part of town, or the drug of choice goes into your body by another route. I should ask Fallon what it is. Ketamine, maybe. When bright young things are buying up betting shops and opening a barber, when the street food gets good instead of just cheap, that's when cocaine and MDMA are everyone's friend. When things are on the downslope, there's ketamine. Ketamine for the ones who give up; night classes and double shifts and climbing the greasy pole for the ones who still believe there's a life for them, whether they're wrong or not; and anger in the middle, pent-up like it is in Jeanine Baskar—under pressure and ready for the flashover. Although now I guess there's the Sleepers, too, like ketamine without the buzz.

Over the brow of the hill, everything changes. The old traces of civic planning fade away and the houses turn to brownfield sites and chickenwire, until you pass the boundary line of the Erskine land, marked by white picket fencing in the meaningless, manicured image of classic Americana, and beyond that the food plant, which is a vast sprawling box of pre-fabricated sections fronted by a stained façade in what someone must have thought was Deco. It looks like a plastic model of an old T-bird you might buy if you couldn't afford a real Christmas present for your kid.

And there at the gates is a picket line: four men and two women in the blistering midday heat, placards resting on the wall behind them, and the gate guard trying to pretend he doesn't know them all by their first names, trying to pretend he doesn't hope they win so he can do better than that plastic T-bird. They see me and muster up a chant so ragged all I can tell is that the last word rhymes with "eight".

When I first walk over, they huddle up like I'm about to beat them. When I'm by myself people don't read how big I am until I get close. My working suits don't look obviously expensive so they assume I'm just large and in this context that could mean brute squad, although surely not all by my lonesome. When I tell them I'm not going inside I'm pretty sure it's the only win they've had all week. One of the men has stitches over one eye. They're tired as hell and, what's worse, they're getting thin. However many years I've been alive, I still don't much like the idea that you can work and go hungry at the same time.

They watch me as I lean against the fence and slide all the way down it like I'm tired as hell too, which I tell myself I'm not. I wait a while before I say:

"Hi, fellas."

"Hi," says the nearest one.

"I'm Cal. Cal Sounder." I put out my hand.

He comes closer like he's found a bear in his garden and wants to drive it off, but he's thinking maybe that's not a good idea. "Patrick."

"Come away," one of the women says to him. "Sarah, get his picture." Another woman, lean and a little younger, snaps a photograph of my face.

"We keep a record of all visitors to the official picket," Sarah says. "Your image will not be accessed unless there is an incident." She glances over at the first woman, the one who's in charge.

"Cal Sounder," I say again, and offer her a card, but she doesn't touch it.

The one in charge has a familiar face, and I wonder if I've seen her in the street, but that's not it. I take out the picture of Ailsa Lloyd and hold it up. That's not it either. Sometimes people just look like they look like someone. I tell her I'm Cal again, like I haven't said it already, and she looks away but finally says, "Alex."

"My mother's name was Alexandra." Which it wasn't, but it probably could have been.

"You said 'was'?"

"Yeah."

"I'm sorry for your troubles."

"I came to talk about yours."

She barks a laugh. "Came to let us know we can have more of 'em, I'm sure."

I shake my head, letting the bump at the back roll against the fence. It has a scientific name that I can never remember because it's just a description in long words, and since I became a Titan my fingers go to it whenever I'm at rest, as if checking I'm still there. I'm still holding Ailsa's picture, so I show it to her. "Know this face?"

"Why the hell would I tell you?"

"I don't work for the Erskine Company."

"I'm sure none of their bruisers would ever lie about that."

"She was murdered. I'm supposed to find out who by."

"A cop? Even better." Some people take a while to understand a death has happened. Some just expect the world to be that way, which looks like indifference until you realise it's pain.

"Investigator. An old lady wants to know who killed Ailsa Lloyd." Let them assume it's a relative, not Martha Erskine. "Ailsa." Holding up the picture.

She gives me a long look. "Sure, I know her."

"So, what was she like?"

"Oooh, you know. All piss and vinegar."

"How so?"

Alex waves her hands at everything. "The picket wasn't her speed at all. Right idea, she said, wrong action. Action like military, you know what I mean? Like direct action, the way people say when they mean smashing things up."

"This woman?" Holding up the picture again.

"Yes, that woman, didn't I just say so?"

Now, why would a real estate agent want to support a strike at a factory in a town she barely knew?

"She just rolled up and told you to get radical?"

"Pretty much straight after they hired her. I figured she was, you know, inclined to trouble."

"They hired her?" I don't figure the Erskines for needing an out-of-town agent to acquire land in Shearwater. I remember Sandra saying some days Ailsa dressed like she had a real job. Alex waits for me to stop woolgathering, then carries on.

"Sure. She clocked in a few days, then right away she was angry. Got in an argument with a supervisor and ten minutes after she was in Basu's office. When he wasn't there for it, she came to the picket. Figured if we were here while he's in the office, we were the hard core. Like he's not worker enough." Alex shakes her head. "I don't see what he's waiting for, but he's the real deal. He was busted for it, back in the day—if he gets arrested again it's a whole thing, but he's here every week like the rest of us. Looks fit to die on the hot days, but we all take a shift."

"Organised labour."

She laughs. "Exactly. But her . . . She was kinduv inspiring, you know? Like she was on fire. Block the road, she said. Put sugar in the tank of a big truck. For starters."

"Direct but not violent." Or gateway actions, escalations to something else.

"Honestly, she made it sound fun. Like we could fuck around and do good at the same time. She didn't push."

"And Basu?"

"He says it's not time to go hard, to hold off. I don't know what time we're waiting for. They don't pay enough money, and what there is just . . . blows away. Erskines own all the property, tourist business means all the shops still open are too expensive. Plus you have to stay on-site for meals and they're marked up all the way, like eating in a fancy place. What you take home at the end of the week doesn't cover what goes out. It's an old song, isn't it?"

"So when Ailsa talked about direct action, were you there for it?"

And now she's ashamed. "I felt like I should be. Like she was going all the way for us and we were hanging in the doorway. But in the end, I told her no. Strike is one thing, that's another, all of that. You get arrested, get on the wrong side of the line, that's all for you. And someone could get hurt. You mess with the tyres on those big trucks and they blow, that's a whole tonnage moving a hundred kph. It can roll, it can jackknife, it can buckle. Even moving slow, that can happen, and you don't want it."

The respect a real worker has for the monstrosity of physical things in motion. Respect you get from seeing someone's hand in a press, from watching a stack come down right in front of you and knowing you would have died. One time a scaffold collapsed in Tappeny Bridge while I was walking by, and I watched two men fall nine floors and then realised the metal tubes had landed all around me and driven like spears into the pavement.

Alex is shaking her head like she's still talking to Ailsa Lloyd, still arguing, because maybe that danger is the marker of desperation that brings rapid change. We're so screwed we'll do something this dumb to tell you so. But maybe Alex and this Rudi Basu are right too—you do that and it goes wrong, you lose big, because now you're the monster.

"Problem is, you don't know where it goes," Alex says. "I told her so. Fuck. I must've sounded like Rudi."

I shake her hand and I don't tell her whether she was right or wrong, because I don't know.

Ailsa Lloyd, workplace agitator.

Heading into town again, I realise the neighbourhood around the food plant looks down towards the water but can't see or touch it.

It's disconnected from the fishing town that used to be, facing away from the plant but shackled to it by topography. White cube houses stare at one another, subdivided again and again until the sleeping rooms are the mandated minimum size and the shared hallways and front gardens are cracked and grey. Decline written in brick.

Two hundred metres on there's a bar on a corner, four tables outside with wooden tops made from recycled doors. I stand and wait and the server stares at me. I don't belong.

"You got a box crate or something I can sit on?"

He nods and brings me out a little wooden folding step that doubles as a stool. When I sit on it, I'm the right height to eat, but I have to sit like I'm a cartoon frog, legs crossed at the ankles and hips open under the table.

"Get your order?" he asks.

"Sandwich," I tell him, "and a glass of milk."

"No milk," he says.

"What do people drink with their sandwich?"

"Beer."

It's not even half past ten. "Water's fine."

"It's good with beer."

"I'll come back another day in the evening and try it that way."

He shrugs and slouches inside. When he comes back, the sandwich is stupidly good: Swiss cheese and some kind of slaw, bacon so thin and crispy it's almost conceptual. I'm starving, and weirdly, from this distance, there's no smell from the food plant: they must pipe it out the other way, and the vapour rises and gets caught by the breeze and dropped on the centre of town. Justice, of a kind.

"Who comes here?"

"People," the server says.

"Got regulars?"

"Families, once a month maybe. Managers from the plant. Some of the union guys weekly."

I'm sitting in the destination food spot in the neighbourhood. Othrys prices, probably, so no one comes every day. Anyone who can afford to has other places to be.

I feel someone coming before I see them: three men in charcoal suits, wool and ballistic fabric weave. The server vanishes inside like a big squirrel into a tree stump.

"Hello, stranger."

Cheerful, authoritative, lightly bullying. I look round and find focus-grouped ethnic diversity in mid-grade tailoring. A street-level enforcement trio, except the mood doesn't feel quite right. There's something else.

"Morning, gentlemen."

"Good morning, sir. My name is Dave Reason. This is Matthew Jimson and Phil Holbrook. We are from Erskine Security." The town muscle, Miles's helpful fellows, just supporting the local cops who don't have the manpower to put street officers on all the streets. Two of them aren't interesting at all. Holbrook has on spectacles: he's management material, figure he's fast-tracked and this is his apprenticeship. Reason isn't even that: a permanently disappointing also-ran who hasn't yet realised this is as high as he goes. Jimson is something else, some kind of real thing: six foot and some small change, dense like hardwood, with the bored look of a guy who one time worried about IEDs and snipers, and now occasionally gets shat on by a seagull. He stands out by the way he fades into the background, not because he's grey, but because he seems not to be noticing you and you find yourself returning the favour. Figure he's the elder brother sent along with the kids.

I smile. "Have you tried the sandwich? It's real good."

"I'm afraid not. We work with the Erskine Company and our job is to ensure there's no trouble in and around their holdings here in Shearwater. Which, come to think, is kind of the whole town."

"Good job. Haven't seen any trouble since I got here."

"That's good."

"I think so, too. Do you guys have, like, cool ID or something?"

He smiles and gets out a slice of plastic on a lanyard—his picture, and an over-worked corporate crest that's meant to invoke history and solidity but makes me agree with Ailsa Lloyd about setting things on fire. David J. Reason, Security. But it's not the same as the white card in my pocket. Reason's is wider, squarer, less like a credit card and more proprietary.

"Gosh. That looks really serious."

"Yes, sir. Now, you mind I ask: when did you get here?"

I take a bite of my sandwich and speak through. "Sorry, this is real good, like I said, and I don't want it to spoil. What was your question?"

"When you got here."

"Few minutes ago. I think they were just opening up. I was hungry, I saw the tables."

"I meant, when did you get to Shearwater?"

"Oh, I thought you meant here, like, this bar."

"No. So when was that?"

"Little while. I'm not counting days, to be honest."

"And what brought you to our shiny little town?"

"I go where the work is. You know how that is."

He doesn't like that I'm suggesting we're the same. He works for the Erskine Company and right now he's pretty sure I'm a stoner or a bum. Sure, I'm tall, but lots of people are. Far fewer of them are Titans, and it takes experience to tell the difference on a single dose. Not a whole lot of experience, mind you, but some. "And the nature of your business?"

I turn and look at him across my plate, make my eyes wide and dumb.

"Sandwich reviewer."

He stares at me long and hard. Behind him, one of the others stifles a laugh.

"Okay, sir, that's real funny, but I'm now going to ask you your name."

"Okay."

He waits. I wait.

"What is your name, sir?"

"Donahue." Like I'm not sure. "I mean, that's my first name but everyone just calls me Hugh."

"That's nice, Hugh, but I was thinking a full name."

His hand on my shoulder now, like he's the principal and I threw mud. I wonder if they picked me up on camera at the plant and came looking. Sure as hell they should have, but you can never tell who's asleep, or lousy at their job.

"Donahue—and then my family name is kinda strange: Djasz," I say, pronouncing the D just enough that he doesn't hear how that sounds. "Like, D. J. A. S. Z."

One of the outriders sighs. I think it's Jimson, seeing where this goes. I look over at him but he's busy fiddling with lint around the buttonhole on his suit. Reason snaps his fingers to get my eyes back on him.

"Is that an overseas sort of a name, Hugh?"

"I don't know. It was my daddy's name, Momma said."

Holbrook says: "Come on, Dave. He's just some kid."

"He's sassy," Dave says.

"He's stoned," Phil Holbrook tells him, "or dumb. Either way, he's not a striker."

"The workers, united, shall never be defeated," I say, like it's call and response, and that's what you say when someone says 'striker'. They all look at me.

"Sassy," Dave Reason repeats.

"I heard that somewhere while I was eating," I say. "Are there real strikers here? Like in books? Can I meet them?"

Reason's about to do something stupid, but Holbrook gets between us, sits down. Figure the army put him through college, now here he is double-timing a street job and an MBA, on his way to the top.

"We don't know where they are, Hugh. But if you see one, I would be real excited to know about that too. Can I give you my number?" He doesn't wait for an answer, slips me a card. Cream, sharp corners. Not as expensive as the one I gave Ashley last night, but over-specced for a foot soldier. A man with a plan. I feel kind of bad about that, but not very. Management in an outfit like Erskine Security is not a job that leaves you with entirely clean hands. Even if they're not strikebreaking, they look after the family interest as much as the physical property, and that means payoffs and intimidation from time to time. Keeping the little people quiet. Holbrook has to know that, but here he is anyway. I wonder for a moment how much slack there is in Tim Iverson's leash. Cop in a town this size, either not much at all or a whole lot, depending on the cop. Depending on whether Martha Erskine's for real when she says she likes independence.

I take the card. "This is nice. Real fancy."

"You go ahead and call me if you meet any strikers, all right? Because I would like to meet them too."

"Okay, sir, I will."

And like that, I've been recruited as a junior member of Dipshit Dave's brute squad, an unconscious asset in the fight against communism and the living wage. Jimson shrugs and walks on with the other two. I'm fairly certain he already knows what's coming, and doesn't care. Perhaps he'll get a kick out of it when Reason and Holbrook tell their boss they have acquired a street-level source named Huge Ass.

Was it a camera at the plant? Were they just passing by, or were they particularly watching the Caffrey? I wonder if Ailsa Lloyd was trying to buy something someone didn't want sold.

The server reappears now that the sun's come out again.

"Those guys do that a lot?"

"Yes, sir. A whole lot."

"They just roust people on the street? Bother folks at your tables?"

"Yes, sir."

"What does your boss say?"

"He says 'shit'."

"Fair enough. You mind I ask you one more thing?"

He does, but he doesn't know how to tell me, because his boss doesn't protect him or his customers from random assholes who ask questions.

"Where would I find a building with blue waterproof paint all over the door?"

"Down by the seafront," he says, a little wary now that I may be an actual idiot.

"Maybe you can think of one in particular? Maybe with one of those slots for a keycard on the door?"

He shrugs. "There's cabins and such all up and down. Once you get outside the town."

I show him a picture of Ailsa Lloyd, but he never saw her before.

I finish the sandwich and overtip, then go down to the beach to stretch my frog legs.

In the sunshine the beach is busy, if not buzzing. There's a workmanlike feeling about the fun going on around me: families with sun shelters and bottles of soda in coolers building castles out of sharp obsidian, wearing gel shoes to protect their feet. The Grand Erskine is just a ruin again, no sign of the lights or the kids from last night. Figure they won't make it until three or four in the afternoon. I realise I'm looking for Ashley and make myself stop, because either I'm hoping to see her in a swimsuit or I'm frightened I'll see her lying cold among the stones. Neither one of those is entirely healthy; both belong to who and what I am.

Ailsa Lloyd, realtor from Othrys on a big job. Ailsa Lloyd, dead-end factory worker in Shearwater.

Ailsa Lloyd, labour activist.

And Ailsa Lloyd, dead on the beach at twenty-something, a bird inked over her heart and Fallon trying to cut round it because there's nothing else left to save.

I look south to the Sleepers, and listen to the sigh that comes off them, the whisper that you hear day and night if you listen, and I wonder if Ailsa Lloyd heard it, and if she did, what it said to her, and what it says to me.

Work the case.

I put my phone between my shoulder and my chin. They recently redesigned the model so you can do that without turning it off with your face. Progress. The line purrs and then clicks as the person on the other end picks up the call.

"Hey, Sporty Jasmine, it's me."

"Boss?"

"You know any other me?"

"Pretty much everyone in the world. What do you have?"

"I have a dead lady with two jobs," I tell her.

"I don't know if you forgot now that you're basically one of the bad guys, but a lot of people die and got two jobs."

"High-end real estate agent and factory worker in a seaside town with no future."

"Isn't the world special? But that does sound a little hinky."

"You talk to Deerborn yet?"

"Yeah, but so far they aren't talking back. I'm on it."

"Work your magic."

"You know it's just actual work, right?"

"Fine, then do that."

She laughs at me and signs off.

I walk along towards the promenade and the half-dozen entertainers busking and doing close-up magic in gold body paint. I show them Ailsa Lloyd's picture and throw money in the hats. They saw the cops on the beach yesterday, and they saw the sad, waterlogged bundle that was Ailsa Lloyd being carried off. No one knows anything. Maybe they saw her before, just passing by, or maybe they didn't. They weren't looking. They had work to do, and so do I.

The keycard. The terminal. The jewellery.

Two jobs, and the picket.

Blue paint.

Torrance.

And someone may be lying to Martha Erskine.

Too many pieces, as always; too much noise to hear Ailsa Lloyd.

I sit down a little way from the sea, and listen to the sound of another world, old and strange and far away, crashing down on the land. I never used to be much for just sitting there. Maybe I never thought I had time. But every wave is different from the last, and the light and colours change even as they stay the same.

How long I sit there I'm not sure. For those moments, by the water, my sense of self is gone, and when it comes back I wonder suddenly if that absence is how the Sleepers feel, if that's the thing they're chasing: the disappearance of a self too heavy to carry. The sun is white overhead, the black sand starting to get hot enough I can feel it through my shoes. Once upon a time this coast didn't get hotter than nineteen or twenty degrees. By three o'clock this afternoon it'll be hot enough to cook on the stones. I get up, and start walking back to Celia's.

And then, through the glare, I see something I never would have expected, or honestly even imagined: a man in board shorts about to go kite surfing.

He's tall and severe and he has scars from a dozen injuries across his chest and arms. One of them is an old puckered bullet wound like a carambola, the tissue weird and pale against the rest of his skin. He got that one in Monrovia, back when wound putty only came in Caucasian flavours, and although I know that, I had not anticipated seeing Emile Zoegar with his shirt off. It took me seven months to find out his first name was Emile.

Still less am I prepared to find him like this, in sea-blue shorts with pink jellyfish, lifting a small child up in his arms, shooing another away from the inflating kite, turning to a slender black woman in her forties with a movement so carefree you'd think he was just an ordinary Joe. For a mad moment I wonder if this is his family, hidden and vulnerable and special, and if I'm now the possessor of a secret so deep I should turn away before he sees me and never let him know I was here. But it's too late: the woman catches me staring and he sees her eyeline, and follows it.

I expect him to go cold and professional in that moment. I don't want to be at odds with Emile Zoegar. I don't know exactly what his skillset is, but I know in the broad generality that he is what you call 'capable'. He is clear-eyed and sure, and he is unfettered by the niceties of the law.

He sees me and an honest smile breaks over the stone face. It is the most unawaited sunrise. He opens his arms and before I know it he is hugging me, his head resting briefly on my shoulder, arms damp with seawater and sweat wrapping around me at elbow height as he laughs.

"Mr Sounder! How good to see you! Come! Come come. This is Josephine Addes, and these are her children Micah and Elle." Twins, I think, maybe nine years old.

Josephine steps forward and it's hard not to notice how beautiful she is, the roll of her hips as she walks across the sand, the play of tension in her stomach as she extends her hand for me to shake. After meeting Ashley last night, I'm better prepared for the chemical cascade inside my head, so I smile and manage not to stutter. Apparently it gets easier after the first two decades, which would be fine, except that I have fifteen years of this to go. I remember Athena laughing at me in the first months after I got out of the tank, my attention-deficit male gaze snagged by every plunging neckline and floating hem. "For god's sake, learn to love it, Cal, or you won't make it." She meant 'make it to your next dose'. Being a Titan isn't just about the drug, it's also finding a way to understand and be in the world despite the offset.

Athena does love it, and she showed me how to love it too. Especially for someone in my line, she said, who sees death more than most people, it's important to accept the vigorous overgrowth of desire and appetite. Otherwise, like a celibate priest, you withdraw more and more from baseline humans and their world.

In that first six months after I was healed, we lived a wild curve of party sex, food and exhilaration. When that slowed, she took me to a place she has out among the olive groves and gave me a very serious talk I still don't properly understand. For Athena, life as a Titan hinges on whether you can accept your own scale. Most can't, and it swallows them, so they take refuge in extremes and caricatures of who they were before the first dose, becoming ever more disconnected and alone, like Stefan with his conscious monstrosity, a mask even to himself. So far, among the Titans, love is the one ephemeral thing, the only aspect that doesn't last. Athena believes it's because people assume that you continue as you are, for ever, but the very nature of T7 is growth and change. It's like walking down the marriage aisle thanking god you don't have to do romance any longer.

"Be the thing we are," she said. "The long, strange evolution into the new. Let the body have the things it wants, the food and wine and the fighting. Cherish the people it desires, and let those perfect moments, new and fleeting friendships measured in days or decades, be part of the long and changing selves we make together."

We were naked on a rug, breathing in the scent of hot air and olive leaves.

"That doesn't make you jealous?"

She laughed. "Very. But also: no. How can I be jealous of a fraction of time? It's too small. It has to be.

"We're going to become other people, Cal, over time. That's inevitable. Those people need to be more complex, more layered, more fascinating. Otherwise what's the point? Did you know most trees start to die when they reach a certain height?"

"I didn't."

"Now imagine you stop that from happening, so the tree grows out and around, and gets older and older, and vines and creepers and orchids grow on it, whole families of animals, generations of them, living on the tree. Not constrained, but endless and varied, changing over time but staying the same. It doesn't look the way it did when it was a sapling, and it isn't: it's become something vaster and more complex, because of unlimited time."

I smiled at her, put my face in her hair. "You want me to be like a tree?"

She bit me, but not hard. "No. I want *us* to be like a forest of them."

And a forest we shall be, if she says that's the way this works.

But even if I had time for sex in Shearwater, it would not be with Josephine Addes, who is so clearly in love with Emile Zoegar, and whom he so clearly loves in turn. Although not, going by the appalling tension of their mutual restraint, that either of them has allowed this to be acknowledged in the light of day. Or even, god help us all, in the dark.

I shake her hand and step back, keeping my eyes above her collarbones, shutting down my awareness of the top half of the swimsuit, perfectly judged between sensible and scandalous. I shake hands with Micah and Elle when Josephine calls them forwards.

"But what are you doing here, Mr Sounder? And why on earth are you wearing a suit on the beach?"

"I'm working. I don't mean to intrude. I just turned around and saw you and . . . " My hands wave off the truth: couldn't believe it was you, like seeing a praying mantis changing a tyre. Didn't move fast enough, didn't mean to disturb your family time. Whatever family time this is, that reeks of unfulfilled desire. Don't want to bring dead Ailsa Lloyd to your party. Above all, don't want to let slip to this radiant, respectable women, however accidentally, that she's hanging out with a guy who does what Emile Zoegar does for a living.

"Oh, well," Zoegar laughs, "then I don't want to know! No war stories for me this week. But come and eat with us one day. We're just off the beach. The children would be excited to talk to a real Titan."

Does that mean they haven't met his boss, the Humpty Dumpty of crime? Or just that his idiosyncratic T7 transformation reads to them as "not a real Titan"? Lyman Nugent—better known as Doublewide—got his dose by an irregular route that evidently did not include the personalisation stage.

I'm trying to say no to Zoegar, but Josephine catches me before I can. "Please, Mr Sounder. Come by any time."

I glance at Zoegar, taking his temperature. He's still happy. Josephine rolls her eyes, then suddenly clasps her hands to her chest as if shocked.

"Oh, my goodness! Emile! Don't tell me you're a criminal!"

And she bursts into gales of laughter. So does Zoegar. I'm standing there watching them crack up like the only churchgoer at a burlesque night. Josephine dries her eyes and leans on my arm. Her fingers are long and strong.

"Yes, Mr Sounder, I know who you are. And I know who Emile is and what he does. What he has always done. So you don't have to spend the meal covering up all his terrible secrets. If you are very fortunate, I will tell you some of the funny ones he likes to pretend never happened."

And Zoegar, instead of looking worried, just smiles even wider like this is the best thing in the world.

"She will," he says. "I've never been able to stop her, at all, in any way."

I have no idea what I'm into here, but I have to find out. Curiosity isn't always a virtue in an investigator; there are any number of fascinating things that don't matter in the solution of a case. But that doesn't mean that I can pass up the true and accurate history of the screw-ups of Emile Zoegar.

Then the wind changes, plucking at the kite, and Zoegar gives a whoop of laughter. A moment later he's flying, almost upside down and full of joy, and Josephine's eyes are bright as she follows his progress out over the sea.

I leave them to whatever the hell it is they're doing.

Away to the south there's a ripple of movement behind the heat haze: like milk spilling on a table. The Sleepers are taking shelter under white survival shades. There are limits, then, to their weird self-immolation, like dying is an aesthetic and they're damn well going to do it right. No bubbled skin and screaming headaches as they go, just a kind of wan poetic exhalation in the dusk.

On the boardwalk, just close enough to the beach to be worth climbing the wooden steps, there's a woman selling iced water off the back of a cycle cart. I buy two. Then, because I'm there, I show her a picture of Ailsa Lloyd, but she shakes her head. She's grey, the way you get grey when you're ageing well through hard work: streaks of dark hair under the frizz of sun-bleached white, white racing vest and shorts, corded muscle on the arms that hold the handlebars of the bike. Smart eyes regard me from under a cheap sun visor.

"She the girl that died?"
"Yeah."
"You going to do something about that?"
"If I can."
"And you can. You're the kind that can."
She doesn't mean Titans.
"Yeah, figure maybe I am."
"What all else can I do, then?"

I ask about the beach kids, but they're all the one to her, seasonal butterflies. She knows Torrance to look at, but not more. Ashley she remembers, as a nice girl who won't hang around Shearwater longer than she has to. "They all go to the Roller," she says. "You want to see the kids, that's where they are." She points vaguely along the shore.

"What about tides? Someone told me there's a guy named Bill Tracey." It was Fish Food, so not exactly reliable.

"Tracey's a good enough man." With reservations.

"I'm told he knows the currents."

She snorts, turns her hand this way and that. "Sure he thinks he does. He's been a captain fifteen years along this stretch. Nine years a seaman before that. He's no amateur, that's true enough. And he's what you call a character. Looks fine in a bridge coat." She snorts. Figure she can appreciate the view as much as anyone, without giving her approval.

"But?"

"But he knows the ocean, far out, and he's a passable pilot, but he ain't from here. Didn't swim the tide pools as a baby like we all do. Didn't ever swim Big Rock Tunnel."

"What's that?"

She laughs, and with a shock I have to revise her age down a decade and a half. She's only a decade or so older than I am, but baked by the sun. "A stupid dare, back when. There was a rock with a three-metre tunnel about two metres down in the bay. You go through it, you're old enough for a beer."

"And now?"

"Oh, one of the tourist kids near died, back when the hotel was open. Martha had it hauled away to deep water."

"Seems a shame."

She shrugs. "It was only ever a real bad idea. Still. You want to know the close water, you talk to Agnes."

"Agnes who?"

"Agnes Agnes. She makes things out of junk, sells them in that little shop. Can't miss it. Only one open on the block, round the corner from the fountain."

I still don't know where that is, and we go back and forth until she throws her hands in the air. "Get on the back. I can explain it to you or just take you there, and this'll be quicker."

I've done more frightening things in my life than hitch a ride on that cycle cart, but I honestly don't remember what they were. My knuckles are white on the metal frame by the time we get there, but the sign is clear and fresh-painted in its own little backstreet, near to picturesque as makes no odds: Agnes Carvalho Salvage & Art.

The water seller waves off my offer of money and rides away slow. Small-town people: either they like you or they don't, and you'll know about both. I ring the bell and a woman opens the door.

Agnes Carvalho has a wide bronzed face and broad shoulders and she wears a leather forge apron over a summer dress. She brings me inside and there's beach junk made into every conceivable thing: old cigar boxes rendered as handbags, big old clam and conch shells become light stands, a cabinet writing desk made of rough driftwood and oxidised copper bands. And, yes, charm bracelets on a cylinder of synthetic velvet, the ends peeling off the cardboard tube within. There's pure art and interior design and piles of rope and wood to take home and use in your own way. Figure Agnes has the broadest possible customer base: the shiny people come for the fashions and the locals for supplies, and that combination in turn makes it real and risky for the money: mixing with breadliners and upcyclers, feeling like you're in the world, not floating over it for a change. Figure she has a second price list, too, for people who can't pay a hundred for an old metal tin with a cheap clock mechanism sintered in, however pretty the pattern of wear and corrosion. Figure she sells the rope cheap to those who need rope, and expensive to anyone who's going to hang it on a wall.

"Nice bracelets," I say.

"Tourist trash," Agnes says.

"You sell a lot?"

"This season it's all that's moving. Barely worth opening for, but what can you do? If I sell one large piece to an out-of-towner, I can put my feet up for a month. If not . . . well, there's always paint and rope and oil to make ends meet. No?"

We walk past the gewgaws and trinkets into a back workshop that smells of dust and hot glass. She has an actual kiln and cooling ovens, boils obsidian and makes her own shapes, but those she doesn't sell here, they go to Chersenesos, to a specialised boutique that marks up a thousand percent and sends her enough, each month, to pay the rent.

There's an unfinished board table with burn scars, and above it: a map.

"Tea," Agnes says, pouring for both of us. Round, thick fingers, strong arms and thighs from lifting and making for years. Soft voice and warm, narrow eyes as if she's always squinting into the sun. There's an air conditioning unit at full blast wired into the kiln: an exchanger to turn waste heat into cold. Otherwise, a room this size would be intolerable in the summer, never mind the ovens.

The tea is mint, fresh, with a trace of something else, maybe Thai basil or anise. When I tell her why I'm there she sighs, but nods a craftsman's nod. Sometimes you make bassinets; sometimes it's coffins.

"She washed up here," I say, pointing. "Near the Sleepers."

"And they didn't move her?"

"Why would they?"

"Why do those people do anything at all? They are very strange. Sometimes they do nothing for days and weeks on end. Sometimes they cry or sing. On other days they build little houses as if they want to live, and then they burn them or destroy them with their hands as if they were a storm."

"She wasn't moved far. Not carried. No signs of damage to the body post-mortem, and there would be. Maybe they rolled her over, went through her pockets at most."

"And you say a few hours in the water?"

"Yes."

The map is a standard survey, one to fifty thousand scale, but very large, covering the whole wall. The coast is along the bottom, the sea at the top. The land area is just as it was when the printer sealed it up for delivery, but the beach and foreshore are heavily marked: wood here, bottles here, good glass, bad glass. Salvage. The names of storms and shipwrecks. A trail, of a kind. The blue ocean section is even more complex, lines of pencil and felt-tip pen laid over one another, colours and speeds, dates and times, phases of the moon. A madman's nest of lines, or perhaps a truth only Agnes can read.

Agnes puts her hands on the map. Her right is on the beach where Ailsa Lloyd was found. Her left hovers, circles, tracing a gyre, tapping and fumbling. Her lips move. The hand strokes, slides away. Finger touches a knot.

"Here is where the decision was made."

"The dump?"

"Oh, no. There are several places for that. Say three. But here is where it went wrong. Your murderer wanted the body to go away, yes? But it came in, instead. This is where that happened. There is a shoal here, treacherous for the bigger boats, good fishing for the small ones. But rivers under the sea meet here, and depending on the wind and the rain, one wins out over the other. This is where she turned again, and came home."

She moves her fingers down towards the land. A single dot of brown in the blue. "This is Cormorant Rock. If you dropped her here, you might think she would go straight out with the ebb tide and into the deeps. She almost always would. Do you think it was a fisherman who killed her?"

"Could be. I don't know."

"A fisherman would know about the rock. But he would also know not to do it there this week."

"Where else?"

"Oh, here." A deep blue stretch, narrow, leading up towards the ceiling, and the wide ocean. "Here anyone with a boat and a chart, if they were not much experienced with Shearwater current. It looks like it goes straight to the deep water, and it does, but only once you get all the way down. The top layers of the water come inshore again."

"An amateur."

"Yes."

"You said three places."

Agnes sighs and brings her hand all the way to shore by her shoulder, the far city limit of Shearwater. "This," she says. "Also here. Anywhere else on the coast, it would either keep getting thrown back in the same place, or wash up further down. That's a very particular destination. That's why I asked if she was moved. Even if you threw her in the water where she was found, she wouldn't go there. It's a paradox of tides."

I look at where her hand is. "Where is that?"

"Well, now it's a Marine Reserve. They take care of fish and so on, give them a place to be. And the land is the same, all overgrown for the biosphere. She likes her privacy."

"Who does?"

"Martha Erskine, of course. That's her house, and that whole promontory is called Martha's Point."

I sit on Agnes Carvalho's porch thinking about that until a green and white check taxi pulls up out front and the driver says he's looking for me. His name's Bø, which is not quite the same as Bo.

I ask Bø if ever he picked up Ailsa Lloyd from the Caffrey. He says Tim Iverson asked him that already and I say then he probably has the answer right on the tip of his tongue. Bø says there are six cars in the Highwater fleet and he only drives this one. His mother drives the minibus for group transfers and his father and brother have the executive saloons. His fiancé, Steven, drives the last car, which is like this one. I say that makes five cars, and Bø says he likes that I'm still listening. The sixth car is another cab, but they rotate them so that they're always in tip-top condition for the customer.

Did he or Steven drive Ailsa Lloyd?

Yes, Bø says. Steven did. Steven told all this to Iverson. I give him money and ask him to repeat it for me, if he remembers, and Bø does remember. Steven drove Ailsa Lloyd four times over four weeks, always to the same address. He can write it down for me, but that wasn't where she went two nights ago. Two nights ago she cancelled the car, and whatever she did, Steven can't say.

54 Oliviera Close, in Sapolo, just beyond the Shearwater line. When I ask, Bø says Sapolo is really a suburb, like Shearwater has those any more. He drives me past, and it's a residential street, dull houses, one of them for sale. She was, after all, a realtor.

Bø takes me back to Celia's through the old part of Shearwater; the half kilometre square of fisher cottages and canneries is all winding alleys narrow enough to shake hands across the street. In other places I've been, the shadows make the ground level cool even at midday, but the hard concrete of the surface here soaks up heat so that even in the shade the old town is a dry, punishing oven that saps your energy and makes you want to lie down and die. It occurs to me, as I walk, that if a person was looking for an opportunity to ambush me, now would be the time, in these cramped little byways, but they don't. Obviously I haven't met enough people yet.

We turn left one more time and then we're coming out into the main streets, and a woman pulling one of those chequered shopping baskets on wheels gives me a look that says I'm up to no good. I guess men in taxis coming out of old town alleyways often are. She turns away, as if it's no more than she'd expect.

I'm just about done when I get through the hotel door, but as I head up the stairs, Miles tells me there's a message from Sporty Jasmine.

"She wants me to call?"

"No, Mr Sounder. She wants you to meet her. At the railway station."

Miles, being Miles, has already arranged a car for me to get there, because he doesn't believe guests at Celia's should walk.

Thirty minutes later I'm standing on platform two, watching Mini Denton in boxing-inflected business casual get down out of the old Transriverine Express, red trim dusty with salt and black glass sand. Behind Mini is another woman, dark haired, younger and confused, wearing a pant suit and a tifafai band to say who she is or wants to be. She has a black bamboo-fibre case over one shoulder, branded with a familiar name: Deerborn Real Estate. She sees me, looks at Mini, and then abruptly starts to run down the platform, bag jouncing on one shoulder, until she's in a flat-out sprint as if the devils of hell are behind her and I'm the last saint in all the world. Her shoes have low, sensible heels and a rubber front sole—realtor's walking shoes—so she runs like a hurdler about to take off until she arrives weeping about two metres away from me and stops cold, not knowing now what to do or say. She has a long face like a disappointed social worker and long fingers like a pianist, and she's willow lean and tall enough that from that distance she can look up at me comfortably. Arriving a moment later, Mini Denton says, "This is Cal Sounder," and the woman nods, and finally makes a decision. She lunges forward and puts her arms around me and cries out loud. Mini, still perfectly calm, says: "She was fine on the journey. Sorry, I should have seen this coming."

I have no idea what's going on. Girlfriend, sister, best friend, colleague. Then the woman steps back and straightens up. She puts out her hand for me to shake as if her whole face isn't streaked with tears to match the damp blob on my lapel.

The woman says: "Hi, Mr Sounder. I'm Ailsa Lloyd."

3

We stash Ailsa in one of the rooms at Celia's overnight. Mini Denton takes the one right beside it, with a connecting door, and in the morning we walk our prize to Dansen's and the guy brings us lava coffee. Mini stares at it a while and then quietly goes to the bar and gets herself a lemonade. Lloyd doesn't. After a couple of sips she looks steadier, more solid. A caffeine junkie, which is no surprise: she has the look of someone driven, smart and just a mite shocky under the skin. Can't say I blame her for that last, but it's gonna take her longer than I've got to process this, and I don't want her forming conclusions before I get the straight answers.

"So tell me, Ms Lloyd: when did you make partner?" I ask, and her eyes open very wide.

"A week ago. How did you know?"

"He's a little bit magical," Mini Denton says, lips pursed above her straw. She doesn't like it when I show off.

"I took a guess," I said. "You want to hear some more?"

She nods. "Now I'm curious."

"You're the youngest they've ever taken on. You had to scream and yell to get them to say yes, but two or three of the top cats think you're worth it, and that matters more than the seven or eight mid-rankers who are pissed as hell they got passed over again."

She laughs. "That's about the size of it."

"And you absolutely have not been murdered."

She shakes her head. "Nope. All here. Head, shoulders, knees and toes."

I take a picture of the dead woman in Fallon's drawers from my pocket and slide it over to her. "You know who this is?"

She nods. "Janey."

"Janey have a last name?"

"I don't remember. Something... chonky and North American, I think. Miller. Mueller. Fuller. She was a temp in the office. I didn't really get to know her."

"Well, she knows you."

"I guess so."

"I'm going to ask you a bunch of questions now in no particular order. Some of them are weird. I'm not doing it to be an asshole, I need you to answer them without trying too hard. Once people settle into a line of recollection, they get to making up things when they don't recall. They patch the gaps and believe that's what happened. It's natural but it doesn't help. Okay?"

"Oh, yes. Of course."

"Did you like Janey?"

"Yes."

"When you were a kid, did you have pets?"

"What?"

"Some of them are weird."

"Oh. Sorry."

"S'okay. So: did you have pets?"

"Uh. Yes. Sure. A pet."

"What kind?"

"I had a lizard."

Mini raises her eyebrows. I didn't have Ailsa down as a lizard kid, either. You don't know people just because you see them.

"Did you socialise with Janey? Go to a bar?"

"Yes. We went to Morgan's in the Brewery District."

"What did you drink?"

"I had margaritas. She had that awful red stuff. Bitter, with orange."
"What was the lizard's name?"
"Lizard."
"That's creative."
Her lips twitch up in a smile. "Oh, sue me."
"What did you feed it?"
"Bugs. I never felt sorry for them. Now I feel bad about that."
"Was Janey hired through an agency?"
"Yes, we always use the same one. Hargreave-Todd. They give us a low rate."

That's a Tonfamecasca holding. In Othrys, lots of things are. I imagine putting handcuffs on Athena, which is a mistake, because then I remember putting handcuffs on Athena two months ago, and the long, slow night we had.

Get your head in the game, Sounder.

I've run out of lizard questions, so I ask about sport. Ailsa Lloyd was not a sports kid, but her brother was, softball. Still plays, still loves it, doesn't care to compete in any structured way. She got all the drive, but she worries, sometimes, that he's happier.

"Janey seem like she wanted your job? Working her way up?"
"No, more like she wanted gone as soon as she could."
I think of the picket line. *All piss and vinegar.*
"She the type to make a fuss?"
"What kind of fuss?"
"Any kind. Someone took her food out of the fridge. One of the boys has lingering eyes. I guess she wasn't there long enough to get passed over."
"'Lingering eyes.' That's the nicest way of saying 'sex pest' I ever heard."
"Thank you."
"Not really a compliment," Mini says. "Ms Lloyd?"
Ailsa blinks. "Oh. Did she make a fuss. No, she was . . . mousey. I barely noticed her until we went out. Then she was hilarious. One of those people who keeps it all inside until five oh one, I guess."
"You have keycards for the office?"

"Yes."

I show her the one from the Caffrey. She shakes her head.

"Ours are like a proper ID. They have the company name, and a picture and stuff."

"And Janey had one?"

"We all do."

"In her photo, how's her hair?"

"I don't— Oh! Janey *Williams*! Oh. You did that on purpose." Another smile, approving. I can see her making a mental note: ask about lizards, hair in photos.

"Thank you, Ms Lloyd." Although I'm not going to get too excited about 'Janey Williams'. Something tells me it's not the last name I'm going to hear.

"Happy to help. I mean, not happy ..." She waves her hands: violent mortality.

"I have one more question, Ms Lloyd, because the cops are going to ask. You know you need to talk to the cops, right?"

"Of course."

"Can you prove where you were two nights ago between ten and five?"

"Oh, yes. That's easy. I have, you know, witnesses."

I figure she was in the office. Conference call with Hong Kong or Brisbane.

"What were you doing?"

"I was having sex."

"With witnesses."

"It was that kind of night." She grins like we've all had them, which looking around the table I guess we actually have. Mini Denton is staring hard at the ceiling, trying not to laugh at my face.

"And someone will be happy to back you up?"

She nods. "I'm sure. There's probably a home movie or two as well."

I drink some more lava. Athena's right. Sex isn't a scarce resource.

"Are you working on a purchase in Shearwater?" Mini steps in, before I can say goodbye. Mini Denton is in the process-orientated stage of becoming a detective. She does not like that I leave detail on the table.

"I was, a couple of months ago. I had a brief from a confidential client looking to acquire various Erskine Company properties either outright or as part of a regeneration partnership for Shearwater. It didn't fly. That was disappointing, honestly. It sounded like it could have been amazing."

"Martha Erskine doesn't share?"

"I don't think that was it. The buyer pulled out. No acrimony, just ... no longer interested in Shearwater. The partners put me onto something overseas instead, and it went really well. I actually just got back."

Mini smiles. "So you had a deal and a partnership to drink to."

"Yes, I did! But I don't really drink, so ..." She laughs, then flushes—not a blush, probably a memory, like the one I just sat down hard on, of Athena twisting and smiling—then sobers. "God. Two nights ago—that's when she was killed, isn't it? Wow. Sex and death." Mini catches it before I do, but only by a second. Her arm wraps around Ailsa Lloyd's shoulders as they start to shake. I pass her a paper handkerchief from the aluminium box on the table.

I get up and lean on the wall beside the door. I call Iverson's number, and he picks up straight away. "Cal?"

"Hi, Tim. I'm having coffee with Ailsa Lloyd."

"You're drinking coffee in the morgue?"

"I'm in Dansen's. Ailsa is too. I'm not a doctor, but I'm gonna say she's alive and well."

A long pause, and then he says something they probably would have burned you for back in the day. Says it quite a few times, actually, which is fair.

"I'm coming over there. Does she recognise our victim?"

"She says Janey Williams did temp work for her a couple of days last month. Says Janey seemed like the type to move around."

Iverson doesn't take long to work that one out.

"Well ... shit."

*

I leave Ailsa to Iverson, with Mini babysitting. She's proprietorial, giving Tim a stern look as he sits down: you be nice to this kid, copper, or it's your ass.

"You got a partner," Iverson says to me, surprised. "I didn't expect that. It's a good call."

"Stray dog," I tell him, and Mini raises one finger to usher me out.

I'm not figuring to do much of anything but walk and think, so right away I get company: an angry little man in hand-cut suit yelling at me as he approaches. Guy's wearing two-tone brogues in a beach town.

"Are you Cal Sounder? The PI?"

I let him get all the way to me so I don't have to yell back. When you raise your voice, even if it's just to be heard, people can read it the wrong way. Or the right one. The guy's still yelling, right up in my face.

"See here, mister! You come see me when your feet touch dirt in Shearwater!"

"Is that right?"

"It is! It absolutely is! You work for the Tonfamecascas and this is not your town!"

"I don't."

"I beg your pardon?"

"I don't work for the Tonfamecascas. I am cohabiting with Athena Tonfamecasca. It's not the same thing."

"Don't shit me, city boy. When your plus-sized feet hit the ground here, I should have been your first call, and you know it."

"I don't even know who you are, peacock, but I'm guessing you don't do a lot of walking."

He'd bristle if he wasn't already all hackled like one of those small dogs that has a heart full of fight and a head full of nothing. "I'm Lance Vesper, that's who!"

Head of Erskine Security. I'd pictured him different: a slow guy without much to say, doing the quiet bad things and not making waves. Letting the young ones bark at the strikers. This item seems oddly peppy.

"Hi, Mr Vesper, I'm Cal Sounder. I'm sorry we haven't met yet, but I'm here working a case, and you're corporate security for the Erskines, who could be involved. I can't be checking in with you like you're in charge."

"I am in charge, Sounder. Shearwater is a company town, and I'm the damn company."

And, look, he brought friends: Reason and Holbrook and their older brother Jimson. Still all calm and quiet, and now he's paying attention I don't like him so much. Those bored eyes are too smart and steady. I'm starting to think he knows what he's doing, and maybe specifically around Titans.

"Hey, boys," I say, and wave.

"You're real funny, Sounder," Reason says. "Hugh Djasz like Huge Ass. Like we're ten years old. Real professional."

"Well, you were making yourselves obnoxious." Looking for a nod from Jimson, but I'm not getting one, just a loose-limbed lack of concern.

"They were doing their damn job," Vesper says. "And if you sass any more of my people you can expect consequences."

"Is that how it is?"

"That's how it is."

"You mind if I ask you a question?"

"So long as it's respectful."

"Where were you two nights ago between ten p.m. and dawn?"

It's interesting to watch him turn red.

"Go to hell."

"Thank you, I'll put you down for no alibi, and since we're doing this: where were all you others? Dave? Phil? Matthew?" Nothing. "For that matter, where was your boss? Does Bail Erskine go out on the town? Does he have a party place on the promenade?"

"None of your damn business."

"Well, see, Mr Vesper, now I think you're pre-judging the situation. I mean, if we suppose Bail Erskine went and strangled a girl on the beach, then he's very much my business. And you know as well as I do that I'm gonna look that way. It's an old story: family man, patriarch, kingpin, sure, but even then, a man has desires, and they can be unpredictable and fierce. Maybe especially then. And sometimes the ladies he directs his attentions to can be unreceptive in unflattering ways, especially to a fellow who's as physically old as Bail. Your man wants a few years of the experiences of genuine age, is what I'm told, and here's one of them: getting turned down by young women. Or maybe not turned down, but when it came to it, well, the frailty of an older libido, if you see what I mean. So maybe he isn't quite as prepared for that as he thought he was. Maybe she makes an unfortunate remark. She wounds his pride, and he responds by murdering her, and telling you to tidy up. It's not like that would be a new tale, so why don't you ease everyone's pain and tell me he was at the Rotary Club with five justices and a famous golfer, playing backgammon all night long?"

"This is my town, Sounder. You don't ask me shit like that."

"You said that before, Mr Vesper, and I didn't much like it then. It's not your town, and it's not Bail's. It's not even Martha Erskine's town. It belongs to the people who live here, and I gather more than a few of them have beef with your employer right now."

Vesper looks around and now we have a problem. Dansen's is hardly an early evening hotspot, but it's not tucked away either. There's a few people idling nearby now, and our voices aren't exactly private.

"Gentlemen," Vesper says. "Explain things to our friend here."

"Oh," Iverson says, coming out into the street. "Hi, Lance."

"Hi, Tim," I say. "Mr Vesper here was explaining how things go in Shearwater."

"And I'm sure he was explicit about the hard separation between his role in securing the extensive holdings of the Erskine family and mine as the appointed chief peace officer of the town."

"Now that you mention it, Tim, we were just getting to that part."

Vesper looks like he swallowed a live animal. He snarls at me.

"If you make waves, you're done here, you understand me?"

"Well, it's nice to meet you, Lance. I hope your nose is okay."

He actually says, "There's nothing wrong my nose." I don't punch him, but I move my shoulder just enough that he flinches. Then I run my hand through my hair.

Through all that, Matt Jimson doesn't so much as twitch.

Iverson takes Ailsa Lloyd and a second coffee in a to-go cup back to the police station, and Mini and I walk around the town centre, not looking at the closed shops and the cracked windows.

"This ever happen to you before?" she asks.

"Did what ever happen?"

"Wrong name on the toe-tag."

"That's a nice image."

"How much does it happen?"

"It happens. Sometimes it's a mistake. Sometimes it's not."

"So what do you think?"

"What do *you* think?" Because honestly, I don't have an idea.

"I think Janey Williams wasn't her name either. I think she was into something. I think she came down here with a plan and it went sideways."

"Everybody has a plan, Sporty Jasmine."

"You're saying don't jump too early."

"No, you can jump all you like. Just know when it's time to jump back again later."

"Here's to the Trinity," Mini says, raising her lemonade. Not the Catholic one, the crime one: sex, money and power. "What do you need from me now?"

"When Iverson's done with Ailsa, take her back to Othrys and have her walk you into the Deerborn office. Talk to the partnership. Get them to ask the client for permission to read you in. If this is about her deal, then it's a problem for them too."

"You think they'll go for it?"

"For me? Hell, no. Since it's you, maybe."

Mini makes company types feel happy and secure. There's something in the way she wears conservative anthracite and flies through a slide presentation that's like milk and cookies to people who routinely work in eight figures. The same people take one look at me and see something that doesn't belong in their yard. They're not wrong.

"What are you going to do?"

"Meet the victim. Again."

Fallon says there was activated charcoal in the stomach cavity.

"You know what that's for?"

"Overdoses and poisonings."

"That, and some women take it when they're drinking in bars. It doesn't do much for alcohol, but if someone slips you something it gets stuck in the charcoal and you go home on your own ticket."

"That's reasonably horrible. Was there anything stuck in the charcoal?"

"No."

"So it was a precaution?"

"Fuck, Sounder, I don't know. I feel like an asshole."

I don't argue. No one likes it when they misname a dead body, but it happens more than you'd expect. The image recognition system isn't perfect, and all the many different agencies and departments have a habit of using their own standards and pictures, with the result that a system that's supposed to be over ninety-nine percent accurate in the real world comes down to more like eighty tops, and that twenty percent is a whole lot of queries per day. Most times the coroner's offices will run a face several times before they write the tag, but when a body has clear picture ID and a case is hot—well, why query a bad system when you already know the answer?

I don't ask her whether Ailsa Lloyd's family just got uninformed of her death, or what they said if they did.

"And no, I have no fucking idea what her real name is," Fallon says.

"You knew someone who knew her." I still have the address in my wallet.

"Angela." No hesitation. I'm glad because I like Fallon and I don't want to ask her where she was when someone was drowning not-Ailsa. "She has a bar called the Roller. It's a heap. And about a lifetime too young for me." But there's something there, some almost-smile.

"Hey, Fallon?"

"Yes?"

"You know two rough boys hang around together? One with red hair, the other older with the words 'Fish Food' inked on his hands?"

"You should ask Iverson."

"I don't want to throw chaff his way. Or get them in trouble they don't have coming. They got that local character feel. Figured you live here, maybe you could tell me."

"I don't know what you think I'm into, Sounder, but two angry men with bad tattoos is not it."

"So that's not the crowd at the Roller."

"That's more the Swordfish."

"And that is?"

"A longliner bar near the boathouses. They come in with a good enough catch, the boys'll burn through a ton of money saying hi to everyone. Then they wake up and they've spent what they meant to save and they drink more to feel better about it, then they fight whoever's nearby, everyone gets stitches and they do it all again."

"They find enough fish for that?"

"Sure, if they go out towards the ice, sure. A month away, maybe. But only the owner captains ever make real money, and not all of them."

"Why not?"

She sighs and looks at me patiently, like I'm from impossibly far away. "Boats leak, Sounder."

I wait, but apparently that's all, so I ask how long before we get a new ID. Fallon's running a deep search through the national police files, the kind they do when they really need to know rather than when they want to tick the box, but by the same token it's going to take hours, even days. Processing time and cycles cost money, and the department never has any.

I call Captain Gratton at the Chersenesos precinct and ask for a favour. He's a friend, or was. Gratton doesn't pass me so many cases any more. My value to him was as an honest broker who was known to be honest, and while no one's suggesting I'm not that guy any more, the optics don't shine the way they did. The guy who said no to Athena Tonfamecasca because she was a Titan is one thing; the guy who moved in with her after she made him one is another. But that doesn't mean we can't help each other out.

"No," Gratton says, "absolutely not."

"How about if I said please?"

"It's Iverson's case, Cal. I'm not duplicating a search he's already running. Twice the cost for the same result so you can have it before he gives it to you, which he will, and you know it. You gave him Ailsa Lloyd, for god's sake."

"I'd have brought her to you if it was your case."

"You'd have made me wait for days. Maybe until you were done."

"I was trying to make a good impression."

"You mean you can't presume on friendship."

"That, and I don't want to lean into the Titan thing."

"It's nice how *now* you're all fucking bashful," Gratton snaps. "Run it through the Tonfamecasca system, I hear it's comprehensive."

That hurts a little bit. I don't work for Tonfamecasca and he knows that. I freelance for them sometimes the way I do for anyone else, but I didn't take Stefan's gold. I'm just living with his daughter.

"It's a single database. Yours is networked."

"You want me to run a deep search, which another department is already running, just so you can keep up with your cop friend in Shearwater. Do you have any idea how much that costs?"

"I can ask the client to reimburse." I want Gratton to run a search because sometimes two departments get different answers. It's in the nature of the mosaic.

"Oh, sure. Then the Othrys police department is taking payment for services from—remind me, who's your client?"

"A person in good standing, well-known in the community."

"And screw you. Do you even know whether they have a criminal record?"

"I sincerely doubt it." It didn't occur to me to ask. "If so, I would expect it to be a very long time ago."

"How long?"

I can't answer that. If I tell him the answer it narrows the field from billions to dozens. With an interest in Shearwater, probably only one.

When I don't say anything, Gratton huffs like I just proved his point. I guess I did.

"Come have dinner," I say, as I leave. "At the apartment."

"Love to," Gratton tells me, and I can hear him making the calendar entry in his head: Tuesday, never.

Fallon was right. The Roller is a heap, and it's so young I feel older than Martha just walking through the door. It's surf-inflected, all shiny wood and Hawaiian prints. There are tropical flowers growing in baskets everywhere and the greenhouse-glass ceiling isn't shielded to keep out the heat, so Angela just opens all the windows and floods the place with aerosol water every ten minutes. It's a steam room, and my clothes cling to my body about twenty-five seconds after I walk through the door. I can already guess who comes here: every pretty person between seventeen and thirty-seven, looking to get hot and wet while they drink, show off their perfect tens. There's a board of instant photographs behind the bar, the chemical kind, not the ones from a mini-printing camera. The definition is worse, but they don't run in the wet. I want faces, I don't care about composition.

It's barely lunchtime so there's almost no one here, but Angela is setting up, watering orchids and other things I can't name. She has a tattoo, like Fallon, and it occurs to me for the first time to wonder how exactly they know each other. I wonder if Angela was one time a mortician too, and decided she didn't like it.

I have a badge issued in Othrys. It says I'm a consulting

investigator, and it has my full name and registry number, 019. I show it to her. I don't know why, but instinct tells me to.

"Hi," she says, hard neutral.

"I'm Cal. Fallon told me you knew Ailsa Lloyd."

Angela looks away. "I just heard she's dead this morning."

"She is, and it turns out Ailsa Lloyd wasn't her name. I met the woman your friend borrowed it from just now."

"Shit. I guess she's having a fucked-up kind of a day."

"A little freaked out, maybe."

"You would be. So did my friend have a real name?"

"She had another name. I doubt it's real."

Angela peers up at me. She has on a tank top and lightweight ripstop pants, perfect for the room and the draught ales, for the surf-momma vibe. Just a hint of street brawler in the biceps and the way she leans onto her toes. "It's like that?"

"I don't know what it's like yet. I know I'm in the third day of a murder case and time matters. She lied about her name, so I'm working it."

"You think she had it coming?"

"Sure, maybe she was a serial killer. Or on the run. She gave a false name, she got murdered, she had activated charcoal in her stomach. I don't know barely anything about her because so far she lied to everyone she met. That narrows her down to a very few kinds of people depending on her reasons. I want to know what those reasons were."

"You know what the charcoal's about?"

"Do you?" Because if this is where she drank, then this is where she thought she was at risk.

"She didn't need it here, if that's what you mean. I see anything even looks like that in the Roller, I'll feed the fucker through a dredger engine."

"So it doesn't make sense to you."

"Maybe she thought someone was going to kill her, you think of that?"

"It crossed my mind."

Angela follows that one through. "Oh. And if that is what happened then it's probably going to be obvious who that is when you find out her real name. So I'm being kind of a dick right now. Crap."

She goes back to the bar, and the silence is so abrupt that for a moment I think she's just lost the thread, like maybe she's coming down off something. Then I realise she's going through the book.

"Keeler, Machado, Lapp ... Lloyd, Lloyd, Lloyd, where are you ... " her finger traces the entries, handwritten in ballpoint pen. "Yeah. She ran a tab and always settled in cash."

"How much cash?"

Angela frowns. "A whole hell of a lot, actually, when you count it up."

"So there's a bank somewhere that knows her."

"There is a bank that knows everyone. But one time she came in here and at the end of the night she used a card. A friend's, she said. Christy Farber." Angela passes me the book, and I write down the name, the card number. First Othrys Mutual: upmarket high-street banking for the young executive set. A cut above Ailsa Lloyd's social grade, and a mile above mine, until Athena.

Christy Farber. Same vibe as "Ailsa Lloyd" and "Janey Williams", somehow. Not ordinary, but not remarkable. Middling names. You might remember, you might not, but none of them makes you stop and ask "who?"

Did Christy Farber argue with her bosses? Did she make trouble and have to move on? Did she get a payout and go looking for another in Shearwater, trip over a manager with a temper?

Anything's possible. Keep going.

I kick off the floor and spin around once on the bar stool, ask my next question.

"She hang out with anyone in particular when she came in?"

Angela nods. "You know how some people are just out there and everything gets wild around them? She was like that. She'd be in here half an hour and the whole mood would change. Not just her table. Everyone just pushing it that bit further, taking risks.

Dancing, another bottle, flirting. Definitely not a going-home-alone mood? The waterfront set lapped her up."

"Who's that?"

She snorts. "You know who I mean. A town this size there's only one clique worth the name. The party people. Some post-grads from the university in Othrys at the weekends, a few local rich kids and a couple of surf-and-code startup geniuses, plus any of the other Shearwater kids they think are interesting this summer."

"Interesting?"

"Fuckable, okay? Jesus. Don't pretend you don't know how it goes."

"I know how it goes. I just don't know how it goes here."

"Well, that's how it goes. Every couple of years the guard changes. Every few months someone gets brought in or drummed out. It's society, anywhere you go."

"Who makes the running?"

"The money, of course. Anyone who parks a big boat in the marina. Anyone from the big houses on Erskine Hill. Anyone who can drop a name and make a splash. The local kids fill in the blanks. Young ones get to the drinking age. Old ones move on. It's a cattle market."

"It ever get worse than that?"

"Not in here." Steel, suddenly, her jaw very tight. "In here, I see anything I don't like, anything I ever might not like, you're done. A week, a month, a summer, life. What I say, goes."

"You seem awful cut-up for someone who runs a foam bar."

She comes out around the bar so fast it's like dog racing. Her face is right up in mine. "Fuck did you say to me?"

I look down into her eyes and she is ready to go. Angela will actually take a swing at me if I push her, and I kind of love that.

"I'm going to find out who killed her, Angela. I can't do that if you break my jaw."

"Not like I couldn't."

"Oh, I'm sure you could, but if it comes to it don't use your hand, use a stick, okay?"

"Fuck you." But she's not angry any more, just unhappy, because there's a dead kid and she's a bartender and the kid was one of her own.

"Angela?"

"No, I didn't."

"Not what I was asking."

"Sure it was."

"Maybe it was. Tell me who you kicked out."

"What?"

"You had someone in mind. Who did you kick out?"

"Oh, half a dozen in the last few years, just on instinct for the most part. One or two pushed their luck with my wait staff, maybe got handsy beyond what my people were okay with."

"Who got the lifetime ban?"

"Pretty boy with dark hair and a trust fund. They mostly do, I guess. Wide shoulders and a boatload of charm."

"Why'd you kick him out?"

"That was all me. I got a feeling off him I didn't like. Kid never heard a 'no' he couldn't turn into a 'yes'. That kind, they have to make a positive choice to follow the rules. He hasn't yet. Hasn't been asked." Unless he has, and I don't want her making that connection yet.

"Where were you between midnight and five two nights back?"

"Here. Cleaning up. Then home."

"Where's home?"

"South end of town, inland. Where the soil actually grows something."

"How do you get there from here?"

"You turn the key and you follow the highway, Cal."

"It's not much of an alibi, Angela."

"No, but I don't care about that, and nor do you."

"I might."

"Sure. Come back to me if you actually think I did it."

"Are you dating Fallon?"

She stops, and grins. "Dating?"

"Yeah."

"You want to ask if I'm stepping out with her?"

"Okay."

"Ooooh, are we holding hands in public?"

"Okay."

"Am I going to make an honest woman of her?"

"Okay, I get your point."

"Are you, like, a thousand years old?"

"It's just a question."

Now she's laughing. "Wow, kid. Just: wow. Your momma did a great job."

I realise we're about the same age, maybe she's got a year on me, but she's seeing the babyface and she hasn't asked herself what I am.

"You got a picture of the waterfront set? This year?"

She goes behind the bar and pulls two photographs off the wall. Blown-out faces, beautiful bodies in beachwear. Ashley, of course, and the camera loves her.

"Who's the kid?"

"Which one?" She leans around me to look at the pictures.

"The one you kicked out."

"Oh." Her finger runs along the line of the party, a couple of them there last night at the Grand Erskine, a few others not. Not-Ailsa lounges on a couch wearing a tango dress that's never been even close to a barrio. She has one hand on her hair and the other resting halfway up the thigh of a snub-nosed boy in a long-sleeved sport shirt. Rich cotton, gold and red and blue with white collars: European rugby, the professional league.

"That's him—Torrance Erskine," Angela says, her finger coming to a stop on the rugby shirt.

Back at Celia's, I call Iverson.

"It's me."

"Well, that's nice. Hi, this is Tim Iverson, who's speaking?"

"Cal Sounder."

"Oh, it's you."

"You're hilarious."

"Yeah, since I made captain everyone thinks that."

"You figure out where that paint came from?"

"Under the nails? I thought a boathouse. I was wrong. Then I thought a boat, but Dijkstra tells me you don't submerge the stuff."

"Dijkstra tells you?"

"He used to be a fisherman till he got pissed off with it. Long hours, he says."

"He got pissed off with long hours so now he's a cop?"

"He makes poor life choices. The paint's watertight and salt resistant, but there are sea things that love to eat it. Strictly lighthouses and machinery above the waterline."

"Sea things?"

"Critters. You want more than that you can go talk to Dijkstra."

"I'll pass. You check the dredgers?"

"No, Cal, because I'm a hundred-year-old incompetent."

"Not the dredgers."

"No. And not the big fishing combines, either. They use a similar paint, but it's orange and comes from China. This one's Brazilian. Bahia Blue."

"Dijkstra know that too?"

"No, that's the chemical analysis. Fallon sent me a boring report because the DNA hasn't come back on the other sample. I don't think it ever will."

"It's great that we know so much."

"Go to hell, smart guy. Say, you met Lance Vesper."

"I feel like I didn't make a great impression."

"That is true."

"How is a guy like that running ops for Erskine?"

"He looks good on TV. Bail has another guy for the real work."

"Jimson."

Iverson makes a clonking noise: nail on the head. "Walk a little careful around that one, Cal."

"Yeah, I saw."

"He got into it with some of the local boys a month or more back, four of 'em."

"How'd that come out?"

"How do you think?"

"I think that one of them got busted up pretty good, stitches but no dentistry. Let's say two more had big fat bruises and one of them turns out not to know how you fight with a bottle, but he'll keep his fingers. Jimson maybe had to get some dry cleaning done."

Again, the clonk. "But that's not why you should walk soft. The fisher boys are natural scrappers and some of the Erskine men have done a tour or two, but in the main the dark secret is they're sensible, ordinary boys. All a long way from what you'd call real hard cases. Jimson, though . . . I'm pretty sure Bail brought him in to mess with me. I think he's had some Paris training somewhere."

Paris. Not the city, but the legend: the man who murdered Achilles. It's smartass military code for someone trained in how to kill a Titan. When I was still just ordinary, I got the basic course from a friend, and for sure I don't want the advanced one from an enemy.

"Duly noted." I let it sit until Iverson knows I'm serious. "By the way, I got another name for you: Christy Farber."

"What's that?"

"Ailsa. Janey. Whoever."

"Huh."

"That mean something to you?"

"Not specifically. Keep going, I'll tell you when you're done."

"Figure you know Torrance Erskine?"

I can hear him not liking the question.

"I do."

"You know he got banned from the Roller?"

"Torrance gets kicked out of a lot of places. Usually more than once."

"I got a picture of him from Angela. Our dead woman has her hand on or about what the judge would call Torrance's intimate region."

"Doesn't mean he killed her."

"Hell, no. But you know it means we have to think he could have."

"Yeah, I hear you." He's making it pretty clear he doesn't want to. Figure this comes under the heading of me being persistent while he pretends to disapprove. *You're gonna owe me for this, Tim Iverson.*

Then he carries on.

"I said I don't know Christy Farber, but I'm not surprised either. I was gonna call you anyway: we started to get face matches about twenty minutes ago. Seems Ailsa is Janey is Becky is Susan ... A bunch of names all over. She must have been pretty good, too, because none of them was ever convicted of anything."

"You're saying she was a con artist."

"I'm saying there's a limited number of reasons a woman takes nine jobs in six months under nine different names. Some of those reasons are sympathetic. Most of them are not."

I guess that's fair.

"Any of those names actually hers?"

"Probably. The only one that has any real history is Mary Ann Grey. Twenty-seven years old. Liked hiking, photography and old comedy shows. Mother still alive, school yearbook picture is the same person."

"Mary Ann Grey." Tasting the name. Three parts, three syllables. Different from the others. Some people do that on purpose, so they remember to live in the lie.

Iverson sighs. "Well, whatever name she's using she's always a low-grade clerical or production line worker, and a pain in the ass if you're her boss."

"Yeah, that tracks."

"It does, but I don't think it was necessarily a bit. Turns out she was born in Tilehurst."

Oh, goddam it.

"And Tim, just because it would make everyone's life that much easier ... I figure there is not another Tilehurst where everything's just peachy and that's the one she happens to come from."

"There is not."

*

Twenty years ago and change my favourite cooking knife slips in my hand, and I can feel the edge—not blunt but not sharp enough to be undetectable in that frozen moment of shock and mistake—as it cuts the callous on my middle finger and the vibration from every whorl and ridge in the skin buzzes in my mind before the edge taps almost delicately on bone. I drop the blade into the pile of potato skins and slap a washcloth around the wound, holding my hand in the air, but I never get it properly checked out because the world has broken so badly that for six hours Athena and I just watch on our medium-size, obsolete TV screen: we watch men and women screaming and falling in streets just like ours, helicopters and smoke and armoured cars, and someone throwing something that we're told later is a petrol bomb, and a man on the ground as batons rise and fall and rise and fall again, and later we see his broken cheekbones in X-ray and the paupers' coffins being carried out of the ash, and blood slowly stops leaking into the little adhesive sutures from the first aid kit, as we realise there will a time before and a time after, and the scar will always remain.

Tilehurst is the shame, the moment more than twenty years ago when the skin came off the skull of the world. Depending on who you talk to, it's either the inevitable truth of the way we live or the perfect storm, never to be permitted again. The end was the Tilehurst Six hanging from a makeshift scaffold in the city's main square, Alton Lidgate in his corporate uniform, his left hand tracing the line of his right lapel, proclaiming that this was order restored and justice done, and then, later, Lidgate himself on trial, where he damn well belonged. The beginning was Tilehurst burning, red flames and the mob in silhouette, not riot but insurrection, and Lidgate's armoured cars and Lidgate's men with water cannons and gas, and then with guns, and torture not even for information but just to put people in their place, and the whisper of graves full of bodies written off as building collapses and fires. The arrival of soldiers from outside, the lockdown, and the whole country angry and lost, the yawning chaos under our feet as we wondered if everything would fall apart now, if it was time to buy shotgun shells and count who you trusted: who was family, and who was not.

No one running a con where they wanted to be inconspicuous would choose to come from Tilehurst.

Athena and I were together when it happened. It was the first time around, before I called Stefan to save her life and built a wall between us for a decade. We woke up as it was just breaking, on every channel on the TV. We sat there in pyjamas at ten in the morning. We stared at the screen and we cried. A lot of folks did. We cried until we stopped, and then we went out to do necessary things, and when we came back it was still happening. The story leaked out in dribs and drabs, spun and respun until it made no sense. Lidgate said he'd uncovered an armed takeover, some kind of coup, almost, by drug gangs seeking direct control of the city. There wasn't anyone to argue because by then he had all the aldermen under his protection, and they nodded and nodded and said their bruises were from gangsters, and shook when he looked at them.

But something was happening. Lidgate wasn't in control of all the neighbourhoods. His armoured cars were stopped by blockades made of street lamps and rubble and school buses; by fresh-mixed concrete blocks still drying, and tyre-cutters rigged from clothes lines and masonry nails. The news shows started to find people willing to go on air and call Lidgate a liar. They said they were just people, but somehow they came to be known as the 1848, the embodiment of a population under the boot heel, a spontaneous drawing of the line. Lidgate said they were shills for drug-barons.

In the month of April, Tilehurst burned for nine days. The smoke alone was a choking pall that drove people from their homes or killed them in their sleep. They lost water after the first forty-eight hours. It was like a war that came from nowhere, weather from the clear sky, and when it was done tens of thousands were unemployed, and homeless, and in jail. A year later, they worked out that

4,331 people were dead. Alton Lidgate died in jail, and everyone but everyone assumes he was helped along.

Tilehurst is the echo of something we don't want to name, the shadow of writing we choose not to read. The city still exists, and they say it's coming back somehow, that it's nice again, alive again, but you still don't say the name lightly. Mary Ann Grey was from a ghost town.

I can hear Iverson breathing on the far end of the phone. I almost ask him where he was back then, but I realise he was here, a few years out of his first dose and already decades in the job. We have a case and I have questions about today.

"Was she on any wanted lists?"

"She is completely clean. Except in so far as her face is associated with like a dozen other people, some of whom exist and some of whom do not, but none of whom is legitimately her."

"Identity fraud. But no money."

"Nope. Just one gig after another."

"Maybe it's not easy to get a job when your real name says 'Tilehurst' as soon as anyone looks." But she had money, from somewhere, this Mary Ann Grey. I think of Angela looking through her account book. Cash, every time but once. A lot of it, but not from the jobs. I wonder whether to tell Iverson, and decide: not yet. "Tilehurst. Jesus."

"I hear you. And it's another motive, maybe. Maybe something happened in Tilehurst and she got away with it. Or she saw something and someone else got away with it, and she's been looking over her shoulder ever since."

"She would have been, what, five years old?"

"A certain kind of person doesn't have that perspective."

Yeah. Monsters. Super.

Iverson must be thinking much the same thing. "You want my job for a month?"

"Definitely not."

"Well . . . shit."

*

"Caffrey front desk?"

"Sandra? It's Cal Sounder."

"What do you want?"

I'm following the money, as you do. "Did Ailsa Lloyd get any deliveries while she was there?"

"You mean like food?"

"Like in the mail. Or special service."

"Oh, yeah. Every two days, a parcel."

"When was the last one?"

"What do you care?"

"Might help me find out who killed her."

"Might might might."

"I'll give you a hundred."

"Get lost."

"Two."

"And when you get there, get lost again."

I get the feeling Sandra Ku does not love investigators on principle. Which is fine. A lot of people do not.

"Sandra, her name was not Ailsa Lloyd. Ailsa Lloyd is a sweet, scared woman right now sitting in the police department talking to Iverson, worrying that someone wants to kill her. The woman who stayed with you was maybe called Christy or Mary or something the hell else. I got no idea."

"Your friend Reason came in here and threatened me, you got some idea about that?"

"Dave Reason? The security prick?"

Long silence. "That's the guy."

"That might be my fault. Did he by chance look like someone chewed him out?"

"Oh, hell, yes. Some kid on the street gave him a fake name. Huge Ass. He was so excited he told his boss, got set straight real quick. Oh. Oh!"

"I have a childish sense of humour."

"You also got that two hundred?"

"I do."

"Last parcel was two days ago."

"You still have the paper?"

"No, she always took that away. But they just messaged me. The next parcel is due in half an hour."

It's late afternoon already when I open the parcel back in my room at Celia's. I'm not sure what I'm expecting—drug shipment, documents, clothes from Mom. The paperwork is drab and mendacious: to Ailsa Lloyd at the Caffrey from Deerborn Real Estate, but I'm guessing it never went through the Deerborn office. Someone called it in, met the courier, handed it over either outside the building or just dropped it into a hopper on a street corner. Maybe even set up a new account so that Deerborn would never query it. Mini will go through the place like a hot wire through wax but she won't find anything. Deerborn is a cutout, not a clue.

The pouch is soft plastic in the courier company livery. Inside is a block of money. It's not enough to shock you, but it buys a lot of drinks at the Roller, or a lot of services of various kinds elsewhere. One every two days. That's an impressive number of zeroes over a month. Whatever she was doing, it was expensive, and someone was paying—but they weren't all that careful about hiding it. They either didn't expect anyone to come looking, or they didn't care if they were found. I like the first one, because dumb bad guys are easy to work with. I don't like the second one at all.

I take out the plain white keycard and look at it. Safety deposit? Safe house? Car, apartment, what? And if so important, why wasn't it on her when she died?

Or did her killer realise that they still had it after the body dump, and bring it back to the Caffrey? Did they plant it? Or did she leave it for someone to find?

Ailsa Lloyd. Janey Williams. Christy Farber. Mary Ann Grey.

Mary Ann Grey, from Tilehurst, where everything burned. Dead now, in Martha Erskine's ocean, twenty-five years and a dozen lives away.

*

In a place like Shearwater the sea is the point of everything, and its presence is baked into all the houses and all the streets. Even now in this candle-end of fishing and mostly empty holiday rentals the salt water still governs the form of things, and so when I walk out of Celia's and head away inland to stretch my legs, west and a little south away from the front, I know it's only a matter of time until the turning of the roads brings me back around to the centre, and the promenade. I step out onto the grey-black of obsidian sand and keep walking until I come upon what I'm looking for without knowing that's what I was doing.

"Well, hi, there, Cal from support services."

I try to keep my eyes above her shoulders, but it's not as easy as it was with Josephine Addes. I don't have Emile Zoegar standing beside me, and if Josephine was heedless of how pretty she is, Ashley is the other thing. It's like trying to ignore a marching band, and my Titan self does not disapprove of the tune they're playing at all.

"Hi, Ashley."

She glances downward at something on the sand, and my eyes reflexively follow, getting caught on the way in curves and skin, the line of the bathing suit and what it does not quite reveal, then caught again by Ashley's own as I'm looking at her hips. She grins like a dolphin.

"Hi." She puts her arm through mine and reels me in, my elbow clamped somewhere noticeably not ribcage, and walks me down towards the water.

"Did you know, Cal, that I checked with City Hall and there's no roving gophers or handymen on the payroll this summer?"

"I never said I was a public servant."

"No, and you're kind of wearing a suit. So what do you do, Cal?"

"I actually need your help."

"So true."

"As a local guide. Paid work."

"You want me to show you the sights? You know we don't really have those, right? It's the beach and Erskine Hill and the broken windows from La Serenissima to the old Hapsburg Casino. That's kind of the whole town."

"I was thinking more the surrounds. I figure you and your friends know pretty much every lost corner of the coast."

"Not, like, geologically, but sure."

"You party, you go by boat. Your moms took you to rock pools and hidden creeks and such."

"You're making my childhood sound a lot nicer than it was." Harder and sharper.

"I'll make it up to you. I'm trying to find an out-of-the-way place."

"I like that idea."

"A blue building covered in weather-fast metal paint. Keycard entry."

"And now it's boring again. All right, what else?"

I think about it. Mary Ann Grey didn't have a car.

"Walking distance from the Caffrey, or from a bus. No more than a half hour tops. Road access, probably."

"Huh. You sure about that last one?"

"No. But I figure if you have a private place, you got to have a way to put stuff in it."

"This is the coast, Cal. That doesn't have to mean a car." She nods to the water.

"I guess not."

"Contraband! Is that it? Long John Cal?"

"Yeah, that'd be nice."

"You know I have just the thing to turn your frown upside down."

"Is it an address?"

"Yep. Mine."

"Of a blue building with a keycard entry?"

Something in her face. She has it, or somewhere it could be.

"You said paid work. How much?"

I think of a number and double it. She whistles.

"That's a lot of money, Support Services Cal."

"Deal?"

"Sure. You bring it by any night after eight. Just call to let me know you're coming."

"You don't like surprises?"

"My place is like an oven. I need ten minutes to get some clothes on."

"Sold. You want the money up front?"

"I don't see you going back on a deal. There's a private beach past the far side of Martha's Point, just beyond the city limits. Bus from Holloway Drive, once every hour. No road access but there's a deep-water channel right to the rocks at the near end. The wreck there used to be a bar, and in the back yard there's an old shipping container. That's blue. I didn't think of it at first because you said a building, but I guess it counts. We tried to get in one time, but it was locked up. New lock, with a red light on it. I don't know about a keycard. I wasn't paying that kind of attention."

"Who's we?"

"Me and Torrance, a while back. Are you sorry you asked?"

"No."

"Liar."

"Was it serious between you two?"

"You mean, like, did I love him?"

"More like were you thinking you might marry him. He has advantages."

"Some women might take offence, Cal, at that implication. Would I marry the money? Is that it?"

"People who think that question is offensive generally haven't gone without."

"True fact. So, no: that's not where we were. And if I was going to marry a bank account, it wouldn't be Torrance's." She turns slightly, and the sun touches her just so as she half-whispers in my ear. "I'd wait for Bail to get his first dose, and marry him." She lets that sink in, then pulls away. "See you some night, Cal from Support Services. Remember: call ten minutes before you ring the bell. Or, you know. Don't."

She walks off along the shore, and the crook of my arm feels hungry where she isn't standing any more.

I take the bus from Holloway Drive because that's what Mary Ann Grey would have done, and I sit on the seaward side, because I figure she did that, too. It's the last bus this evening, and there's almost no one else heading this way: just a few old folks going wherever old people do. Canasta, maybe, or carpet bowls. I look at the faces, each one alone on a bench seat staring downwards into wrinkled hands, and realise they're not that much older than me.

The bus pulls up at the city limit marker and I get out. The old people don't look up.

Martha's Point is behind me, fenced off, serious about conservation and biodiversity. I wonder if Martha ever gets out of the water now, or whether she sleeps on her back looking up at the sky the same way I do back home, but where I have the buzz of Othrys all around, Martha has the sea. I wonder if, whatever she's done to herself, in a couple of hundred years I'll be doing too. If Athena will be happy as a sea person when we get too heavy for dry land. The cube law is unforgiving.

I wonder if Mary Ann Grey's body was dumped at Martha's Point, and if it was, whether she wants me to tell her, and what she'll do then. Is that why Vesper doesn't want me around?

Perhaps I'm sleeping now.

This isn't part of Martha's land, but it's hidden by it on the map. Here it's obvious, and boring, but you have to look hard at the paper or the screen to realise it's separate. I walk down towards the water, jump a broken fence into an overgrown yard, pebbles and scrub plants and black sand, and there it is: a standard international transport container about twelve metres long, flaking blue paint and a single red light on the chest-height door handle, like an eye.

I slip the keycard through the slot. The lock is set too close to the wall of the container, and my fingertips catch the edges of the flaking paint. The rust gouges at the quick, and I look down and see blue beneath the line of the nail.

I push the door and it swings open. The metal takes a long, slow time to reach its widest, and when I go in it's like stepping into a sound booth or a refrigerator. The walls are thicker than the usual container, and the space is an even temperature rather than the oven I was expecting. There's a cooling unit and even a dehumidifier. Someone's decorated so it's like a little apartment, drab rental colours and an efficient carpet taken up from a lobby somewhere, the cut edges rolling up against the first few centimetres of the walls. For a moment I wonder if this is the right place, or if I've walked in on a creative solution to the Shearwater property market. Not that there is one.

There's a low table and chairs, a filter coffee machine and a stack of books. The back walls have three couches arranged in a U and tangled sheets and cushions say they've done duty as beds. There are clothes and shoes and a washbasin upside down in the corner. Bachelor living for the secret society set.

There's no mystery around what society. There's a huge red star with a hammer in it, bold and go-fuck-yourself, spray-painted on the wall over the nearest couch. It's gaudy and absurd, and if I owned this place, I'd want that painted over and made good. I find myself looking around for more of the same: plushies and T-shirts and action figures, Karl and Joseph and Che. In the centre of the room there's a hand-press on a trestle table and a stack of printed matter: agit prop for the new age, cartoons of Ancient Greek Titans devouring children in togas. The bearded figure on the right isn't Zeus, it is indeed the founding sage of revolutionary communism, explaining the metaphor for the hard of thinking.

That's fine. I don't care if someone with a boy-crush on Karl Marx and access to stationery wants to hate on the Titans. Athena's the only one I've met worth a damn, and it's not like I'm objective about her. Her mother's more like Martha, disappearing into the strange and new; and Stefan's a bona fide horror who just happens to like me, for a given value of like that includes watching me die if that's the way it goes. So sure: let's talk about how the Titans consume the bodies of the young, and never mind that by any reasonable standard the revolution has a tendency to do the same. I just don't care.

But I do care about the workbench, and the eight barrels of something which may or may not be wired up to two neat sticks of fudge wrapped in plain paper. I say fudge but it's more like marzipan. If I lean down and smell it, I'll get a whiff of almonds. Not that I'm putting my face anywhere near. It's superstitious of me, because so long as I'm inside this room—inside of fifty metres—it really makes no odds whether I put my head near the explosives or not: if they go off, I'll be the first Titan on the Moon.

Now I know why the container has high-grade atmospheric controls: you wouldn't want the plastic to sweat. And it hasn't, so far as I can tell, even in the summer heat, but that isn't a reason to stay here for one more second. Almost, I walk straight out again, but then I stop. The thing about bombers is, they love tricks and traps. And they particularly like logic gates: if, then, and, or. *If* you open the door, *then* come in *and* go straight out *or* touch a particular thing.

I look down at my feet. I have to wonder if there's a pressure switch somewhere under the carpet, or more than one. Is there a safe route, and I just happened to walk it coming in? Or does the first sequence of steps prime it and the second detonate? What if I'm standing on the plate right now, and it's the act of leaving that finishes me off?

I stand there working it through: there'd need to be a safe-mode switch deeper in the room—except maybe that's what you'd expect and it's right by the door. Maybe it's the light switch. Or maybe that's a direct detonator for the stupid. Maybe maybe maybe, and I realise I'm just walling myself in. There's no point going on with this. I still have to leave. My phone isn't going to punch through the metal walls, and I don't want to be here when they get back. I crouch down, leaving my feet exactly where they are, and find the light trace of oil and sand which is my footsteps. I put one hand very softly in the toe of my nearest print and feel for a difference in texture, in what lies beneath. For a moment I think of touching Ashley like this, feather light and exploratory. That makes me think of Athena, laughing, and how I miss her. I put my weight into my fingers and lower my eyes as close to the surface as I can. There are ripples but no obvious pads, but then again, a switch can be tiny, a radio transmitter the size of a bug, and if you step on it the circuit breaks. Boom.

I decide to do it smart and cautious, so I stand and pick up one foot and put it down where my print is, and then the same again, one, two—but by three, I'm running, and then I don't even try to retrace my steps, I just lean forward as far as I can and throw myself out of the door, flat in the sand and then up, on, scrambling away from the enormous bomb. I keep running, floundering across shifting obsidian gravel into the scrub beyond until I'm standing breathless in the trees, calling Iverson, and the blue container is still blue, and the sky has no smoke in it and I'm not on the moon.

It takes nineteen whole minutes for Tim Iverson to get there, and I count every heartbeat of it. I'm not ashamed of being afraid, but I am ashamed of putting myself in that situation in the first place. I was careless, like a kid who thinks he's immortal. Bad habits creeping in at the edges: Titan thinking. Just putting off biological age doesn't make you deathless. Just being physically twenty again shouldn't make you dumb.

When Iverson comes, he comes with uniforms and a crew of bomb cops in big, stupid-looking impact suits like inflatable sumo for parties. In Chersenesos, the suits are dyed blue so they look official, but here they've bought surplus and they're desert brown, except the sergeant in charge, who wears arctic. I wonder how often she has to deal with something in this line: once, twice a year, an unexploded vodka still in the back country, maybe every so often an agricultural hydrogen tank. One summer in Chersenesos, Gratton's team was called out for 500 bottles of over-fermented ginger beer. We all laughed, but when ten of them went up, the little glass needles shredded the drone and came halfway through the visor on Gratton's observation gear. Mostly like that: dangerous, but not.

And then from time to time something more deliberate, where you have to hope the person who made it was careful and clever and good enough it won't fire just because someone in the northern hemisphere uses a cellular phone, but at the same time you hope they're not so good they're better than you.

"Get the fuck back," the team leader tells everyone, conversationally, then looks at me. "You: report." She comes up to my rib cage, but she's in charge as hell. The name badge on her shoulder says 'Iqaluq', no initial.

I tell her about the layout, the press, the workbench. She looks at Iverson.

"Preserve as much as you can," he says.

"We'll take pictures as we go in," she tells him, like that's probably all he's getting.

In the end it's better than we could hope for: the gear is laid out ready for assembly, but nothing's connected. The barrels are still empty, even if the two little sticks of military plastic by themselves are already enough to blow up a building. It's not a bomb yet, it's a plan, with ingredients.

People who handle explosives have to be methodical, so if something isn't right—if you need extra loops of wire, or more tape or solder, or just lunch—you don't start the process of putting everything together. I guess it makes sense: the overwhelming number-one cause of death among bomb-makers is bomb-making.

On the downside, the same thoroughness extends to obfuscation. The men's shoes are clean inside—Iqaluq thinks they wore plastic bags over their socks—and the whole container has been doused in what Fallon refers to as a spitball: DNA collected from multiple sources, usually bars, and replicated so that now, as Fallon tries to identify the people in the container, she's getting thousands and thousands of names. Not hard, or even expensive.

Back room biowork you can buy in any town with proper criminals. I wonder out loud whether we can run down the seller, but Fallon's ahead of me. It's bespoke, she says. Unbranded.

Iverson frowns along the beach. "You see what I see?"

I see a big metal box with a bomb inside. "I don't know."

"The bomb was going to be assembled within the container."

"Seems like."

"Which means it was going to be detonated inside the container."

He's right: again, you don't put the damn thing together and then carry it out with your friends. Once it is what it is, you want to leave it very much alone, and far away.

"A ship?" Maybe one of the dredgers. Imagine it going up in the middle of the bay, the mediapathic horror of the kids on kiteboards, the weird backdrop of the Sleepers on the evening news. Shearwater as context—a town slipping into the abyss.

Iverson shakes his head, looks inshore. "The Erskine plant," he says. "Got to be. But don't tell anyone I said so, at least, not anyone in town."

"You think you can keep a lid on this?"

"If I want to. For a while. I don't know if you noticed, Cal, but I have some connections." The Erskine family, who half do and half don't think of him as one of them. I wonder what that's like, and then realise I don't have to.

"It's a bomb, Tim. Possibly political. You have to call the Supras."

The Supra-Cantonal Investigative Authority, every cop's ultimate boss, whose Othrys office looks like a black armoured tomb, get very touchy about terrorist plots.

Iverson smiles a fey little smile. "Let me do that right now." He mimes picking up a phone with one hand. "Hi, is that SCIA office for East Coast Six?"

And now the other hand. "Yes, it is, Tim Iverson speaking."

"Tim, it's Tim Iverson, local law enforcement. We have something you need to be made aware of."

"Thanks, Tim, I'll be right there."

He puts down both phones, and shrugs.

"You're deputised," I say.

"A lot of cops in small towns are. And by the way, Cal, on that score: we are going to talk about you keeping back something like this," Iverson says.

"Aw, come on, Tim, I didn't know it was something like this until it was, and then I called you because I'm not a damn fool."

"You got anything else I need to know?"

"Such as what?"

"Such as something like a giant fucking bomb, Cal!"

He's taking this a little worse than I expected. I guess that's fair. He thought he had a murder to deal with. Now it's this. Radical escalation.

I think of the refectory hall full of people, the big trucks that come and go full of vanillin. I see the bomb go off, and the consequence. If that's the dawn of a better day, you can keep it: small-minded bullshit murder on a grand scale, no more changing the world than stamping on a man's back in the gutter outside a dive bar. Except that's something I've seen, human and horrible and personal. This ... this is new.

"No," I tell him. "Nothing like that."

Martha Erskine's investigation just got a whole lot bigger. Where does Mary Ann Grey fit into a bomb shop? Did they kill her because she knew too much, or did someone else kill her because they found out? And who are *they*, anyway? Three working men in their prime who don't smoke, don't care for beer, don't have so much as a swimsuit magazine. All right, maybe they're vocational soldiers of the cause, serious people without vices, although if they are, you'd expect more of them than to allow a loose end like this. And I don't like their shoes. Those shoes are mid-grade muddy, not clean the way you wear your Sunday best, and not soiled the way a pair of shoes gets when you do real work. They're grimy, like a middle-class boot after a day hiking. Like that star and those pamphlets, the container is a comic book in three colours, a superhero in a tight suit dishing out lessons in good honest thinking as he knocks down the bad guys. In the revolution according to the container people, guns get fired and no one dies; bombs go boom and only the wicked suffer. It's ridiculous. Is this how real revolutionaries think? I always assumed someone like that had more going on, a real plan, but maybe it's just blow shit up and hope like hell, and anyway it's more fun than work. Sure: it's not like the Titans of capital are geniuses either. Half of them act the way they do because they've seen it in movies. Is this the same?

A cartoon of resistance drawn by someone who doesn't know what it's for.

4

There's a slow train in sixty-five minutes but with Mary Ann Grey's key card in my pocket and a container full of bomb just outside town, I don't feel like waiting. I should have given it to Iverson but I didn't think of it and he didn't ask.

I call an executive transfer service Athena uses from time to time. She loves the ease, but I know the pilots.

"Zaher, it's Sounder."

"Hey, Sounder, what's up, man?"

"Is Billy Hussein working today?"

"Sure, Billy's in saddle. What you got?"

"I need a lift out of Shearwater and back to the city."

"Rafiq is closer, man."

"Rafiq Aziz?"

"Naw, that asshole crashed a goods quad full of lemon juice and milk, stank up a field north of town so bad even dogs won't go in there. We fired him hard. This is New Rafiq. Rafiq Malarmé."

"I thought you were trying to kill me, offering me Rafiq."

"Would I?"

"So New Rafiq is okay?"

"Hey, Billy! Sounder wants to know if New Rafiq is okay!"

In the background, Billy's voice says yes. Someone else—I'm guessing New Rafiq—says to go fuck myself.

"Thanks, Zaher, now the guy thinks I'm an asshole."
"Hey, I can't help if my pilots got good judgement."
"You're an asshole too, you know."
"But neither of us is an asshole like Old Rafiq."
"God, I hope not. Ask New Rafiq if he will please fly me back to the city in one piece for money."

New Rafiq evidently will.

I bill it to Martha Erskine's expense account. A quarter hour later a drone taxi drops out of the sky and I get on board. Two seats, plus room for luggage. New Rafiq is indeed okay, but I get the sense he's messing with me a little for my lack of faith. My stomach turns over as he banks on final approach and I'm looking straight down into the pool on the Conlin Street Tower two hundred metres below. Martha overtips him, because I can hear her laughing every time I have to swallow as the little machine goes tight around a corner.

Othrys in the summertime is a flat-iron heat. The breeze blows off the boiling land onto the lake during the day, and at night as the steel and concrete city cools, the clay beneath and the clear water beside give up their heat to the dark, keeping the temperature high the whole twenty-four-hour cycle. The apartments along the Plutus open their balcony doors; the Chersenesos towers spread their feathery arrays of heat exchangers out to run air conditioning systems for Titan residents and their rich ephemeral friends, and down in Tappeny Bridge the kids break open fire hydrants to spray the streets with water and keep them cool. It's not even illegal once the gauge hits thirty-eight Celsius: the lost water is cheaper than the dying.

Almost every building is a mass of vines and creepers, their roots in planters along the front curtilage, growing up towards the sun, so that from the farms to the Chersenesos batholith and from the west canyons to the Viderfluss, the whole city is one ferocious growing thing. At four o'clock in the afternoon, two or three times a week, it rains in torrents for half an hour, and the streets are slick with flower mulch, nectar and dust. You can smell summer in the city, sickly sweet and acid at the same time, and it makes your mouth water for something iced and hard to drink.

New Rafiq sets me down by the statue of James Baldwin, which is pretty much the only statue in Othrys I can stand. The Baldwin Plaza is the smallest open public space where the company will allow a landing, and the furthest into the city. In winter it's a quarter-hour bus ride from the Lacarte Free House, the communist bar where the Costanza brothers talk revolution and serve beer and vodka to poets and stevedores alike. In summer it's thirty minutes because the drivers can't let the tires run hot.

Tony, behind the bar, nods her head when I arrive. I have a history here that isn't awful, and the brothers think it's funny that I still come in. Even funnier that I kind of agree with them on a lot of things. The PR team at the Tonfamecasca Company don't think it's funny at all, but they get paid to worry.

It's gotten so there's a spot I like at the Lacarte, where I can see the door and talk to Tony at the same time. I sit down and take a moment to see who all is here. Two long tables full of construction workers, yellow hats on hooks under the benches. A trio of university students with too many books on the table and a whole loaf of black bread and pickles to go with their drinks. Some ordinary locals who just come in because it's close. The usual hard core at the big table under the arch, bearded and pissed off with everything. Lousy tippers, but they're talkers and believers, hermits of the Church of Karl. Marto told me he doesn't feel he can keep them out. And then there's the sextet in the corner, wearing mid-grade suits with no ties and no jewellery, talking and writing and answering phones. You might think they're managers, but you'd be wrong. National labour organisers don't come in Bolshevik cosplay. They're too busy trying to see it done. The woman in the window seat catches my eye, and I wave. She nods back. Even union presidents occasionally have lost cats and wayward spouses.

"What can I get you?" Tony asks, from behind the tall glasses.

"Dark wheat, some revolutionary socialist gossip and someone who's good with electronics."

I take out the keycard from the Caffrey and put it down where she can see it.

"That's not electronics. That's a card."

"Containing electronics."

"Barely."

"But I need to know what the card knows."

"Will there be wage slavery?"

"Well, since that person owns the means of production and will be paid full value for the product of their labour, I'm saying this is an enlightened and appropriate proletarian arrangement."

"Oh, hey, Sounder, you solved capitalism. You know what this opens?"

"A bomb."

She stares at me. I'm pretty sure it's the first time I've surprised her.

"Like a *bomb* bomb?"

"Like a shipping container full of explosives."

"Wow. Are you okay?" She looks as if she wants to check me for signs of blowing up. That's dumb, but I still have the same reaction about once or twice every hour, so we're dumb together.

"I'm fine." For a given value.

She picks up the card. "No prints?"

"Look at you with your forensic lingo."

"Jackass."

She flips the card over and looks closer, then pulls a space gun from under the bar, grey plastic and a purple emitter: an ultraviolet lamp for testing high-denomination bills. She pulls the trigger. The card goes dark pink. She flips it over and something shimmers on the surface of the card.

One. Eight. Four. Eight.

Tony slaps her hand over the light, and her voice comes out in a furious whisper.

"Jesus fuck, Sounder!"

"Sorry." I've got my hands up like she's going to smack me, and I'd somewhat deserve it.

"You're sorry? You're not even surprised. Did you know?"

"There may have been some other indications."

"Like what? The fucking Red Army Choir?"

"My murder victim was from Tilehurst." She starts to wave that off, and I have to tell her what else was in the container with the explosives.

"Are you out of your mind?"

"Keep your voice down."

"You're gonna come in here asking about that?"

"Who else is gonna know?"

"*You* are gonna come in *here* asking about that?"

"You think it's provocative."

"You *don't*?"

"I don't care! I just walked out of a big metal box with a respectable-size ammonium nitrate bomb in it, and the only serious target anyone can think of is a food plant full of ordinary working assholes who make flavourings out of plastic junk. So I'm a little short on deference right now to everyone's feelings about the glorious solidarity of the International!"

She looks at me long and slow, all the anger ebbing away to something that isn't calm.

"Well, saying that is not going to help."

"I was hoping maybe you'd ask for me."

"Fuck you so much."

"Will you?"

"Absolutely not. I'm going to talk to Matias. If he's okay with it, he can ask for you."

Matias Costanza, the angrier Marx brother. "Marto's not here?"

"No, he's on holiday. You just wish I'd ask him cos he reads too many old Hammett novels. Marto has a man-crush on your sorry gumshoe ass. Go on, get in the back before I change my mind."

She moves away down the bar, fluid and unconcerned like I didn't just ruin her day.

*

SLEEPER BEACH

The back room at the Lacarte is a beer cellar and bootstrap propaganda press like something from prohibition or wartime. There's a drinking water tap and a small sink, a pair of cot beds for late nights and as I see the flags I realise that the container could have been patterned after this. It's a miniature of the same installation with explosives instead of beer barrels, and for a moment I think about getting down on my knees to look for pressure pads. I don't know if that's trauma or just bad manners, but I don't do it, and a moment later the door opens and Matias comes in.

Matias Costanza looks like your big sombre uncle with a surprisingly pleasant singing voice. He wears a boatman's jacket open and denim he patches himself, sashiko style. On slow nights you can see him in the corner with a table lamp, peering down at the geometry of prudence and thrift. Unlike Marto, he doesn't talk so much, and unlike Marto, he doesn't think I'm funny. Tucked in behind him there's a boy almost as skinny as Matias is big, with a shock of midnight hair and sad Iberian eyes.

"This is Paulo," Matias Costanza says. "He can maybe help with your keycard problem. Paulo, remember what I said: set your rate, stick to it, and if Mr Sounder isn't prepared to pay it, walk away. That's what the union is for."

Paulo nods.

"I thought you'd invite me to leave," I say.

"Did you?"

Matias sits down. Paulo hovers, not sure if it's his time.

"Do your capitalism, for Christ's sake," Matias growls, "so I can stop feeling sick and have a drink with this asshole."

I tell Paulo what I'm prepared to pay and his eyes get briefly very round. He says that would be acceptable. I give him the card.

"I want everything you can tell me about this. How old, where does it come from. Is it just a keycard or is there other data? Can it tell me where it's been? I need a summary I can understand, and I need to know where to go to get more. Okay?"

From one of those stupid quarter-size backpacks Paulo produces something cobbled together from offcast digital junk. There's a little cubby for the card. He looks around and sits down on one of the cot beds. The junk box goes ping.

"My brother thinks you're a socialist and you haven't realised."

"Pretty sure he thinks that about everyone."

"Occupational hazard."

"If so, I don't always live up to it."

Matias sighs. "Socialism isn't Santa. It doesn't keep a naughty list. You want a drink?"

"I have one."

"How the fuck do you have one and I don't? Is this my bar or what?"

"Beer is theft."

He helps himself to a bottle from a crate and pops the cap on the edge of the table. One swallow, and then he bows his head.

"Tilehurst? You sure?"

"I'm not sure about anything. But it's there somehow. Have you ever been?"

"I went one time, about ten years ago. To touch the stone. It was nothing, just another town. But also not nothing. Like a ghost in the air, or a stink. Tilehurst drew a line, Sounder."

"What line?"

"You know what line. The same line you have a problem with. The one between us and the speciation rich."

"I'm guessing 'us' is ordinary people. Do I get to be part of that any more?"

"That's a question for you. Do you know the answer?"

"If you draw a line down the edge of the world and tell me I have to stand on one side or the other? How the fuck does that work?"

"Probably quite badly." He drinks again. "She saved your life."

"Yes."

"And made you a Titan."

"Yes."

"And before that, you saved hers by doing the same."

"Stefan did it."

"You knew he would."

I don't say anything.

"But then afterwards, when she was better, you couldn't be together any more. Why was that, Sounder? Was she just too tall?"

I chose for her because I couldn't let her die, and she never looked back. And then I felt she was on the far side of something.

"That," Matias says. "That's what Tilehurst did to us. All of us. It drew the line."

"It wasn't even a Titan thing."

"Doesn't matter. It was a money thing."

We sit there not angry but not talking, looking for a way back to the middle ground.

"Uh. Excuse me?" Paulo, with the keycard in his hand.

"Hey. What have you got?"

"Nothing, Mr Sounder. It's just a card. This year's software, pretty basic security, printed and set up on a portable machine. No company details or anything. It's . . . ordinary."

"If you were doing something secret, is this what you'd use?"

"Yes, I guess. It's clever because it's not smart. It doesn't connect to anything or tell me anything now that it's here. I could get past whatever it locks in about a half a minute, but with just the card . . . it's just a card. That's good practice. Sensible design."

"It doesn't say 'Down With Capitalism' in the firmware?"

"No." He looks confused. "I mean, I didn't check. Do you want me to run a deep scan of the code? I can do that. Otherwise I should cut the fee. You're not getting anything."

"I asked you to get me whatever information was in the card. You did. Value received. But sure, run the scan."

Matias scowls. "Don't teach him that capitalism gives a shit, Sounder, just because you do."

But I make Paulo run the scan, and it comes back empty.

Everything else in that container was showing off. Flags, papers, working men's shoes. The damn card has the publication date of the *Communist Manifesto* on it. But you go down a layer and . . . nothing. No frills, no pretty pictures, no traces. Anonymity by silence.

Matias rubs his hands as if he's cleaning them. He has tattoos on the knuckles, but the fingers are soft and fat, almost like a child's.

"The bomb was all built inside the box?"

"Yeah."

He shakes his head.

"There's not many targets you could take that container to that wouldn't be workplaces."

"I can think of one, maybe two."

Martha's Point, or just Martha. What would an explosion that size do to a Titan in the water? Hydrostatic shock? Maybe I'm looking at it all wrong: it's not a bomb, it's a depth charge. I ask myself why someone would want to kill Martha, but the answers are so many I have to stop. She's a four-dose Titan. That doesn't happen without some friction.

"What do you want, Sounder?"

"I need someone to talk to. About Tilehurst. And if there's anyone who might build something like this on your side of the line, I need to know that, too."

"On my side of the line."

Shit.

"You know what I mean."

"Do you?"

"I just want to know if there's someone here in Othrys who remembers. For the rest, if you can't, you can't. I'll try to stop it anyway."

Matias draws a breath like it hurts.

"I know one guy. Firefighter, back then. Not much now, to be honest."

"Will he talk to me?"

Matias extends his hand, palm down, and tips it one way, then the other.

I push my luck. "And the other thing?"

He shrugs. "Hey. You want to ask the room, Sounder, you be my guest. See what that gets you."

*

The Clearline is a square tower shaped by social architect Cheri Hayle, who also built the water treatment facility half a kilometre away, and she used the Clearline as a bracket for her grand design. That's what the name means: there's a clear line between the two, and she thought that in that space, between homes and work, she'd make a thriving polity of ordinary people, a culture of mutual support and assistance which would spread out along the lake until Othrys was a fine and pleasant land. She even thought the Titans would end up following along, carried on the tide of architecture.

Instead, the city just drowned the Clearline and its new ideas, and now it's a black-stained fortress glowering down at a sea of low-rent commercial, petty crime and fast food. The treatment plant is mostly automated, so the jobs blew away, and the hope with them.

I take the stairs to the seventh floor, because I don't trust the elevator one bit, not even with the shiny municipal plaque with the service dates etched on. Particularly not.

There's a slim, drab woman in blue overalls washing the floor with a grey mop as I go by, and we do a little dance around one another: sorry, sorry, thank you, hi. She's smiling as I turn my back, and it doesn't look like something she does a whole lot.

Apartment 709 has a name under the bell: Mirador, S. The S is for Simon. I don't ring the bell because Matias said it upsets him. It's wired to the phone, which is plugged in on the far side of the apartment from the door, so he has to choose whether to leave it ringing or take for ever to limp over there and back again. Instead, I just call out:

"Mr Mirador! It's Cal Sounder," and by the time I'm saying "Sounder" he's already there, like maybe he didn't have all that much else to do today, and maybe he was waiting.

I go inside and the word "apartment" seems a little grand. It's a single room with a galley hob and a toaster oven, then a chair and a bed, and a sliding door for a bathroom I'm guessing is about the same size as a closet. It doesn't smell good, and nor does Simon Mirador. He needs help to take a shower, and he doesn't get it but one day in five. They change the dressings on his legs every forty-eight hours, so the jockstrap flavour of the air is mingled with the tang of disinfectant.

"Come in," Mirador days. "Sit yourself down." He should be on a Zimmer, but he's not, he's using two sticks, wooden and homemade. Matias said he was a carpenter, and I wonder if he did these himself, taking back control.

He used to be a tall man, as baseline goes, clear over a hundred and ninety centimetres, but now he bends one way and the other, like an olive tree. He asks me what I'm doing here, and I tell him about a dead woman and a bomb in a box, and the stupid pamphlets and the flag on the wall.

"You want to know about Tilehurst," Mirador says.

"That's right." I had it in mind to offer him booze, or coffee, but now I see him I think that would be wrong. There's a jug of ice water on the counter, a half a glass by it. Herbs in jars for tea, and a stack of white pharmacy bags for his burns. Decades-old burns that have never quite healed right, with all that we can do.

He sees me looking.

"I wouldn't take it," he says.

"I didn't mean to stare."

"That's all right. You stare all you damn well want. I wouldn't take it. They offered it to me, said I could have my life back, all I had to do was give them names. I said no."

"What names?"

"Anyone I knew who was in the fighting. On the union side. Looking for the ringleaders, they said. A fact-finding, they said. I said the facts were that Alton Lidgate burned my home. Alton in person, you understand me. I said I saw him. They said that can't be. I said I did. Well, okay, they said, you did, then. Now, what else can you tell us? I said no."

No to T7 therapy, microdose for skin regeneration on his legs. Skin and quite some muscle, by the way it looks. Would have been fairly new back then. A lot of politics to get it for just some guy with burned legs.

"I said no," Mirador repeats, and I realise it's the truth of his whole life.

"You happy with that choice?"

"Hell, yes. You happy with yours?"

I almost tell him I didn't make one, but I can't. Looking into those mad brown eyes, I can't. I didn't make a choice then, but I've never regretted it that one was made for me.

"Yes."

He nods. "You should be ashamed." Not like he's angry, just a fact.

"Maybe I am. But I like being alive."

He watches me for a while, and I try not to blink, like we're in school.

"All right, then," Mirador says. "You're wrong, but you ain't a liar or a coward. And Matias Costanza says you're doing your best."

"He's a romantic."

Mirador laughs, dry and hacking, and flops down into his chair. There's nowhere for me, so I stay standing, and I figure he likes that.

"What the hell do you want to know about Tilehurst for?"

"Does it matter?"

"No."

I wait, and he waits, and then when he's waited enough, he just starts talking. His voice is strong at first, but gets reedy fast, and I wonder if it wasn't just his legs, but his lungs, too, that got burned when he was trapped in a house in Baker's Yard, on the Tilehurst mountain side. Trying to save a family, having to accept two out of five.

Reedy, so I pass him the water, but it doesn't much help.

"I went there for quality of life, you know that? Fucking schools and little bars, parks. I wanted to get a dog. Slow down. You know?"

I don't, so I nod.

"Fucking Tilehurst. Sure, quality of life, if you're in the right position, on the right side of the Rinsom-Walker company, then you can have your quality, your glass of wine at five o'clock. Your kids can pay for lunch, sure. If you're management. Otherwise it's just another fuckin' hole in the ground where you dig and dig and never find the bottom. You know they rigged the survey so that more poor people would come and fill their workhouses?"

I didn't know. It sounds possible, but maybe like too much effort. Probably they just made it up.

"It was a grab," Mirador says. "Not land but workforce. They wanted more head of population to make higher local unemployment, drive down wages. That's how they said it—'head of population', like when beef farmers talk about steers. Then they had it, and the infrastructure couldn't cope. City budget wasn't big enough, local taxes were too low. Not enough firemen, buses, power. The water system was at capacity, food they were shipping in daily from the coasts but it was getting hung up in traffic and if the trucks ran out of fuel the refrigeration'd fail and boom! Now it's just swill. So sure, build a bigger road, but that costs. That's fine, they're tight with the banks, so they tightened borrowing, cut wages ... bam. Like it was real clever to fuck people that hard and increase shareholder value. Like no one had any choices. No pushback. You know? So we pushed back. Not so hard at first, then harder. But it was a righteous push, no foul. You hear me? It was all clear water."

But Tilehurst was a rotten borough just like Shearwater is. The company men knew that and they put the screws into the factory workers deep, thinking that being the only game in town made them kings and princes. Which it did, and if they knew history at all they'd know that kings and princes walk a fine line, and when they step over it, the price is always high and hard.

Before hardly anyone outside of town even heard of Tilehurst, the execs at Rinsom-Walker bought themselves a month of strikes and pickets, protests in the street. But righteous, like the man says. If it had happened elsewhere, both sides would have come to the table, the way Rudi Basu is doing now with Bail Erskine, slowly but slowly dragging him to the water and showing him the cup, and the way Bail Erskine is doing with Rudi Basu, standing off a ways and saying he's not thirsty, not at that price, and the thing is so long as no one goes nuts, neither one of them has to get everything he wants for them both to get enough.

That said, there's a certain manner of person who thinks a deal is when they get all the toys and the other kids just have to give them up. Tilehurst had a man named Alton Lidgate, and he wasn't looking for the same thing as anyone else. Alton Lidgate—Simon Mirador hawks and spits—Alton Lidgate was a man to fight a war just because, but if there was one thing he wanted more, it was to smash the Tilehurst unions.

"It's fucking congenital with them. Old Man Lidgate read a book on the early Pinkertons and thought it was a business plan. Brought in all his kids, trained them from early. Like prayers. Smash the reds, smash them dead. But it's more than that. He wanted to step up: turn a service contract into a seat on the board. Physical violence into economic power. Not like that's never been done, right?"

"And on the other side?"

"Fuck you mean, the other side? You going to tell me it was six of one? Like I wanted to be in a fucking war? We were workers! Okay? Just people getting the fuck along, trying to save and prosper, like our parents told us. You work, you get paid, you save and one day you have a nice house, nice clothes, your kids go to a good school, grow up proud and live longer and they don't have dirt under their nails or burns on their arms and they run the world. That's the promise, right? Prosperity in the next generation. Except now what does that mean? The old rich don't die, they just get bigger. There was no other side. There was just people. Fuck. You want to see?"

"See what?"

"See what it was, asshole. What Lidgate was."

"Yes."

Mirador gets up and it takes a long time. He shuffles to the cabinet and gets a brown cardboard shoebox twenty years old and puts it down on the coffee table. When he opens it, the shoebox is full of crap: pieces of string wound around a man's hand and tied off, letters and a couple of medals out of the boxes, a mug, a cloth badge meant to be stitched on a sleeve. I see the Tilehurst firefighter sigil, fraying and discoloured with age. He fumbles and swears, then withdraws a drive card and one of those memento screens old people have for photographs and video clips instead of a terminal, block bezel and rubberised thumb-size buttons. He hands me the power cable and I have to get down on my knees to plug it in. Mirador smirks, presumably at a Titan on all fours. Maybe just because to some part of him I'm still the heat, private or no.

I get back up and the clip's already playing, handheld: a phone or a vest cam. There's a hubbub of noise, people yelling. It looks like we've just gone into a private house, barging through a cracked-open door and straight to the living room where a family is eating: an older man, probably grandpa, a couple and three kids, the youngest still in a high chair. The woman's black, her clothes traditional East African, maybe Sukuma style; her husband is more modern, and going by his accent, as he raises his voice to ask what the hell is going on, KwaZulu Natal.

Our group doesn't answer, this is a fast press action: secure the room, the corners, the doors, check the other floors but there's no one there, and by the time the boys come back from the attic, Alton Lidgate has already stepped in front of the camera and he's beating the old man. Behind him you can see his sons, like photofit copies in uniforms for kids, faces avid with paternally mandated rage. Lidgate gets so wild the high chair topples over, and when the father lunges to catch it, he takes that as hostile action. His hand touches his jacket lapel and snakes out, and I know what's coming, I saw the razor blade for just an instant before it vanished into his palm. It's a doorman's trick from the wrong kind of bar: a blade sewn where someone grabbing hold of you will cut themselves on it, but you can flip it out so a flat slap will blind or disfigure. If you get the neck, it'll kill real fast, real messy. Lidgate lays open the father's cheek clear to the bone. Nerve damage, likely: often times with a cut like that, you can't smile any more when it heals.

Coiled bloody around the child on the floor, the father weeps, rage and shame as our heavy boots begin to strike him, and

Lidgate tells us to turn off the damn camera, and what the fuck are we, a moron? The last thing we see is the two families, one looking down at the other, as Lidgate turns back to his work.

The clip finishes, and the fat memento screen goes grey.

"I had that," Mirador says. "I had it and they wouldn't do anything about it. The judge wouldn't accept it in evidence."

"Do you know what happened then?"

"More of the same, for fuck's sake, what do you think?"

"Did they live?"

Mirador shrugs and starts to cough, finally spews something into a second glass hidden down by his feet for a spittoon. I want to hear more about Lidgate, feed my anger, but that's not why I'm here, gathering evidence for the righteous dismantling of a dead man. I don't think it will even help Mirador feel better, by now it's just a sore in the soul. While he's talking, I have to do right by Mary Ann Grey.

"Tell me about the 1848, Simon."

"Fuck you."

Still waiting. Got all the time.

"Fuck you, Sounder."

"I don't want names. And I'm not a cop. I don't give a shit if someone shot up a patrol car twenty years ago. I just need to get what happened."

"No one knows what happened. It's all gone anyway."

"What happened that you know?"

"A ceiling fell on me, you jackass. I got burned from my ankles to my ass. Lost one testicle to fire. Okay? And one fucking lung."

"What about the other one?"

"What other one?"

"Your other testicle. Could be very important to the investigation."

He stares at me for a long, long time, and then he starts to laugh. It's such a horrible noise, I wish he'd thrown me out.

"Jesus, kid. You got no limit, do you?"

"My girlfriend says I'm very goal-oriented."

"I bet she does. Jesus."

He laughs some more, and spits again, different colours this time.

"You're talking about the 1848."

"You think I'm just going to tell you shit now?"

"How about if I promise not to help you at all? No money, no coincidental offers of new muscle grafts. No gratitude, even. Just you tell me and I take what I need and forget the rest for ever."

"They got new muscle grafts?"

"Fuck, Simon, I don't know. You want me to find out?"

"Of course I fucking do. My life is shit and it hurts all the time and you're right. What I got to tell is worth less than nothing. My wife was right too. Fuck."

"I'll ask around. Maybe there's something. You can sell me something that's not worth anything for whatever I can do to get you in a programme. Which you know is probably nothing. I'm not Tonfamecasca."

"You're Tonfamecasca enough."

I start to argue, but if everyone around me thinks it that hard, then maybe I am. In which case, let it be worth something.

Simon Mirador shuffles over to his counter and boils a kettle. He stops it when the dial says 80º and makes genmaicha, tea with roasted rice. We sit and watch it swirl and settle in a glass pot, and by the time it's ready it's like we're friends, like I'm the nephew he never sees. War stories and bad memories and tea. He almost falls on the way back to sit down, and I almost try to catch him. He sits down and glowers: *Don't you fucking dare help me.*

"There was no 1848. I mean not like people say now, not at the time. There was no committee, and there sure as hell wasn't no plan. There was just some people shit-scared and desperate and dumb enough to take on the Lidgates. Which is some serious dumb, you get me, because those fuckers came heavy. Like warzone heavy from the start. So people got to organising hospital tents and shower stations for the gas, new clothes in bags, a bunch of sizes, and if you knew where to look, you could get help. Like that. And a lot of us in the firefighters, we were in that. Paramedics too. The cops not so much, but more than you might think. Ordinary people when they could, like if they would have a back door onto another street, or maybe they'd even make one. But it was never a conspiracy. No T-shirt, no votes."

I think about the Lacarte Free House popping up out of nowhere because it was needed. Spontaneous revolution in a limited space. That's how the books say it happens, but you never see it, and it doesn't tend to last.

"How'd the name happen?"

"Oh, that was some bullshit. There was a guy, an enthusiast. Man had a whole shelf of books, waiting his whole life for an actual revolution. That moment when everything he'd always said would be true, and people would finally take notice and behave the way they were supposed to. Far as he was concerned, we didn't already know who we were, and how we were getting fucked, we just thought we did. Called us the vanguard, wanted a cell structure so the cadres couldn't be rolled up all at one time, so that after Tilehurst we could spread out and preach the word. Seed of the revolution. Like this wasn't going to be over in a month anyway, like they wouldn't send in the tanks. Oh, Comrade Mirador, even tanks shall avail nothing against our resolve. You know what resolve can do against an APC? Fuck all. But it was like this was everything he'd ever wanted. The historical moment all laid out and ready to go. He started calling anyone he met a soldier of the 1848. Started calling the news as the official cadre communications officer. Called Alton Lidgate, demanded a parlay. Said if we had a name, we weren't just some guys any more, we were a faction. A force."

"You remember his name? This enthusiast?"

"Said you didn't want names."

"Don't figure you care about this one."

"Fuck, no, I do not. Aloysius Grey."

Grey, like Mary Ann, but it's a common enough name.

"He have a family?"

"A wife, sure. A kid, I don't know. Maybe."

Mirador sighs, not like he's tired, but like there's plenty to sigh about.

"You married back then?"

"Yeah."

"Burns a problem for that?"

"Naw. Not the burns. My attitude, after. I wasn't sound. Expressed some stupid opinions on the spur of the moment. Pain talking. She went down south. Anyway . . . Once it had a name it was a criminal conspiracy, see? It was a threat to stability and blah blah blah. So then, the tanks. Local cops wouldn't do it, so Lidgate got to bring in his own people. We pushed back, tried to block the roads. I think . . . he wanted that. He wanted to be in a war. But it burned too hot, because we wouldn't lie down. It got too loud."

It's "we" now, for the first time.

"They set me on fire," Simon Mirador says, hands wide like everyone's here. "Me and the whole damn town. And people were screaming and dying and I didn't move fast enough and maybe I didn't clip my mask or maybe it came off when I hit the ground."

Tilehurst burned, and Simon along with it, and the pictures went out on your screens every hour of every day until even in Chersenesos people were sickened and crying, and someone— maybe Stefan, maybe not, but someone like him, all meat and power and calculation—made a call: this is too much, too close to the bone. Bring down the curtain.

See that it doesn't happen again.

Getting off the bus at Gull Town, west of the batholith, I can taste the clear water of the Plutus cooling the air. It's what makes Gull Town a better neighbourhood than Tappeny Bridge—that and the new run of Goan food places up and down Fore Street, before it crosses into the harbour district and the warehouse conversions eating into the lakefront from the Chersenesos side.

Orhan's office is cleaner than it used to be. Gull Town is prettier and richer. I like to think that's Athena feeding the Tonfamecasca Company purse back into the city, tying Chersenesos into the world.

"Cal, Cal, Cal. How come we never see you no more?"

"I was here a month ago, Orhan, give me a break."

He grins. "Touchy."

"I'm missing my old friends."

"You're missing when they didn't have to deal with you being what you are now."

"Oh, sure, tell me the straight truth. That always makes people feel better."

"Give me work and I will pretend you are still as short and temporary as I am."

"Can you find the 1848?"

"No. Also not Mr Streetlight. Nor can I get you a date with one of the Fate sisters." Urban myths of a world with Titans in it: a madman twenty feet tall with hands like loops of wire for hanging late walkers in the night. The older sisters of Stefan's clan, so big and weird they live in the lake now, and eat swimmers who pass by overhead. Although having met Martha Erskine, I'm revising my opinion of the impossible, and the second in particular absolutely feels like something Stefan's crazy relatives would do, if they existed.

I hand him the parcel of cash from the Caffrey. "That's yours if you can tell me where it came from."

He looks at the label. "Some dive motel in Shearwater. Is that all you needed?"

"Before that. It says Deerborn Real Estate, but I'm pretty sure they never saw it coming or going. I need to know from whom, to whom, and for what purpose."

"That is a great deal of 'whom'."

"I also eat with cutlery now."

"Obviously that's a lie. Come on, what else?"

I show him a map of Martha's Point, and touch the beach due north with my finger.

"Find out who owns the land."

"Is it ... Martha Erskine?"

"This land."

"That's not land, that's a fly speck."

"It's a building plot on the water. A bit of scrub."

"You want to know who owns a bit of scrub."

"I do." I think of Zoegar in his board shorts, and a traitor part of me has to ask. "Also: find out whether Rudi Basu, the union boss in Shearwater, is in bed with Doublewide."

"See, that you should have asked me first, because that's the part where someone comes and shoots me in the face."

"No one's going to shoot you in the face."

"You got shot, like, two times already."

"Yeah, but I kinda always knew when it was gonna happen."

"You know who you know, who you could ask?"

"Is it Doublewide?"

"It is Doublewide. You could go ask him, instead of me."

"He's a little upset with me right now."

"But he won't shoot you."

He probably won't shoot me. "Maybe I will."

"Or why not ask Ostby?"

"I don't trust Ostby."

"You used to trust Ostby."

"I used to use Ostby even when I didn't trust him. Anyway, he quit."

"Ostby quit?"

"So he says."

Orhan shakes his head. "Times they are a-changing."

In my memory I see Mary Ann Grey and the bruise across her back that Fallon thinks is from a boat's anchor. I think about Torrance Erskine and Simon Mirador.

"I dunno, Orhan. They look all kinds of familiar to me."

I'm not sure how much I mean that, but it's true that the patterns repeat. You start to see them as an investigator, and as a Titan it only gets clearer. It's part of why the old ones have trouble with names: it's honestly hard for them to remember which iteration of the same story they're dealing with.

I walk into Tonfamecasca Tower and put my card on the reader.

The gates open to the executive section. I have high-level access now, whether I want it or not, although for the highest level you don't get a card. The system just knows who you are. I get into the elevator and push the button, and as always I wonder if the machine will spit me out, or just take me up all the way to the top and drop me. Stefan Tonfamecasca is polite to me now, or at least he no longer raises his voice above the level where it's physically painful to hear him, but it's a mistake to imagine that makes him cuddly or safe or even human. Stefan is himself, only and always.

The elevator moves, the briefest vagus discomfort letting me know I'm travelling, and then I'm there. The door opens. He's had the whole place redecorated again. The floor of the cupola is matte black, some kind of hyper-absorbent material so that stepping onto it feels like a leap of faith, and nothing has any edges any more. It's more nauseating than the journey up: proprioception struggling to make sense of an environment without cues. I could be in free fall, in space. I wonder if he likes it because it makes him think of weightlessness, or because the absence of external benchmarks makes him and others more conscious of his scale.

In deference to sanity, he has at least evened the floor: there's no sunken lounge area to fall into, and the furniture is just ordinary black in the field of darkness, so you can see the contours before you crash into it. Just. A black plane, the sky above and the lake beyond, and Stefan himself, sitting in a chair, reading a book.

"This is a surprise," he says, not looking up.

"I came to ask you something."

Now he does raise his eyes. "You don't mean a question."

"I also have a question."

"Start there."

"Alton Lidgate."

"That's not a question."

"You knew him?"

"I met him."

"What did you think?"

"If he'd been even a little smaller, I'd have squashed him with a shoe."

"That doesn't actually tell me if you liked him."

The rumble of a laugh. It doesn't hurt, and I wonder if that's because he's being careful or if I've just got that much more mass than when he flattened me with his voice.

"On this occasion, you may deduce that I did not. A tiny man full of tiny angers and small ideas that he took for the scale and measure of the world. Loathsome creature. To call him a cockroach is a gross insult to my least favourite arthropod. Now. Why are you really here?"

"I'm working up to it."

"Surely not . . . permission? Oh, please tell me you're not about to ask me for her hand?"

"She'd kill both of us for even entertaining that conversation."

"I'm so glad you noticed. But what else can it be, Cal? What can I possibly give you?"

"I need to talk to Glass."

The interest in his eyes goes out, and they get very hard.

"Why?"

"Because I need to know about Martha Erskine."

"Ask the analysis division."

"I'm not that interested in ROI."

"That, at least, is not news to me. I assume you came with an alternative that I will hate slightly less."

"Get me in with Rinsom-Walker."

Stefan stops. I mean he actually stops. It's one of the creepy things high-dose Titans do; they're big and slow and when they pause to think, the rhythm of their bodies doesn't quite read as alive, like a whale wouldn't if you were so close you couldn't see what it was, just a wall of barnacles and weed. In the black gloss emptiness of Stefan's cathedral to himself, he almost becomes two-dimensional, a giant made of math.

"Tilehurst," he growls.

"Tangentially. And only maybe."

"Why is it always old sins with you?"

For a moment, I tell him the actual truth. "I don't know. Maybe because it's the only kind Titans have. Or maybe it just works out that way."

We sit for a while, and I realise that one day that act of just sitting will turn—for Athena and for me—into the very thing I was wondering at in Stefan, that strange atemporal stillness. I can feel the whisper of it in my bones, midway between meditation and the dive reflex.

"Anthromachy," Stefan says.

"What?"

"It's a bar, Cal. An achingly pretentious bar. Kathleen Walker is a creature of habit. I'll let her know you're coming."

"You didn't say no about Glass."

"I used the word 'alternative'."

"Yeah, but you had to know I'd go with both."

He glowers, then laughs again, in his chest. This time my teeth vibrate.

"Honestly, I'm still dumbstruck by the idea that you'd come to me before, rather than after."

"I don't absolutely have to piss you off at every opportunity."

"How interesting that you should notice that. Cal?"

"Yeah?"

"One of your most charming features has always been that, capable as you are, you have absolutely no circumspection whatsoever. You are a blunt object moved by an idiot, smashing through the world. All the complex plots of a dozen geniuses could come to grief simply by underestimating your rejection of the idea that a straight line is not the quickest route between two points. I take comfort in your sheer predictability. It makes you safe to have around."

"Thank you?"

"You've surprised me today. Twice, actually. You are growing as a person. Go and see Glass, then. Have him tell you whatever you want to know. And why don't you come and join me for dinner when this case is over. Just us boys."

"Sure, why not?"

"Do you still like the apple pie from Crispin's?"

I feel a tingle along my spine. I used to eat that when I was ten years old. Stefan didn't know me then. Nor did Athena. The only way he can even have that name is from a deep dive into my life, and the only way he'd have it at his fingertips like that is if he'd actually read the analysis, as opposed to letting his security people do that for him.

It's one thing to pay special attention to Stefan Tonfamecasca. That's like checking the weather forecast before you go out in a boat. It's another to have him pay special attention to you.

"They closed years ago."

"Yes, but Arnold Crispin lives in Hollymore, and he was kind enough to sell me the recipe. I'll have the chefs prepare it, hmm?"

"I hope you gave him a good price."

"Arnold thought so, and that's what matters, don't you think?"

He waves his hand and goes back to his book.

"You're going to visit a long line of broken people, Cal. You always do. I'm very interested to see how many times you can experience that before you understand my position a little better."

Anthromachy is a fifth-floor wine bar themed around variations of summer. White wine, white leather, white light, everything balanced on a knife-edge of over-ripe, but frozen permanently before it can cross the line, which makes the downslope look even hungrier. If there's a place in the universe farthest from Victor's, the Titan dive where I once fought two wannabes for the right not to fuck them under a table between the fish and the foie gras, it's here. A server in catwalk monastic leads me to Kathleen Walker's table, and I can hear Stefan laughing all the way from the cupola.

Kathleen Walker is seven feet tall and looks fifteen years old. She's wearing designer military pants with an XXXL white T-shirt I've seen on street barrows: Bo Peep manga holding a sheep and a tiny farm in the palm of one hand, blue letters under the cartoon face—"Young Money". I realise Kathleen has the same hair as the image.

"Ms Walker."

"Mr Sounder."

"It's good to meet to someone else who has resting babyface."

"Fuck you, too."

"I don't mean anything by it."

"Get yourself a drink and don't bullshit me. I'm ten thousand and four years old." She can't be a day over 150, and it's weird watching her try to be young. Or maybe I'm watching her be what she is when I can't let go of the idea that she's not.

"You're definitely giving off that ten-millennium vibe. I think it's the hair and manga combo: super old lady."

She nods as if I've been nice. "And you're very young. Emergency dose, he said, like Athena."

"Yeah."

"And you're the kid who called him when she was dying."

"Yeah."

"You realise what that means to him, right?"

"It means I'm a giant pain in his ass."

"Oh, yes. Keep doing that, Mr Sounder. It's very smart, because it lets him pretend he doesn't owe you."

"I think we got past that when he saved my life."

"Oh, that's sweet. Do you think he values your life the same as hers? No, of course not. She's his favourite child, the one he truly loves. You saved the world for him, and what's some T7 set against that? A few minutes of bookkeeping. No, you may feel even, but Stefan is still way underwater with you, pretty much for ever. And people like Stefan really hate debts they can't repay."

"Do you?"

"Like poison." And for a moment, I see Kathleen Walker peering out of those huge blue eyes, like a snake in a hole.

The server brings a glass with wine in it, cold and sharply yellow. I taste pine esters and Savatiano.

"From Geneva," she says, smacking her lips. "A revival."

"It's very good."

"That's why I don't wear lipstick."

"I hadn't noticed."

"You fucking better have."

"All right, I noticed. You have a great mouth."

"Thank you. I think we've done the sex chit-chat now. Stefan says you've got questions, so . . . hit me with your best shot."

"How did Tilehurst happen?"

She bursts out laughing, then chokes and laughs again. "Oh, shit! Fuck me, Sounder, where's the fucking foreplay, Jesus!"

"You said—"

"I know what I said. Motherfucker, I am Kathleen Walker of Rinsom-Walker. You're talking about the worst thing that ever happened in my long life and you just—throw it out there. Is that it?"

The worst thing that ever happened in her life, not anyone else's.

"Yeah, Ms Walker, because what I ought to do is go back over every piece of paper that ever existed and speak to everyone who's still alive, and I ought to find the one line through all of that which ties you to what happened so that you can go have your next two doses in jail."

She cocks her head. "Why don't you?"

"Because I thought about it and I checked it out, and I know you saw me coming. Not me but everyone like me, conceptually. You and your subsidiaries own all the jails listed to hold convicted Titans. There's probably a suite waiting for you at every one of them just in case. Is that right?"

"Something like."

"If I even lived long enough to get you to court."

"Oh, not you, Mr Sounder. I'm very fond of Athena. I used to babysit her, back in the day. But others, perhaps, yes, other people might have bad outcomes."

I get up. "Never mind, Ms Walker. I'm sorry to have wasted your time."

"Oh, sit your ass down and stop being so precious. You're supposed to be a man of the world. I'm not even close to the worst person you've ever met. You've got experience beyond your years. I respect that, and you knew what I was before you came. And you still did."

I did. I don't have to like it.

"It was my mistake," she says. "Me, personally. I let all that happen. I didn't order it, but it's on me. And yes, I do care. There just isn't anything I can do to fix it, so I don't try. Now sit the fuck down and listen to what you came for."

She tells me the story everyone wants to know, and there's nothing I can do about it.

A long time ago, back before T7, even, when mining was still done with shovels, the Walker family made its fortune digging a hole in a pit full of blue clay. In that clay was a large selection of shiny rocks which, when you took them out of the clay and polished them up, millionaires would pay for to hang around their necks or wear on pinky rings, or stud the hubcaps of overpowered cars, and back then people just weren't too bothered if there was a war in the neighbourhood, or if a lot of the folks doing the actual digging didn't come home one night.

A little less long ago, the Walkers put some of that easy money into lithium mining, and then other things used in electronics, and finally they got into making things as well, and they settled on a no-account town in a gap in the mountains to build a new campus. That town caught their attention by offering a string of breaks on tax and local law and all sorts of other things they liked, and all was well until one day it wasn't, and they started to get some friction with the people working for them who suddenly couldn't afford their own streets, or their own restaurants, or even just to stay alive in the town they still believed was theirs. They took it into their heads to protest their wages, and they got good and loud.

At that time the boss of the whole family was Michael Walker, but Michael delegated a lot to his daughter Kathleen, who had all manner of impressive management qualifications and a literal lifetime of experience, and Kathleen ran the numbers and decided to fight the corner. Knowing it wouldn't be popular, she called in a specialist named Alton Lidgate. She hadn't worked with him before, but she'd heard good things. And Alton Lidgate showed up, and understood the assignment.

"He looked so chipper," she snarls into her revived retsina. "A little peacock fucker always playing with his buttonhole and his tie. You know what a tie is for, Mr Sounder? My therapist told me: it points at your dick. Alton Lidgate couldn't stop playing."

I think of the blade in the lapel and wonder what Kathleen Walker's therapist would make of that.

"Little peacock fucker," she says, touching her own chest where the jacket ought to be.

It wasn't long before Lidgate vehicles were keeping the peace the local cops couldn't, driving around neighbourhoods cooling off anyone who got rowdy, and seeing to it that the workers who'd been browbeaten into crossing picket lines could do so without consequences. It wasn't a stable state, by any means, but Kathleen knew the poor people would run out of money faster than she would, and for a poor person, running out of money meant running out of food, rather than just having to reassess strategic options.

Alton Lidgate had it all in hand.

"And then the motherfucker tried to fuck me," Kathleen says, loud enough that the server comes over with the bottle, and a bowl of vegetable crisps and something hummus-adjacent which tastes like lime.

"Motherfucking motherfucker," Kathleen says, and it occurs to me that if she really pisses them off, she'll just buy this place and tell them to keep her table open.

Alton Lidgate made a play for a seat at the big table. He didn't want to be just a contractor any more. He wanted into the partnership. If Rinsom-Walker was under siege, he reasoned, the company would need a man who understood sieges. All he had to do was provide a war, and he delivered one. For fun and profit, he hanged six people in the town square, and set the world on fire.

"It nearly worked! I made it so fucking easy for him," the old lady says, and just for a moment I think I really can see her age, in the crumpling of her big, child-like face and the self-pity in her voice, before I realise that's just her. She was always this person, and she'll never change.

I hand her a napkin and she starts to cry into her cold white wine.

I cross town slowly, and I can tell I'm dawdling. I don't care. Sometimes you take some time. I do it now, wandering for an hour, then two, letting the street remind me who I am. I see kids throwing water balloons, a parking warden ticketing a supercar and people laughing. I see an old man and an old woman carrying a dinghy down to the cold water by the mouth of the Viderfluss, and when they set sail and instantly fall in, and it's the finest time they've ever had together until tomorrow—and no body washes up on the shore, no one chokes their neighbour or burns down the whole neighbourhood—finally the city washes away that old monster's tears and the taste of her revival wine.

I call Mini Denton and download everything I've learned. I add to her chore list: check in with Orhan, tell me what he finds.

"You going back tonight?"

"No. Got house calls to make. You're coming too."

"I am?"

"That's what sidekicks do, Sporty Jasmine."

"Sidekick, my ass."

"It's French. It means co-equal partner in training."

"My mother's French."

"Then you know. Meet me at four, I got one more thing to do here first."

"You don't need help with that?"

"Nope."

"See you at four."

Sporty Jasmine has good sense. She doesn't argue, she just hangs up. It's not that it wouldn't be good to have someone else in the room, catching inferences. It's that I don't want Glass getting sight of Mini Denton. There's too much there for him with to work with, and even now he likes to work.

Back down into the other city, the one where I make my living. The place where Stefan didn't say I couldn't go, and I should worry, soon, about why.

Reggie Glass has hands that don't work: Parkinson's, fairly advanced. He holds the cup as if it was a bird, and lifts it to his lips with the caution of someone who's been burned many times and can't resist trying again. His eyes are almost entirely swallowed in the wrinkles of his face, and his silk dressing gown has holes around the folded cuffs. Some of them are from the embers of his cigarillos; some are just from moths. The fabric is stained yellow with time and nicotine: backstreet chromatography. The little room is so hot I'm resenting him for drinking coffee, but the very old notoriously don't give a damn, and Reggie still less than anyone I've ever met, because the world truly does hate him. He's over a hundred, and getting the best healthcare there is—Stefan's sense of irony at work. The best healthcare, but no T7, not now or ever, because the Titans as a group won't have him.

Reggie Glass is a gossip, which is like saying Joseph Stalin may have been responsible for some political murders. Reggie is *the* gossip, and historically also *the* blackmailer and extortionist of Othrys society, the man behind the stories that wrecked lives, broke companies, finished careers. None of that would matter in the normal run, but Reggie didn't restrict himself to the normal class of celebrity. He built up a library of uncomfortable and horrible secrets about men and women over two hundred years old, and he began to use that to choose outcomes, pick senators, parlay knowledge into physical power, and at a certain point he became sufficiently effective that Stefan took notice, and cut him down. From one day to the next, no media outlet would take his calls, no politician would admit knowing him. The phone company lost his account and couldn't re-establish his connection to the web. A long time ago, in a bad country, they called it Zersetzung: decomposition, but made transitive—a thing that one person does to another. Like biological entropy, Stefan returned Reggie Glass to the soil, and all the information that made him what he was got devoured by worms. He still hears everything, and what he doesn't hear he can guess. People come to him, like I do, for secrets and lies. But he knows the limits of the game now, and that he's lost the only part of it that matters, and that broke him all the way down. What remains has manners and enough money to get by, and skin so meagre and translucent you'd take it for jellyfish in one of the all-night Chinese bars along Midcity Drive. I bring him chocolate orange peel in a gift box, and I have to help him with the lid.

"Martha Erskine," Reggie says. His voice is high and uneven, but getting stronger as he speaks. His hands uncurl, too, and he can manage the chocolate. I once met a concert pianist with Parkinson's; the only time she could use her hands at all was when she played, and then she was almost as good as she'd ever been. As soon as the music stopped, the blessing was over. With Reggie Glass, the music is when he's telling tales, and if he's hurting someone that way, he can very nearly use chopsticks.

"She's been around a long time. One of Stefan's very first commercial clients, along with that husband of hers, the one who died."

"How?"

"Fell off a cliff, I believe, in the Alps."

"Pushed?"

"Stupid. Mountains don't forgive stupid."

"What about now?"

"I don't imagine that's changed."

"Martha. Now."

"Oh, the usual. Arguments about money with the workforce. Tawdry. I'm not sure that's even her problem any more. She's withdrawn from the day to day, leaves all that to Bail Erskine. Many times grandson something something MBA. Only a few years younger than I am, that boy. Real shit back in the day, too. Mellowed now. Only hurts people on purpose, and almost never for fun. I liked him back when, I must say. We ruined more than a few together."

"Withdrawn how?"

"Every how. From the business, the day-to-day ennui, but also the way they use that word as a euphemism. The rumour is she's losing her marbles. Delicious, if true. Always so difficult to know whether T7 will take care of that, and of course, she's old already, four doses like Stefan. Cardiovascular issues must apply. A delicate problem."

"She seemed perfectly okay to me."

"You met her? I want detail."

"You got chocolate orange peel."

He sniffs. "Paltry."

"You want another box?"

"Yes, I do. And cherries in kirsch."

"Your nurse told me no booze."

"They don't count, because she hasn't thought of that yet. Have them sent round tomorrow. Perhaps the courier will be young and foolish and stay for an hour or two, and I can hear all about life among the young."

"Done. Tell me."

"She sleepwalks," Reggie says. "That's the word."

"A lot of people do."

"Yeah, but it's the wrong word. See, ordinary sleepwalking is a problem with the shutoff that stops your body responding to any commands your brain gives while you're dreaming. You're asleep, experiencing the dream world, but moving around in the real one. This is the opposite, or the same but coming from the other side: she goes to sleep while she's just doing ordinary stuff, like she has narcolepsy, but you can't always tell just by looking. Externally nothing changes, but inside... She still experiences the real world, but she responds like it's a dream. You get why that's alarming, right? A fourteen-foot woman in charge of a multibillion industrial complex wandering around like Alice through the looking glass. She's a high-dose Titan in the first place, so everyone else seems a little thin to her anyway, but when she's sleepwalking she might do anything. Set herself on fire to catch bugs. Declare a trade war with China. Who knows?"

"Is she violent?"

"She's anything, Sounder. She lives in the magic world half the time, maybe more. Has she been violent, I've no idea. But could she be, in theory? The way I hear it, absolutely anything is possible."

Perhaps I'm dreaming now.

So perhaps not Doublewide's arm, after all, but the friendly embrace of Martha Erskine, wrapping Mary Ann Grey about the middle to draw her down. It's not hard to picture the scene: Martha dreaming about something, reaching out and snaring the girl, smothering her by accident and then diving down into the deep so that she drowns. Letting her body go with the current, and then waking a moment later, maybe while Mary Ann Grey was still just in sight, too scared of what she'll find to go after the bobbing thing on the tide. Getting the news a couple of hours later and calling me. Calling me ... why? Because the security boys are saying it's Torrance and they'll take care of it, and she doesn't know if they're protecting him, or her, or doing something else, keeping her on a throne she can't hold, for some advantage of their own. A deal with Bail. With an overseas buyer jockeying for power on the Othrys shelf. With anyone.

With Athena.

Except Athena told her about me. Set the idea, some time back: if you're in trouble and you want truth, you call Cal.

Martha called me because she didn't know herself, didn't trust herself, and she didn't trust the family security people, or the family themselves, to tell her the truth.

Reggie smiles. "I can see I've made quite the impression. I shall buy the newspapers and watch what comes. I like to add to my tally occasionally, even now. Don't forget the cherries, Mr Sounder. I'd hate to think of you as a welcher."

One day, Reggie will die of old age, and the world will get incrementally lighter for it.

5

I have a fistful of maybes, and with those and some change I can buy cheap coffee. Maybe Mary Ann Grey was Aloysius Grey's daughter, and maybe he was there, on the ground, when Tilehurst burned. Maybe Alton Lidgate made a play and killed the town, or maybe Kathleen Walker is a liar even to herself. Maybe all of this means something about the dead body on Fallon's slab and the almost bomb that almost blew up. Or maybe Martha killed her and Lance Vesper will set up Torrance and nothing will happen, or maybe Torrance actually is the killer and the shipping container belongs to another story altogether. Maybe and maybe and I don't know.

I go back to the apartment in Chersenesos, hating how cold and empty it feels when Athena isn't there. She's on a four-day team-building trip with the new Tonfamecasca board: one other Titan and five baseline humans, mostly lawyers. They're going to play ping-pong and eat noodles with their fingers. Athena says doing something calm, nice and embarrassing is more effective with these people than all the laser-tag and rafting in the world. I lie down on our bed and inhale the air, catching the traces of her, missing her, knowing she'll be back so soon that the moment of separation barely exists at all.

Days matter, because every instant of life is worth treasuring—that's the underlying truth of being a Titan, after all, that avarice for time. But here's Athena's point, the one I can't deny: that days of being apart don't matter, because we have so many others. If she took a six-month trip and we were ordinary people, that would be one hundredth of the time we could hope to spend together. Precious time. But for her and for me, it's likely not even a fraction of that. Four days is nothing.

The consequence of our longevity is that the old patterns fail. Titan lives are still a new thing in their own terms, still rare and still untested, still not understood. There are new dynamics of self and desire and friendship and love, and so far every single Titan has failed the test. There is not one single conventional partnership among the few thousand living that has lasted more than a hundred years. Most are as fleeting as ordinary marriages, or even worse. Asking one person to carry your whole emotional weight for a millennium is probably impossible. Look at Stefan, ever more strange in his cathedral, ever more unmoored from common humanity. You might as well love a mountain or a sea. And yet he needs love, clings to Athena, to the few others who know him as a person—even in his weird, terrifying way, to me. Stefan is master of the world, but he's alone.

Athena believes the way forward is expansion. Acknowledgement of difference and deliberate self-insertion into ordinary life. Have friendships with the people who come and go and let yourself recognise that that's what they'll do. Take lovers among the ephemera and cherish the joys and the inevitable losses, and consume those relationships as part of the greater growth, the sprawling novelty and affection that comes with an endless life and a body ever more vast with each new return to youth. But never misunderstand the difference between the two: a great love of decades is the stuff of human poetry, but there aren't words yet for what it is to love a Titan for ever. We don't make many poets. Or I should say we haven't, not yet. That's the challenge: not to steal back twenty-four hours from a management retreat, but to conquer twenty-four hundred years, and beyond into whatever weirdness lies over the horizon.

Whatever it is Stefan thinks I'll learn from people like Reggie

Glass, I want to learn Athena's lessons instead. I pick up the phone from beside the bed, and dial. When she answers I hear the smile in her voice, tired but glad.

"Hey, you. How is it?"

"I spent the day finding out about horrible people being horrible. Stefan thinks I'm growing up. And before you ask, it was disconnected and it did not go off, so I'm fine."

Her voice goes a little sharp. "Before I ask, *what* was disconnected, exactly?"

"The bomb I found in a big box."

"The word 'bomb' is the key player in this conversation, mister."

"I know."

"It's the headline, Cal. 'I found a bomb.'"

"That's why I wanted to get 'disconnected' in first."

"I'm accepting your logic pro tem, but I have conditions."

"Okay."

"You are not to find any more and you are not to get exploded."

"Okay."

"Also, you wear the suits I got you."

"Okay."

"Apart from that, what's Shearwater like?"

"Pretty and pretty broken. You know what the Sleepers are?"

She's heard rumours. She always has. She hadn't understood the scale.

"You want me to do something?"

"Such as?"

"Such as find out who they are one by one and fix what's broken with money."

I wonder if that would work. Three or four hundred individual interventions. Thirty million and change, taking an average, to solve every one of their problems and set them up in the world again, not just getting by for a month, but stabilised. Well within the realms of the possible, if she chooses to do it. An obvious answer—unless, if she chooses to do it, her action just creates three hundred more. She follows my silence.

"You think it won't work if it's a Titan."

"Maybe. Leave it with me. How's the retreat?"

"You know what I want?"

"A holiday in an A-frame with a water door into a thermal spring."

"Oh, that is much better than what I wanted. Let's do that."

"Is it too late to add in some sex?"

"It is not too late. Is there no sex in Shearwater?"

"I believe the bylaws permit it."

"Rural living by the sea. Sunshine and blue sky. I envisage you on a sandy bank with a beautiful shepherdess consoling you in my absence."

I think of Ashley, and having to call ten minutes before dropping by. "It's not really sheep country."

"That was very quick, Cal. It sounds like you have someone in mind." Laughing gently at the traces of my old-school human-baseline fidelity, when we've done together all the things we've done. "You're wool-gathering. She's not part of the case, I take it."

Reality check: Ashley, in a jealous rage, holding Mary Ann Grey down in the shallows with a wooden spar, swimming her body out to sea like a lifeguard in reverse. But whoever killed Mary Ann Grey was physically strong and most likely bigger than she was. Ashley's about the same size.

"No. It's a small town, but no."

"I wouldn't want her distracted from the things she needs to be concentrating on."

"And those are?"

She laughs again, and I can feel it in my tongue and my lips, the ache in my fingers to touch her. She knows how I feel about that laugh. Close enough that I can hear the texture of her mouth, but far beyond the reach of my arms, she settles down to tell me things that make me glad and alive.

In the morning I take Sporty Jasmine and we retrace Mary Ann Grey's steps, heading out into the between country where she made up her lie. Mini Denton still uses Mac's car: a black road-legal military thing that looks armoured but isn't. Unlike everyone else who has one, she can actually drive, and the smoked windows and matte paint job give the thing what she calls 'cruise authority'. No one really wants to find out who's inside, so when she signals, other cars just get the hell out of the way.

"Where to?" she says, as I get in.

"You want to pick?" I show her Iverson's list.

"We head for Johan Heights," she says, after a moment. "There's a couple of places on the way."

"Any particular reason it's Johan Heights?"

"I should have a married a guy called Johan."

"Who was he?"

"He wasn't Mac."

She turns the wheel and I manage not to say that life is long, because mine is and hers isn't.

On the inland side of Othrys, in the spaces that aren't yet towns but have gone past being drive-thrus and malls, Mary Ann Grey worked a dozen jobs in half as many months, crissing and crossing the country like a drunkard weaving a quilt. We drift from one to the next, an hour here, an hour there, the valley country flat and boring in between, the mountains always on the horizon but never getting any closer. The food is awful and different every time we stop, the only constant certainty is grease and parking lots.

Johan Heights, when we get there, isn't much higher than anywhere else for a hundred kilometres. It's almost aggressively the same as all the others, and all the others are the same as each other: prefab gothic, wall dividers poorly located to create shadows and airless rooms, stark white drywall and endless glass doors with endless black roller blinds like something by Herzog. The chairs in the waiting rooms have so many stains you could think that pattern of damp, coffee and bleached-out fungal propagation was some kind of aesthetic, until you look close and see the lines of underlying colour at the seams: pale honest blue. A dozen identical bosses with different faces but the same beaten mood, the same simmering rage at Mary Ann Grey's sass. The same amazement that she had the stones to quit and move on. The same damp, vindictive pleasure, immediately swallowed, when they find out that she's dead. It gets so if one of them was genuinely sad that'd make them a suspect.

And the story never changes, it just gets layered on thicker and thicker. Bad mustard on bad ham. Sometimes she was open about it, sometimes she was covert, but wherever she went, there was trouble at the mill. The only thing she ever did wrong was give a false name when she took a job. Everything else was by the book, right and tight, but she never lasted long and the only thing she didn't kick up a fuss about was leaving. You have to figure that was part of whatever she wanted: come, and go, and leave nothing but resentment. I find myself wondering if she paid tax on all those different tiny bits of income, and if so how she got around all the different names, but at the next job I talk to the paymaster who says she never collected her cheques, and when Mini goes back along the line, that's the pattern again. Not one of those jobs ever paid a red cent for Mary Ann Grey.

"I'm from here," Mini says in the car, when I ask her why so quiet. But when I ask if she wants to swing by somewhere, she says not really here, just all of them.

We don't talk for a while, and then we do, about inconsequential things, until we both know we're fine. She drops me at the train station, then turns and heads back to Othrys, following the money. I take the express over the mountain pass to Tilehurst.

You can't easily see a scar on a city once they've built it all up again, but you can feel the absence of what was there before in the way long-time natives look around it, have to force themselves not to hunt for the seams. When Tilehurst burned, a whole swathe of neighbourhoods just stopped existing, and half of the new parks are unmarked graveyards, the trees and grass growing tall with their roots reaching down below the imported loam to the layer of bone ash beneath. The houses came back, as bricks and steel will, but the chains were broken: the small daily rituals that make a city what it is. Life changed and shifted and the past blew away on the hot south wind.

A new ring road is already in place, bounding the city's sprawl, and outside it are the box towns where the new labourers sleep before they travel in on buses and trains and trams to serve the new gentry in the shiny investment streets where they used to live. The developer calls the box towns the Diamonds, but mostly the people just know them by the number of the road you take to get there. Where do you live? Out in the Five. Down by the Seven.

I don't know if that's surrender or resistance. Maybe both.

Lila Grey's apartment is in a serviced block in the Nine, sandy yellow brick and two ways in, one for the premium dwellings, which have access to a rooftop spa and a gym, and one for the other eleven floors. I don't know how it goes, but Mary Ann Grey's mother has one of the good ones. I go up in a fake service elevator, wooden slats and iron gates and a panel of buttons in ornamented brass where the real thing would have cracked plastic replaced so many times that none of them look right.

I walk down a corridor past the indoor tennis club, white light and potted ferns, until I find the corner apartment, and the nurse answers the door.

"She doesn't know," he tells me, in the hallway. "I've told her, but it just rolls off. Then sometimes she does know, but if you talk about it, she won't hear."

I go in to talk and listen anyway.

The old woman is sitting upright in her bed, but you couldn't say she was sprightly or even really alive. There's a place between life and death that looks like an eternity of both. That's where she is, Lila Grey, and the longer we talk the less I understand. She tells me she's in contact. I ask with whom and she laughs like I've said the right thing, like finally, someone understands. She tells me she's been waiting for me to come, she's prepared a message. The nurse has it, on his table. It's long and complex, but I'll know what to do with it. I say thank you, and ask about her family.

She tells me proudly that her dead husband was a hero of the revolution, like it's the first thing that matters. She tells me it was like the great Soviet battle at Vitebsk, where the German tanks were held back by a dozen cavalrymen for three days. The horses died, they ran out of ammunition, they fought Panzers with swords and kettles and spears made of pine. In the end they had nothing but courage, and finally not one was left alive, but they saved the defence. They were dead saints of Mother Russia, her family came from there once. Her husband was like that. He was a saint, too good for the world and too generous, and of course everyone envied him. She's not religious, but envy is a sin, the worst of sins because it makes people cruel to the kind.

Then without a pause she tells me everyone hated that man, and so did she. She lifts her left arm in her right and cradles it, then chops down hard between the elbow and the wrist. She tells me Aloysius Grey was a pillar of the movement in the streets and a violent bastard in the sheets. Not like her husband, she says. Her husband was gentle and they told such awful lies about him, made him sound like a monster. Poor Aloysius, they told so many lies. She glances down at her hands, old and weak, and tells me to dim the light. The light is too cruel.

I'm not sure what will happen, but I ask if Aloysius was cruel.

Her face comes clear for just a moment: "Never," she says. "They said it about him, but he never raised a hand to us, that was a damn lie."

And now I don't know. With the same perfect certainty, she tells me there's an iron bird standing in the doorway and it won't leave her alone. It squats on her chest at night. No one believes her when she tells them, can I see it? When I say "yes", that's worse: I'm lying, she can tell I'm not looking at it, I'm mocking her, but it's there, black feathers like razors and the stink of burning. She points her finger and then says it's good to see me again, and how was France? She tells me the nurse steals things, but it's not his fault, they're so underpaid.

I ask if her daughter was a happy child. Yes, of course. I ask if she's happy now. And I can see that Lila Grey has no idea, and knows it, and in that absence she sees herself as she is, sees the yawning endlessness of her personal purgatory, and she's appalled. Her hand shoots out towards me as if she's drowning and I take it. I'm about to tell her I'll help, somehow, I'll get her out of this bed and down to the garden at the very least. She's about to tell me what she wants, what she needs. In this single instant there's the hope of resolution.

She smiles and asks why I look so sad. A moment later she's talking about Mary Ann. She's remembered a whole life that never was, all swim team trophies and perfect kids and a two-car garage. She draws me close so she can tell me a secret. When she whispers in my ear it feels like she's going to take a bite out of it; she's so close, so avid. The secret pours out of her, vital and urgent, but it's the heroes of Vitebsk she's turning in, not her husband.

"Ten years later, they turned up drunk in a whorehouse outside Volgograd! Can you imagine? All lies. The whole thing, all lies."

We sit and I let her talk, the certainty in me dwindling with each moment. I started out thinking I'd sift gold from the river of her memory, however turbulent, but I was a fool. Lila Grey is a mirror of whatever I want to believe. If I stay here long enough and feed her the names she'll indict every suspect, every player in the game. I want to get out of here so badly I can taste it in my spit. I want to stay and listen, and help her say one thing that matters, because it's all Lila has left.

In the end, Castor the nurse comes back, and I draw him away.

"Is this what it is?" I ask him, and he nods.

"All the time, day after day. You kid yourself that it'll be better tomorrow, but it won't. That's yesterday you're thinking of, and you're just trying to go back there."

"I'd like water now," Lila says.

"Warm or cool?" Castor replies, and she says he knows how she likes it. Castor pours two glasses, and she tuts at the first one: no, no, no, then takes the second one and knocks it back.

"Slowly," Castor says, without hope, and then sighs as she coughs half of it into the towel over his arm.

Back in the hallway, I ask him if he knew Mary Ann before she left, if he knew Aloysius. He shrugs.

"The husband was already dead. Long time back. The place was like a shrine. Just pictures everywhere, except in the girl's room. That was all pictures from magazines, all over the walls."

"What magazines?"

"Movie stars and parties. Gossip. Clothes. All the best places to be seen, like she was going to walk in and join them."

"She ever try?"

He shrugs.

"They have friends you know about? Family friends?"

He nods this time. Castor's waiting for something.

"I need to talk to them next."

"You could try asking her." Thumb over his shoulder. "She might just say 'yes' at the right time."

But when I do try, Lila shakes her head hard. That's private, she says, otherwise what if the iron bird goes to visit them too? She'd be embarrassed to send them an iron bird. But there was something she wanted me to know. She's been putting it all together.

I ask what. What do I need to know.

Lila's face is full of guile. I know what, and she knows I know, and that's all a pair of knowers like us need say.

I go back out and find a thick stack of spiral-bound notebooks on a side table. I pick up the top one and open it: a line of dots and squiggles, occasional single letters underscored. I half wonder if the crazy old girl has made up a cypher, but I know better. I turn the page, more of the same, then all of them. From time to time, she almost seems to be writing in English, but when you look harder it's just white noise in black ink. Notes from an empty place.

I take the notebook from the very bottom. Her hand was stronger then, but the content is the same: a line of As, like practice for a test, then a line of Zs for balance or because the shape pleased her. Her own name, her daughter's. Never her husband's. Pictures of flowers like something scratched on a cave wall that no one bothers to show to tourists.

Castor looks over my shoulder. "No good?"

I show him, and he nods. Then, cautious: "Often times she says things no one but me understands."

"Is that so?"

"It is. Everyone knows. So if you need, say, her address book, well, maybe I heard her say you go get it."

"Is that what you heard?"

"It for sure could be. Understanding her doesn't come easy, even to me."

"Did Mary Ann understand her?"

"Mary Ann never came back here but once, and Lila spat on her. Called her a monster. Said she killed her father. The kid just looked at her a while and then walked out."

"You're not playing straight with me, Castor."

"Whaddaya mean?"

"You want me to think she didn't say anything to that?"

"The kid?"

"Is anyone else in this story? Of course, the kid."

"I don't recall."

"Someone said that to me, I'd express myself pretty freely. You want me to believe Mary Ann Grey just took it?"

"It's her sick mom, man, and she says all kinds of shit. After a while you just roll it off."

"It's just everywhere I go I hear about how Mary Ann would fight anyone, anytime. She was a fighter. And here we are and her mom says something like that, I don't see her just rolling it off like you say. I see her as the kind can't sit for it."

Castor shrugs.

"She said something like 'fuck his revolution and fuck you too'. I think it was just the worst thing she could think of."

"And Lila was upset."

Castor points towards the bedroom. "What do you think, man? How I even know for sure?"

"This is all just coming back to you now?"

"Call it a free sample. You want the address book?"

"Yes, I want it."

He says a number. I say a very different number and he doesn't like it. He wants to know if I'm kidding around.

"That comes with a bonus, Castor."

Now he's interested again. He gives me the line I'm looking for. "What bonus would that be?"

"I don't slap you so hard you go out of here through that window."

He gets a pugnacious look, and then a scared one as he tries to imagine how it would actually go between us.

"There's no need to be like that. You got expenses, Mr Detective."

"I got expenses and fiduciary obligations, but most of all I have a sense of things and how they ought to be. I don't mind you lying for me so I can take that book and find who killed that mad woman's daughter. I figure if she was in her right mind she'd be okay with that. But I do object to you making too much money for selling her out. So I think you're gonna give me the book and I'm gonna give you the few bucks your soul is worth, and you're gonna hate me and wish you had the means to knock me on my ass, but tonight when you're sitting in whatever shitty bar will have you, drinking Lila Grey's address book and counting the pennies, you'll know what you are, and that's a better world. Now give it over or I really will slap you."

He doesn't move, and I slap him, fast but not hard.

"That's a downpayment. You get me, Castor?"

"You're a son of a bitch," Castor says. "I'm just trying to make a living."

"I know," I tell him, "and I respect the hell out of the part of you that takes care of that old woman in there. But I can see the gaps on the walls where the other part of you already sold her pictures. Give me the address book before I dwell on that too much."

He gives me the address book and I give him what I think his integrity is worth in folding money. It'll buy a round of drinks so long as he doesn't go anywhere worth drinking.

*

sit in what passes for a bar in the new Tilehurst. The lights are bright and the plastics are clean so that it's like an airport lounge or a fun park. The waiter gives me what she claims is draught beer. It tastes the way pleather smells.

The handwriting in the address book is clear and round, with a whole lot of names crossed out. I take pictures of the pages and send them to Mini Denton, tell her to trace them all and find out who is still alive, who remembers the family. Figure it's Tilehurst and Aloysius Grey was maybe some sort of a minor protagonist in that story, got beat down by the Lidgate boys and didn't die, kept his secrets behind his broken teeth. Like so. Figure that means a lot of the people he knew are going to be dead or moved on or just plain broken like that fireman back in Othrys. Still more will lie about him because of what he is, or because by now they truly think they were buddies back in the day. And some will lie because they hated the bastard and don't want to say. A whole load of bullshit to walk through in case someone dropped a diamond ring, but that's what junior partners are for.

Mary Ann's page in the address book is like a bookie's betting sheet, one number after another, and the old lady's writing gets shakier and shakier until the last one is in someone else's, maybe Castor's. I look at the ink for the last entry Lila Grey made with her own hand, at the shape and the way it sits a little uneasy on the page, like maybe she couldn't really see the little lines or couldn't hold the pen steady, and I go looking for others like it. There aren't many and half of them are doctors. Most of the rest are groceries. Under E, for emergency, I find one more. I call it, using the house phone for cash.

"One oh two eight two," a woman's voice says.
"Hi, this is Castor, Lila Grey's nurse?"
"What can I do for you?"
"Lila has tachycardia. She's going into hospital at five."
"Understood. The policy will cover it."
"She wants to see Mary Ann."
"That won't be possible."

"I know that. The cops told me. But she won't know if you send someone else, she's all the way gone. Listen, do I still have a job?"

I try to make myself sound whiny and bullshit, like Castor. It obviously works.

"I'll have someone come by."

I put down the phone and the waiter brings the check. Pretty sure she overheard the conversation, because she leaves the tip on the counter and walks away.

The car pulls up a half hour later. I'm sitting on a bench down the block reading a newspaper I bought in the same place as the cheap camera I'm using to take pictures. I traded the kit for a discount on a respectable pancake lens the guy promised would make clear images at range, and now it's in my hand as I turn the page on my newspaper, snap snap snap as the car pulls up and a woman gets out. She doesn't look like Mary Ann Grey, but she's dressed like her and has her hair the same way. I make sure to get her face and the number of the car, then walk away. There's nothing more to learn here, and as soon as Castor opens the door they'll be looking for me, whoever they are. I phone the number through to Orhan.

"I need to know who."

"And I am not the Department of Motor Vehicles."

"You need me to hold your hand while you pay a clerk to give you a credit card number so you can do your thing on the credit card number?"

"I am business-to-business, Cal. This is consumer-facing."

"You're worried about getting shot."

"I am a little bit worried about getting shot."

"Call Sporty Jasmine, have her get whatever she can and give it to you. You go from there."

"Sporty Jasmine?"

"Mini. Taormina. Whatever."

"I know, Taormina. She was here telling me to go faster on the other thing. You want that I should ask her to get shot?"

"No one is going to get shot."

"That is always what people think before they get shot."

"Speaking as someone who has been shot, I have to say that is not true."

"Oh."

"You gonna call her?"

"I feel she will think less of me."

"That probably *is* true."

"I'll get your information."

"The who, Orhan. Get me that. And all the other stuff. But start with the who."

"To be clear: who sent the untraceable cash bundle and also who owns the company that owns the company that owns the land that isn't Martha Erskine's; and now also who pays these medical bills and who drives this car?"

"The company that owns the company?"

"You think I sit on my ass the whole time you're away?"

"No, I just hadn't appreciated the complexity."

"Well, now you do. This is expensive because it's hard."

"Can you do the car thing?"

"Are you paying?"

"Of course."

"Then I can do the car thing."

I run through some shoe leather getting to a few of the really old addresses in Lila Grey's book, the ones in faded ink, and when that gets me nothing but young professionals in converted retail and shared apartments, I try the ones crossed out with new addresses given in the box towns. There I talk to three grown-up children and two surviving principals, and what I hear is just about the same from all of them: Mary Ann Grey never had one good word to say about her father, and Aloysius Grey would never shut up about his glorious revolution. The way he talked you'd think what happened in Tilehurst, between the red streets and the burning roofs, was a win for everyone. To hear him tell it by the time he died, you'd think the 1848 carried the field, and he was the only member: doctor, strategist, soldier and getaway driver, Aloysius Grey was all of them, and the law never came for him after because the Man couldn't touch you when you were, with all your heart and soul and fire and belief, not just yourself but the People as well.

History notwithstanding.

And Mary Ann Grey? One day she just wasn't around any more, and her old man didn't mention her name. I like to think she broke a bottle over his face before she left, because one night he did come home with stitches on his bullshit smile, but honest to god, I got no idea. Maybe someone with less cause and more choler just got tired of his noise.

So where did she go? Once upon a time, Mary Ann had a boyfriend over in the Three, in a white building with twenty-nine floors that looks like a water bottle at a high-ticket exercise class. His name is Doug, and next year he'll be thirty. He got married at twenty-eight, to a woman Hanaa, who plays violin. She's practising upstairs while I ask her husband about Mary Ann Grey.

"Have you seen her recently, Doug?"

"I have. She came by a while back. It was kinda odd. Sweet, I guess." He has on spectacles and a leather apron, because Doug is a silversmith at a place that makes rings for executives who fancy themselves bikers. While we talk, he's polishing a miniature nude, Psyche on her back. There's a matching Eros cooling on the bench, and if you buy them both they make a crude little replica of that statue by Canova that's so good it outright oughta be banned.

"How so?"

"She met somebody. A big family kid from the Shore, she wanted to—I don't know, I guess: see if I'd think less of her for being with him. Because of what happened here. I said, go for it."

"And do you think less of her?"

"Maybe some." He laughs. "But I want her to be happy. She always seems so alone."

"Always?"

"The last few years, anyway."

"You're in touch."

"She calls me from time to time—late, early. When she's walking or in the bath. We talk. Sometimes messages from wherever she is. Stupid stuff, pictures of dogs in costumes, all that. I send some back. What friends do."

I look at Doug, and he's got a slightly queasy smile. "Doug, man to man: is there unfinished business between you two?"

He looks away. "Not . . . it isn't a thing. It's leftover, and I don't feel like I can shut it down. We just never said goodbye."

"And more recently, you find yourselves saying hello at all?"

"What? Oh, you mean—no."

"You sure?"

"Yeah, absolutely. No way."

I look at him a while, working on his commercial porn jewellery and living his life. Sure, he could come down to Shearwater and they could make love on a lilo. Maybe every hour of a long night he's supposed to be at some ring-maker's conference. And then maybe she says she's going to tell his wife and he strangles her there and dumps her there and here I am. Honestly, I don't see it. I don't believe in many things, but I think I do just about believe in Doug. I check, anyway: I ask where he was when Mary Ann Grey was killed, and when you do that, people know, or start to know, that the person you're talking about is dead.

"I was here," Doug says, before his brain catches up. "It was date night. We made . . . roast crispy duck. Getting the skin right is crazy, you have to do this whole thing. Wait, why are you asking me that? Is she okay?"

"Not so much, I'm afraid."

"She in trouble? I can come down there. My wife won't mind."

Figure she might, Doug, if she's a smart sort of woman.

"I don't think there's much you can do, man."

Doug nods, and I see him age right there in front of me, from being that generation where your friends don't really die, to the one where they do. It's not a big step from there to the one where you will, and that's where real age starts.

At least, that's what I hear.

"Her dad break her arm?" I ask. Doug doesn't know for sure,

thinks maybe. Thinks just about anything of old Aloysius Grey, who he has down as a number-one bastard, full of flash and grease and hot air. I try something else. "You ever talk politics with her?"

"She hated all that."

"Hated like wouldn't go there or couldn't stay away?"

"Both, I guess. But it wasn't ... she wasn't Aloysius. You know, like what they say? Give me a single point and I can move the world? She didn't want to move the world, Mr Sounder. She just wanted not to have it move her."

So what was she doing in Shearwater with a bomb and a load of pamphlets? But Doug isn't going to be able to tell me. I'm getting a sense of it now, of Mary Ann and the way it was. Some people you know because they're right there, they live loud and colourful, they leave traces everyone remembers. Others not so much, but still the shape of them sits in who they knew and what they did. And then there's a very few who only seem to exist by the life they don't lead, the choices they don't make: you get to know them in the sound of all the pets they never owned that didn't bark, the tables they never danced on, the weddings they never had.

I come out of Doug's apartment and look at the sky for signs of rain. There aren't any. Heaven is a blue-white arch of heat compressing the whole world, dry air rising off stone and the occasional wilted tree the city council put in a concrete box to pretend Tilehurst really is a living space again. I walk, and I have to take my hands out of my pockets so they don't sweat. I hear cicadas from a green upscale garden and I wonder how much they spend on irrigation.

On the far side of the road, a woman says my name: Sounder. She's middle-aged and sensible, but waving like crazy to get my attention, like something's going down and I need to move right now. I look one way and see an oncoming commercial truck, step back to cross behind it when it's gone.

"Are you okay?" I call to the woman, and she shakes her head.

"Help me," she says, but when I step into the road behind the truck and try to go to her, the doors open and someone lays a leather skin full of little metal balls across the back of my head. They call it a blackjack because that's what happens: blackness, and the knowledge that you've fallen among thieves.

I'm a damn fool, and the woman is smiling as they put me in the back of the truck.

When they get me out of the truck, I'm just about okay enough to walk by myself, but the back side of my head feels white and cold and my neck has a warning line of sweet overstretch down the spine. When I move too fast it feels tired, and I can't say I disagree.

The boys walking me to wherever I'm going don't like it when I look around, which is fine because it still hurts, but I can smell damp walls and human beings, and beneath that there's a smell of hot metal like an old-time printing press. I don't recognise the place because this isn't my town, but I know what it is: a nowhere land. You get them, in the gaps between closed-down and reopened, before the demolition crews come in to turn a playground into a mall or a school into apartments, these run-down plaster-peeling industrial lots, full of spiders and rats and shadows, and that's where we are. In one of the places that's not off-grid so much as off-label, where no one sees what goes on because no one wants to. A hospital, maybe, back in the day, or a really nasty college.

The first room we go through is a dormitory, more a flophouse, but that makes it sound squalid and it's not. It's clean and dry with neat rows of beds, each with a locker at the foot, and now I'm thinking barracks, or monastery. There are curtains making shared rooms for couples, and one whole wall is a kind of memorial, painted wood-effect and gold, the names of the fallen, except when you look closely you don't know them. Not war heroes, not criminals or cops. Just names, like from a phone book. At the far end there's a crowd of people, young and old, reading books, and a murmur of discussion, notes on pages. Someone says something earnest about praxis. The word means 'practice', the application of a theory in the world, but god forbid you just say that. To a certain kind of person 'praxis' is a shibboleth. It says you've chosen a side of Matias Constanza's line. They stop talking to watch me as I go by.

"Hi fellas," I tell them, and they don't answer so I try again. "Long live the revolution. The fire has not gone out."

One of them raises his fist in salute. The others glower at my suit and my Titan body.

"Sure," I tell them. "Wouldn't want to feel solidarity with the wrong sort of person. Might get counter-cooties."

One of my walkers nudges me along. "Don't do that."

"Do what?"

"Don't make fun, smart guy. Those are serious people having serious conversations."

"What if I want to have a serious conversation?"

"Then you're in luck."

We go through the door and up some stairs, then down again into the next part of the building.

This one's less crowded and more businesslike, just a few rows of those serious people bent low over work benches making things with tubes and springs and sheer grey extruded stuff from boxes packed with popcorn. I take a closer look as I go by, eyes still half browned-out by the rap on the noggin, and the guy walking me grinds something hard and cold into the soft place below my ear. Bad practice: never touch the man you're guarding with your gun. Once he knows where it is he knows how to take it off you and after that it's a whole narrative for you both. Unless his head still feels like a three-day hangover. Maybe I'd try it anyway, but it's not like we're alone. There's two other guys walking escort for a total of three: call them Adam, Butch and Charles.

"Don't touch me with that," I tell Adam. "Did you crack my skull, you son of a bitch?"

"I think you got male fragility," Adam says. "You whine a whole lot."

"Gosh, I'm crushed."

"Yeah, keep talking and you'll find out what crushed is."

I look down at the table and see what the thing is being built.

"Is that where you got yours? You trust these assholes to make one that won't jam and blow your fucking hand off?"

The guy at the workbench looks up. "I have made three hundred of these, and tested them all personally. They do not jam and blow your fucking hand off."

"Mika says they don't jam," the guy says. "Good enough for me."

"Lebedev Generic PL-15 Micro, version nine," I say. "People call it the AK of handguns. Small enough to go in a pocket. Not a marksman's gun, but much lighter and more durable with the new ceramics, detector invisible, and you can get parts anywhere so long as the original maker stayed within tolerances. Good choice for a revolution."

"For the many," Mika says, proud.

"Good choice for high-level crime, too, of course. Necessary compromises, sometimes, to fuel the fire. You stockpiling against the day or just moving product?"

"I told you to quit your smack talk," Adam says.

"Plus also: fuck you," Mika adds.

"Fuck me? How about fuck you, dealer?"

"Dealer? You want to talk about who's a sellout? Who's in hock to the fucking monster machine?"

"Mika . . ." the guy cautions.

"The nerve of this guy, coming in here and calling me a fucking dealer," Mika says.

"And fuck the corpse of your revolution in the eyeholes, buster." Which is one of those statements that makes a silence in the whole damn room. "Oh, wait, you can't, because it's in the morgue back where I'm working and it looks like a girl who spoke your language and someone put out her lights. You know what else they got there? They got people they call Sleepers on the beach just waiting to die of the whole world, yet somehow that's not important to you, just like it's not you down there picking crabs off of a dead woman's face, it's me, and if anyone figures out what happens to her, that'll be me too, and maybe it'll turn out that one of you saints of the new International, who was supposed to look after her, just up and strangled her because she wasn't interested in giving it up to his heroic passions. I'm pretty sure her hero dad smacked her around when she was just a kid. Anyone tell me that didn't happen? No, you can't, because you got no idea because you don't give a shit. What do you think, Mika? You want to tell me how building Lebedevs in a derelict does anything about any of that? Call me if you think of anything, deadbeat. I'll be sure and tell her mom you said hi."

He's halfway around the bench before I've finished and Adam has to catch him. I lunge past like I really want to get into it. Butch and Charles get hold of my arms, but because I'm still punch-drunk and groggy from the blackjack we all go down in a mess, with me as the ham in a revolution sandwich. My head slaps into Butch, bloodies his nose. At the same time my left hand snags in his jacket, wrenching the thumb out of the socket and dragging the fabric around his waist. He looks ridiculous. The noise of my thumb going sounds like gristle and ping-pong. I yell and shake my arm this way and that, dragging the jacket off one of his shoulders, making the dislocation worse, which makes me yell more. Butch all but throws Mika back behind his workbench, tells me to stop being an asshole, then grabs my arm and untangles me but tweaks my thumb and I want to vomit. He can see what's happening and jerks back, swearing, so roll I away and spit, then lie on my side with acid in the back of my nose. When I open my eyes, I'm looking at the business end of a Lebedev.

"Don't move," Adam says. "At all."

"He started it," I point at Mika. "Tell him. Can I get a little help here?" Waving my thumb.

Adam gestures, and Charles, the one I didn't land on, comes over and pops my thumb back where it ought to be, like killing a rat. I yell again, because it hurts and it's okay for them to know that, and they all get nervous because they don't want me to throw up on them. People are strange: these guys are proud of their convictions and they'll kill me if they're told, but the idea that I might puke completely wigs them out.

I look over at the guy with the bloody nose, down at my thumb and sigh like I'm giving something up. "I'm sorry, man, I got no beef with you. Nor you, Mika. I get that you all believe in what you're doing here, I just got emotional. It's been a day."

They don't meet my eyes, don't laugh.

Slowly, paying real attention to the gun in Adam's hand, I get up and walk real careful to wherever it is we're going, and no one says anything while we get there.

"Dina," my escort says, in a brown, rectangular room. There's nothing about the woman waiting there that says "Dina". The name is all wine and olive groves. The woman isn't. There are papers in front of her, and the way she touches them says they're her real friends.

"He give you any trouble? I thought I heard something."

"Doctrinal argument," Adam says. "No harm, no foul."

"I dislocated my thumb," I add, "you can write that down if you like."

"Thank you," Dina says, but not to me. She leans back and looks at me for a really long, silent time until I feel like a fish in a tank. "You really are one of them, aren't you? This voice of authority you have, so naturally assumed. How old are you?"

"That feels like a personal question."

"I'm trying to be friendly, Mr Sounder. Isn't that what you'd prefer?"

"I'm in my forties."

"Are you sure?"

I shrug. "I remember most of it."

"But you've been through Stefan Tonfamecasca's process. There's an issue with memory sometimes, as I understand."

"Sometimes. Not in my case."

"That must be nice, to know things with such clarity. You're wrong, of course. Not about yourself—I doubt Mr Tonfamecasca would waste time on messing with your head. But you're wrong about everything else, in small but significant ways."

"And you know what those ways are."

"Oh, no," she spreads her hands. "I only know that they exist. That they must. Power doesn't allow for a vacuum, does it? It floods in and fills the spaces. Tears up anything in the way."

"Sometimes."

She steeples her hands the way a bar fighter puts them behind his back when he's trying to be better. Dina's a teacher, but the dangerous kind, brittle and angry before we begin. "What was life like when Stefan Tonfamecasca was young?"

"Pretty much like now."

"Really? How do we know what things were like four centuries ago? Or is it five?"

"We have these things called books. Search engines. Museums, yet."

"Ah, yes. Sources. Records. They can be tampered with, falsified, we all know that. And even at their best they represent an opinion, a subjective angle of view. But we don't have to rely on them any more, do we? We have Titans. A very few, very old people who were actually there. But then it occurs to me that they, too, have an angle of view. They're people of power."

"They are."

"*You* are."

"If you prefer."

"I definitely do. You are influential, as a group and as individuals. So how would it go if something happened, say, a hundred years ago, and a Titan wanted it to be remembered differently?"

I start to say there are limits, and then I think about it. Not a hundred years, maybe, with information passed directly from parent to child. But two hundred? Yes. In a span like that almost anything could be rewritten if Stefan wanted it. After the generation that saw it died, and when their children were dead too, he could just change what was recorded. What was taught.

"How is that different from a world without Titans?"

She nods. "Not much, I suppose. Except that it's the same people, time after time. The same agenda. A refining process."

"If it happens."

"You think it doesn't?"

I think the world I live in belongs to Stefan. It hadn't really crossed my mind to wonder how long that's been so. He's a line that extends as you look at it, in both directions from the middle. The closest human approximation to infinity.

Dina nods. "As it happens, I wasn't really asking if we live in a fabricated history. I was asking why today is the same as however many hundred years ago. There was a time when a decade sufficed to change everything. And yet very little has changed, according to those museums and books you mentioned, in all those years. Why is that, do you think?"

"Maybe it's a perfect world."

"Sass? Is that really your best answer?"

"I don't think my answers are all that important in this discussion, Dina. I think you already have your own and you want to tell me what they are. I don't object to that at all but I don't see that we have to waste time with me telling you mine just so you can tell me I'm wrong."

"All right. I think Stefan Tonfamecasca is a weight not just on economic justice but on development. I think he's the reason we live in a temporal monoculture as well as a lateral one. The reason we're increasingly homogeneous, culturally speaking, around the world is the same reason we still live the way people did before T7 existed. Because the way things are right now suits Stefan Tonfamecasca personally, and everyone answers to him in the end. Or rather, in the avoidance of the End. In living, he—you all—make us not in your own image but unconsciously in the image of what you find easy to deal with."

"You're way over my head."

"I don't think so. Tonfamecasca isn't even a real name. There's no language on earth, no home country that would produce it. It sounds exciting everywhere. And no one ever asks where he comes from, because the past is behind us, and the only thing that matters is how far forward into the future we reach. Which of course means that the person who matters most is . . . Stefan Tonfamecasca. You see? That's his priority, and it frames everything. And if you, Mr Sounder, were to replace Stefan, then I imagine over time everywhere on Earth would become some sort of irreverent speakeasy. Does that strike you as a good thing?"

"Would life be better if the world were an irreverent speakeasy?"

"Yes."

"Maybe it would."

"Exactly. You don't particularly care, but on balance that's how it seems to you. And Stefan likes things—consciously or not—the way they are, and so everything is bounded by that casual preference. How does that sound?"

I think Stefan just painted his bedroom black and feels more and more like geology. I don't know what that means if Dina has a point, and I don't really like asking, so now I'm stuck with her crazy in my head. There's a certain kind of person can ask questions that won't go away. They make good detectives and they're a colossal pain in the ass. Being one is not easier than knowing one.

"I don't think it's inevitable. Titans aren't all alike."

"Ah, your lover. And you. One of these things is not like the others. A slow, over-arching change to the order of things, is that it?"

"That's more her than me."

"You help people. Do the job that's in front of you."

"The second one more than the first."

"Liar." But she doesn't seem offended. "Do you think you're unchanged, though? The same Cal you were ten years ago? Nonsense. Your voice rings out, Mr Sounder. You speak as a token, an avatar of the secular divine. The great god Titan, walking with men, down among the little people. A demi-god. A noirish Hercules. Are you careful with where you put your feet, so that you don't crush the ants?"

"Lady, you use a lot of words."

"Yes. What choice is there? How many battalions has a former professor of literature?"

I look pointedly back over my shoulder at the room full of guns. She snorts. "Don't be absurd. That's not a battalion. That's barely an argument."

"I don't feel entirely comfortable with people who can look at a thousand guns and think: 'that's not enough to make my point.'"

"Oh, yes. I'm a cult leader. A madwoman. I must be. No one rational would take on the system. It's so enormous, so dominating. There's no point in my preparations, so I must be bent on a noble death. There it is again, that certainty of your own power. *You* can't fight the system, so no one can. If the system can't be fought, it must be ameliorated, and to do that, you need to borrow its power. Collaborate, but in a good cause. Is that about the size of it, Mr Sounder?"

"About that."

"Boys and their toys. Did it never occur to you that a direct trial of strength is not required? Battalions, indeed. How many Titans are there in the world? Two thousand? Two and a half? And most of those first dose. Almost ordinary. Certainly vulnerable to conventional injury. A pretty girl in a hotel room with the right gun and the resolve to get it done. A handsome young man with dark eyes. There are billions of ordinary humans, Mr Sounder, and only a very few of the Titan class. Perhaps twenty or thirty of the most ancient who'd take more killing. For the rest . . . you could all disappear in a single night."

"Build a paradise on mass murder. It's a great idea, I wonder why no one ever thought of it."

She considers me, and I don't know what she sees but I return the favour. She has grey hair, shiny and quite short; round, white cheeks like frozen apples; brown, shuttered eyes. Her hands are strong and calloused, with scars, and I see ink just above the cuff of a faded chore jacket, denim so old it's turning white. The ink could be prison, could just be old and bad, but it's interesting it's still there. Memory scars, then, of something too important to leave behind.

"All right," I say. "Why are we talking?"

"I hear things, Mr Sounder. This enterprise is long-term. Slow and steady, not flashy. Opportunities may arise along the way, and the whole thing may forever be unnecessary, a side show to which I foolishly devoted my life. Perhaps the people will rise up against you. Perhaps you all will come to understand the fundamental wrongness of what you are and remove yourselves to an island to live your long, strange lives without the rest of us, and we'll come to consider you like Galapagos tortoises, precious and rare. In the meantime, I listen and I hear things, and you are in the midst of events that I find I want to know about."

"I don't work for you."

"No. But you must be permitted to trade information."

"That's only good to me if I get out of here."

She nods. "True."

I wait, but that's it. "This is where you tell me I will."

"Actually, all I have to do is leave the option open. You'll take it, because it's the only game in town."

"Screw you."

"Yes, I thought so. An exchange of information, then. I'll even let you ask the first question."

She waits, and she's right. It is the only game in town.

"Are you in Shearwater?"

"No."

"Not anyone from your team?"

"No."

"Anyone you know about? Like you but a separate organisation?"

"You can say '1848', Mr Sounder. The sky won't fall."

"All right, what about the 1848?"

She sighs. "I wish. In twenty years, Mr Sounder, of living in the post-industrial cracks, I've never seen anyone but us. The search for communist life in the universe carries on. My question: what do you want from Lila Grey?"

"Her daughter died."

"I know."

"I'm trying to find out why."

"Because we live in a world of structurally enforced alienation that kills all of us, one way or another. Us, but not you."

"I don't think a judge is going to sign an arrest warrant for alienation. If you had a great big bomb, would you look to use it on a high-dose Titan?"

"Probably. But not today. On that one night, yes. There's no point getting you one at a time. Stefan Tonfamecasca will just make more. You're a hydra, sprouting heads faster than I can cut them off."

Something occurs to me, and it comes out before I can stop it: "Are you Flens?"

Flens: one of the nightmares of the new world, the baseline human who kills Titans in their homes, leaves them jointed for Stefan to find. I always assumed Flens was a sexual sociopath, if she existed at all beyond the whispers of cover-ups and blood baths, the ambient tabloid hiss of not-quite-news. Now I wonder if she was something else, more clinical and experimental: Dina trying out themes and processes, establishing response times.

"Is that your question?" I'm sort of interested, and I think she might actually tell me if she is, but then again: I'm not here hunting fairy-tales. I want to know who killed Mary Ann Grey, so I shake my head.

"It's not my turn, anyway."

She nods, as if granting absolution. "Do you feel different now?"

At over 215 centimetres tall, I've no need to ask what she means by "now". I say yes.

"How?"

"More complicit. More alone." I'm surprised by how easily that comes out. I haven't told Athena. I'm not sure I've told myself. "Have you been to Shearwater? Stood on the beach?"

"I have."

"You've seen the Sleepers?"

"The broken product of the same system you collaborate in when you work with the hierarchy. A slavery so absolute that it distances human beings from the act of life itself; the victory of capital in the very depth of the soul, and the triumph of despair."

"I thought that was supposed to lead to enlightenment." In the book, that's what it says: suffering makes us wise, and we come together as a natural consequence, take ownership of the world. Maybe it will one day, and I just have to live long enough to see it.

I wait for her to say something about how she'll save them, but when I look into her brown eyes I see nothing but vindication. It doesn't occur to her to give them blankets, to wonder if they could be woken up, or healed, because their sleep demonstrates that everything she believes is true.

"Why do you care?" she asks. "They're no different from any other baseline human: ephemeral and small."

"Why shouldn't I care?"

"Because you don't belong to them any more. You're separate. Different."

She glowers at me, and I glower back.

"Did you know Aloysius Grey?"

"I did."

"Did you know he broke his daughter's arm?"

She turns her face away. "Propaganda. Psy-ops."

"Lila told me, just now. Almost the only thing I got from her that made any sense."

"Lila's senile."

"I have to ask: did you know then, too?" And this time I can see the shame before she shoves it down. "I'm already contracted to find out who killed Mary Ann Grey. If you're not in Shearwater then you're not behind the container bomb and you need to know who is. If I take you on as a client, I don't discuss it with anyone."

"I've just told you I'm preparing to kill you and everyone like you."

"I don't think you can get to most of them. As for me, a lot of people I meet are planning to kill me. I can't be choosy about that or I'd get no conversation."

"And your fee?"

"You can pay what you think the service is worth, when it's done."

"An honour bar?" She shrugs. "I spoke to the Costanzas about you, they're big fans."

"I like what they do, too."

"Left anarchic mutual support networks at a local level. Mitigation, not revolution. Attractive, but in the end . . . a cloud of false hope in the mind."

She doesn't care about the Sleepers and she doesn't care for the Lacarte. And she hasn't said yes to my offer.

It occurs to me to wonder, as I look at her snow-apple face, how crazy she is, and how hard it is to be inside her head.

"I think I'm going to leave now," I say.

"Are you?"

"Yes. One way or another."

"I'm fascinated to know how you expect that to work."

"One of two ways. The first one is I get up and walk out of the door. I don't see anyone here as I go, and I'm terrible with faces so I don't know who you are. I go and do what I can for dead Mary Ann Grey. It doesn't do you any harm because you're not in it. And maybe one day you need me or someone like me, and you call. Or vice versa, who knows?"

"Or?"

"Or there's the other way."

"Yes, so I gathered. I'm just curious that you think there's some leverage you can apply."

"You're my leverage."

"Me?"

"I get up, I hold you in front of me, and when the boys come through the door I shoot them down." I reach into my pocket and let her see the little gun I stole from Butch when we went down on the ground and everyone was getting excited about social justice and my thumb and his face. That's the trouble with lightweight ceramic. If there's a lot going on, it can take you while to realise it's not there any more.

"Sixteen-round magazine," I tell her. "Figure I can make a hell of a mess here. I'm sure your boys are willing, but the thing is, I've got training and they haven't, and I'm resilient and they're not, and in the end they're going to choke on shooting through you."

"They are believers," she says.

"But they're dumb, Dina, and when you're dead, this all will come apart. Someone'll sell all the guns to the street. Whatever communications links you've got with your people undercover will stop working and fall away. This whole thing you've done will just be secret history, and the Titans won't even know they've won. They tell me that's what happens, by the way. We outlive things so fast, sometimes we don't notice they're gone."

I point the gun at her and wait. Time is on my side.

6

I step off the train at Shearwater Station, remembering real Ailsa Lloyd running towards me, seeing the reverse angle along the platform. I wonder if Mary Ann Grey arrived the same way. I imagine her coming down the same platform alone, with all her ghosts, and disappearing into the shadows of the holiday town.

Dina wouldn't have given a damn, any more than she cared about the Sleepers. People with great work to do so seldom have time for the small. They leave that to people like me, who don't understand the important things. Me, and Fallon, and Sporty Jasmine and Iverson and all the other assholes who pick up the pieces of things others broke. I honestly don't know if she's right and I'm wrong, I just know I can't do it like her.

Mary Ann Grey did not work for Dina. I believe it. And Dina has no idea if there's a real 1848 operating in Shearwater, but she doesn't think so. I believe that too, and while I believe she wouldn't have told me if she'd meant to let me go, I also think she told me in case she did.

I get out my phone. By the time I've dialled, I'm in the street outside and there's just enough shadows and grey mist that I feel stupid walking around with it next to my ear. I won't hear if someone comes up on me. They might come up on me to get the phone. I let the call go through anyway because I'm too damn tired to be smart.

"Hey, Orhan."

"You are a very impatient client, Cal."

"I have time constraints."

"You, less so than literally anyone else I have met in my life."

"All right, I just want to know things now, not tomorrow."

"You get that I am cooking dinner right this second, yes?"

"You're making tagine, Orhan, it's not like you have to tend it all that much."

"How do you know I'm making tagine?"

"Your mother's in town and you always make tagine."

"I somehow believed it would be more impressive than that. Like you have a surveillance drone that follows me around."

"How do you think I know she's in town?"

"I told you she was coming."

"Sure, if that's what you remember." I can hear him wondering, and I wish I hadn't said it.

"You told me, Orhan. I'm just a guy. Now, please, it has been a long, weird day. Give me something."

And he does. He tells me who pays for Lila Grey's medical.

I ask him to say it again, and when he does, I don't like it any better than I did the first time.

Mary Ann Grey crossed the country making trouble as loud as she could, and she came to Shearwater with that legend wrapped all around her, and down by the water there's a blue container with a bomb in it and all the makings of a revolution. Down by the water, and not far from where you'd put her in the water if you wanted her to wash up where she did. Not far from Martha Erskine's house, if you wanted me to look that way.

"Bail Erskine," Orhan says.

"Sure," I say, at last. "Why not?"

Because: why not?

At the simplest, Bail Erskine wanted a trouble magnet. He wanted someone to draw out anybody thinking real bad thoughts while he and Rudi Basu locked horns over clauses and paragraphs and everybody's lawyers sang base. The poor man's razor says to stop there; don't buy more trouble than you can afford.

But you could not, along any axis, call Martha Erskine a poor man, so that is for sure not where it stops. Some cases are just like that: every break looks like another hill you got to climb, and then suddenly you're at the top and the whole world is just laid out in front of you and you wish it wasn't.

I'll look forward to it. For now I need to eat, and sleep, and not smell like the back of Adam's truck and the dust on Dina's gunshop floor.

I walk down to the main street and into the police station. Iverson's not there; Dijkstra tells me he eats most nights just around the corner, a casual kind of a place up an iron fire escape on the side of the old corn market. Not that anything illegal happens there, it's just you could walk past it a hundred times and never know to go in. Spicer's, Dijkstra says. Luandan, with beer.

When I get there, Spicer's is box crate and steel, actual sawdust on the tiles and the rich smell of pine wood rising from it. The owner's brother has a carpentry shop on the inland side, close to the highway where he can watch the trucks go someplace else with the things he makes, and wonder whether he should be there too.

Some kind of irreverent speakeasy.
Goddamit.

Iverson sits at a little table by himself, reading. I figure it's going to be a crime scene report, but it's not, it's just a paperback with lines creased on it where someone carried it in their pocket day after day. *After All* by William Matthews. Poetry. Go figure.

"Hi, Cal," Iverson says. He looks like I feel.

"You mind if I join you?"

"I guess not. Maybe we can take a minute before we talk about the case?"

"I don't want to talk about it at all."

That makes him laugh. Then he looks at me properly, and sees the new bruises. "What the hell happened to you?"

I really do think about telling him the truth, but old habits die hard. "It turns out I'm an asshole."

He chuckles.

"Yeah, sure, laugh at my pain."

"Hey, you made it funny."

"Just tell me what to eat so you don't have to carry me home."

"People would talk."

"I'm pretty sure they will anyway. In the name of mercy, Tim—"

"The calulu's good. So's the cabidela. Stay clear of the muamba unless you're not afraid of dragons."

"It's that hot?"

"It is that hot."

Figure it probably isn't, but I can try it another day. We do small talk about the food until Iverson's inner cop gets the better of him.

"So what the hell happened to you?"

"Argument at my knitting circle."

"I was asking out of concern, Cal."

"I was answering the same way."

"Sure you were."

"But if we're working, then the good news is that Bail's paying Lila Grey's medical."

"Bail Erskine?"

"Yes, Tim, Bail Erskine."

"How is that good news?"

"I just figured it would sound better if I said that."

"You were mistaken. How long?"

"A year, maybe more."

"Fuck. You want to do my job while I go away somewhere?"

"You asked me that already."

"Did you say yes?"

"No."

"Then I'm gonna keep asking. What do you see?"

"I see ... Bail paying for Mom's medical. Then I see Mary Ann making trouble at the factory and sleeping with a junior Erskine."

"You think he planted her on Rudi or on the boy?"

"Sex, money and power."

"So, Torrance is a sideshow."

"Which doesn't mean he didn't kill her, just that I don't figure Bail bringing in someone like Mary Ann to screw him. Or her going along with that. Follow the trinity."

"You know, in actual modern policing we don't talk about sex, money and power any more."

"Do we not?"

"We talk about M. I. C. E."

"I'm assuming this isn't a put-on."

"Money, ideology, compromise and ego."

"So . . . sex, money and power, but all grown up?"

"Vesper was right, you really are a smartass. Tell you, when we get to the end of this—and we will, Cal—when we get to the end of it, the motivation will be one of those things."

"You know which it is?"

"No. Do you?"

"I do not."

We sit there and look at nothing for a while.

"You got more?"

"No."

"Can we just eat now?"

We do. We put the world away outside the doors of Spicer's and we eat and we drink, and after a while we start talking again, and I ask Iverson about himself.

"You ever get married?"

He stops, beer halfway to his lips: a dark wheat, rich and fine in the glass. "Yes. Separated."

"She live nearby?"

"Not for a while now. She was ninety-one. Had a good innings."

I stare at him. "Shit."

"You're . . . really not used to the age thing, are you?"

"I guess I am not."

"She ditched me two years after our son was born. Before you ask, he lives over on the west coast now. Children of his own. I . . .

never really got back into things, after that. And then . . . " Not the classic collapse of a Titan marriage, just an ordinary human mess, but that means it was a long time ago. Iverson got his first dose at seventy-eight. For epilogue, he's waving his hand up and down, the universal sign language of first dosers: this happened, and it changes things.

He's more than thirty years in. "It still doesn't fit?"

"Oh, I like it just fine. But the offset, you know?"

"Not yet."

"No. I guess you're still . . . mostly in touch with the baseline?"

"And just out of touch with most Titans. Mr In-Between."

He laughs. "Jeez, Cal, you should be a cop."

We toast to not fitting in, and get more pãozinho. Halfway through the next beer, I tell him about Mary Ann Grey not fitting in either. He sighs and his head drops low for a moment.

"You got kids, Cal?"

"I don't."

"Oh." He looks at me. "Oh, no, because you're barely older than you look."

I spread my arms, yes. It throws him that I'm forty-one, just like it throws me that he's not fifty. We're looking at one another from opposite ends of the telescope, but at least it's the same one. Martha sits in one of those huge observatories on a mountain, and she can see other worlds, but not me.

"You gonna hit me with some Titan wisdom now, Tim?"

"Would if I had any."

"Damn." I was slightly hoping that he did.

"Make it work with your girlfriend. It doesn't get easier with time."

"Are you . . . with anyone?"

He shrugs. "I'm significantly not with someone. Like specifically. But I keep trying."

"How long's that been going on?"

"Twenty years or so."

Barely a heartbeat. I wonder if I ought to tell him what Athena says about growing the soul, but he's older than both of us combined, and a cop, and a captain. Don't see him taking life coaching from a stranger across a restaurant table. I smile.

"What do you call that, like a romance of attrition?"

I've crossed a line, the way you can sometimes and have no idea it's coming; my smart mouth putting a needle hard into his pain, and for a minute I think he's going to swing at me. His face twists with real anger, but he's old and smart and measured, and—by good fortune or proximity of selves—we've turned into friends these last days. Nothing like standing within the blast radius of a fertiliser bomb. Nothing like accidentally pushing someone's buttons and having them decide to let it go.

"I'm sorry, Tim. Sometimes the inner asshole's got no class."

He laughs, raises his beer. "Then you and he are both gonna drink with me, Cal, to the fairest of the fair, who mysteriously cannot see my good qualities in the bright noonday sun. To Dixie."

We drink. If he'd hit me, we'd have to hug now, so thank god for small mercies.

"Her name's Dixie?"

"It is."

"Nice name."

"I'm attracted to her, Cal, I didn't get to christen her."

"Tim, are we talking about Dixie Erskine?"

"We are."

"Aren't you her nephew or something?"

"It's a Titan family, Cal. There are so many branches on the tree, genetically I'm probably no closer to Dixie than I am to you. As for socially . . . well, it's not like the Iversons have egg nog and stockings at Erskine House each December. We are professionals and they hire professionals."

"Is that the issue with your girlfriend?"

"No. Unfortunately, I'm pretty sure the issue there is me."

Without being asked, Spicer brings more beer, but also more food to soak it up.

It's been a long minute since I've gone head-to-head in an

undeclared drinking contest, but the key is generous cheating. I have my water glass in one hand and my beer in the other, and I wave and gesture and drink, but I drink from the first and use the second to express myself. It's just a habit: when I'm working a case and I don't know who all is watching, I stay in the safe zone. I think of Mary Ann Grey with activated charcoal in her stomach.

Have to ask: did she think of it because she was a woman living alone, drinking in a town she didn't know? No. She thought of it because she was in this game, one way or another. All those bit-part temp placements she led us to with the credit card at the Roller, just in case we didn't find them otherwise; a legend for a girl. And what's the legend? A hard-working kid from Tilehurst with a hero dad she hated, can't shake what he taught her about the workplace and her rights, can't hold down a gig for all the handsy bosses and short-cuts, washes west to east until she gets here, just looking for a place to hang her hat. A righteous woman looking for an honest job.

How much of it is true I don't know yet.

But suppose it is, or nearly is, what happens then? Who blows up and who wins? And why did Mary Ann Grey lose so hard?

The clock speeds up, and I'm laughing at Tim Iverson's war stories: the time Vesper threw up on his shoes at a ball; the kleptomaniac beach volleyball team; how a herd of wild pigs got loose in the casino. Iverson's got that off-the-hook edge to him now, volume control's gone, but Spicer doesn't seem to mind. The other tables are empty, and I realise it's time to pay up and move on. Iverson excuses himself for the first time the whole night; his pelvic floor must be made of steel.

I call for the cheque, Spicer waves me away. "He runs a tab," the guy says, "and I give him an honest discount because he comes so much."

"He like this a lot?"

"Naw, man, you made him laugh tonight as much as I ever saw. It's good! I like when he laughs. Some nights it's like feeding a dead guy. I mean not dead, but ... maybe he speaks one or two words the whole night, beyond the orders."

"He ever bring a girlfriend?" Because I'm a bastard and people lie.

"Don't I wish? For him I wish, but also for some woman. He's the right sort. But no. He comes in with that Dixie, and no offence but she's no good for him. All the time Dixie Dixie Dixie. Every once in while someone else, I get excited, maybe this is different, but no. Just friends, and the way he says 'friends' he don't mean the kinds of friends who turn into something more. Friends to talk to about serious things. Work colleagues, I guess. That Iqaluq, a few times. I like Iqaluq. She orders big. I think maybe they're having a thing. Then what do they talk about?"

"Is it police work?"

"No, sir, it is so much worse! They talk about Dixie." He throws his hands in the air. "The man is his own worst enemy. A good-hearted smart dumb son-of-a-bitch. He got all the bullshit Scandinavian gloom and no N'Zeto, that one."

True enough, I suppose. Even mostly drunk, Iverson is just more Iverson: louder, more emphatic, sadder. You have to think the last one would fade away in the right company.

"How's he get home?"

"He lives a block over. Never so trolleyed he can't walk. Sometimes I walk with him, when we close up together. My place is seven hundred metres further on." And five hundred metres the wrong side of the main avenue, in the narrow streets where people hang washing and the rooms are small. I know, because I checked him out before I came.

"He stays that long?"

"Oh, sure. Every couple of days he literally washes his own plates, a few more, we talk. It's nice."

Nice for Spicer, and nice for Iverson, who has nowhere better to be nights than up to his elbows in detergent suds, talking to a guy who thinks of him as a good client.

Athena's right: the most dangerous thing is the habit of loneliness.

*

I don't sleep well. Since I became a Titan, my dreams have been bright with texture and power. For up to a decade after you get the dose a big chunk of what's in your skull is effectively newborn and behaves that way, seizing on everything it encounters and building structures which make no sense, demolishing them and starting again. The effect is worst in the first months and tails off, but what lingers is the dreams and nightmares of a child.

Tonight, I'm back in the blue container and Mary Ann Grey is sitting opposite me. She looks like Dina the revolutionist but much younger, for a moment so young that her arm is still in a cast. Then she's in her twenties again and I ask her things and she answers, but from moment to moment I don't know what either of us is saying. I write it all down on a spare page from Lila Grey's address book but when I read them back the words make no sense.

Then I feel the container lifted and swaying, I feel us carried on a ship and then falling, and the smash and splash as we land. Water starts to come in, swirling around us and washing the shoes and the paper and the plastic into a spiral. It's warm and thick and when it bubbles up over my head I find I can breathe. A moment later I look at Mary Ann Grey and see the panic and I realise: she can't. I swim to her and try to breathe air from my lungs into hers, and for a moment she's Ashley and I don't know if I'm saving her or tearing off her clothes, and then she's Athena and she's lifting me out of the water and compressing my chest and her mouth is avid and everything is wonderful and then it's just night in a mid-grade hotel, and so late that it counts near enough as early.

I sleep again, better but not long, put on some clothes and drag myself out into the world to find Rudi Basu.

The Shearwater union chapter has offices by the old fish market, and to get there you have to walk the length of the working harbour: a stone arm that runs straight across the southern corner of the bay beyond the Sleepers' beach. The dredgers moor up on the outside of the arm when they need to, but their home base is actually a hundred kilometres north; the marina, next door, has a few cracked old pleasure boats drifting at anchor and one all the way sunk, with just the masthead poking out of the water and gulls laughing at it all around.

The fishing port is different, still alive if only barely, with a double line of open-front warehouse structures right on the water and basket winches for bringing up the catch. There's a couple of white metal sails sticking out the back landside, fenced off because they get hot: the rear end of refrigeration heat exchangers. The boathouses are further along again, with slipways running down to the water and a big longliner pulled up on one of them with men refitting the deck and repainting the name: *Evermore*. Figure the fellow telling them all what to do from halfway up the side must be Bill Tracey, who looks fine in a bridge coat and maybe knows the offshore water but not the inshore—depending on whether you credit Fish Food—meaning he might have just the right mix of pride and ignorance to drop Mary Ann Grey's body so it'd wash up where it did. Him and all his crew, and anyone else who doesn't meet the standard as set by Agnes, of Agnes Carvalho's Salvage & Art, which is probably almost the entire population of Shearwater, and Othrys, and the whole entire world.

There's a boat unloading, fish mixed with strips of plastic, the winch basket mesh wide enough to let the streamers drop away so that the dying megrim and bright orange gurnard look like they're getting a parade. Used to be a catch like that was worth tens of thousands internationally, but not any more, not from here. I watch the crew and they watch me right back, even with their shoulders turned away and their hands busy.

"Who're you?" one of them calls out.

"Sounder," I say. "Detective. For the dead girl."

They all twist to look at me now. Finally, another man yells back. "We got Iverson for that. What do we need you for?"

"You don't. But I go where I'm sent."

The second man seems to think about that, then loses interest.

"You're not welcome," the first man says.

"It's better that way," I tell him. "Lot of times people don't like it when they find out what really happened with something like this. If I'm not welcome in the first place then nobody has to feel bad hating me when it all comes due. But if you find you got a story you don't want to tell Iverson, you can tell me and I'll make it matter."

Another basket rises from the hold, belly-white and mottled and flopping.

I go up the steps and through the black-painted door with the number on it in white.

Inside, the office is quiet and full of purpose. There's a big ocean fish stuffed and mounted on one wall, the eyes dull against the gloss plaster. I half expect it to sing.

"Help you?" a thin man says, looking up from some kind of chart.

"I need to see Rudi Basu."

"Talk to Sal." He indicates a square-faced woman with crinkly hair and hypothyroid eyes. "Hey, Sal!"

"I heard, Chin. Keep your pantyhose on. You looking for Rudi?"

"I am."

"You look like trouble, kid. If I get him to make time for you will I wake up tomorrow feeling like an idiot?"

"I don't know. How did you feel this morning?"

Outside they're loading another basket of fish. The winch creaks. Someone calls out to his mate: "Hey, jackass! Watch where you swing that thing."

But no one in the union office is making the slightest sound whatsoever, and Sal's eyebrows are way up on her high bulldog face.

"Fuck did you say?"

"You wanted to know if you'd wake up feeling like an idiot. I can't answer that question. Maybe you never doubt yourself at all or maybe that's the first thought through your head each day. Maybe you weren't really asking but I don't know that either. You want to take a swing you go right ahead. I won't hold it against you. But when you're all done I still got to talk to Rudi Basu about a dead woman on the beach, and some other things that go along with that."

She looks at me long and hard and I look back, and I won't say it's like love but she sees me. I figure that's permission enough and I go to move past her.

Her fist lands in my stomach with her full weight and conviction behind it. It's nothing like Stefan laughing, but all the same it rocks me onto my other foot. I settle, then nod.

"Now you can say you made a Titan step back. Can I go in?"

"Aw, crap, you're Sounder. I heard of you."

"What did you hear?"

"I heard you weren't a total asshole."

"That's an exaggeration."

She barks a laugh. "Take a seat."

Over in the corner there's a small bench for visitors and a drip machine with a clear jug half full of something black and acrid. I sit down and ask how's the coffee, and now that we're all straightened out Sal gets bold and talkative. She says the coffee is as terrible as you'd figure but at least it doesn't taste of fucking vanilla. It's hard to get things to taste right in Shearwater because the air is saturated with flavours. She says if I was to visit the actual plant I wouldn't taste straight for two hours. She says she hasn't had vanilla ice cream or anything vanilla since three days into the job. No vanilla, no strawberry, no peach. She likes lemon. They don't make limonene here. They could, but they don't. Every Erskine food plant has at least one flavour it just doesn't make so the people who work there have something left to enjoy. The union wants to make it three, according to Sal, but management is holding.

"Not for long, let me tell you," says a deep voice behind me. I turn round into a face that looks like funerals in the rain. Rudi Basu has long jowls and no kind of smile until you see the eyes, sharp and pale like a husky's, calm like old ice. He sticks out his hand and we shake. There's an old scar on the outside, a short snake of stitches from the wrist to knuckle of the index finger.

It must have been deep at the time, because the line is narrow. Something sharp as hell.

Basu hasn't my height, but I'm pretty sure he's not giving away much in terms of mass, and if plenty of it's fat, then plenty of it's not. He says his name and squeezes once, like the first time you sit down in the driving seat of a German automobile. "Shearwater Agrichemical zero-one. I hear you are looking for me."

"I have to figure you also know why."

"The woman from the beach."

I show him Mary Ann Grey's picture.

Basu peers at the picture a good long while. He's not a man in a hurry. Not everyone's body reflects who a person is, but Basu's does. He's a man to plant his feet and let the world wash over him, and when it's done with all its folderol he'll still be there and he won't likely have changed his mind. A deliberate man. I bet he hasn't made an impulse purchase since he was ten years old.

Not the kind of person to raise his hand in a moment of anger and kill someone, and for sure not the kind who lets her wash up in the wrong place after. Which either means he didn't kill her or he had reason and she washed up right where he wanted her to.

Basu's done with the picture. "I met her. Young woman with plenty to say. The kind of lived experience that makes people think they're old before their time, but when you're older you look back and think you were just hella pissed-off. Smart, for sure. Driven, too. Maybe not both at the same time. Sal?"

Sal peers over his shoulder. "Oh, that one. She's dead? Well, that's a kick in the canoe for sure. I liked her. She had trouble in her old job."

"More than one."

"Lot of people who have that problem have it more than once, Sounder, on account of there being an almost infinite oversupply of shitheads in positions of power."

True enough, but not many of those people have messenger parcels full of cash sent to their hotel rooms, and none of them have Bail Erskine playing bank for their medical.

"She ever mention being from Tilehurst?"

Basu's face flickers. "No. You telling me she was?"

"Seems she was Aloysius Grey's daughter."

"That I did not know."

"You ever run across him?"

"So far as I know he was never in Shearwater."

"I meant back in Tilehurst. You're from there too, right?" Instinct, or maybe just a guess, but I'm not telling Basu because I'm right—I can see it in his eyes.

And now the rest of his face is catching up. Turns out surprise makes him look a little less like a turtle from a cartoon show. "Yes, I am. Me and a couple of others in town. Old men getting on with new lives. Now, how the hell did you know that?"

I give him the detective look: don't make me tell you it's my job to know things.

"She didn't mention it to you? I hear she was all in favour of some direct action on your strike. She never said 'Oh, Mr Basu, what about the revolution?'"

"Oh, sure, she wanted to block the roads with a hay rick, like in a movie. And I hear she talked like a real Bolshevik with my shop floor. The inevitability of the historical process, the suffering of the worker triggers a moment of enlightenment across the world and suddenly it's there for the taking. Peace and prosperity for all."

"You're not a believer?"

"I don't believe anything is inevitable, Mr Sounder, least of all peace and prosperity. I think both of those require effort. Energy expended, every hour of every day, to keep the top spinning on its point. And I think if suffering reliably made people wise, the world would have been a paradise a thousand years ago."

"You tell that to Mary Ann Grey?"

"Thought she'd have plenty of time to figure it out."

"She was pretty."

"I suppose."

"You didn't take the time to impress her. No war stories?"

Hands clasped across his stomach, comfortable. "Oh, no. Not my speed."

"What is your speed?"

"Something a little more age-appropriate."

"She was an adult woman. You weren't tempted? Talk about what it was like, fighting on the streets. Maybe tell her she's right. The struggle goes on, and Lance Vesper is the next Alton Lidgate."

And now those husky eyes meet mine like they're seeing me across a distance and he rubs the scar. Figure I know where that came from now.

"Mr Sounder, I think you just tried to shit me up. Throwing that man's name in my face. That's a cheap shot."

"I don't think that's quite an answer."

"I'm not too old to feel desire, Mr Sounder, but I am sure as hell too old to wrap myself in the red flag to get laid." He draws a breath, then another. "And if you put Lance Vesper in a pan and reduced him down to a jelly, and then you got every other Lance Vesper in the world and did the same and you made all that jelly into one man, that man would not be one tiny part the bastard that Alton Lidgate was."

I think about telling him Stefan shares his opinion, but what's he supposed to do with that knowledge? Say thank you and doff his cap?

"She have strong opinions on the Erskine Company? You talk about the plant?"

"Sure. She wanted us out on strike. So do about ten percent of the workforce at any given time. Make it thirty right now, with Bail screwing around."

"But you don't?"

"Everything has a time, Mr Sounder. We might get there, but not yet. Go too hard, some people don't show. Go too soon, no one has the stamina to hold out. So: first we pinch the hose, then—if we have to—we turn off the tap. Everything has a time."

"Speaking of times, what about eighteen forty-eight?"

"Publication date of the *Communist Manifesto*. Most people

think of white supremacists or Beethoven. Honestly an interesting litmus test by itself."

"The group."

"You mean the Tilehurst cadre? Like, secret handshakes and tunnels? You have to know it wasn't like that. No conspiracy, just survival and making shit up as we went along."

"I mean like a warehouse full of men and women making compact Lebedevs."

Basu's eyes get shady and closed. "I know who that is. She doesn't operate in this town."

"As a courtesy."

"Perhaps she'd say that. I think it's because fishing towns don't do as they're told by the literature she reads."

"But you know her."

"I'm a union boss, Mr Sounder. I know everyone in the space."

"Lyman Nugent?"

"I know the name. We don't move in the same circles."

Doublewide would say he's in everyone's circle, they just don't know it yet. But that's not the point, and what Basu just said wasn't strictly a denial.

"Did you have any pets when you were a kid?"

Basu doesn't know what to do with the question, doesn't seem inclined to argue. He shrugs. "A dog."

"I met a woman recently who had a lizard."

"I don't really know what she'd get from that."

"Me neither. Dina says she's never found the 1848."

"By any measure, she's the closest thing I've ever seen."

"But not the actual thing."

"Do you really believe in fairy tales, Mr Sounder?"

"No. But I believe in a dead woman strangled on a beach, Mr Basu, and I definitely believe in the eight barrels of maritime diesel and ammonium nitrate in the blue shipping container she was visiting."

His eyes get wide. "No shit."

"It'll be in the news when Iverson can't keep a lid on it any more," I say. "Sooner if someone tips Jeanine Baskar to it. Figure she'd love to give the *Mercury* that kind of scoop."

Basu shudders. "Sal, tee up a meeting for me with Cathy Logan. We'll need to get out in front of this. The union lawyer," he adds to me. "This kind of shit always comes back to lawyers. And Baskar will come as close to saying I'm part of it as she can without getting sued."

"You have history?"

"Only the cease-and-desist kind."

"So you didn't ask anyone for a little off-book help to put pressure on Bail? Even by mistake?"

"And get this? No. I don't know about you, Mr Sounder, but I can't pull a full-fledged terrorist group out of my ass."

"Except you know Dina."

He waves that away. "Dina misses the point. If the revolution ever comes, it won't be Lebedevs that matter. It'll be organisation. Infrastructure. To whoever keeps the water and power switched on, the spoils. When the hammer comes down, that's what matters."

I just nod, because I think he's right, and Basu stares at me the way he didn't when I asked about his pets.

"You know, I find it fascinating that you still believe you'd be under the hammer, rather than behind it."

"I know how it goes, Mr Basu, as well as anyone."

More consideration. Then: "You want my phone records? That kind of thing?"

"Iverson might, but he can get them his own self. Where were you five nights ago?"

"Negotiating."

"And four?"

"Negotiating the same damn clause."

We shake hands.

"You ever wonder whether the world would be better without Martha Erskine?"

He grins. "Sure. But mostly Bail. He's a pain in the ass."

"Why? What does he want?"

"In the end? Martha's job."

"Can he get it?"

Basu spreads his hands: *Who the hell knows?*

Sal shows me to the door, and as she turns away there's the weird tang of dessert in the air, the whiff of vanillin. Of course: she works at the plant, even Basu still does. Good union people never stop working, even if it's only a few days a month, so that they know what the shop floor feels like, eat the same food and piss in the same washrooms. And here, they breathe the same air and can't taste white chocolate or plain fudge, and everyone else knows where they got that smell. I wonder if Torrance tasted it on Mary Ann Grey, if he knew his family's factory on her skin. Then I think of Athena, and the stories her skin tells, and a moment later of Ashley. If a person touched his mouth to Ashley's neck, would she be flavoured with Shearwater's air, or not? Has she ever worked a summer job at the plant?

"Hey, Sal. Am I right in thinking that's Bill Tracey out there?"

"Probably," she says. "If not, you can try the Swordfish, table next to the pole."

When I get to the Mahalo boathouse, the *Evermore* is locked down and the main doors are shut. I knock, but no one comes. I walk down a narrow alley and then across a road that's thick with grey sand and fragments of the cardboard they use to pack ice around the catch. It can be any cardboard, but nothing printed, or the ink gets into the flesh and you can't sell it. The packing men tear off the glossy smiling faces of fake families on the other coast and fake prosperity on this one and throw them away, and when the wind blows it snatches the pieces from the dumpsters and rolls them along gutters and drains until the sewers in winter clog up with white teeth and branding. The Swordfish Tavern is one floor on a corner, peeling blue paint over bad concrete. The door is a metal mesh over chipboard, no glass.

Inside, the Swordfish is dark, warm and quiet. A cork board

shows the due dates of return of three longliners, and the names of the crews. Somewhere there's music, thin and lo-fi. I take off my jacket and grip it like a wash rag as I go to the bar, and I don't even try to be nice when I tell the barman to pour me something. I have business here and it has to look that way. Anything else and I'm just an asshole in the wrong room.

I lean on the bar and wait while the guy takes the longest time to get my drink, but one of us doesn't care about the clock and one does, and in the end he pushes it across the bar.

"Anything else?"

"I'm looking for the captain of the *Evermore*. Heard he and I might be able to do good for one another."

"What kind of good?"

"The kind where you do the right thing and get paid."

He laughs. "That's not something I hear too much."

"Me neither."

"Tracey ain't been by yet. Maybe in a while."

There's a single steel pole on the left side of the bar and a clear space with a circle of linoleum cut into the wood floor. Two tables on the far side against the wall and a door to the bathroom. I sit down to wait. The barman tells me things I don't intend to remember that mean nothing to anyone who wasn't there.

After half an hour, Bill Tracey still doesn't come by, but when I get up and look out of the window, someone else has. He's sitting with his back to me and his legs hanging down off the outside of the dock towards the water. He has a tackle box and a short, thick rod for sea fishing. It's not the dainty kind you see from millionaires in chest-high rubber boots, but the kind you have if you know where there's mackerel close in by the shore. I wouldn't recognise him except that he turns his head into the wind. Of all the things I would have expected right here, right now, Matthew Jimson fishing off the Shearwater sea wall is not one of them.

I tell the barman I'd appreciate it if he told Tracey I was looking for him, and I go outside and say hello.

"Good morning, Mr Sounder."

Wide shoulders, rugged face with some weather on it. When you see Jimson not wearing corporate anthracite, you realise how much he doesn't belong in an office. He should be jumping out of a helicopter into a burning field.

"Mr Jimson."

He has a pocket knife open in his lap and he's cutting a length of light line and tying on the float and hook.

"I actually enjoyed the joke, you know. Donahue so he wouldn't notice, plus that spelling to appeal to the latent xenophobia. You read him just right, and it landed perfectly. He reported to Vesper face to face, and it wasn't until he'd said it twice that he realised how badly you fucked him. Hugh Djasz."

The voice is like the man, all smooth without stress or sharp edges, and still it carries like he's the hero and everything else is just room tone. Good guy vocals from a mid-budget movie, the kind of delivery you've just got, or paid a lot of money to learn.

Jimson shakes his head slowly without taking his eyes off the fishing line. "Fuckin' hilarious."

"I figured you wouldn't let it get that far."

"There's no learning without the possibility of failure, I guess. It's not like anyone died. But don't let Dave Reason catch you napping. I don't think he's appreciative of the lesson."

"Tell him I get childish when I'm nervous."

"What could you possibly have to be nervous about, Mr Sounder? You didn't feel just the teensiest bit embarrassed screwing around with a kid like Reason, given who and what you are?"

It occurs to me idly that Matthew Jimson is big enough that he could be a Titan, if he was a small guy before the dose. He has the volume, and in the suits he wears, with just the right combination of formal and slouch fit, you can't tell if it's meat or bone. If it's deliberate, it's very well done: a tiny extra tool for the projection of power.

"He's not just a kid. He's himself plus you plus the whole Erskine machine."

"And you're whatever you are, Mr Sounder. Cohabiting with

the most powerful woman in the world. You brought a whole new meaning to punching down right there."

"I'd feel bad about that, Mr Jimson, if it wasn't for the dead woman and all the bullshit."

He bobs his head. "That's a fair point."

A gull lands by him and pecks once at the bait bag in his box. Jimson reaches over and twists its neck once, then tosses it into water and pats his hands on his pant legs.

"What would you have done if Iverson hadn't come out around then?"

"Walked away. Would have looked unprofessional if I'd knocked over two Erskine boys on my second day."

"There were three of us, Mr Sounder."

"I figured to leave you standing, Mr Jimson, since you were the grown-up in the room."

"Is that right?" The barest tension in his shoulders, a flicker of anticipation. Matthew Jimson quite wants that fight. More than that, he thinks he can win. Paris training, Iverson said, and it must have been pretty good, because Jimson's not an idiot. If he rates himself, then I do too.

"It is. Now I have to assume this isn't a chance meeting. Did Lance Vesper ask you to come breathe down my neck?"

A brief instant of contempt. Jimson doesn't think any better of Vesper than I do.

"I thought it was time we talked," he says. "About Mary Ann Grey."

If Bail knew Mary Ann Grey—if she was his creature, to whatever end—then Matthew Jimson knew all about it.

"All right," I say. "Who killed her?"

"Torrance Erskine," Jimson says.

"Why?"

"Sex game gone wrong. Or maybe romance gone sour. One of those things rich boys do."

"Is that right?"

"It is."

I could ask him why Bail is paying Lila's bills, but I don't, because I like it that I can see what he looks like when he's lying. "If you could prove that, you'd just tell Iverson."

"I'm not in the business of proving anything, Mr Sounder. My job is to keep the Erskines out of it. Torrance is the guy, and you can't have him."

"Oh, I see. You want me to know the fix is in."

"That's correct."

"So who's taking the fall?"

He shrugs. "An out-of-town drifter. One of the men on the beach. One of the women, even. Hardly matters. They're all the same. Washed-up and crazy."

"I haven't spoken to Torrance yet."

"And you won't."

"Figure I owe it to my client."

"I guess they'll be unhappy."

"Sure, if I don't do my job."

"But not so unhappy as if Bail Erskine takes against them, of course."

"A powerful man, is Bail Erskine."

Jimson catches my indifference. "Huh. I did not think you were working a Tonfamecasca angle here."

"I'm not."

"I guess you'd say that."

"Are you fishing for something in particular?"

"Dinner, of course."

"That's nice. I see what you did there. You ever dabble in politics?"

"Liars disagreeing with one another is still just lies." A moment later he clambers to his feet and picks up the rod. I see the float and the flash of the hook as it goes past my face. I don't twitch, but only because it wouldn't do any good. Jimson has fast hands. He watches the cast out and down into the water. "A drifter, Mr Sounder. From out of town. Don't try to talk to Torrance. His mother has a string of lawyers, and if they come up empty there's always me."

"I do appreciate the input, Mr Jimson."

"Thank you for your time, Mr Sounder."

I watch him for a while longer, mostly so that I'm not running away. There's nothing interesting in watching another man fishing. I head back to the road, thinking about Jimson and Torrance and Bail and Mary Ann Grey.

Liars disagreeing with one another is still just lies.

I get on the same bus I took two days ago to the beach where the blue container was, and it's got the same people on it now, with the same whisper of lives set in unchanging patterns. From the port it ducks inland to a school with high fences and grey slabs for outside space, no colour in the whole campus. Then it comes back to the sea for the Sleeper beach, from a time when that was where south Shearwater had barbecues and Sunday afternoon walks. Now it's that strange white forest, sighing, and no one does anything. It just grows when a new person gets off this bus with nothing left to push back against the world, and shrinks when someone walks into the ocean or dries up and blows away. And here am I, doing exactly what everybody does, and watching it fade away in the right-side mirror of the public bus.

I push the bell one stop before the private beach. It's a straight, empty road with no reason for the stop you can imagine, until you realise it's there for the people who work for Martha, unseen below stairs. Courtesy or utility or both, never to be untangled or examined. I look along the promontory for the house, although I already know you can't see it from the road.

Martha's Point has high walls and unforgiving gates. A sign reads, Private: Marine Reserve. They're not serious defences, they're invitations to fuck off, so I don't. I find a place where a tree grows close to a post and step from one to the other, up and over. There's no wire or spikes at the top. Cameras somewhere, but I don't care if I'm seen. Martha can yell at me for my lack of propriety if she wants to, but I'm pretty sure that's what she's paying for.

I walk in plain sight up the drive, retying the knot in my tie.

When I need to make an impression on people who pretend they don't do that, I like the ventaglio.

It's a long way from the gate to the point, and the drive isn't much primped or pruned. On either side the ground is overgrown, bushes and low cover under the canopy of palms and figs, every so often an old, old olive. I wonder if Martha planted them herself, long ago in the before times, and has watched them grow ever since. Again, I think about the offset: how is it, living in a world where you can watch the growth of trees, but adult humans just flick by, here and gone in the equivalent of a decade or a little more. Do you end up more comfortable with olive groves than people, more concerned for their wellbeing? Do you, for example, close off the road and let them grow wild all around, so you can feel you're not the only thing your age in the world apart from Stefan Tonfamecasca? And if you do, how does it go, then, when you start spending more and more time in the sea? Is there anything below the waterline that grows as long and slow as olive trees? Is Martha shepherding a reef down there, watching the coral spread back, bright and rich over the white husks of the past?

I come over the brow of a little hill, and find the waterline and the house together, the one wrapped around the other like a cat around a stove. At either end there's a garden bubble, a dome of glass like Stefan's cupola, but the land side of the house has no windows, just a smooth white curve and a giant brown door.

I knock, and the door opens, and a small white woman with grey hair in a headscarf looks at me and says: "oh", as if I'm selling something she doesn't want. She opens the door anyway.

"Come in, Mr Sounder."

"You know who I am?"

"By implication."

Whatever implication it is, she doesn't love it. She steps aside and I walk through a doorway that makes me feel small, like a child.

The old white lady is called Mrs Seraphine, and she makes to be something between a housekeeper and a house pet. Once upon a time she was Martha's executive assistant, and when she retired she just somehow never left. She had no place to go to, no family any more, and no desire to get a pilot's licence or learn to rumba on the beach, or fall in love with a schoolteacher and move to somewhere in flyover country where she'd never see another Titan again. She tells me all this in terms, blunt to the point of rude, except the only person who could really take offence at the descriptions is Mrs Seraphine herself.

"I'll see if Martha wants to talk to you."

"Wait."

She stops, and turns.

"I'd like to talk to you first, Mrs Seraphine."

"Go ahead."

"Is Martha going to have another dose?"

"I couldn't say."

"Yes, you could."

"All right, I could, but I won't."

"How long has she been afraid of sleepwalking?"

The narrow face scowls. "Barracks rumours."

"How long?"

"That's not what it is."

"I know. How long."

"A year."

"She spoke to Tonfamecasca." To the doctors, the aftercare team. I have their number in my wallet. We all do. You'd no more not have it than leave the house without your shoes.

"First thing. They were ... equivocal."

"They don't know if another dose will help."

"They expressed some concern in that direction. Also the cube law. Martha would be ground-breakingly large."

"But she can swim. That reduces the cardiovascular issues."

A smile. "Yes, she can."

"How can she swim? After-market extras?"

"That I really don't know."

"I'm not here to steal her secret sauce. I wouldn't understand anyway."

Mrs Seraphine sniffs, either at my ignorance or my dissembling: I don't need to understand something to commit it to memory.

"Why is Bail in charge?"

A flash of scorn. "Who else?"

"You."

"Oh! Nonsense. That's not a job any wise person wants."

"It comes with promotion prospects. T7."

She shrugs, and I realise that headscarf is more than just neatness: a nod to some kind of orthodoxy, but giving no clue as to which. "I'm not so eager to postpone my appointments as other people, Mr Sounder, in this modern world."

"Did Iverson call you?"

"About this Mary Ann Grey?"

"There was a bomb found on the north side of the point two nights ago. In a shipping container."

"We heard, of course. A possible threat to the plant. Captain Iverson is even-handed, but he does not forget the flow of obligation in this town. That's part of why he's the captain."

Part of why he's still the captain, at the age he is. However much Iverson wants to pretend he doesn't take sides, he can't pretend he doesn't have strings. Everyone does.

I run my hand through my hair, feeling like a kid talking to the nurse. "Iverson thinks the target was the plant."

"You don't?"

"I wondered whether it might be different. I thought, what if that container was taken out of there by boat, the way it came in, and what if then . . . at a certain time and place . . . it was pushed off that boat and detonated under the water."

Mrs Seraphine didn't get her job with Martha by being slow on the uptake. Her eyes get wide for a moment.

"Do you have any evidence for that?"

"None at all. But it occurred to me, and I figured I'd pass it on."

She glares at me as if seeing me for the first time, starting at my feet and reaching the hair on my fringe before coming back to my face. Almost no one does that. People say they look you up and down, but they don't. You have to make a deliberate effort to go from toe to top, and when you do, you pay more attention because the arrangement of things is new. I just moved from black and white to colour in Mrs Seraphine's picture of the world, and I'll never go back. She'll pick me out of the landscape from now on, register what I'm doing. Executive assistant, companion, house pet, bodyguard: all retired, but all still here.

"You've got a very nasty mind, Cal Sounder. Read a magazine or something. I'll come back and get you."

She nods with approval, and walks out of the door.

There are no magazines, and I have to figure if there were they'd be like the ones in waiting rooms: decades old and weirdly specific. Back issues of *Pro Golf Weekly* and *Shore Longline News*, or some kind of fashion magazine featuring gingham and olde-worlde stylings that cost more than a new car. If old Titans don't understand human lifespans, how bizarre must be consumer-oriented glossies, with their flickering bright lights like the leaves of trees in a fast-motion film of autumn.

I read the dictionary. It's the last one they published in print that's supposed to contain all the words in the language. So many of them don't mean the same things any more. Infer; purposefully; beg the question. The edges of the book are deckled, left deliberately ragged to give an impression of artisanship, because not even this volume is old enough for that to be an actual artefact of the production process. It's an affectation so old that it's now authentic in its own right. It makes the pages hard to turn. I look up 'Titan' and there's nothing about T7. I try 'communist' and there's a prim little entry about holding goods in common as contrasted with Proletarian ownership of the means of production. I wonder if the Lacarte's tendency towards mutual aid rules them out. I'd love to go back and tell them they're just Kropotkinites, after all.

"Come with me," Mrs Seraphine says. I didn't even hear her come in.

It's easy from the road to misunderstand the scale of the house, because you assume unconsciously that the door is built to human dimensions, but it's more than twice the size. From the waiting room we walk down a long corridor to the seaward side, all glass, curved and perfectly clean to the point of invisible. We wind our way through something between a sitting room and a terrarium down and down to the water level. Outside it's just water, not the gentle shingle of the Sleeper beach, but the stark continental drop-off from just a few metres beyond the line of the house: obsidian sand and then a deeper dark that must go down a half kilometre before it levels off. There's a sea gate instead of a door, and a wide, deep channel of water rolling back and forth to the edge of a steaming pool, where Martha Erskine is waiting.

She opens her eyes, and for a moment doesn't seem to see me at all.

"Mr Sounder," she says, still looking through me. "What an unexpected pleasure."

Mrs Seraphine is gone again, that spooky sidestep out of the sightline and into the blind spot. I feel an itch between my shoulder blades and manage not to look round. She won't be there, anyway. I'm pretty sure Mrs Seraphine doesn't take cheap shots. Figure her for a very simple killer: a brush-past and a pinprick. Something stark and unfixable in the blood, neither invisible nor needlessly painful. I take a breath and ask my question.

"Why do you think you killed Mary Ann Grey?"

She doesn't acknowledge it at first, but I've seen Stefan take an hour to decide what he wants to say. When you're this old and this powerful, no one jogs your elbow, and silence is a tool in itself: the quick so often answer their own questions and give away their intrigues as they fall headlong into it, panicking at a quiet that seems to accuse, when all it is is the sound of a bigger, more patient mind taking its time.

"She was here," Martha says.

I wait, again.

"They all came, those bright-coloured fish."

She means the waterfront set, but I don't love the image:

bright-coloured fish teeming in the bright warm water, while below, something huge watches.

"They came and they played. Walked among the trees. I let them do work for me. Forestry. I pay them. Too much, of course, so that the local children can treat their sophisticated friends without being scared of the bill. Sometimes they just come and work and put it away like squirrels. Go to college, leave town for ever—or until they come back, old and wise."

Baseline old.

Her eyes aren't fixing on anything. Is it memory or sleep? Is there really any difference for her any more? I think of Lila Grey, alone in her old apartment with Castor in place of Mrs Seraphine. How far apart are they, if Martha can't wake up? And if she can't, who's preying on her? There'll be no missing pictures here. No one would dare, with that guard dog stalking the corridors. Is that why she stays? What does Lance Vesper think about it? Isn't that his job?

"She lingered, and we talked. I don't recall what it was about. Love, I think, and history, and suffering. It hadn't occurred to her that I knew what that was, any of it. And I will admit, it took some remembering. I was young when I was poor, Mr Sounder. So very young, so long ago. I've been a corporation for most of my life, and that's not about to change, whatever Bail may think."

"Bail wants the big chair."

"Oh, sure. He thinks he does, because he's never sat in it. Do you know what the Erskine Company is, Mr Sounder?"

"A conglomerate. Plastic to chemicals, energy and food. Mining to chemicals to things. Chemicals to medicine and bioplastics."

"You're a schoolboy with his homework."

"You're a teacher looking for wrong answers." Everyone sees the babyface.

"Hah. True. It's a machine, Mr Sounder. A machine for making a particular product. All that power and effort goes ultimately into one thing."

"Money."

"No. Oh, no. Money is just a precursor, a necessary condition. The machine makes Titans, Mr Sounder. Titans worth the knowing. Once or twice in each generation—and the generations do get bigger as time goes by, and so much more diffuse—but once or twice, there's a prospect. Someone you might one day be grateful to share a century with. Someone the more exciting for their distance from what we have been. Oh, and wild cards, of course. The ones we bring along for the ride, like Dixie, because you just never know what's going to matter. Do you?"

"I guess not."

"Your Athena saved your life for love, but she made you a Titan because you're interesting. There's enough of you to make more of yourself over time, not less. To fill the shoes you've been given. And enough of her, for that matter. Very interesting girl. You see?"

Yes. "Not yet."

"Well done. Yes, Bail wants my job. He'll grow out of it. I might even give it to him, for a while, just to watch what happens. I watch everything. And that was why I had the party in the first place, and she came, your Mary Ann Grey."

"You liked her."

"Oh, yes. We all did. It was a dinner party, you know, all the local friends. Have you met them?"

"Who?"

"My family."

"Not yet."

"Go to the house, introduce yourself. Take their temperature."

I nod, and don't speak. She hasn't lost the thread, I'm just hearing her think.

"The silly boy was here with her, the pretty one."

"Torrance."

She waves the name away. There are so many young people, so fast, so pretty, so similar, and soon enough they're old. Faces in the crowd.

"They were bickering and he left in a huff. She stayed. I didn't ask what it was about. Young people. I assumed sex, but I might have been wrong. She stayed and we talked and then—well. Then at some point I just stopped noticing."

She shrugs, and water laps and washes in the pool. Not entirely water: it's viscous around her shoulders, oily and thick. She's human, after all, she can't spend all day every day in the water and not get dried out. The stuff in the pool must be good for the skin. It looks heavy with salt, too, keeping her buoyant. Likely this is where she sleeps, warm and cosy as the womb. Her eyes flicker drowsily now, and her voice gets deeper. It's breathy, but I can feel it in my chest today, like Stefan's: dangerous and strong. She's been making a conscious effort to keep it light, and that caution is fading away. I make a note to ask Fallon whether Mary Ann Grey's eardrums were broken. I don't know whether the sea would have done that, anyway.

"I have moments, Mr Sounder."

She stops. I wait. Never interrupt your client when they're telling you what the hell is going on.

"Moments I don't remember—or I do, but they don't feel like me. She was here, and then she was dead, and where she washed up was where things go from my sea gate. So I wondered. I fretted, as old people do. And then I noticed this."

There, on her extended arm, a little tiny line of scratches. Could be three, like three fingers of one hand. Could be something else again.

"When I saw these, I saw her face, just a flash like the moon on the waves, but green in the black. Skin under water, in the night. She went down into the deep, beneath me. Reaching. And I watched her go. So I don't know, you see. I don't know if she fell past me and I was halfway sleeping, or whether I was the one who pushed her down."

Or whether she was there at all, whether it was a waking dream, and those scratches came from coral or obsidian sand.

Martha Erskine looks up at me from the pool and her eyes are very dark and human, very frightened in the warm day. She wants me to tell her she's not going mad, that she didn't dream-murder another human being for no reason at all. But I don't know the answer, and she isn't paying me to be nice.

"What did you do then?"

She blinks.

"What?"

In conversation with old Titans, almost everyone lets them dictate the flow, the direction. It's not even a conscious choice, just mammal obedience to something huge and dominant in the room. They get used to it, and very uncomfortable when it doesn't happen, like old people anywhere who are accustomed to the deference of the very young.

"So you looked at your hand and you saw scratches and then you—let's say envisaged for now—you envisaged Mary Ann Grey dying. Did you tell Iverson?"

If she did, he and I are going to have words.

"No, of course not."

Because Titans that age just don't submit themselves to a process they might not ultimately control. That goes without saying, and again: they don't like being made to say it, to assert the exceptionalism they think is just the natural order.

"Vesper."

"No."

"Because he's not family."

"Exactly."

"But you told someone. Apart from Seraphine."

"I tell Seraphine everything."

Not that she needs you to, not by now. By now a security professional like Seraphine is in every nook and cranny of Martha's life by default. You'd have to burn down the house and start fresh to root her out, and even then: check your slippers and your mirror.

"And who else? A doctor? A friend?"

Does Martha even have those? Is there a knitting circle of four-hundred-year-old women who drink sherry, talk dynastic succession and play pinochle on high days and holidays? My mind's a little blown at what they might say to one another, between the dropped stitches and the stock tips: the best sexual techniques when you look twenty and mass more than a rhino; which designers scale up this season; how to break an economy without leaving a mark; and who does the best wet work when you absolutely want something to go away.

"Bail," she says at last. "Fiduciary responsibility."

And Bail sure as hell wouldn't tell anyone, unless it needed fixing, and then he'd talk to ... surely not Vesper? No, someone colder and sharper. Jimson, of course. Bail would tell Matthew Jimson. *Liars talking to one another.*

"And then you called me."

"Yes. I—if I did it, it changes things."

If she did it, she can't trust herself any more. She has to hand over the reins for real.

Most likely, as it so happens, to Bail Erskine.

"All right, Martha, that's what I need for now. Thank you for being candid with me. Now, I take it you still want to know what happened and you don't want comforting lies, is that right?"

"Yes."

"Then I'm still your guy. You're still my client, you own the answers I find. If you want me to pass them to anyone, I will. If you don't, I won't." Which I have to say to be sure of walking out of here past Mrs Seraphine.

"What do you think?"

"I think you didn't kill Mary Ann Grey."

"Why?"

"I don't know."

"So it's meaningless."

"No, it means I think you didn't do it. I just don't know why yet. Mrs Erskine, how do you think most murders are solved? The hard ones, I mean, not the stupid ones where you just bust the guy with the blood all over him."

"I suppose you look for evidence and assemble it to find the truth."

"Like a puzzle."

"I suppose."

"That's what most people think, because we all like to believe that reason holds the key to understanding the world. Murder is shocking, even though it happens all the time. Death is very big and we are very small, even if we're Titans. It's comforting to believe we can make things safe and predictable again by thinking hard. We can find the secret pattern that makes the world make sense. And sometimes, maybe it even works. But the real world isn't orderly. It's made of chances. Rain falls on the dead as they lie there in the alley, and all that magical forensic stuff just bleeds away into the sewer. Animals carry off the wristwatch that stopped at the time of death. Witnesses get hit by cars just because sometimes cars hit people. Sometimes the motive makes no sense; people kill for money without knowing they won't get any, and you never find out that they expected to be rich. We pretend we can unbreak the vase, but sometimes all we can do is imagine how it fell. So what it comes down to is that you sit in the place where it all happened and you see how that place works. You meet the people it happened near, and you watch them being who they are. You find the traces of the person who died and ask how they lived. In the end, you know where to look before you find the thing you're looking for: the loaded gun, the torn cloth, the note written in blood. There's a hundred stories in Shearwater this summer that could end up in someone dying, Mrs Erskine. The way I read this one, it isn't about you."

And that's something else the old ones have real trouble with, because everything is about them.

"Call me Martha," she reminds me, because it's the only thing left she can control.

"Of course, Martha. Now ... invite me to go by the house, please."

"You're already here."

"Not this house. Erskine House, on the hill."

"I already told you to go."

"And I want you to invite me, so that when I say I was invited, I'm not a liar."

There's a pause, and then she says, like we're meeting in the street: "It's so nice to have you in town, Mr Sounder. I do love it when Athena comes by, and she speaks so very highly of you. You should swing by Erskine Hill and say hello to everyone. I don't get up there too much these days, but it's a fine old place. See what stories they're telling this summer and come tell me all about them."

Her face flickers again, sharp now, the dream washed away. Beneath the oil and salt, something big in the shadows, watching the reef, taking its time.

7

Let's say Martha did kill Mary Ann Grey and let's say it wasn't just because she's crazy and the porpoises told her to. Suppose Martha knows something, or knows it sometimes, and that thing was so bad that Mary Ann Grey had to die. How would that go? What even bothers a Titan that old?

Mary Ann crossed the country this way and that, making trouble in a dozen jobs under a dozen names while her mother's care came from Bail. Grant her good faith, and his, and say she was what she seemed. She came to Shearwater for the bomb. She came to kill Martha, or blow the Erskine plant or do something that explodes Martha's bad secret, and somehow Martha found out and killed her first.

But all that would be something you just hand over to the cops, even to Vesper. He's got to be good for that much. There's no need for Martha to drag Mary Ann down and down, full fathom five like the man said.

And Martha doesn't remember doing it. She remembers Mary Ann falling past her, already gone.

Say Mary Ann belonged to Bail from the get-go. Say he wants to crush Rudi Basu's strike action because somehow it's so damn bad it needs breaking. Maybe it just offends his ego—the last letter in Iverson's shiny modern quartet of motives: Money, Ideology,

Compromise, Ego. I can't help feeling they're all just ways of saying the same thing.

So Bail runs Mary Ann into town, and when she gets here she's supposed to link Rudi to the bomb in the blue container and down come all the cards in the house. That explains those clean executive work shoes and the movie-set vibe from all the shiny pamphlets. But then why does Mary Ann Grey stay at the Caffrey using Ailsa Lloyd's name when she should be in a working dorm somewhere, getting to know the working stiffs and living the role? Why does she jeopardise the whole operation by blowing money at the Roller with Torrance? Is that what drives Bail so crazy that he murders her? And if he did, then why is the cover-up just so damn bad?

If Torrance killed her, I'd buy the lousy aftercare. I'd buy the crime itself, too, all stupid and full of anger. Torrance finds out that Mary Ann is lying about her whole life and gets so mad he just drowns her after Martha's beach party. Bam. Down she goes. But if that's actually what happened, why is everyone telling me so? Do they really think I can't do anything about it?

I throw lumps of black beach glass into the water and feel stupid for a while. I look for Ashley among the few swimmers, but it's just the office workers swimming with their eleven o'clock coffee. The perks of living in a town with no business to speak of: no urgent meetings. Just one day after another of this. It's hard to see how Shearwater stays empty, come to think. You'd figure all the start-ups would be here: surf and sun and empty lots, but they go where the money is, all clustered on the fringes of Othrys, chasing Titan finance for their IPOs and Titan eyeballs for their business plans.

And speaking of finance, it's time I talked to someone who knows what lives on the underside of the rock. I get on the horn and tell Zoegar I need to see his boss.

"I advise against it."

"So do I. Call him for me, please."

"I cannot guarantee his disposition towards you, Mr Sounder. You crossed him."

"Yeah, but he crossed me, and nobody got hurt."

"Apart from those who died."

"That was one guy your boss did not like, plus nearly me. How is that skin off his nose?"

"I do not entirely disagree, but nor can I say that he shares your view."

"So call him."

I can hear Emile Zoegar shaking his head, but I know he makes the call, because a little while later a black town car pulls up outside Celia's, and some time after that I'm sitting in an inland farmhouse made of rough yellow stone, waiting for the Humpty Dumpty of crime.

Watching Doublewide walk anywhere is unsettling. The first thing you see is a fat man with a crazy fat head and shoulders like the carcass of a steer. In winter he wears green velvet, but in the summer he has on a white linen farmer's shirt with fishtail labourer's pants and tan suspenders which only emphasise the vastness of his stomach. Perfect tailoring, and if I had to guess, I'd say made of the same blend as my suits. Maybe the same tailor: Doublewide can do due diligence on ballistic fashion just like Athena's people can.

The second thing you notice is the lightness of his step, like he doesn't weigh the better part of a quarter ton. He has small feet in pale leather shoes, and he moves orillero-style, proud and smooth like a professional pallbearer or a man palming a knife.

In the end, though, it doesn't matter how many times you've met him or how hard you try, you won't stop yourself staring at his arms. Lyman Nugent—Doublewide—is a Titan, but not the regular flavour. Some combination of genetics and skullduggery threw a spanner in the works, and he has the mass but not the height. The only place his body stretched was his arms, long and folded as if he's a mantis, or a bear begging for figs in a pit. He sits down opposite me and leans his face on his hands like a kid in school, but his elbows rest on the ground outside his feet. He doesn't speak.

"Hi, Lyman, it's me, Cal."

Dark, glittering eyes in the folds of flesh, empty of expression. Almost anyone who makes the connection will think twice before killing me, in case Stefan takes exception, but Doublewide isn't afraid of Stefan. Like me, he gets a kick out of standing up to the king. Mind you, he's also some sort of a king in his own right, and he cares about dignity. I keep talking.

"I know, it's been a while and we didn't exactly part as friends, but if you just sit there, I'm gonna have to apologise, which as you know I'm horrible at. I'll mean the hell out of it, but you won't hate the experience any less."

Still nothing. All right, then.

"Mr Nugent, I'm here today to express my humble and genuine—"

His eyes widen. "Oh, dear god, stop." His voice hasn't changed, plummy and full-lipped, a voice for ordering off-menu.

"Are you sure? I've got a whole speech. I memorised it."

"Your cruelty knows no bounds, Mr Sounder. I surrender. Please: don't apologise any more."

But there's something in his voice that's almost a smile.

"I'm honestly sorry I screwed you. I had to, but for what it's worth, I actually do feel bad about it."

"You appreciate that I sent a Titan to kill you."

"Yeah, sure, but if you'd actually wanted me dead you'd have sent Emile. That guy was just a big strong jackass."

"I understand he acquitted himself tolerably well."

"For a given value that includes him getting eaten by a bear and me not dying."

And now the smile is there in his face, folded like sourdough. His hands, still touching at the heel, flap together to make a little round of applause.

"Capital! Capital, Mr Sounder, I confess I have missed your company. You are a liar and a cheat and a good fellow for all that. And you met Emile on the beach! I've never dared go along. Does he really wear a pink bathing suit?"

"Not that I've seen, but it's definitely within the mood."

"Astonishing."

"You find that as weird as I do?"

"Almost certainly more so, knowing him as I have for many years within a very specific range of circumstances which rather preclude both bathing shorts and the colour pink."

"He could carry off his whole thing in pink."

"No, the garish psychopath mode is not for him. He'd rebel at the sheer ham of it. Great Scott, the very idea. Have you ever contemplated such a thing? For undercover work?"

"Not so much."

"And quite right, Mr Sounder, quite right, it would spoil you for ever more. Now, as we begin: a glass of beer from the excellent barrels down below. I would say wine, but the summer heat makes me crave the smack and bite of a traditionally brewed lager bier in the fashion of my Slav ancestors."

The beer is excellent, because Doublewide knows that life is short, and doesn't care to waste it on anything less. He doesn't count coins, not just because he's rich, but because he's only interested in substance, which is probably why I'm still alive, and why we're talking as if we're friends.

I guess I care about substance too.

"Now, sir, you took a risk, though I flatter myself you did not regard it a great one. I like to think you esteem me sufficiently to know there was never truly bad blood between us, only expedience and form. No vendetta. Bygones are bygones."

Sure, they are, now that I'm keeping high company. But never mind that.

"You sent Zoegar to Shearwater."

"No, he was visiting his lady friend."

I wait, because if we're talking, we have to get past this.

"Oh, well, if you must. I asked him if he might bend his mind to a minor matter, while he was there."

"Might you be prepared to tell me about that minor matter?"

"I would not choose to repeat our prior regrettable interaction, sir. Perhaps you might tell me first why you wish to know."

"There was a dead woman on the beach."

"Ah! The sorrows of the sea."

"She was murdered."

"The land, then. Quite so. And you are to uncover the narrative of her sad demise. For the local police?"

"Private client."

"But not Tonfamecasca."

"No."

"A trade, then. Let us discuss the place in general terms. Mutual marginalia may be revealing for us both."

"Here's a freebie: someone put a very big bomb in a blue box by the water."

Pale eyebrows rise on the huge head. "Oh, dear. Related?"

"She had a key to the box."

"I dislike explosives. Effective, but crude and attention-grabbing. My own business will be more difficult in consequence of these shenanigans." He raises his voice. "Pierre?" The guy who brought the beer comes back.

"Another glass, sir?"

"Yes, but also please inform Ms Cattermole that there will be considerable attention paid in Shearwater over the next while. Our business may become a little more visible than we'd like."

Pierre slips away.

"You gave me a name, Lyman."

"One you are quite at liberty to research, Mr Sounder."

"Meaning it won't tell me anything."

"Meaning what it will tell you is quite benign. But there's no need for you to scrabble through the paper trail. Ms Cattermole is one of my legitimate amanuenses. I had it in mind to buy some property in Shearwater. Leisure, office buildings and accommodation."

"Buy it with clean money, run dirty money through it, make a loss on the refurbishment and claim the break, then sell it on."

"Oh, Mr Sounder, there's no poetry in your description. You entirely miss the elegance of the financial dance."

"You know a lady named Dina? Mid-sixties, strong opinions on employment rights, makes a lot of guns?"

Doublewide frowns. "We have ... spoken occasionally, as the captains of ships in the fleets of opposing nations not for the moment at war. The scorn she reserves for me is perhaps the greatest of all: the lumpen monster feeding on the bilgewater of the system. Hers not to ask the causality of my life, or its aspirations, only to judge its present. Rather harshly, I must say."

"I thought that bomb might be hers. Still could be, but she says not."

"It's quite in her vein, surely?"

"Especially if the target was Martha Erskine."

"You think it was?"

"I think Martha is the target of something. So does she. But then she pretty much always must be, and I don't know if it was that."

"Have you met Bail?"

"I have not met Bail."

"Quite an interesting character. He declines T7, you know."

"Not permanently. Just for now."

"He wants to give the appearance of a clear head. He can't take Martha's crown if he's a neo-adolescent bedding everyone in sight and beating his chest on the docks like Hercules, now, can he?"

"He probably could."

"Indeed, he overestimates the amount of attention people pay to his private life, a common failing among inconsequential men of power."

"How did you come across a fellow like Bail Erskine?"

"A more probing question, Mr Sounder, more ticklish." He waggles his long spider fingers. "But since we're such good friends, and you're playing straight with me, I shall tell you. No charge."

"Why do I think passing on the information itself is what you get out of this?"

"Because you're not a fool, sir. Now, whisht and pay heed while I spin my yarn."

"Last time you did that, it got me in a lot of trouble."

"But also to the truth, no? So then. Whisht."

"I don't know what that means."

But I do, so I shut up, and he talks.

"Some time ago, Mr Sounder, I had a hankering to increase the diversity of my holdings in the daylight economy. There'd been something of a kerfuffle a short while before—you know how these things go: a large-scale event sends the money boys into a kind of funk, they get the jitters and start contemplating their souls, or at least how over-extended they are, and how if everything came apart tomorrow their liens and credits might not add up any more to the sum of their debts. It's a silly moment which comes around every so often, predicated on a collective loss of nerve, and whenever it does come around, what emerges is that things are worth roughly what you'd expect them to be, and anyone who has allowed themselves to believe otherwise is likely to have a difficult time, while anyone who has capitalised on that understanding will be in good stead; but the astonishing thing is that the world broadly continues to turn. Very little of consequence has actually occurred.

"What does tend to happen, however, is that certain less scrupulous fellows, who have engaged in Ponzi schemes and alternate wily exploitations of the cupidity of others, are exposed for what they are: scam artists and flim-flam men, and in that revelation, of course, it often turns out that a truly huge amount of money has not been stolen so much as it never existed at all, and then a genuine, if local and short-lived, crisis may occur, as indeed—at that time—it did.

"And I took it into my head that I would like to explore the kinds of holdings that are mostly not subject to such vagaries: sensible, infrastructural firms that own things and make things and do things that are permanent. Food production and the ocean economy are very much in that category, as are multi-centenarian family firms like the Erskine Company, which, after all, inevitably takes a long view. So, I put out some feelers, and found that I did not, after all, wish to place my money in that area, though the offer was very much on the table, if you see what I mean. Indeed, it was that very willingness which excited a mild attack of the willies in me, and caused me to scratch the surface a little more deeply."

"Erskine's in trouble?"

"No, no. Erskine is somewhat leveraged, to be sure, but in real terms the family could buy the loan and the company would be in debt to its own shareholders. Not unusual—and quite tax efficient, if they could be bothered, but there's really no reason why they should be. A shame, to my eye: all the dividends would technically be repayments for a while, and not subject to the normal taxation of capital gains. It's no skin off my nose, but I dislike seeing the revenuers get more than they absolutely must. It's not as if our politicians actually do any of the things they're supposed to with the money, after all, or we'd have more railways and schools, and fewer casinos."

"But something isn't right."

"Well, I've described the on-paper reality, but I think what's on the ground may be a little different. You can't tell exactly from the outside, but by implication, I think Bail made some poor choices as part of the expansion of the Erskine Company he undertook to modernise and circularise its workflow. He made some bold seed-capital bets which didn't pan out. Again, it's nothing serious from a dynastic point of view, but for a man who wants to be the next shot-caller it's an embarrassment."

"It hasn't come out."

"No, he's been very adept at concealing the issue."

"He put his hand in the pension fund?"

"Nothing so crass. You recall the economic stutter I mentioned, which ironically claimed the lives of the young businesses Bail put money into?"

"It was about a half a minute ago you mentioned it, so, yes, I remember."

"That problem went away because the international banks changed their perspective on certain kinds of money. In short, they allowed a great flood of post-criminal cash and specie into the legitimate system. Grey money into clear, if you like. Then they changed their perspective again and behaved as if nothing had happened. In fact, they were quite keen to close the specific avenues they had opened, and rather unkindly passed some of them to the financial crimes investigators of various countries, which is what I personally had rather expected. But it was, in its own way, rather a splendid solution; since the dark money was money that already existed, but was inaccessible to the daylight economy, it didn't constitute quantitative easing as such, but rather a kind of unlocking of artificially sequestered funds. Governments taxed it as best they could, the while pretending they had no idea they were taxing blood diamonds and slavery and so forth, and in the end there was actually an increase in reported revenues that quarter across the world. Everyone was happy, and the wheels turned—I say 'everyone', but what I mean is everyone not directly the victim of some savage act far away. On paper, once again, no crisis measures were taken."

"How does this tie up with Bail?"

"I'm pretty sure Bail did something similar on a smaller scale. He allowed inward investment from, let's say, dark grey investors. Perhaps he didn't conduct quite as much Know Your Client research as would be normal, and they, in exchange, did not ask why the paper value of their investment halved overnight. A perfect meeting of interests, you see."

"But now he has those dark grey investors as shareholders."

"Actually, he's smarter than that. He's ringfenced them in a kind of escrow structure. They can't sit on the board, but he has to buy the shares back before he can sell—not that he ever would. That doesn't matter, because he has the original amount of money he wanted to cover his—well, his ass—so he doesn't have to fess up to the whole business, and at the same time those dark grey people get their money legitimised at a fifty percent haircut, which is absolutely as good as it gets, especially after you claim relief on the loss."

"And that scared you off."

"I don't like muddy water in my drinking glass. I have plenty of muddy water. I was looking for the clear stream. If I want—well, I do want to play in Shearwater, as you see. I'm thinking of buying the Grand Erskine. What do you say? The Royal Nugent Hotel?"

"Peachy. Although the local kids will hate you—it's where they take one another's clothes off."

"Do you know, that might be enough to talk me out of it? I do so admire the enthusiastic fornication of youth."

"What're the consequences for Bail?"

"On the family side it, no doubt hinges on whether they decide to treat it as bold or crass. As to the bargain itself . . . it sort of depends who he's dealing with. If all they want is money laundering, it's a one-time thing and that's fine. But how often do you meet someone in that category who actually doesn't want more than they're paying for? Closing the door is always so much harder than opening it."

He smiles, reminding me that he's in that category too, and all he's paying for is the beer.

"Can you swim, Lyman?"

"I don't know. I've never tried."

"Martha Erskine can swim."

"I heard she likes to play among the whales."

"And you didn't happen to be in Shearwater recently?"

"No. I can prove it, if you need me to, but the surest thing is that Mr Zoegar asked me to stay away. Keep clear of Miss Josephine. I understand." But though he hides it well, I can see that it makes him sad not to meet the woman in his friend's life. Whatever those two share, it's deep and old and means more than money or crime.

The hardest thing about being a Titan is making friends, but the hardest thing about being an investigator is finding out that monsters have hearts as well as jaws.

The long, black towncar drops me at Celia's and my hotel room. I need an hour not working. Miles says the Shearwater Spa opens on a day's notice, and the hotel library is three glossy coffee table books about places Celia has travelled to. I ask Miles if there really is a Celia or if she's just branding. Miles laughs a hospitality laugh but doesn't actually answer the question.

This is the other reality of towns like Shearwater: there's nothing to do. Sooner or later you go down to the sea again, because that wide expanse of don't care is all the fun there is. Curiously, it's almost enough. The waves are never the same from moment to moment, endless variations of light and depth.

Perhaps that's what the Sleepers see, staring out at it until they die, and perhaps that's why I'm standing in the middle of them, my street shoes and socks dangling from one hand. Like Martha Erskine, I don't really know how I got here, or what I was thinking when I pressed my toes into the half-eroded, half-sharp scree of the beach, but now I'm looking at them for real, for the first time, and they're as strange and similar and different as the sea.

The nearest ones are glassy-eyed and silent, not looking at me or away from me, just not looking. They're dusty white with salt and a fine powder of glass. The combination is abrasive, so the ones who've been here longest have angry sclera and pink tear tracks from the corners of their eyes downward, like the saddest clown make-up you ever saw. I force myself to see faces, not masks: a man, young and hungry-looking, completely rapt in his contemplation, male pattern baldness thick with sand; a woman with a stack of family albums unopened on her lounger, who looks like she oughta be baking cookies for her grandkids; a run of three-time losers and petty thieves I almost recognise from bail flight posters, clustered together as if they've turned to stone; an executive in a smart suit, what they call anthracite. He must be cooked, and the sweat is running down his face over cracked lips, grey hair and grey skin and grey dust and still holding a briefcase as if it matters any more. How many secrets could you hide in this crowd? How many answers are dying here, to questions that aren't police questions, just something more fundamental and desperate? And did one of them kill Mary Ann Grey for some reason that'll never make sense to anyone?

I raise my voice, diffident, almost, for the first time in five years.

"My name's Cal. I'd like to talk to someone about the woman who died here. I don't mean to disturb what you're doing. But she wasn't looking for death and she still found it. Will someone talk to me about that?"

There's a shuffling, like if you're in church and someone's praying too loud or singing the wrong words. That isn't done. Don't touch me with your inappropriate. Don't be here in my space. Don't be, at all.

"Cal Sounder. I'm a consulting investigator in Othrys. I try to make things better, best I can. That's my thing; I try to help."

I hadn't thought how feeble that would sound. How much more so now than when I was twenty percent smaller.

I walk in amongst them, looking for eye contact, not finding it. A fat man, or was, his skin hanging looser now that he barely eats, yet still not slim because he hardly moves, glances up at me only to look away. With a shock I realise he's barely thirty.

A woman with two children sits looking out at the water. The kids looks as if they've given up trying to attract her attention, as if her world is dragging theirs down and they don't know what to do about it. I sit down in the dust in front of her, hoping the waves won't splash me from behind.

"My name's Cal," I say again. "What's yours?"

The woman doesn't answer, but I see one of the kids notice me. Notice, and hope. He puts his hand out. It looks like he's begging but I think he wants to shake, or play, or hug, so I stretch out towards him. The woman's arm comes up.

"Ricky," she says, "come away."

"Hi, Ricky," I say. "I'm Cal."

He nods. I've said it three times, and he's not a fool.

"You hungry?"

He nods again, fast. Very hungry.

"Well, let me get you something. You think your sister's hungry too?"

Around me, I can feel them all taking notice. Not like one at a time, but like one huge creature that's feeling an itch or a bug and doesn't like it.

The girl looks around. "I could eat," she says. She must be seven years old. Thin but not appallingly so. Can't have been here long, or maybe the kids are managing somehow. Maybe the food carts on the promenade sneak them leftovers at the end of the day. Kids are resourceful when they have no choice. They recognise necessity and they don't care much for anything else.

"Come away," the mother says, but there's no weight in it. Me stealing her children is just another thing the world has done to her that she can't stand or do anything about, even if it's just for a quarter hour.

I look at Ricky and then at the spot where Mary Ann Grey washed up. "I'm gonna go sit over there and eat. But I always over-order. It's a vice I have."

Ten minutes later I'm back with a bag full of sandwiches, and Ricky and the girl are eating and not looking out to sea. I bought water, too. Figure the kids would have preferred pop, but I don't know how long they've been without and I don't want them to vomit. I give them the sandwiches in halves, one at time, and I keep them talking so they don't fill up too fast.

Yes, they've been here three weeks. Yes, they go inland and eat at one of the bars when it closes late and there's stuff left over. They drink water from the public taps by the showers. It's warm on the beach and they each have their own blanket for night-time and they share a sunbed. Their mom brought them here when it all got too much. They don't actually know what that means, what "it all" was. One day they were living in their house, the next they were here, and she doesn't do much any more but stare. They're waiting for her to get better, but they're not sure, any more, that she will, or what to do if she doesn't.

So all that said I get to asking them about Mary Ann Grey, because I'm not a tourist or a health worker. I have a job to do, even if it makes me feel like a heel.

Ricky doesn't recognise the picture. His sister does. She says the lady swam a lot, played volleyball. She had pretty friends. She had a boyfriend.

I show her Torrance's picture. She nods, then isn't sure. Maybe the lady had two boyfriends, or maybe the other one was just a friend who was a boy. It's not one of the waterfront set. Ricky's sister hasn't ever seen him except when he came with her and they talked and walked along the beach. Maybe he was the lady's dad. I get the feeling Ricky's sister would be okay if the guy had been her dad. I wish I had pictures of Bail Erskine and Dave Reason, just in case. I wish I had pictures of the 1848, but I wish that anyway. But Ricky's sister is still young enough to see faces in the clouds without trying, and everyone who isn't her mom or her brother is essentially the same. It wouldn't tell me anything I could lean on.

I still wish.

I tell them they can eat at Celia's any time, day or night, on me, for as long as I'm in town.

"Are you a Titan?" Ricky says. It's the first question he's asked, and I don't know whether to lie.

"Yeah," I say at last. "Is that good or bad?"

He shrugs. "I don't know."

That makes me laugh. "Yeah. Nor do I."

We chat a while, and then I walk away along the beach, and I can feel his eyes on me all the way to the trees. I don't look back, because if I do, I'll spend the whole afternoon and the whole damn night just talking with him and his sister, and that won't put either of us in a better place.

Some voice inside me calls me a coward all the way back to my hotel box, and keeps saying it while I take a bath and let myself sleep until the evening, when it's time to go dine with the Quality.

Erskine Hill is steep and wide, a central avenue cut right up into the eucalyptus and pine, stilt houses and cantilevered balconies hanging out over the scarp slope, casting short shadows over the black Shearwater soil. The county has been stripped. No lynx, moose or bears. They were hunted out a hundred years ago, and not reintroduced. Now it's just foxes and feral cats, and small snakes. Occasionally a wolf pack drops down from the north, and has to be gently nudged back towards the circle.

I ring the bell and a manservant answers the door. I don't know any other way to describe him. He's a man, he's wearing a long coat and a tie.

"I'm Cal Sounder. Martha said I should drop by and say hi."

Manservant doesn't find that odd. Professionally doesn't—it's part of his thing.

"Yes, sir. And: hi to anyone in especial, sir?"

"Bail, for sure. Torrance, if the kid's around. I'm in town on business, but Martha suggested I swing by the house."

"Martha Erskine, sir?"

"You know any other Martha who's going to invite me up here?"

"No, sir. May I ask how you came to be speaking to Madame Erskine?"

I'm tempted to tell him I hopped the fence and broke into her waterpark, but I don't. "It was in the nature of a private matter."

Manservant reads something into that, doesn't matter what. Somewhere inside, I have to assume one of Dave Reason's classmates is right now calling Mrs Seraphine, and Mrs Seraphine is making like the question he's asking is so damn stupid she's worried it's contagious. If the manservant has an earpiece, it's a very discreet one. I'm thinking just a buzzer inside his coat: one for yes, two for no, three for run like hell. After the briefest imaginable pause, he opens the door wide for me to go in.

"I am Macklin. Please wait in the green lounge, sir. Someone will bring you tea directly. I will see if Mr Erskine is in the house." Because billionaires, like the daughters of overprotective fathers, are often not in if it doesn't suit.

The green lounge is small and cosy, something between a waiting room and a giant walk-in closet for people and things. It only has one door. The far wall is pure bookshelves.

"Hey, Macklin. You get these by the yard? Which of them is the spooky secret passage?"

But he's already gone, and honestly I'm glad. Joshing the hired help was funny when I was just some guy they could throw out. Now it's punching down, but I can't quite shake the habit.

The door opens and a woman comes in with a silver tray. The

teapot is made of silver too, tall with ornate trim around the base and a wooden handle: actual Mexican Empire ware. As she sets it down she looks up at me for the first time, and I realise it's Ashley.

"Can I offer you some lemon or milk with your tea?" she says, then recognises me, too. "Oh, shit! What are you doing here? This is where I work, for Christ's sake!"

Before I can tell her I'm working too, the door opens and Torrance Erskine comes in, and right behind him is Dave Reason and a guy with a dog on a chain.

Torrance looks at me and says: "What the fuck are *you* doing here?" And bless the kid he is actually ready to go, hands up in a not-terrible boxer's guard. Reason steps round him and puts one hand back onto Torrance's chest, the other into his coat shoulder for whatever he's got there, what he wants me to think is a gun, but all this is so much security theatre because Torrance is a rich kid playing at being his daddy and you get Dave Reason in a pack of twelve, but even if they were both Olympic-terrifying I'd still be looking at the dog.

It has a huge wide head with eyes half closed like a viper. It has a lolling smile that says nothing but marrow, and a weird pink nose on the front of a grey and liver face. White eyes with huge dark centres stare out at me, and behind in the corridor there are four more just the same, but this for sure is the alpha, or however that actually works with dogs, and it is big and heavy and wrong, and right about the same height as my chest.

Once upon a time there was a project in China that increased muscle and bone density in dogs. Supposedly it was just an experiment for human medicines, but all the world looked at it and saw a riot dog for a country with a stern understanding of the relationship between the government and the governed. Stefan told me that he always thought it was a prototype, proof of concept for a space-migration therapeutic. Not that the riot thing wasn't a bonus. When T7 was in the pipeline he did experiments on dogs too, and the strange, wild consequences have passed into folklore around Othrys: the Devil Dogs of Chersenesos, lost and howling on the mountainsides north of the city.

I've always figured there must be something in it as a matter of history, but I surely never expected to meet one, let alone five, yet here they are: dogs twisted and huge, out of proportion and yet not, and something in them speaks to something in me and knows we're related, children of the same test tube.

It's not a family connection I want to lean on too hard.

Down around waist height, something makes a noise like a combustion engine for a big truck, and I realise the Devil Dog is growling deep in his chest, and look away before I meet his eyes.

"Who the hell are you and what do you want?" Torrance Erskine says, from behind Reason's arm.

"I told you. I'm Cal. I'm not here for you." Although I can be, if it works out that way.

"I'll be the judge of that," Torrance says, which makes no kind of sense at all. Figure between now and when I saw him on the beach, someone broke the news about his girlfriend. Figure if he didn't kill her he's grieving, and if he did kill her he probably still is, but freaked out and terrified into the bargain.

There's a time to walk softly and a time to make some noise, and it seems to me that if I want any kind of answers out of this crowd, this is the second.

"I don't think you will," I say. "In fact, I know you won't. You're a kid, and your family is a few hundred years old and some of the originals are still around. You're basically a pet for the next four decades, if you even make the cut after that, which you're not showing a lot of signs of doing right now."

I see Ashley's mouth dropping open. Figure Torrance doesn't generally get handed the long brown envelope of home truths. I want to say he bristles, but it's more like he's about to have a fit. If I wanted to know about Torrance's temper, there it is.

I raise my finger. "And before you say I don't know you, I absolutely do. I know you by the way the world moves near you. I know more about where you stand than you do. You are so fucking disposable that your family's corporate security—probably Dave's boss and Dave's boss's boss—is right now telling the actual Erskine elders you maybe murdered a woman who was your lover, and that's almost the only thing they have ever heard about you. Your grade point average barely made it to Bail. He sure as hell never passed it on because to most of the family it's white noise. You're an ephemeral. So when Dave's boss Mr Vesper—who is a colossal disappointment, by the way—when he goes for tea and chit-chat with the gods? They might as well just give you a barcode like you're a courier pack arriving from Chersenesos. I figure the way they see it, this is just your standard sad story: rich boy gets put in his place by a pretty girl, loses his cool and kills her. Then he calls someone to help him deal and they completely screw it up."

I look at Dave Reason, since he's right there anyway.

Reason, to my amazement, absolutely loses his shit. Honestly, this guy. He runs at me, hauls off and throws a punch bigger than the dog. It's so wide and slow I have time to notice he's slipped on a pair of cheap metal knuckles in his pocket, super unprofessional, and I like him a little more for that because it's smart, for a given value of smart that includes Dave Reason. I move my head because, crappy or not, that's going to bruise, and then I hit him once in the ribs, hard.

Titan hard.

I don't want to actually rupture anything inside of him, so I telegraph it enough to give him time to tense up. Dave Reason goes backwards through the air and does not touch the ground until his calf muscles intersect with the line of a reproduction French day bed and he falls into it, actual tears in his eyes, clawing for breath. Someone somewhere says "oh, shit" in an impressed way, and then everything is quiet again. The dogs are fascinated, but not much moved. You don't own a dog like that and let it get excited at a few punches. You train it and teach it so it'll sit through a bombing, then bite grandma's head off on command. But the dog man doesn't say anything. He just watches, and so the dogs watch too.

I wonder how old they are. Older than me? A century? Two? Five?

I point at Torrance. "Expendable."

At Reason. "Dumb as mud."

I look around at the dog man, grey haired and impassive and near as jowly as the animals themselves.

"And you," I say, "you haven't looked at either of them for instructions, so maybe you want me to think you're a dog flunky while you take notes, but I figure you'd be Bail Erskine."

The old face crunches into an expression that has all the characteristics of a smile. "I guess I might, at that."

He lets go of the chain and for one horrible moment I think I've overplayed this and I'm about to get turned into bonemeal. Then the dog huffs and slumps down onto the carpet.

"Goddam lazy mutt," Bail says, as the others wander in behind the alpha and find corners and cushions to drool on and the room all but fills up. "They're all the same, Mr Sounder. They look a good game, but unless one of them steps on your foot they're not much of a threat. Chronic arthritis. And narcolepsy, of all things. But I can't say I don't love them, all the same."

His eye picks out Torrance with disfavour, and the comparison goes unsaid. Bail sighs.

"Torrance, please apologise to Mr Sounder and thank him for an object lesson in family politics."

Torrance looks all kinds of pissed off. It hasn't registered yet that Bail just told him everything I said was true. Adrenaline, privilege and testosterone; I honestly don't know if there's a dumber cocktail. Still, he'll be watching this replay in his head over and over today, and sooner or later maybe it'll get through the shame and he'll actually hear what I wanted him to know. Or Ashley will tell him, if they're talking again.

"I apologise, Mr Sounder, and I do thank you for explaining things to me so clearly."

Wherever Torrance goes to school, it makes for excellent liars.

"Good," Bail says. "Now, go put on something smarter for dinner. We have a guest." And just like that, everyone leaves.

Bail walks me through the house like he doesn't notice it any more: this huge power building full of wood panels and gold leaf. Old money screaming its name at every turn. A lot of things change in the world, but some things don't. One of them is how dynasties use space to make you feel small: they make you walk a long way indoors to talk to them, hang art you've seen in museums. Your footsteps echo and you feel like a bean lost in a tin, and then you arrive at something like a throne and the dynamics of the room make clear the relationship: you ask, and they decide.

Erskine House wants me to ask nicely for food to feed my children, but that's not why I'm here.

We get to where we're going and it's a switchback: a small, neat little room with a pretty modern table in driftwood and dinner laid for six. Nice move, making everything cosy beyond the formal black and white tiles and the polished brass, soft furnishings here so it's intimate and quiet. The kind of place where you feel you've been taken inside the circle, where you can be a little honest, a little forthcoming. Bail lifts a Sam Sanghera jacket from the back of the door, throws it on over the rumpled shirt. From flunky to master by adding one unstructured linen coat worth two grand and change. He kicks two chairs away from the table, and sits in one of them, starts talking as soon as his ass makes contact with the wood.

"All right, Mr Sounder. You come," he snorts, "highly discussed. What can I do for you?"

"I was really hoping for 'recommended'."

"If that's the road you were aiming to travel, son, I'd say you're a little lost."

"You think I can get back on it?"

The door opens and Torrance steps inside, followed by a Titan woman with a hand on his shoulder. With a perfect athletic figure in a single-strap gold sequin dress and a blue silk scarf draped around a neck like something made in dark emperador, she reads as baseline thirty, fine-boned like a heron. I still don't see the relationships straight off, the way I would have without T7 in the mix, and my mind comes up with possibilities: big sister, roommate, governess, dom. She turns and I see Martha in the line of her face, and it clicks: mother. She looks as if she likes me about as well as you'd expect.

Bail, still pondering my last question, shrugs.

"I sure as hell wouldn't start from here."

And it looks like that's the bell for round one. Macklin the manservant appears through another door, patiently starts pouring sparkling water into glasses. Erskine House casual: one flunky between six.

"This is Dixie," Bail Erskine says calmly, gesturing to the woman in gold, "Torrance's mother—and my great-aunt, I believe." Another thing about Bail that's weird. He's baseline, so he doesn't have a Titan's issue with family relationships, still uses all the old familiar words. Figure it's a little tiny power play, like the dogs: here's a man who keeps Titans on leashes. Or maybe it just amuses him to tell Dixie she's an old lady, even if she does look like a young one.

"Mr Sounder," Dixie says, like she'd say it's raining. We shake hands, which is to say I shake hers and she gives me the corpse grip, flaccid and unenthused.

"Who are the other two?" I ask.

"Captain Iverson is coming, and I have a morbid fear of odd numbers, so I'll ask Ashley to join us. You met her on the way in. She's working here this summer, but she's also a family friend." I wonder if that's the term for anyone on staff Torrance has sex with, or whether they really were family friends before that.

Dixie sits down as far away from me as she can, Torrance next to her. Ashley appears through the same door as the manservant.

"Sorry," she says, "I didn't have anything else to wear."

She has on black trousers and a punky T-shirt, her work jacket thrown over with the collar up. Good improvisation: if you didn't know she'd been below stairs ten minutes ago you could take it for a carefully selected look.

"It's fine, Ashley," Bail says. "Oh, no, if you wouldn't mind, I'd like Captain Iverson there." Leaving her only with the seat between me and Torrance. There's a soft footstep behind me and I recognise the absence of affect that distinguishes Jimson in any room.

"And this is Matthew Jimson," Bail adds, "who's working security here tonight. Matthew will take care of us all if there's a terrorist outrage. Or a fire."

"We met," Jimson says. He rubs his left hand on his right shoulder, like he's loosening up to hit me.

"He happened to go fishing in the harbour when I was there on business," I say, in answer to Bail's eyebrows. "Did you catch anything, Mr Jimson?"

He shrugs. "Enough to be going on with."

Macklin reappears, not with caviar but with Iverson, looking harried. "Sorry, Bail," Iverson says, sitting down. He grins around the table. "Hi, everyone. What are we eating?"

"Starter: vanilla lamb noisettes," Bail Erskine says. "You'll love it, Mr Sounder. Speciality of the house."

Macklin reappears a moment later, and when the covers come off, I smell Mary Ann Grey.

"Hi, Cal," Ashley says, between mouthfuls, but I'm pretty sure she means: *What the fuck is going on?*

"Hi, Ashley."

"I hear you're a private investigator."

"Actually, I'm a violinist, but I have to pay the bills."

She starts to say "really?" and then catches herself. Iverson's face on the far side of the table quirks. Amusement, but also something else with more wear and tear on that I'm provisionally calling "age". He looks over at Dixie in a certain way, and she looks back in the negative. Iverson's face doesn't really change, but I can feel his regret somehow, in the slight shift of his body. For all that she's clearly telling him to get lost, what's between them is an unvoiced tension loud enough to feel like a connection—and there is something on the other side of that coin, because she likes watching him try and fail. How long have they been doing this? Iverson, at Spicer's, said twenty years. They're old enough to be my grandparents. In Titan terms we're all the same generation, but I still think of twenty years as a long time, which puts me in the same conceptual box as Bail, three decades my senior, who's Dixie's great-nephew. Titan offset, as seen through the lens of multiple generations.

"Mr Sounder is known for having his own particular way of doing things, Ashley," Bail says. "Even when he's dealing with very important people."

"Especially then," Iverson murmurs.

I look at Bail. He shrugs.

"Come on, Mr Sounder, out with it. You dropped Martha's name at my gates. What are you doing here?"

"I wanted to meet you. Get the lay of the land."

"And how's the land looking?"

"Well, I found a bomb in your town. That was exciting."

"Yes, indeed. I do so enjoy sleepless nights."

"I would have thought a man in your position lived on his nerves. High-stakes finance, and suchlike."

Was that just a flicker of tension? Not sure.

"You're used to the hurly-burly of Chersenesos, of course, but the Erskine Company is rather more sedate. I don't ride a tiger, Mr Sounder, I drive a mule train. Less exciting, but it gets where I'm going, all the same."

"Even mules kick out from time to time, Mr Erskine."

He shrugs as if I'm not putting my finger in an open wound and jiggling it around. "Not mine."

I give him a minute. He doesn't feel the need to fill the silence. He's Bail Erskine—that's someone else's job. Dixie takes up the slack.

"Do we know anything more about the bomb?" Aimed into the room at large, in case Iverson wants to come in, or Bail has something to say himself.

When no one answers, I stir again, just a little.

"Captain Iverson thinks it was going to the food plant. I don't know about that." Iverson makes a fuck-you-very-much face at this little drive-by. Pretty sure when he imagined me making trouble with the gentry, he didn't intend to be there when it happened. Bail eyes me thoughtfully over a red slice of lamb.

"I assume you have an alternate theory?"

"That's kind of my job, Mr Erskine."

I watch him enjoy the formality for just a moment: a Titan sitting at his table offering him polite deference. He's just heard that I sass Stefan whenever I want to, and I think he's drawing the conclusion that I'm showing him more respect than I do the Tonfamecasca patriarch. Maybe it even seems that must be because he's still baseline: he hasn't taken the easy road even though it's there for him. It doesn't seem to occur to him that I just don't care enough to get in his face. Just like it hasn't occurred to him that I wouldn't be here if his boss trusted him to get it done. Bail exercises great power, and he's forgotten that it's not his, it's borrowed.

I hold the moment, and then play long into the grass. "I'm honestly curious to know what Mr Jimson thinks."

"Mr Jimson?" Bail prompts.

"It's a mistake to imagine terrorism obeys conventional thinking," Jimson says. "They could load it up on a truck and smash it into a port from the land side. Throw a college party on the beach right next to it and then blow it up. Take the whole thing to the other coast before they wire it up, or detonate it going over a hydro dam in flyover country. Send it to Chersenesos, even."

He looks at me, and I know I'm supposed to be thrown by the image of Tonfamecasca Tower in flames, but Jimson isn't seeing Stefan for what he is. He's seeing an empowered, achieved Bail, assuming limits that aren't there. Chersenesos spirals inwards to the tower plaza, the entire urban map of the peninsula quietly redesigned to stop any vehicle gathering momentum, and the fountains and landscaping in the plaza itself amount to a jagged field of bear traps which make it impossible to cross at any speed. A transport truck like the kind you'd need for the container would get hung up on the water sculptures, and the blast from that distance wouldn't so much as crack the security glass. Over time, Stefan has turned the entire quarter in which he lives into defence in depth. People could die, of course, but not many, and Stefan wouldn't notice until he looked down from the cupola and saw that his little ant farm needed tidying up.

Athena would be safe.

I look back at Bail. "It occurred to me it might be for Martha. Either by land or dropped into the water where she swims. I don't how bad it would be."

Bail's easy sense of fun evaporates.

"Bad enough not to be an idle speculation."

"You mind if I ask you a question, Mr Erskine?"

It calms him this time, that little flutter of pride at being the boss. "Go ahead."

"Does the Erskine Company have any holdings in Tilehurst?"

Near as I can tell, Tilehurst doesn't mean anything to him beyond what it means to everybody. Down the far end of the table, though, someone shifts. Dixie, maybe, bored out of her mind. Or maybe Jimson, responding to his industry's most famous screw-up. I wish I'd thought to get up and walk around, like a detective in a movie, so I'd know for sure.

"Macabre," Bail Erskine says, but like he'd say the wine had hints of blackcurrant. "I don't think we do. I'll have someone look into it, if you like. Sure as hell not much, though. Though the city council does come sniffing around looking for new infrastructure. Jobs and such."

"But you've had some labour trouble here. Strikers."

Bail Erskine doesn't seem concerned. "Lots of thunder but no lightning. It'll blow over. Or at least, that's what I would have thought, until all this." A look at Jimson, who nods. A dollar will get you ten that he told Bail what Vesper would want him to, that the security arm is under-resourced to deal with low likelihood/high-impact risks—like bombs in shipping containers, and once-in-a-lifetime rioting burning your city to the ground.

Well, that's interesting, but I'm not asking Vesper, I want to hear from Bail. I put my hand out less than half a metre from his face, blocking his connection with Jimson. He blinks. It's so rude he can't quite believe I meant to do it. Down the table, Iverson shuts his eyes. Yeah, well, you asked for it.

"Mr Erskine, did you have a pet when you were a kid?"

"I had anything I wanted, and too much of it. It took me forty years to get over my happy childhood."

"Did you ever happen to have a lizard?"

"A what?"

"Ailsa Lloyd had a lizard."

"No, I did not. But I wouldn't order anyone murdered on that basis. An overreaction, don't you think?"

"Where were you when Mary Ann Grey was killed?"

"Asleep, I should imagine. Alone, alas, but not unwitnessed. The security people, you know."

Meaning that Bail's alibi, if he needed one, would be a group of people whose job is protecting him.

"If you'd had a lizard, what would you have called it?"

"Rex, probably. I was an unimaginative boy. What is all this?"

"Did you ever meet Mary Ann Grey?"

"I don't believe so."

"You never slept with her, for example?"

"Torrance did."

"That hardly narrows the field. Do you take lovers, Mr Erskine?"

"You don't mean lovers, Mr Sounder. You mean do I have sex with young women in the locality who are impressed by my wealth and power."

"Well, do you?"

"I have done, in the past. At the moment, no. Although I do intend to, in the future. When I take your—friend—Mr Tonfamecasca up on his offer of a medical intervention. At which time, I have to say, I feel Torrance's tediously notched bedpost will pale into insignificance at my excesses."

I turn my head to look past Ashley at Torrance. He stares down at his food, eating mouthful by mouthful. He's practised at this: public humiliation. It's not just me who picks on the kid. Or rather, it is, but Bail's indifference is the same thing only worse. And this, in front of Ashley. If I was Torrance, I wouldn't kill Mary Ann Grey, I'd kill Bail, but maybe that's whose head he held under water, and then he woke up.

"I'm just wondering if you were lovers, Mr Erskine, because you were paying Lila Grey's medical bills a year ago, before Mary Ann Grey ever came to Shearwater."

"I doubt that."

"And yet I know it's true."

"Probably you're mistaken. I'll look into it."

"You wouldn't know something like that off the top of your head."

"I have a lot of money, Mr Sounder. Really a lot. As you'll come to know, money in quantity doesn't sit still. It goes places and does things, and the more of it you have, the more people are empowered to move it around, point it at problems and opportunities. You say I was paying medical bills in Tilehurst?"

"I do say."

"I'll talk to the branch office and find out why. Quid pro quo, community outreach, some oblique form of bribe to a local politician. Sometimes just straight good works for the hell of it."

"You're saying it's coincidental."

"I'm saying it's small money, Mr Sounder. A merely rich man might need a reason to commit to such an arrangement. Even a very rich man would know that he was doing it. I do not. At this time, I'm probably paying a few hundred bills like that just from my own accounts. Several thousand more from the firm, a thousand again from the goodwill trusts. Sometimes it's liability or settlement. Mostly just because it's there. Dixie's sister met a woman in a wheelchair who wanted a dog; my mother knows a man whose grandson can't afford college; the fish chef has cancer and needs a novel treatment. On and on and on, the responsibilities of being there and being empowered. Which is why I find the younger generation so dispiriting." He glances along the table. "They're not fitted to become what they must."

Torrance helps himself to more lamb, as if he can't hear any of this, or as if he's heard it so often it doesn't matter. I bet it does, all the way down to the soul.

Bail, chewing: "He reminds me of me when I was that age."

"Honestly, he seems like an okay kid." For a murder suspect, anyway.

"Oh, well, maybe I'm wrong. I was an asshole back then. Never saw anything I couldn't have. Drank it, snorted it, fucked it, bought it, sold it, spent it, wrecked it. I had a regular bed at Iverson's because he didn't like having me in the cells."

Iverson covers his face with his hand.

"That right, Iverson?"

"That's right, Bail."

"For Christ's sake, Tim," Dixie says in disgust. She puts her hand on Torrance's. "Bail's being shitty because Mr Sounder's here. He doesn't like to be put on the spot. It doesn't happen to him, you see, Mr Sounder. Martha doesn't choose to, and Tim hasn't the backbone. I'm just family, not an executive. A civilian. So it goes. There's just Bail and his money men, and the company."

"Why don't you tell me about Torrance, Ms Erskine?"

"I don't have anything to say to you, Mr Sounder. You're a momentary annoyance. You'll buzz off back to your shiny towers and your sugar mommy any day now, and my life will carry on regardless."

Bail chuckles as if she's made his point, then turns like the most genteel sort of viper. His smile never gets any less real as he answers my question for her.

"Torrance wants to be admired. He doesn't have much to be admired for except good looks and money, so that's what he trades in: a kind of microscopic celebrity."

"Did he kill Mary Ann Grey?"

"Ask him."

"For shit's sake, Bail," Dixie says. "The word you're looking for is 'no'. That's what you say when someone asks you if my son is a murderer. You say 'no'. And fuck you, Sounder," she adds, after a moment. "Fuck you for encouraging him."

"And what happens if he did?" I look at Iverson direct, but it's Bail who answers.

"Much as I'd like to make a point about feckless youth to my extended family, Erskines do not stand trial. If Torrance killed her, then the whole thing goes away."

"And yet if you weren't contemplating just letting him drown, you wouldn't entertain this conversation."

"That's a particularly tasteless metaphor in the circumstances."

I look over at Torrance. "The first time I saw you, you screwed up because you were too proud to take advice from someone who knew what they were talking about. I got all kinds of sympathy with that. I have done some dumb things in my life, so I want you to hear me when I say this: literally the only thing between you and a murder trial is Bail not wanting to take shit from Dixie over breakfast muffins. Tim over there is sweet on her, so I have to imagine she's more than a coat hook. Talk to your mother. Look me up and see exactly what kind of asshole I am. Then come and find me because I will help you if I can. Even if Bail says not to."

Bail Erskine's old man lips stretch tight, chapped white against white teeth.

"You'd be leaning hard into your connections at that point, Mr Sounder. I hear that's not something you like to do. And then, the word is Stefan is entering a new phase. Becoming . . . odd. Athena is stepping in. The velvet glove. Perhaps that's all there is now: just the glove."

Well, that's offensive. More important, he's leaning into it because it's the raw nerve in his own life, and people like Bail always assume those are universal.

"Touch of projection there, Mr Erskine."

"How so?"

"Oh, I don't wish to be rude, sir. This isn't really dinner conversation."

But he wants it now, to hear it said and to crush it, here, in his home, in front of his people. "Please. Say your piece."

"Well, if you insist, sir, then here it is. I read where your accounts were a little on the hollow side. No fault of yours, just bad timing, maybe some unlucky investment choices. That could happen to anyone, but I have to ask: who did you get to fill the gap?"

"Your information is incorrect, Mr Sounder. Slanderous, even. Wherever did you dig up such trash?"

"From a mob boss."

Bail laughs, light and relaxed. He's an excellent liar. I wonder if that's school or experience. "A very trustworthy source."

"A complex man, but that doesn't change the reality. That you're not willing to take the T7 dose because you don't want to risk being seen as unreliable right now. Not when Martha is maybe slipping a little, and that top job might actually be on the table."

And now, abruptly, it's not fun for him any more.

"Martha's fine. She's actually older than your Mr Tonfamecasca, you know. Was older than him, baseline, before they were both dosed. She'll go on for ever."

"I'm sure she will, sir. But maybe not in the job. The high-dose Titans are still something of an experiment. And I hear she's ... sleepwalking."

Silence. Iverson has his eyes fixed on the pepper pot and looks like he's praying to some cop god that no one asks for his opinion. Dixie, Torrance and Ashley just look confused. I can't see Jimson, but it feels almost supernaturally bland in the dead space behind my back, like I'm being shadowed by herbal tea.

"Tread very carefully on that score, Mr Sounder. Martha is the ultimate authority in the family. In the company. We keep careful medical watch on key individuals, and her mind is in tip-top condition."

Yes, it is, but I'm not sure it still works the same way as ours. I'm not even sure if her strangeness has to be physical or if it's just an outgrowth of the offset. Bail's still talking like he's in charge. Perhaps he really thinks he is.

"Interview Torrance. Go where you like. You've earned that much leeway with finding the bomb. But there are limits. Don't make a scene that I have to tidy up."

He puts his napkin down on his plate: so there.

I expected more somehow.

"Well, that's my cue to leave. Thank you all for an entertaining lunch. Oh, hey, Torrance?"

The kid doesn't look at me.

"I meant what I said. Come find me. If I get out of here without your elderly cousin releasing the dogs."

Bail Erskine gets up from his chair. He makes a ceremony of it, as if he's going to slap me with an opera glove. "I like my dogs, Mr Sounder, but they are anything but fighters. If it comes to that I will just have someone shoot you in the head. You're a first-dose Titan. You go down just like anyone else."

"So do you, Mr Erskine, come to that."

Jimson flows into the space in front of me so fast I can barely follow it. The punch isn't hard but it's efficient: a stinger to distract and lock the muscles. I get my hands up anyway and block the next one and the next, and he ducks fast to avoid my reply but I almost have him. I feel his hair and the warm air where he was, but he's gone, out of reach. It's less that he's quick and more that he moves between perfectly natural postures. Hitting me is one, and this is another, and he's just going back into it. The gun in his hands is a Wilson Combat 9mm, the new model. Ergonomic as hell, no protruding parts to spoil a quick draw, double safety and the pull factory-set at two pounds. A professional's gun, because if you're not a professional you'll either forget the second safety or shoot yourself in the foot. Not that I need that to tell me what Jimson is, not now; full Paris training, for sure, and better than I ever was. I look down the black tunnel to a sharp, fast death, and on to Matthew Jimson's eyes, like glass beads on a string.

But he's not killing me here and now and everyone knows it. Not least because, fast as he is, we're a lot too close together for the gun to be a guarantee of anything except chaos. Although Jimson looks like he really wants to, so I talk to him direct.

"Tim Iverson is sitting right there. Ashley works here but she doesn't belong, and Macklin doesn't strike me as a natural accessory to murder. Dixie doesn't like this thing you have for Torrance and I'm pretty sure Torrance can't keep a secret any more than he can fly. I get you're edgy about the situation and you don't like that I don't back down when your boss tells me to, but I am plum tired of having guns pointed at me this week, and of getting the runaround and the high hat. You're fast and I'm big, but more than that I know what's in your bag of tricks and you have no idea what's in mine. Now put that thing away, or I'll put it away for you."

We all play the staring game for while, until Bail Erskine shrugs.

"I just want to make the situation clear, Mr Sounder."

That makes me laugh, and I see them all flinch, even Iverson and Dixie, as it comes out low and deep.

"Then I wouldn't start from here, Mr Erskine."

I put my back to Erskine House and walk down the hill alone. The itch between my shoulder blades stays there until I reach the place where the smaller houses start to pop up along the road, and then feel salt spray as I turn a corner. I walk between clapboard houses with single bedrooms and rotting balconies looking east, perfectly tended flower baskets cascading down to the gutters at the edge of the road.

Bail and Martha and Jimson and Iverson, and Mary Ann Grey is still dead. She wasn't what she seemed; that much is obvious by now. But what did she seem, and to whom, and when? And who got angry when they found out, or scared, or always intended it to end this way?

She lied her way across the country, under a dozen names. She lied to almost everyone while she was here. She was pretending to be a real estate agent, pretending to be a production line worker, pretending to be a spy or pretending to be an idealist. She left the Caffrey to meet someone, wearing ordinary clothes. She died in them, but I still don't know where or why. I call Mini Denton but she doesn't answer. After a moment I dial another and hear the call go through.

"Mr Sounder?"

"Hi, Emile." We don't ever use each other's first names, but I've met Josephine now, and met her kids. I know one of his biggest secrets and there's a way of seeing the world where that changes things. I owe him safety for them all, and reciprocity of trust along a new axis that's not professional, and he owes me the same. If we acknowledge it, the line pulls both of us in new directions, not all of them easy, or good.

I hear him take a breath. Then:

"Hello, Cal."

"Are you busy?"

"The children are in bed. Josephine and I were talking."

I can just picture it: a metre apart on the same couch, each drinking mint tea and discussing gallery openings or fish recipes, and the sexual tension wound so tight it's like living on a guitar string.

"I need to talk to someone who's not an Erskine. Or maybe just not from this town. I don't know."

"Are you in trouble?" Alert, abruptly, to something in my voice.

"No, just . . . I went to dinner at Erskine House. It's exactly how you'd think."

"How would I think?"

"Horrible, perfect, full of Erskines. Wasted on them."

"Josephine says ring the bell. Pessoa Street, number three."

I turn off the shingle and along the boardwalk, and Pessoa Street is right there behind the old casino. Number three is two floors, old stone and white paint. I ring the bell. Zoegar appears in the doorway.

"Come in, Cal."

I go in and sit down and I start out thinking I'm going to discuss the case, but I don't. Instead, we talk old times and old sorrows, and make the memories sweet again. I tell them about the day I called Stefan Tonfamecasca to save Athena's life, knowing it would draw a line between us, that it was a liberty she might not forgive and a change I might not understand. I've almost never told that story, of the moment the phone rang and the paramedics told me she was under the wall, she was alive, but just barely. The knowledge that it all rested in my hand in that one hanging instant, and the certainty of what I would do, and what it would cost.

Zoegar talks about Monrovia and the smell of ekop trees, the business he was in and the song his mother sang when he was a child. Josephine actually knows it. They knew each other from the age of nine, and he was best man at her wedding, best friend to her late husband and the father of her kids, killed one day in a stupid accident by a falling shop awning, and Emile has looked out for her ever since.

They pour me a glass of something I don't drink and then we do a few sentences back and forth until I just dry up and stare. Sitting in Josephine's parlour I find myself staring at the stuffed bear left carelessly on the empty chair and all I can think of is the Sleeper kids, Ricky and his sister, out there night after night with their mother who just wants to die, except that's not true, it's just what everyone says about them. She doesn't want to die, and she doesn't want them to die either. She still takes care of them: come away, she told Ricky, when she saw him talking to a stranger. She doesn't want to die, she just doesn't know any more how to do anything else.

I say all this to Josephine Addes like I expect her to know how to fix it, and her eyes don't move from my face until I'm done. There's sympathy there, but not pity, not for me. Well done, Cal. Now you know what the problem is. How are you going to fix it?

"I have to leave."

Zoegar raises one hand. "Cal, there's nothing tonight."

I shrug, because I know he's right, but it doesn't change anything. Josephine nods. "Go with him, Emile."

We walk down the beach until we come to the edge of the Sleeper camp, and then I walk on through them as if they're all equally precious, and equally unexploded, until I find the lounger where the kids are sleeping. Ricky is the big spoon, and his shoulders look very small for the job. I twitch the blanket up over him but it slips back down, so in the end I just take off my jacket and wrap it around him and I leave it there. Maybe I'll get it back and maybe I won't. It sounds generous, but it's not: I have another. And another, and another, if I need them. It's not generous. It's just the closest I can get to human. I see Zoegar out beyond the ring of white sunbeds, expression invisible in the dark.

I stand there a while wondering what else I can do, and watching Ricky and his sister sleep, and I know I can't help them unless I can help their mother and I don't have any idea how.

Ricky opens his eyes and looks up at me, unsurprised. "Hey, mister."

I get down so I can whisper. "I'm going to do something to help."

"Okay," Ricky says. "Now?"

Yes.

"No. I have to work out how."

"Okay."

"I mean it, kid." Not words. Something real.

"Okay."

We sit there for an endless time, and I keep willing him to believe: I'm going to help. I am, I am, I am. And then, because I am what I am, I realise there's something else I should ask him:

"Your sister said she saw a man with Mary Ann that wasn't Torrance. Did you ever see him?"

"Do you want me to say I did?"

"It's not a price, Ricky. It doesn't matter whether you saw him or not. I'm still helping. But it helps me if you tell me straight. Did you see the guy?"

"I think."

"Can you tell me what he looked like? Maybe what he was wearing? Fisherman's boots, beach sandals?"

"Smart shoes. Black. Like my dad, for work."

"Clothes?"

He fingers my jacket. "Like this. Kinda."

"And his hair?"

"Yeah, neat."

"Silver?"

"Nope. He wasn't that old. Like he was old but not old." A real grown up, but not an old man. His mother's age, not his grandpa's. Anyone from thirty to fifty. Me. Jimson. Miles, from Celia's.

"I'm going to back to sleep. Is that okay?"

"Sure."

"Will you stay a while?"

"Sure."

The moon comes up while I stand there, and when it does the sound of the Sleepers changes in the silver light, so that it's less fitful and more together, and I wonder if they all care about one another, or whether the point about being a Sleeper is that you can't care about anything any more, because if you cared about anything you'd care about everything and that would drive you crazy and you'd turn into someone who just sits in the black glass sand by the side of the warm water, waiting for the summer to strip it all away.

If I was the 1848, I'd be here, on this beach, with these people. This is where I'd begin everything. Not with bombs in containers. And if I was a bright young believer in a just cause, rolled into town on another mission, that's what I'd tell whoever I was working for: right here, right now, because if the revolution can't do this, that's not what it is, it's just a wrapper for the same world in a new flavour. I look at Zoegar. If I was him, I'd do it just the same. This would be the beginning of my gang, my cartel: the most loyal bunch of crooks there ever was. Why does no one who can do something do anything?

I stand there and I still don't know.

Just like I still don't know who killed Mary Ann Grey.

8

In the morning the phone rings before I'm really ready, while I'm still putting on my shoes. As always, they seem further away than they should be, but that feeling itself is getting familiar, and now I think that if my body miraculously went back to its old size I'd find that just as strange. I tie the laces without snapping them, and feel a small rush of pride. Most Titans use high-strength fibre in boots and shoes, but to me that's just refusing to learn. Something else a lot of Titans do, I suppose.

I pick up the phone and look at it, thinking of breakfast. "Sounder."

"Cal, it's Tim Iverson."

"Hi, Tim, what's cooking?"

"You sound like hell. Get your game face on, I need you for something."

"Thank you for your concern, I also feel like hell. What's happened?"

"Apparently, your grandstanding yesterday had a positive effect. Torrance Erskine wants a meeting and he wants you there."

"Do you?"

"I should have said he won't do it unless you're present. His mother agrees."

Dixie, for whom Iverson has a thing. Super. "Torrance decide I'm the good guy?"

"No, he still he hates you." I can hear Iverson gritting his teeth on the other end of the phone. "But he also thinks you're authentic. That's the word he used. Authentic. I'm, what, sixty years older than you and I've been an actual police detective for twice as long as you've been alive, but you're authentic. I do not know how that works."

"I stepped on his sense of invulnerability yesterday. I guess his balls are still aching. Then Bail told him I was right, then I stood up to Bail. Then I stared down Jimson's gun. To a kid Torrance's age, that's pretty much sorcery."

"You did all that to get him to think?"

"Absolutely."

"I figured you were just free falling through your own bullshit."

"Well, it's a shame you're not authentic or you'd see how hurtful that is."

"Fuck you. Stop eating your croissant or whatever you big city boys do and get on the road."

"Where am I going?"

"Well, now, Torrance's momma, who is very much concerned for his well-being in the face of an unjustified suspicion among certain contract employees of the Erskine Company, is going to accompany him so that I don't accidentally put his dick in a vise and extract a—now, what was her word?—a 'meretricious' confession."

"That is not my fault."

"Keep telling yourself that. Do you know the precise meaning of the word 'meretricious'?"

"I feel you've recently looked it up."

"I did, Cal, and I was insulted in my small-town way. It means that something is superficially attractive or significant, but ultimately possesses no integrity. The origin of the word is in the Latin for a prostitute, which exemplifies a distressing societal prudishness against sex work and quietly proposes that my services are for sale, and taking it all in sum, I believe I'm straight-up supposed to be offended. What do you figure?"

"I think maybe this temporary friction between you and

Torrance's mother is a potential reset, and after maybe she'll be able to see you in a new light."

"It isn't and she won't. In the meanwhile, because this will not be a formal interview, I have asked Torrance and Dixie Erskine to join me at the boathouses, where I happen to have business today discussing tide patterns, and where, as it happens, Torrance himself is also something of a fixture."

And if it's not in the office, there won't be a recording, at least, not a fully official one, so things can be said which otherwise might have to be denied.

"Someone else told me Torrance hangs out at the boathouses."

"It's part of his thing. He likes to play mechanic. I hear he's okay at it, but what he really likes is to be Frog Prince for the girls. The humble local kid in overalls who turns out to be the heir? He runs that a few times a summer. Bill lets him hang around, wipe himself with a greasy rag."

"What Bill?"

"Bill Tracey, Cal."

"Oh, for god's sake." Bill Tracey and Torrance know each other. Of course, they do. It's Shearwater. Everyone knows everyone, and Torrance is a bored kid with no sense of his place in the world and Bill Tracey looks fine in a bridge coat. A pirate captain. Now I really do need to go talk to him.

"What the hell have you got against Bill?"

"Every time I try to talk to him, he's not there. I don't know if he even has anything to tell me."

"Oh, Bill can tell you plenty, Cal. He is not a man short on conversation. I'll take you round to see him later—when you feel like you're drowning in sea dog, wave, and I'll fake an emergency."

"Not a problem. We authentic folks have a secret language."

"I realise, I should not have told you that. When Bill moved here twenty years ago he'd never been on a boat, Cal. He's not even as authentic as you are."

"It's in the blood, Tim, you wouldn't understand. Bill actually likes Torrance?"

"Who knows? He certainly seems to, but Torrance likes the Mahalo, and he's an Erskine. In Shearwater he pretty much gets what he wants."

"Except you're going to make him have a conversation he doesn't like."

"I am. Him and his mom who is unhappy with my meretricious investigation. We will sit in the damned ugly and uncomfortable little cafeteria they have there, and Dixie can enjoy what I take to be the first folding steel chair her ass has been in for nigh on fifty years, while I ask Torrance to tell me all about his relationship with the murder victim. Get Miles to lend you a cushion. Actually, get two."

I tell him I will, and he says to be there in a half hour.

I go down to the beach and look for Ricky and his sister but I can't see them. The Sleeper woman has moved from her lounger and there's someone else there now. I wonder, briefly, if she just got so angry she found herself and went home. Maybe that's how it works. Maybe I should stay here and just annoy these people into picking up their lives again. Preventing deaths rather than investigating them would be a nice change of pace—but if I wanted to do that I should have gone to medical school. Too late now.

Except: it isn't too late.

I'm looking out at the water and it's still today, but now it's also four years ago and Athena is smiling as she rests one hand on my chest. We're on another beach, a white one, and somewhere across the bay I can see dolphins. In twenty minutes, we'll be in the water, and ten minutes after that we make love on a towel, and she rolls over into the lunch basket and we can't stop laughing as the perfect, expensive picnic scatters around us. She pushes me onto my back and threatens me with crème caramel and grape juice as she takes us both over the edge.

And then into the water, and back to her, resting one hand on my chest, her face sandy and salt-streaked and serious.

"Being a Titan is hard," Athena says. "You know why?"

I look around at paradise. "I do not."

"I don't mean it's a hard life, Cal. I mean it's difficult to do well."

"Doesn't feel that way."

"Not yet. But it will, eventually, because there are no excuses any longer for not doing what you want."

"I think that's about being rich."

"It's the same, Cal."

"Not for me."

"Yes, for you. Almost anything you do will attract money, because you're a Titan. You can't evade that and there's no point trying. Banks will loan it to you, investors will offer it to you. People will give you free stuff just to walk by their store and be seen. If all you do is take whatever money you're offered at the rate they give it to you and invest it in Tonfamecasca shares, you'll be a millionaire ten times over by the end of the year. It's already happening. So, what do you want?"

I say I want her, and she laughs and says she wants that too.

And now on this different beach, I understand what she was saying. I don't have to do what I've always done. I made a choice, but I can unmake it now. If I want to stay here and aggravate the Sleepers until they wake up, I can. If I want to be a doctor, it's only a question of time. Lawyer. Oceanographer. Surf bum. Artist. Musician. Goat herder. Every path is mine for the taking, one after another or all at once, to the end or to some incomplete place before I change my mind and pick another, and even that serial defection would ultimately become a thing in itself. When I was at school, they told us that Athanasius Kircher was the last man who studied every aspect of human knowledge. After him, there was simply too much to contain in a lifetime. I could put that theory to the test.

I see Ricky among the Sleepers, holding his mother's hand. Still there. Apparently, I'm not annoying enough to create spiritual awakening after all. Scratch one vocation, leaving only all the others. I try to go to them, just to say hi, but now the Sleepers near me turn and look, and then they get up and block my way. They don't look at me or tell me to stop. They just stand there, like a wall, and I can't get in. They're not even all facing in the same direction. It isn't resolve, exactly, just presence. I remember Simmonds telling me on the very first day: don't interfere. I thought then he meant because it was rude. It just now occurs to me that it might be dangerous too. If I push them, will they fight me? Or will one of them just walk the kids to the water and hold them under until I go away? I honestly have no idea what these people are, or where they draw the line, except that in some way they're drawing it here, and now, in front of me, and I don't know if I can—or should—cross it.

I follow the path I'm on, between the sea and the sun loungers, twenty minutes to the boathouses and Tim Iverson's meeting with his angry ex.

The south beach trails off into rocks and seagrass, and just beyond the first layer of flat volcano basalt split by rain and tide into sugar-loaf chunks, there's the line of the harbour again, where Basu's office is, and the bobbing shanty that is the Shearwater fleet. The big dredger is there at anchor, a round-ended black centrepiece to the whole crowd, white and orange trim like a liner in a child's picture book. It's called *Ophelia*, and every second day it goes out into the channel with two jobs: to cut a clear line through the silt and debris that would otherwise choke the bay at its mouth, and to filter microplastic out of the water and bring it inshore to the Erskines for revision into synthetic flavours chemically identical to the ones that grow on green things in other lands.

Part of me wonders who named the ship; Ophelia is mostly famous for drowning.

There's a water gate at the harbour mouth to keep out the storms, each arm of the wall indented to allow the huge wooden blocks to be craned into place and protect the fleet from the battering of the sea. Still wood, not carbon fibre or anything more exotic, because the old ones simply haven't broken or decayed, and why replace something that looks set to outlast the industry it serves? The shallow fan-shape of water inside the wall is echoed in the Shearwater old town, the one-bed cottages and tiny townhouses, once famously bright coloured, now worn and salted to pastel, glowering down into the clear sea. The only public space in the old town is the weighing station for the catch; where every other place I've ever been has a market square, here the market is tomorrow's problem, and people meet at the water where worth is tallied openly and everyone knows if you're up or down. Except that in Shearwater, 'up' is mostly a memory.

At the far end are the boathouses, five in a loose row, with slipways for relaunching and cradles to draw the boats out of the water, to scrape off barnacles and weed, to recaulk and repair and refit beyond the reach of the most dangerous, most corrosive, most unforgiving environment within the planetary envelope: the pretty sea all the tourists come to dabble their toes in.

In between the third and fourth boathouse, there's a low stone building with a garish sign that says, "Coffee". I'm pretty sure that's not coffee by any Chersenesos reckoning. There'll be a metal pot full of grounds, sugar and eggshells, and they'll pour it off through a sieve and into a cup. Serve with black bread, pickles and—if it's after nine—vodka or raki. In other places I've heard it called policeman's coffee, because the white liquor is invisible and odourless on your breath, so a working copper on his beat might stop in for a winter warmer and have his sergeant none the wiser. Here it's just coffee, and anyone drinks it who wants to.

I walk around the edge of the harbour, wondering if I'll walk into my friends from the first day I was here. I duck my head so no one will recognise me, then realise how absurd that is, and walk on. The cafeteria door is open, drawing the brine and sulfur odour of the docks in with the cool air. Fans on the ceiling turn just to emphasise how much difference they don't make. And over in the corner, at a long table, Tim Iverson sits with Torrance and Torrance's mom Dixie, and the conversation is already not going well.

"You can talk to *me*," Dixie says, and Iverson says no, he can't, he needs it from Torrance.

"Well, I'm his mother."

"And he's twenty-eight years old, Dixie. There's no way he doesn't answer for himself."

In a lot of ways, Dixie Erskine would make a fine pair to Iverson. She's tall like corn, rippling with outrage and certainty, and has no intention to lie down and let anything happen to her son. Her resolve is the mirror to his, and they'd be appallingly perfect together: a new release of humanity leaving the rest of us behind. Like him, she's over a hundred and looks permanent, not so much born and renewed as printed on the world. And as for Iverson, he's every bit the scion she is, old and young at once—and carrying the same inevitability, for all he's set himself up as the counter to the Erskine writ. Sometimes you can't be the opposition without also being the thumb that closes the hand.

Torrance, meanwhile, looks scared of both of them, like a wooden ship at anchor right between the Cyanean Rocks. Their ancient youth is compressing him back into his teens, stripping away the decade which at his age is the difference between a man and a child. I realise we're all treating him like that, as if he has no sense of his own life, and yet, when that was me, I was fully confident of my agency and self. Is it the offset, or just ordinary time in the world that leads me to think he hardly knows who he is?

And how much brass does he need, in this insane moment, to sit between three Titans and try to hold the line on his own behalf? To even propose it and make Dixie wear it. I don't like the kid from first principles, but right now, for the first time, I'm finding a little respect for him.

I walk over and I don't sit down.

"Hi, Torrance. My name's Cal Sounder and I'm sorry I look younger than you but I was dosed in ICU because I was all kinds of dying and now I have resting babyface, but the thing you need to take on board is that they're both over a hundred years old and I'm still less than two decades from where you are. It just this second crossed my mind that you should be in charge of your own decisions, so here's my suggestion: let's you and me go for a walk while Tim and Dixie tear strips off one another, and you can tell me what you actually know. No lawyers and no recordings, no comeback. I want whoever killed Mary Ann Grey. I don't believe that's you and I don't much care about any of the other shit. And then we walk back over here and you work out what you want to say to Tim." Most of which is actually true, and as for the rest, well, that's what we in the profession call "a lie."

"Sounder . . . " Tim Iverson says in disgust.

"How dare you?" Dixie says. "That's against the law!"

"No, it's not. It might be if Iverson did it, but I'm not a cop. Also, this is Shearwater, and with due respect to Tim, nine points of the law is Martha. We can take it up with her whenever. Torrance?"

The kid gets to his feet. "You're the guy from five years ago? The Tonfamecasca guy?"

"I'm the guy from five years ago, anyway."

He takes a couple of steps towards me. Dixie starts to get up.

"Sounder," Iverson says, "this isn't what we agreed."

"It's not what you want but it is one hundred times going to go better than what you were going to do. Your judgement is off because of Dixie. So's yours," I add to her, "and I don't even know why that is. Stay here and deal with your unresolved sexual tension. Torrance and I will have a grown-up talk now."

Dixie huffs and Iverson sighs and collapses back into the chair, then takes off his jacket and passes it to her for a cushion. For a second she doesn't look like she hates him. We leave them as they are, and wander out of earshot, staying in sight of the table like toddlers. Torrance is holding a go cup of the cafeteria coffee.

"You drink any of that?"

"No."

"Wise man."

"I didn't kill her."

"I wasn't kidding. I don't think you did. But why do your family's security people think otherwise?"

"You said they were just setting me up."

"But they think you're good for it, all the same. Why you, when it could just be any poor sap?"

"Because I knew her."

"You slept together. More than once?"

"A few times. A lot of times, actually."

"Like sport sex or something more?"

"More." The word comes out in a whisper, and when I look at his face it's pale. When he turns his head there's a glint of water, and I realise there are actual tears on his cheeks. Oh. Torrance Erskine really liked this woman and he hasn't been able to say it out loud since she died. Is that why she didn't leave the Caffrey? So she could keep on being Ailsa Lloyd for Torrance?

"You were making a play for Ashley when I first saw you."

"She said no one could know." And she made it stick with him, so hard that he was faking it with Ashley even after Mary Ann was dead. Or just so deep in that strange place after death that he would absolutely have fucked someone to feel something, even if it was self-hate. Probably both, and he has no idea how to untangle them.

"She said I had to keep hitting on people, so that no one would figure us out." His voice gets quiet when he says the important parts, so I have to lean close to hear. Part of me keeps thinking it's a trick so that he can put a knife in to me, but it's not. It's real, and unrehearsed.

"She thought someone would notice?"

Which would mean there was someone close by with reason to care. Not Dixie, surely, and not Bail. Someone she knew was there, who had reason to be in her affairs. Now, if I knew who that was, I might have an actual suspect—apart from Torrance himself, who looks a whole lot better for the actual crime now that I know he was in love. And: in love with whom? Ailsa? Or Mary Ann? And just when and how much did he know?

"How'd it happen? You and her."

He looks away to remember and that reminds me of the Sleeper kid, Ricky. Sad eyes that ought to spark, and the weight of Titan business on shoulders that shouldn't have to carry it. Torrance is a rich boy, but seen from beyond the offset he and Ricky are interchangeable, and he's been made to live that every day of his life. "The first time was just what you said. We were at a party. I asked her and she said yeah. We left and we..." he shrugs, trying to find a way of saying "did it" that isn't actually those words. "Then... again and again and we got talking and... we had stuff in common. I liked her. She liked me. It... mattered. No one else knew her the way I did. And she knew me, too."

"Tell me."

But this new Torrance, who I guess is the underlying old Torrance, is an Erskine—and a real one. "Will you trade?"

"Trade what?"

"I want to know about being a Titan."

"You know a bunch of Titans. Your mother, for a start."

"That's family. It's not the same. And you were right. The other old ones don't talk to me. I think this is as many words as I've ever said to any of them."

"Then you should talk to Martha."

His eyes go wide, like I've suggested he burn down a church. "Like that'll happen."

"Don't ask. Go to her house. Sit on the beach and yell at the water until she comes out."

"That's so not allowed."

"Why is that, do you think?"

"I don't know."

"It's because it works, kid. And because she wants to know when you're interesting enough to go do it."

"Didn't you just screw that up by telling me?"

"Are you actually going to go?"

He hesitates, then shakes his head.

"Then I guess I didn't. Sure, ask me anything. But I want a proper answer from you. What was she like?"

If Torrance, nervous, is a change from the bratty kid on the beach, Torrance thoughtful is like a long-term patient finally getting out of bed.

"She was... older. Not like years, but experience. Things she'd seen. She had scars from fights. Like real ones. I think she must have had it tough. You know. As a kid and stuff."

"She ask you for anything? I don't mean money," because he's already bristling, ready to go.

"No. She said she shouldn't be doing it, but she wanted to. That I was the one thing in her life that was just for her. She said there was me and there was stuff she had to do, that she believed in."

"She ever mention the 1848?"

"Is that Bach?"

"Yeah. His famous opera about labour relations."

Torrance looks like he's actually trying to remember. He shakes his head. "Sorry, I'm not great at classical music stuff. Like, I know I should try to be? But I just like what I like. Which is guitar, mostly?"

He looks ashamed. Figure Dixie has views, or Bail does, or someone.

"And you called her Ailsa."

"In public."

"But?"

"She told me it wasn't her name. I said what was her real name and she said she didn't remember. Like she'd left it behind somewhere on purpose. I know it now, like everyone does." Everyone who gets access to in-progress police reports, which, yeah, in his life is pretty much everyone. I wait and let him say it out loud.

"Mary Ann Grey."

I wonder what it's like, learning your dead girlfriend's real name that way. I have to figure not great.

"So you didn't call her Mary Ann and you didn't call her Ailsa. How did that work?"

"She had me pick something for her, just between us."

He'll tell me the name if I ask, but it doesn't matter. He can have that much. Maybe he's even owed it, because this was real all right, one way and another, even if she thought it wasn't. Talk to anyone who works with undercovers: the real trouble starts when they get to carving out a space that isn't who they are as a law officer and isn't who they are as a crook: their special place where they don't have responsibilities to anyone.

And later, when it's quiet and there's time, I need to ask myself when I began subconsciously comparing Mary Ann Grey to a cop. In the meantime, Torrance is due an answer.

"Go on then, kid. Ask me about Titans." I figure it'll be sex. It almost always is. Athena, talking, back on that same white sand beach.

"What are the three motives for murder, Cal? You called it the Trinity."

"Sex, money and power. But they're not exclusive. Just the most common."

"Titans are money, Cal. You see that, right?"

"Yeah."

"We're also power, by the same token. Physical strength, durability. But also connection, proximity, resources, reputation."

"Yeah."

"So most of the time, Titans don't have to worry about those things, at least externally. Between ourselves we bicker, but killing another Titan is a no-go."

"I did it."

"You weren't a Titan then."

I nod.

"And then there's sex."

A Titan after the first dose goes on something of a tear. However old you are, you are not ready to be saddled with teen hormones generated at twice the baseline norm for a period roughly equivalent to human adolescence and young adulthood. Which is to say that Titans have a great deal of sex.

Athena's second rule: we are bigger than we were. We accept what we are, the scale of our bodies and our extension in time. For the first hundred years, take as many lovers from the ephemera as you can. Share them, adore them, grieve for them. Each one makes you more a Titan, adds to the patchwork beauty of your life. Accept them, too, for what they are: brief, splendid, and gone. After that, after the third dose ... who knows? That's another gateway, and the number of people who have passed through it is still only in the low hundreds. We'll have to make it up as we go.

The third rule is that I have to wear the suits when I'm working.

Torrance gets himself together. I'm waiting for one of the obvious ones, so I'm not ready when he says: "Is it worth it?"

I stare at him, wondering who suddenly put a deep thinker into the body of the jackass who couldn't handle Ashley's instructions about the light board. He needs to talk to Athena. I'm the guy who only just realised he could be a doctor if he wanted to, and she's looking forward into a journey of a thousand years. Of for ever, if she can make the technology happen, and you have to know she can. She's the smart one, not me.

I open my mouth to say something, and then the world turns upside down.

I see the plume of flame curl out of the fifth boathouse like a flower, red fire and black smoke expanding, the shockwave almost visible in the air, and I wrap my arms around Torrance and turn my back. A dog far bigger than even Bail Erskine's says "WOOF" and then we're flying. I see the window glass in the cafeteria buckle inward, hope like hell Dixie and Iverson aren't dead now, and my mouth finally catches up with the instruction I gave it before my feet left the ground to say, "What the—?"

We hit the asphalt and flames wash over us on their way someplace else, roaring and so hot it's like a turning on a spotlight and seeing everything in new colours. I keep my arms around the kid, my stupid big body on top of him and finally that extra twenty percent is good for something. I feel fabric crisp on my back and legs. But the suit doesn't catch fire and nor do I, it just feels as if I'm roasting, and all the hairs on my exposed skin wither away.

The flames pass, the wood of the cafeteria charred black and smoking, the heat now localised behind me at the boathouses, the sea air painful and sharp on where my hands and neck are already turning pink. Plus one ankle, where the trouser leg rode up. Scalding, not much worse than a sunburn, and painful, which is ideal because it means the nerves are fine, I'm just going to itch like a bastard tomorrow.

Iverson reels out of the cafeteria, gun in hand, the only person dumb enough to run towards the fire. He has one arm up to shield his eyes. He helps Torrance to his feet, then me, staring at my weird naked forearms and the charcoal that used to be a human place. He goes on towards the boathouse, feet skittering on debris, wrapping something around his face. I open my mouth to tell him not to be an asshole, he can't go into the building. The whole thing is coming down, and even it doesn't the roiling toxic smoke in the air will kill him so bad even T7 might not fix things.

"Holy shit," says Torrance. There's blood on his face, but not much.

And then, impossibly, someone comes out of the boathouse, hardly any more a person at all on one side of his body, the other side a bearded guy in overalls, living his every step towards us like climbing a cliff face, and screaming. I'd scream, too, if half of me looked like that. I can't believe the poor bastard is walking. More survivor's guilt: it would take what I got to save his life, and that's not on the menu, not even if I begged. There are lines Stefan won't cross, and this is one.

He comes towards us and his unburned hand rises. I figure it holds a saw or a scraper, but Iverson is faster. His gun comes up, level and steady, and his weight falls into his feet. Cop training, bedded in over decades.

"Drop it!"

The thing is not a scraper. It's a black plastic handset with a red button, like a movie prop, but I've seen them before in the real world, and detonators do look like that. Some of the construction models come in yellow and black stripes with rubberised handles, but on the whole, what you expect is what you get.

"Drop it!" Iverson says again, his voice getting tenser.

I'm not sure the guy can. Maybe he can't even hear, but Iverson doesn't have a choice about what happens next, and only a few seconds before it's time. He has to assume further explosives are in place and he can't know where. What just went off in number five was obviously premature, but where's the rest? Four, three, two and one? The cafeteria? Or somewhere else within a mile radius? A bank, a bar, a school?

Iverson waits as the man staggers another few steps and says something that might be "bastard". He might be looking at me, or Torrance, or Iverson, or he might be talking to his own corpse-half that won't stop slowing him down. Perhaps the first word was "stupid" and he had a partner back there who didn't check the current before placing the final charge. Iverson doesn't know any of that. He doesn't close his eyes. He says "drop it" one more time, knowing what's coming, and then he fires.

The first bullet takes the dead man in the head, the second and third go into the chest as he falls. It's backwards, but understandable. The reason you aim for the centre mass in the first place is that when you're terrified you get tense and shoot high.

The detonator skitters away and nothing else goes boom. I hold my breath, but we're okay, we're still okay, we're okay, and we're ... okay.

Iverson is on the phone, calling his team, calling emergency response. Doing the job.

Dixie comes out now, grabs Torrance, screams at me. Torrance screams back at her, and then she's hugging us both, her hands grabbing at her son, then at me, at the places where my skin is angry, where Torrance's is not. Thank you, thank you.

I don't know whether I'm more embarrassed than Torrance, but for a moment we have something in common.

I look back at the burning boathouse, and only now, late and late, do I see what it says over the door.

Mahalo Ltd.

And the boat sliding down the slip, on fire, is the *Evermore*, though not apparently for much longer.

I walk back into the cafeteria and go behind the counter. I turn on the water and sluice out as many cups as I can find, watching tiny diamonds of broken glass whisper into the drain.

In the distance I can hear sirens, but they're under water and everything's weird. Iverson's talking and I know what he's saying even if it sounds the same: *Cal, we have to move. There could be more of whatever the hell that was.*

In his face, and in my head: the image of the blue container, and Iverson's certainty that it was destined for the food plant, and mine that it wasn't. I look out towards Martha's Point, expecting another plume of fire, but as long as I wait, it doesn't come. There's nothing from the far side of the city, either, no column of burning vanillin. No thunder, and no screams from the beach. I look along towards the Sleepers, wondering if someone's cold enough to target them. Silence.

Iverson has his phone in his hand, the gun back in its holster now. He's called someone, giving orders. Evacuate, evaluate, respond. He looks windswept and competent, on top of everything. He won't feel it until later: the weight of having shot a man down, not knowing whether he had to. It won't matter that the guy was dying anyway. He says something in my direction and I shake my head. That makes my ears pop, agonising, and now that I can hear it's way too loud, but I'm back in the world. Iverson laughs, then starts to cough, dry and harsh.

"Drink this," I tell him. I fill a cup and pass it over. He tries to wave it off, then takes it and sucks it down. He gives me back the cup and doesn't look over at the man on the ground.

"You hear what he said?" Iverson asks.

"I thought it was 'bastard'."

"'You little bastard,'" Iverson murmurs quietly, one Titan to another.

"So not you or me."

"No."

"Might could have been anything. Anyone."

"Might could."

"You know who he was?"

"Oh, yes." He glances at me. "Longliner named Bill Tracey."

*

I've given my statement, such as it is, to Iqaluq. Iverson, being the shooter, can't investigate himself. Iqaluq turns out to be a hardass, with no compunction about asking the bad questions: do I think Iverson was right to pull the trigger? Did I also hear the words Iverson says Tracey said? Do I believe in what I saw go down?

I realise I should have expected this from Iqaluq, this painstaking granularity. She's a bomb cop, after all. She goes from beginning to end, looking for each piece as if she was picking it out of the walls. She won't tell me anything. I'm not a suspect, but I'm not in the job either, and this is the real deal now. I ask if the bomb is the same materiel we found in the blue container. She doesn't answer, but I see the confirmation in her face before she can stop it. She tells me to think carefully, let her know if I've missed anything out. She doesn't trust me, and by the numbers she's probably right. On another day, I might be hiding something, but this time I saw what I saw: Bill Tracey, half dead. I only wish I could forget it.

Now I'm walking up and down the beach, pounding the sand, and it's not working. In Othrys I'd be walking the long, grey streets between the high-rise towers, down to the treatment plant at Tappeny Bridge and along the water, staring across at the cold peaks on the north shore. I'd be smelling concrete and asphalt and the oil they use to cook fast food, the scent of herbal cigarettes wafting out of the Lacarte. I'd be lying looking up at the sky between the towers, scowling at Stefan's latest choices, his insinuations, his endless needling, pushing back and blaming him for everything that's wrong, finding to my disappointment that yet again he's not at the centre of things. Maybe he is, today. Maybe the fact that he has nothing to do with any of this is a clue, and he personally came down here and strangled Mary Ann Grey out of pure malice at the world, and dumped her carelessly because he doesn't give a damn, and then he finagled Athena into dropping my name to Martha so that he could watch me spin and spin. It's Titan thinking, like stress eating for the ego, nursing the idea that I'm the centre of the world.

I push it away, and look up along the beach to Martha's Point, then down towards the Sleepers and the Mahalo in flames, and that brings me back to Bill Tracey. I sit down in the spiky sand at the water's edge, with the Grand Erskine behind me, wrecked and beautiful with its empty windows and rich colours. Or is it already the Grand Nugent, and Doublewide hasn't had time to change the sign?

Bill Tracey has been here since the beginning. Fish Food told me to go see him, but I didn't because why would I listen to that guy. His name just kept on cropping, and I still didn't go see him it was always local colour. Local colour should have been reason enough, but I had my eyes on Mary Ann Grey and Torrance and Tilehurst, and some guy who looked good in a bridge coat wasn't enough to take the time. Now it turns out Tracey knew Torrance, who was stepping out with Grey, so maybe he even knew Grey. Hell, maybe Grey fell for Torrance at the Mahalo, the Frog Prince thing. And Tracey knew tides well enough that he could think he knew all the angles, and I have to ask myself: did someone put Fish Food my way? Was it, for example, Bill Tracey? If I'd gone to see him, would he have had something to tell me? Something to drop into conversation like it didn't matter? And if I go looking now, will I find it, or did it just get blown up and shot to death right in front of my face? What would Mary Ann Grey have told me, if I'd spoken to her before she died?

Who should I be talking to now, before they're gone?

Iqaluq won't have me anywhere near Bill Tracey's little fisher cottage on the southern bluff, and to be honest I wouldn't go in there before she does anyway. Meanwhile, the whole town of Shearwater is shocked into a kind of stasis by the noise and the reality of the bomb. Two of the shuttered boutiques on the waterfront have blown-out windows, and the pall of smoke rising from the Mahalo Boathouse and the *Evermore* in the water washes over the town, banishing the smell of vanillin and sending even the Sleepers up along the beach away from their sun loungers in a long, coughing tail of empty eyes. The men and women on the lonely benches, waiting for work, have the look of confusion you see on ordinary folk when the sky falls: they're pleased it didn't fall on them, but guilty because they aren't hurt and others just like them were, and confused because somehow the world has changed and they can see the cracks in it for the first time. I sit down next to two I've never seen before, a man in a straw hat with a handkerchief tied around the crown and a woman carrying a dog the size and colour of a litre bottle of beer.

"Hell of a thing. You folks okay?"

On an ordinary day they might not give me much of an answer, but today is a day of misrule and the givens are taken away. I have black dust in my pores that I couldn't get out with the beach water tap, and my suit has needles of metal still in the weave. I smell like accelerant and roast pork. That has to be good for something.

"You were there?" the woman says.

"Wish I could say I wasn't."

"Jesus."

The man takes off his cap and looks at the inside like there might be something written there that isn't washing instructions.

"I hear Bill Tracey died."

"He did."

"They're saying he was the bomber."

"I'm sure they're saying plenty. No one knows spit right now."

"Anyone else get caught in it?"

"I don't know. If they were inside the Mahalo, then yes. Or on the *Evermore*, most likely."

"I got friends on that boat."

"I'm sorry. I hope they're okay."

We sit there, all of us looking away from the world now and somehow down into the guy's hat. There are dried sweat stains on the band, suncream and nicotine. Finally, I take it away from him and put it on my head.

"How do I look?"

He laughs. "Ridiculous."

"Thank you, sir."

I pass it over to the woman.

"I'm not putting this horrible thing on my head." But she does, and the man says she looks fine. I think he means fine like excellent, because she almost blushes. I realise they were courting on the beach: love after baseline sixty, another thing Titans forget is real.

"You all happen to know where Sam Kyle might be this morning?" For a moment, the name doesn't fix. Then I gesture at my hands: "Fish Food."

The woman nods. "He involved in this somehow?"

"I don't think so. I just want to ask him about Bill Tracey. I been slow on this job since the beginning and I don't choose to miss any more doorways."

"The Star," she says. "The Swordfish won't have him no more. He gives you any trouble, you tell him Mabel Zakary says to behave."

I thank her, and head off down a side street, following her directions and wondering at the idea of the place you go to when they kick you out of the Swordfish.

The Star is a rough-edged cellar bar that smells of talc and stale beer. There's not even a pole, just the holes in the floor and ceiling where it got ripped out. Fish Food and his buddy have a table a couple of metres from the hole, well within what would have been wriggling distance. I have my hands in the air for peace before he even sees me, and when I drop Mabel's name he shrugs.

"My cousin's widow," Fish Food says. "She really tell you where to find me?"

"Sam, I'm not here to make trouble for you. I just want to know about Bill Tracey. You know what I do?"

"You're a gunsel for Tonfamecasca."

"Did you just say 'gunsel'?"

"I said it."

"Sam, I'm not offended by the word, though I am no kind of gunsel. I just don't think I've heard anyone use it in real life."

He sticks his jaw out, doesn't speak.

"So . . . I'm a private investigator. I'm also Athena Tonfamecasca's boyfriend, but I don't work for Stefan. Right now, I'm looking to find out who killed a woman named Mary Ann Grey, washed up on the beach some days back. You know about that because I told you."

"We heard," the friend says, when Fish Food doesn't answer.

"And it looks like now I'm also trying to figure out who blew up Bill Tracey and the Mahalo. So I don't know if any of that means much. I was just sitting on a bench with Mabel and her friend, trying on his hat."

Fish Food stares at me. "You put on that hat?"

I shrug.

"You're out of your mind, putting your head in that thing. Ain't that right, Ryan?"

The friend nods and now we're veterans together somehow, brothers of the hat. I don't know how that works. When a bomb goes off everything changes, everyone gets shaken loose. You don't make big decisions that week, maybe that year, or maybe you make the ones you don't have the courage for when fire isn't falling from the sky.

"Cal Sounder," I say, putting my hand across the table. It's bigger than his, and he stares at it as he takes it, and I make sure to give an Iverson shake, solid but light.

"Ryan," he says. "Galway."

"Hi, Ryan."

"So I came to town and you boys were almost the first people I met who weren't on a slab. You tried to send me to Bill Tracey. I didn't go because I got sidetracked, and now I'm thinking what would I have found out if I had?"

They look at each other.

"You think we knew Bill was into something?"

"I don't even know what I think any more. I found a bomb a few days back and I would have put money down it was never intended to be used. Now this. I got no idea. Your friend Bill kept on coming up but he seemed like a sideline. Area man looks fine in a bridge coat. Now he's dead and I feel like a fool. How old was he?"

"I guess sixty?" Sam says.

"But strong," Ryan agrees.

"Yeah." Both of them nodding. Figure Tracey for one of those annealed indestructible baseliners I used to think of as natural ageing done right.

"Strong enough to get us all into a fistfight with an Erskine Security man," Ryan carries on, rubbing his jaw like it still hurts. "But not strong enough to win it."

And there it is. I manage not to swear or jump up out of my chair. I tell myself to take it slow and maybe it's still nothing, and maybe it really is nothing, but that's crap because I know it's something, I know it all the way down to the soles of my shoes. This is why I'm here.

"How'd that happen?"

"The Erskine guy, he was sitting at the bar. Tracey went up for drinks. Then they were fighting, like two words and: bam!"

"And you all piled in?"

They both look like they want to say they were never here. "Not at first. But after a minute, honestly, Bill wasn't doing so well."

"Why not?"

Sam Kyle shakes his head. "Guy was a fucking monster."

Ryan shrugs. "We coulda had him."

But they absolutely could not, and Sam is telling me with his eyes. They never had one single tiny atom of a chance in hell, and Sam knows it because he is old enough to have seen that kind of thing once or twice before: Bill Tracey, sixty and a civilian, up against those too-fast hands and Jimson's body like a bank vault door, and when Sam and Ryan and some other sap piled in they were just more punching bags, and Jimson didn't so much as sweat.

Because it was Jimson. I don't even have to ask, but when I do, of course it was. And what the hell was Jimson doing here? It's one thing him coming out to tell me the score, but in the run of things the Swordfish is the kind of place that's definitionally beneath his notice. Nothing Erskine-related happens here. Company man, solo, at night-time in a longliner bar—you have to call that looking for trouble. Maybe that's it: Jimson just treating himself to the pleasure of beating a man down. You've got an ugly face. I don't like your bridge coat. I hear your sister has a frequent flyer program.

"Tracey tell you why it kicked off?"

"No, sir."

"You ask?"

"He didn't want to talk about it. Said it was old business, he never shoulda done it."

"He got family here?"

"Tracey? Naw, he ain't local."

I keep hearing that. Local but not; only lived here twenty years, practically a stranger. Fish towns, like Titans, take a long view. "What about things he liked to do? Places he'd go that weren't here? People he'd meet? Girlfriend, boyfriend, that kind of thing?"

"He'd go to the union house. He was kinduva pain in the ass about it."

"About what?"

"Said we should hang together. Like group up, not like hang out. The independent fisher boats, he said we oughta make a concern. He was tight with that Basu guy from the plant."

"How'd that go?"

"The other captains said we had a trade association, don't need no union."

"Sure, works great if you're a captain."

They laugh, but I can smell it now, like the burning boathouse on the wind.

"He just up and call in on Basu to talk about that?"

"Naw, they knew each other. 'In another lifetime,' he said. The way old people do."

Basu and Tracey. That ought to make a triangle with Lyman Nugent, ought to be a smuggling operation, one big enough to mean something, but Nugent says not. He's a liar, but I took that for true. Basu is from Tilehurst. Bill Tracey wasn't local. Mary Ann and Aloysius Grey.

I can smell it.

"What about the Erskine kid? How'd Tracey end up playing babysitter?"

Sam shrugs, and for the first time I see him looking like a real person.

"Torrance is okay. Like, he's an asshole everywhere except the Mahalo, but you put him in front of an engine and it's not the same. He's got the ear, he can hear when something's off in the drives just by listening, the way some can. Bill gave him a place to be himself. He was like that. Did the same with me and Ryan. Kept us in work when he could."

Ryan nods.

"What about the girl?"

"What girl?"

"The one Torrance fell for." I show him a picture. Sam puts his finger on her face like it's a thunderbolt.

"Ailsa?"

"Yeah, sure."

"Wait, she's dead?"

Sam Kyle, you are one slow-of-thinking son of a bitch. That is the first thing I ever said to you.

"Yeah. That's why I'm here. Originally."

"Aw, hell. That's the woman on the beach? They were good together. Better together than apart, by a mile. That's a goddam crying shame, is what that is—" Honestly it's starting to look like he might do the crying himself—but now his brain's working it seems like it won't stop. "Wait, you don't think Torrance killed her?"

Did Bill Tracey think so?

You little bastard.

But Tracey was missing half his head and the rest was burned and bleeding out. Who the hell knows what that meant, if Iverson's even right about what he heard. "I actually don't, but you see where folks are gonna ask. Her, now Tracey. Torrance is the third guy in the room."

"Naw," Kyle says again, and when he dries, Ryan steps in.

"They were nice. I mean, to other people. And together."

He flounders for a way to describe two young people filling the holes in one another's souls. He's probably all of two years older than Torrance, and hardly marriage material just yet a while.

Sam wants to know how it went down at the Mahalo, and I tell him what I told Iqaluq. They're both suitably impressed by Iverson taking the shot.

"Just like that?" Ryan says, miming a single shot. I tell him it was three.

"But I don't know about just like that. Pretty sure he hated it. But he did it, and without more than a breath to think it through."

They're both nodding like I've told them something they long expected. I wonder if Iverson's morning just settled a dozen bets: would he ever bring down the heavy end of the hammer, if he had to? Would he really shoot someone he knew? People always wonder that about local cops, and the answer is pretty much always yes, because in a small town, unless you're the wrong kind of cop entirely, by the time you've drawn your weapon your choices are pretty thin.

"You like Captain Iverson?" Sam says.

"I guess I do. There's not a lot of people I find easy to talk to." Him and me both, and I need to get some quality detecting time with Iverson after this. Something's tickling at my mind, that smell in the wind, the question I haven't asked, the memory I can't connect. When did it start? This feeling of something I should have seen already? I had two thoughts at once and I went the wrong way, meant to come back to the other and forgot. Mary Ann Grey. Bill Tracey. Rudi Basu. Torrance. I should have asked Basu about Torrance, but that's not it, and I still can. Why is my head full of the Roller? What would I have asked Tracey, if he was here, telling me this story? Tracey and maybe Basu, who knew him from way back. Way back when, exactly?

Or way back where?

Because right now I would bet the contents of Stefan's wallet that Bill Tracey was from Tilehurst, like Basu and Mary Ann

Grey. Like Simon Mirador and Dina, he lost people. He came to Shearwater and made a new life. A few weeks ago, he started a fight with Matthew Jimson, and today Tim Iverson shot him in the head—though be fair to Tim: by the time he drew his gun, Bill Tracey was long past putting on his fine bridge coat ever again.

I raise my glass to Sam and Ryan, and we drink in silence for a little while. I don't know that you could call it drinking together, but we're all in the same place thinking similar things.

Back at Celia's, I'm suddenly groggy and exhausted, every part of me aching. When a bomb goes off in front of you there's a time before and a time after, and the two are distinct, like the blast fractured a pane of glass in your soul, but it's the body that surprises you, over and over, with how much it soaked up and how much it wants to pretend it didn't. Fight and flight every which way and all at the same time, because bombs don't make sense to the terrified mammal inside. I can't help but dwell on the strange, hard border of the blast, the outer limit of destruction, like if someone had up-ended a pudding basin over the boathouse and scythed away the rest. Inside the circle, space became violent and strange, twisting matter into new shapes, bisecting human bodies but leaving their owners briefly alive. Outside, we were cut and buffeted, but not destroyed. Lines of power radiated, blowing out one window but leaving the next, ripping slates from the cafeteria roof but sparing the weathervane on the remaining half of the Mahalo. Explosive yield, Iqaluq told me, is unpredictable, and the path of explosions likewise, small factors in the land and the make-up of the bomb and the substrate changing how it behaves. Sometimes, Iqaluq said, you can be quite close and survive, while people further away get turned to jelly. It all depends. I asked her on what.

"Bomb gods," Iqaluq said. "Or maybe science. I don't know, Sounder. I just cut the wires."

Miles brings me the telephone: I asked him to call Sporty Jasmine for me. Far away in Othrys, the world is unchanged, unexploded. Things are still real there, where here, objects you would have thought of as solid are thin as mist. Way back when, that was actually a reason soldiers of the revolution used explosives: to demonstrate the transience of material things and shock the proletariat into a new understanding of physical production. Tony told me once. I wonder if she's ever seen this, if she lives on this far side of the bomb.

"I got blown up," I say to Sporty Jasmine. "How's your day going?"

"Not as exciting as yours. Your friend Iverson's on the news."

"How's he look?"

"Like a guy who shot a guy and got blown up."

"They show Torrance Erskine?"

"Cute little bastard. His mom's fucking terrifying."

"She is that. Iverson's sweet on her."

"Yeah, you can tell, even in the pictures."

"You think he's in with a chance?"

"He just arrested her son, so maybe: no?"

"He did?"

"I guess he had to. Sounds like Tracey said something that pointed the finger."

"I guess he did."

"You think it was for real?"

"I think . . . there's more ghosts here than the bottom of Othrys."

Mini Denton doesn't answer for a while like she's thinking about that. Figure she doesn't much like it.

"I spoke to Orhan," she says. "The money pouch is a dead end, he says can he keep it anyway?"

"No. It's money, not a puppy. What's he got?"

"You sound off. Are you sure you're okay?"

"No. I'm all kinds of fucked-up. I think I know what's happening and I hate it."

"Well, now you have to tell me, otherwise it's like a movie."

"No, because if I tell you and I'm wrong then in the movie I'm the asshole partner who was never really any good. You know what happens to that guy?"

"Pretty much the same as happens to the asshole partner who doesn't tell the detective about the vital clue he just uncovered."

"What did Orhan say?"

"He gave me an address. Says it's owned by the same outfit as the one you gave him, where the container was. Says he can't find out who that is, but maybe you can."

A trail, which I should immediately hand on to Iverson, even if I don't know yet that it's relevant. I get Mini to give it to me, then tell her to pass it to the cops via the tip line.

"They won't process a tip right now, Cal. It'll take a couple of days before they even start going through that pile."

Yeah. I tell myself Iverson has his hands full, that he said we'd follow our own leads and see if we joined up. Pretty obvious he wasn't thinking of this moment when we had that conversation.

When she tells me the address, I don't recognise it, but when I look it up, I do. The Old Lighthouse, on a one-lane track that barely has a number, let alone a name, backs onto Oliviera Close, in Sapolo, where Mary Ann Grey went once every week by cab. Where she very markedly did not go on the night she died.

"Tell Orhan he can keep the puppy."

"Okeedokey. You going to tell me now?"

"Now I don't know what to tell you. You should get down here. It's going to break loose."

"It already exploded, boss man."

"Yeah."

I'm still exhausted, like when you've been out in the cold so long that all you want to do is bathe and eat and sleep for days. I get into bed even though it's the middle of the day and close my eyes, and that's all I know for six hours straight.

I get woken up when Fallon walks into my room and tells me she's giving me a medical check-up.

"You're what now?"

"It's mandated. Put your role-play back in your pocket."

"What?"

"How many fingers am I holding up?"

"Three fingers and a thumb, smart ass. I'm not concussed. I'm sleeping. Was sleeping. I got blown up, did you hear?"

"Hence the medical check-up."

"You do dead people."

"I'm the official court medical specialist for Shearwater. I examine the living and the deceased according to the legal requirements governing their situations. Take off your shirt."

"No, I meant that insultingly because you woke me up. You do dead people."

"That's hilarious, I've never heard it before. Take off your shirt."

There's another joke I want to make, but I can't put it together fast enough and then the moment's gone, so I take off my shirt. Maybe a check-up isn't a terrible idea. Fallon stops kidding around the moment I start playing ball. Her gaze gets . . . I guess the word is "clinical".

She listens to my chest. I wait for her to notice the scars, before I remember I don't have them any more. T7 is a thief of memories. She puts her finger on my stomach where I got shot one time. "Pain?"

"No."

"Itching? Phantom wound?"

"No. It's just gone."

She shakes her head. "Freaky as shit. Put your shirt back on."

I do, and she has me take off my pants, walks around me looking for shrapnel.

"You should have needle fibres in your skin. All the others do."

"You got a scalpel in that bag?"

She nods, and I take it, run it across the pants lying on the bed. I go too far and the scalpel clips a little hole in the sheet without so much as a sound. Fallon picks up the pants. There's not even a mark.

"What the hell?"

"Working clothes." Athena was very clear about wearing them.

"Your work is fucked-up."

"Says you." I put my pants back on. "How am I doing?" I ask.

"You have no chance with me, Sounder. You're not my flavour of pie."

"That's totally inappropriate humour, Dr Fallon."

"From which you may deduce that the check-up portion of your day is concluded. You are in good health and you are discharged."

"I was blown up. I still have ringing in my ears."

"It'll fade in a few days."

"Can you do something about it sooner?"

She hands me a sticking plaster. "I thought you'd ask."

"Oh, ha ha." But I'm grateful, all the same, that she took the time to prepare a joke. "Hey, Fallon. You know Tracey?"

She nods. "Not well."

"You gonna be okay doing the cut?"

"There's nothing horrible in doing what I do. It's just the truth."

She holds my gaze, then walks out. I don't know how, but she knows I know something, and that I wasn't sure what I was going to do with it. But I can't do less than her.

I put on a different suit and I walk out along the Sapolo coast path like the tourists don't any more. The path must have been one time quite something: it runs all along the high hills south of the town and on and on above a glittering grey black strand. Go far enough in this direction and the only thing between you and the equator will be thousands of miles of empty blue sea, and from time to time a dredger rocking and groaning as it gathers in all the old sins. In some places the soil has washed away, and I have to climb up and around. Once I go all the way down to the beach and then back up, and the glass here is sharper than out front of the town, cutting into the soles of my shoes until the blades hit the woven ballistic lining and break away. And then I round a corner and the lighthouse is right there in front of me, a white concrete shoebox surmounted by a white tower. The lamp room is round, with blue trim and a wide window on the sea.

I try the handle, but there's no give at all. I move out around the side of the porch, hunting. The walls are dressed stone painted white and sealed, and the whole place feels solid and for ever. It might seem backwards, but Titans build temporary structures so they can tear them down when they're bored or when the occasion demands. It's only baseline humans who worship architectural permanence, the way you love someone who doesn't love you back. The lighthouse was made with centuries in mind, proofed against erosion and wind, and then the reason it existed simply blew away. Who needs a tall tower made of rocks, a lamp spinning on liquid mercury to light your way, when you have geolocation instead?

The first window is shuttered, and the next, but on the seaward side the rust has eaten through a hinge and the peeling wood hangs down at a drunken angle. Looking through into the front room I can see an oaken table and a high, old-time chair. Behind it on the far wall is a single framed photograph, a family group. Under it, draped over the chair, is a red sailing jacket: the kind Mary Ann Grey wasn't wearing the night she died. There's a laptop terminal in front of it, closed flat like a bible in a hotel room.

Everything I was expecting and hoping not to see. I'm older now than I used to be, so I don't break down the door; and I work for Martha, so I don't call Iverson. I slip away as if I'm the one who did something wrong.

9

I call Fallon and ask if the body showed any more bruising after I last saw it. Sometimes that'll happen. She says yes, and I tell her where, and she says yes again. Then I call Mini Denton and tell her what I want. She doesn't sound happy about it and nor am I. She tells me to be careful and when I say I will, she says no, actually be careful. When I say yes again she obviously doesn't buy it, because she does me dirty and calls Athena, who calls me.

"Is it bad, Cal?"

"I told Martha we pretend we can unbreak the vase, but sometimes all we can do is imagine how it fell."

"And this time?"

"This is one of those times and I don't much like it." I don't like it at all.

"Is it going to get worse?"

I don't answer because I don't want to say "yes" out loud, and she says as it happens she's had to cut the retreat short to deal with a problem in Chersenesos. We laugh about how multinational corporations are just so damn needy. It's not a big deal, she says, she just wants to be in town for a thing. She'll never admit the thing in question is me.

"Do what you have to, Cal," she says. "Just the big stuff. Let the rest take care of itself."

So I dial a new number that I don't want to. It takes a while to go through. Figure it's passing from one relay to another, handsets taped together in boxes bolted against the beams of industrial sites, one burner handing over to another, to another, to another, clones and false trails to fool scorpion masts and the like, and the best part is probably no one's looking.

"Hello, Mr Sounder," Dina says at last. "I must say I'm surprised."

I tell her what's about to happen, and she asks why.

"So that if I die, someone will kill the bastard."

"I'm sure your girlfriend would oblige."

"I'm sure she would, but it would hurt her and it'll make you happy."

She snorts. "This is how the structure sucks us all in. All the options serve its ends."

"I don't really care, Dina. I just wanted you to know. If I live, do you want to do some good in the world?"

"I already am."

"I mean in partnership. There are things that would make other things better."

"Mitigation is not the answer, Sounder."

"All or nothing?"

"All or nothing." Hard and sharp and pretty much what I was expecting.

I call Tony at the Lacarte. I'm telling myself I did it this way round because I believe she'll do the right thing, but now as I dial I realise it's because I'm scared she won't.

I hear the sound of drinks and glasses, and someone laughing, and then she comes on the line.

"Tony?"

"Cal?"

"If I say that there was a woman who was the child of some no-account red firebrand with heavy hands and she went the other road and got herself dead in a corporate power grab, what does that mean?"

"It means we failed her," Tony says, without hesitation. "That's on us."

"She was an elective enemy of the revolution."

"Matias already told you: socialism isn't Santa. Some asshole can call her a class traitor if he wants to. I don't see it that way."

"So we can bury her in a revolutionary grave?"

"Are you okay, Cal? You sound all kinds of weird."

"I'm fine. Just feeling old."

"You're not that much older than me."

"I am today."

She sighs. "We all know about days like that. Did you just call to ask me if we should forgive the dead?"

"I've solved this case and it isn't going to change anything. A lot of times it doesn't. I want to do something that will, but I don't know how. I don't even know where to start."

"So you're calling a friend."

"Someone who actually does things."

"I hate to break it to you, big guy, but that is how you start. Tell me."

"I need help. There are kids who need help."

When I say "help" my voice cracks a little bit. I bite down and get myself together. Ricky's fine, even if he is small. He was fine before I got here and he'll be fine tomorrow morning.

Tony says: "Tell me."

I tell her about the Sleepers, and the black glass sand, and I tell her about Ricky's shoulders and my jacket and the moon on the sea.

I wait for her to ask me again what I want, because I still don't know.

Tony doesn't ask.

"Stay on the line, Cal. Okay?"

"Okay."

A moment later, I'm talking to Matias, and I don't know what he's saying, not really, but it must be that he asks me questions, because it all comes out of me again. The boy's narrow shoulders, and the walking dead woman who still had enough in her to say, "come away". The throng of them, discarded and abandoned like the Grand Erskine and beautiful the same way: waiting to come alive again, if anyone cared.

"I thought someone on our side would see a beginning," I tell him. "It's the first thing that made me ask about my victim, about whether she was real. She walked past them and didn't get involved."

He doesn't remark on "our side" and nor do I.

"Cal, thank you," Matias says. "Do you understand? Thank you for bringing this to us. I know you had other options. We're on it now. It's a done thing."

"Please don't take too long," I say. In a month, the weather will change, and those blankets—and those shoulders—will start to look even thinner. I start to explain again, and Tony very gently cuts me off.

"Cal."

"Yes?"

"Catch your bad guy. We've got this."

On to the easy part. I see how the vase got broken. Now I just have to show everyone else.

I sit on a metal chair at one of the beach bars that just about opens by the boardwalk and wait, and after a while I see Ashley coming. She's flanked by two friends, all in summer dresses, but looking serious, like they're going to a funeral. She sits down at my table.

"Well, shit," she says. "You know how to make a mess."

"People always think it's my fault, but I just show up when things are messy."

She regards me for a while and I feel it, the moment when the tension between us goes loose. Athena would roll her eyes: you waited too long, idiot, and now the real world is here and you're not having any fun. Lesson learned, I swear, and yet I never seem to actually learn it.

"This is Diane," Ashley says, "and Chi."

"I'm Cal Sounder," I say. "I'm a private investigator." I don't often say that out loud.

Ashley's friends nod. Chi is older, late second half of the twenties. Diane is younger, maybe on her first job. I tell them I want to confirm something about Mary Ann Grey.

"I liked her," Diane says. "I didn't at first, but then I did. Was it bad, what happened?"

I mean: yes. It was the worst thing in the world. "I guess it was pretty quick." Lie. "But it wasn't good, you know. She was murdered, and she knew it was happening."

Diane flinches, and I feel like a ghoul.

"Do you know why?" Chi says.

"Yes." They wait for me to tell them, and I wait for them to realise I won't. "She had money," I say, like it's a question.

"Plenty."

"But she lived at the Caffrey."

"She said that was temporary."

"And Torrance was the only person she saw? Romantically?"

"Yes," Diane says.

Chi bobs her head one way, then the other: maybe.

"There was someone else?"

Chi wrinkles her nose: not sure. "I saw her walking with someone once. Wrong body shape for Torrance, more like a swimmer. They were down on the beach, he was walking sea side—like a gentleman, so she'd not get wet feet?—and just . . . you know how people walk when they're in tune?"

"Yes."

"Like that. I asked her about it later, and she laughed. She said Torrance didn't have anything to worry about."

I ask about her pets, and she looks surprised. Then we talk childhood for a while, and what it was like. She gets slower and calmer. Memory comes online, colours and scents. I ask her if the sea smelled different then from how it does now. I ask her if she remembers how it smelled the day she saw Mary Ann Grey walking with another man. I ask if she remembers Mary Ann's perfume, her sun lotion, her soap. Underneath the vanillin, her sweat on bright days, her breath when she was drunk and happy on the dance floor.

And then, when Chi is deep in memory, I ask her about the man; the length of his stride, his height versus hers, his hair, his gait. Was it someone she'd seen before, and if so, where?

I already know the answers, but she tells me anyway, and stares like I'm wizard when I fill in the blanks. You mustn't do that when you're gathering evidence for a criminal trial, but I'm not a cop, and I'll put money down this never goes there.

I burn time waiting for Mini Denton's call, and when it finally comes, the shadows are getting long on the empty beach.

She tells me I'm right. The lighthouse belongs to a shell company, which is owned out of an empty office, which is managed by a shell company, which answers to a lawyer. From Orhan's angle it's untouchable, but if you already know what to look for, you can unpick the knot from the other end.

It's an old shell, an old deception, and the tax records aren't as well hidden any more as maybe they should be, as maybe they would have been twenty years ago. Like Shearwater, there are cracks all through it, and the water's getting in.

It's almost closing time when I stop by the hardware store and pick up a handheld wire-seeker, one of those little orange doohickeys construction workers use so they don't drive a nail straight into high-voltage current and find themselves doing their next project for Saint Peter. This one has a robust, military look, camouflage stripes of green across the orange, as if I'm going to be hiding from snipers in a fruit bowl. I pick up a storm lantern which uses chemical glow sticks, and as much instant high-strength adhesive as he'll give me. Which turns out to be plenty, because junkies are a major customer demographic for him these days. I have to go back in for a disposable pen. I almost forgot.

It's a fine night for burglary: no moon, and plenty of rush and flow from the sea to cover any inconvenient noise. I've borrowed a car from Celia's: black, because the colour never goes out of style. The old lighthouse is a cool seven hundred metres along from the road, and it's different at night from during the day. Figure in wintertime the track is a freshet, and the fast-flowing stream has washed parts of the surface away in chunks, so getting to the property itself is like walking on a space rock. I have a glowstick in the lantern, one so deep into red it's almost invisible. It's what you use for this kind of work if you're old-fashioned enough to think night-vision goggles are ridiculous. It also doesn't stop you from hearing, or blow up bright if someone ignites a flare in your face.

The lantern lights my way just about my own height in advance of my steps, but the upside is that most humans will miss it even if they happen to be looking the right way.

The lighthouse itself is still stone and white paint, like permanence in a bottle. Someone valued that fortress defiance, and made it a place to inhabit: the most defensible summer house you ever did see. But the thing about people like that is that they hedge. They make plans even against their own fallibility, against the day.

I crank up the wire seeker and wave it along the wall, at the guttering above and the soil below. I listen to the whistle of the little orange box. I find two coins in the soft earth, and a cheap, pretty earring with coloured glass beads. Not Mary Ann's, that I know of, and I wonder if it's just dropped, or whether this is part of something else, some old, bad story no one has ever told. I keep moving along the wall, guided by the sound, and two metres further on there's a loud squeal: a metal downpipe, thick and cool in the night. I dial back the sensitivity on the box and run it up and down, and there behind the pipe, up above where a normal person can reach, on a rusty masonry nail, there's a key in a little plastic baggie, like cocaine for locksmiths.

I run the seeker around the edge of the door, and find alarm contacts top and bottom. I let myself in and wait to see if a siren starts to wail, but nothing happens. There are white dust sheets over most of the furniture, and the layer of dust on them is thick. I can smell woodworm and damp, and something scuttles busily away from the sound of my feet. You don't generally let your place rot and hold on to an alarm subscription. Besides, the man who owns this place wouldn't outsource work like that.

The shoebox at ground-floor level is a lounge kitchen in nautical tchotchke chic. There's an actual helmsman's wheel at one end, and peeping out from under a sheet is the side of a sofa in blue and white sailor stripes. The stove is old black iron, there's raffia on the floor. There's the red sailing jacket and the terminal right in the window where you can't miss them, and behind me the old picture, just enough to hint at a hidden truth. A spiral stair leads up, and that's where I go. Human beings in crisis head up, like monkeys into trees, and by the same token the intimate spaces of a house are usually on the upper floors, with the street level reserved for casual guests and trades. When SWAT flushes a building, there's always one guy crammed into a corner at the very top. Even quite sophisticated offenders do this: mammal reflex, involuntary stupid. We think of secrets in the cellar because we like to bury them out of sight, out of mind, but the truth is when it comes to it most people keep theirs close, in jewellery boxes and wall safes, folded into paperback books. Cellars are for bulk, for shelter against hurricanes, and by necessity for kidnap victims. Everything else—babies, treasure, porn stashes—gets hidden where we can put our hands on it, where intruders have to get past us to find it: bedrooms, offices, lofts. Towers.

The stair rail is cool in my hand, and something creaks as I climb. I'm a Titan, and it's just metal set into stone, old and by the sea. There's a puff of dust at one of the joins, white paint and mortar.

The next floor up is beautiful. I wasn't expecting it, because I was thinking about murder, but I should have known: the same long hall, but above is the opening to the tower, three mezzanine landings with little bedrooms hugging the high walls, all the way up to the light room, so that you can see to the very top. There's a sense of scale and possibility here, of a future.

The room itself is panelled in light wood, with a long dining table directly beneath the aperture, a glass wall with one return looking out to the endless sea, and even now, on this dark night, the water picks up the starlight all the way to the far horizon. At the other end, tucked into the stone corner, there's a writing desk and chairs, and that's the first place I start to look. I open the drawers but everything's old, no sign of modern life at all. Dried-out pens, ancient peppermints, a chocolate bar half unwrapped and put away again, now all but mummified by time. A sketchpad, and some halfway-respectable drawings: a pretty, austere mother with a winter smile, and what seems like a dozen kids. The father must be the artist, because there's nothing of him, just one study after another of growing children and pride. The clothes say decades gone, even if I didn't already know who they were.

I let the stairs take me on up the tower, to the mezzanine beds. Under mattresses and in cubbies I find a dozen old romances and intrigues, but still nothing I can use. A cache of boiled sweets, an envelope of first teeth, a broken watch strap and a garter belt in white. Marriage, and children, and the clock of time.

I go on up to the top, where in olden times there was the lamp, and it's a den with arrow-slit windows, and a telescope pointing out and away. I look through it, but it's just waves, no magic revelation.

Until I turn around, away from the view, and find the picture at long last: a portrait in the classic style. The thing I wasn't expecting is that he's short. He's just a little man, busy and hyperkinetic. I take a long time looking at the portrait, seeing the changes, the shifts, being sure I'm not mistaken, even though I know I'm not.

"I know you're there," I tell him, and for the first time, I hear him breathe.

"Hi, Mr Sounder," he says, that soft voice even softer in the dark, almost as quiet as the sound of his feet keeping position as I turn around.

I've been calling him Jimson, and thinking he was a basically a little fish, even though I knew he was more than that somehow. I even told Martha Erskine it wasn't about fingerprints or evidence, it was about inevitability—and here we are, inevitably, and this is the beginning of the end.

"Matthew Lidgate," I say, and I've barely finished the name

before the little knife flashes out of his jacket lapel, just where his daddy used to keep the same damn thing. It goes from my shoulder to my wrist like water running downhill. He draws it back across my stomach and up the inside of the other arm, then steps back to watch me die.

I look down at my expensive shirt, and I can feel the lines drawn on my skin, long and perfect down the veins and arteries, across the muscle of the abdomen. I'm an anatomical sketch. It hurts like hell, and tomorrow I'll have some really nasty bruises, but I'm not cut. Working clothes, of course. If Jimson gets his weight behind the knife, he can maybe drive through it, but he won't be peeling me like an apple with those clever little flicks of his wrist. If this was going to be a smart, pretty fight, I'd never have let him get close. I already know he's faster, better than me. His daddy insisted on training. I spent a long time learning to fight Titans before I became one, and I know how that goes: the commitment, the cracked ribs and broken hands, the black eyes and bruised bones. The days sleeping it off, stretching it out and going again, and he took all that on and asked for more. Much more than I ever did, because all I wanted was a hole card. Matthew wanted love and affirmation, and a kid who doesn't see much of them will do a whole hell of a lot for those things. If I let him make the running, I'm going to die.

But you have to know I'll cheat.

This isn't going to be a smart, pretty fight. Not a duel between men of purpose. Just me being what I am, and him being him, and we'll see how that goes.

I look at him, smooth and supple in the shadows, and wonder how I ever missed it, that avid shine behind the cool. The youngest of four sons, all of them lined up to be just like their dad, blooded at Tilehurst one by one like society hunters who take their first deer at fourteen. Aloysius Grey hurt his daughter so badly she joined the other team, but Alton Lidgate was smart enough to hurt his so they'd thank him instead.

I dip into my pocket and throw the wire-seeker at Matthew's

face—he looks just like his father when you see them side by side, like in the family portrait downstairs—and he barely moves; just enough to let it brush past him and shatter cheap against the stones around the fire.

"The way I figure, Matthew—you don't mind if I call you Matthew? The way I figure, Bail was looking for money to launder and you had money that was all dirty. That was where it started and it was good for both of you. If only you'd just left it there."

He comes in again and I hunch, like I've got boxer training and that's all. I throw a couple of jabs, then snatch my hands back when he waves the knife as if I don't know what to do about it. I throw a stupid, slow stamp, the kind fist-fighters learn when they're looking to go four-wheel drive, and only just get out of the way of a silver line heading for my eyes. Or, not entirely out of the way. There's heat on my ear, a sting like a shaving cut. It starts to throb. I play dumb, and hope like hell that's not exactly what I am.

"Hey, that was a good one! You want to try again? I read where Paris training is real dangerous for men like me, but right now you don't seem all that."

"Keep talking," he says. "It's fine."

So I do. "When you looked at what you had with Bail, you saw a way to get back in the game. The big table. The same scam your father tried, that he couldn't bring off. That's how you were going to be a bigger man. Create the crisis, then provide the law and order. Mary Ann Grey makes it look like there's a revolution coming, and you step in to save the day. Hooo man, did that ever get messy."

His feet hiss across the floor as he steps, and this time he catches me, not with the knife but with a shot to the floating ribs that's only just off target enough that I can take it. I let him see what it costs. He's wanted this since he saw me, never mind I was a pain in his ass. He just likes to win. Maybe he gets that from Alton or maybe it's all him. The expression of power is the feeling of breaking bone, the knowledge of injury on the other guy's face.

I give it to him, tempt him with it: my very real fear, the knowledge of how beaten I am if I can't change the game. I feint once, twice, and he leaves an opening only an idiot would believe. I step in to take advantage and he lands another hit to soften me up, then gets a grip on my arm and tries to run along it with the knife to find my neck. I ward him off, just, and blood flows again as the edge catches the back of my forearm below the cuff. More punches. I block what I can, which isn't as much as I'd like. Feel something pop where it shouldn't: cracked rib. Keep going. I don't let him see that, but he sees it anyway, goes for it again and I almost fall on him when it hits. We end up leaning towards each other like college wrestlers, the blade floating in front of my face, my fist in front of his, clenched with effort of holding it back. I misjudged him. Arrogant: Titan thinking. It hurts more when he hits me, and I was expecting it to hurt a lot. Those ribs are going to be a problem if he keeps hammering on them. But if it wasn't like that then this wouldn't work. If he didn't think he could win, I wouldn't believe I could beat him, and now this is where I wanted us to be. Everything else was appetiser: this is where one of us turns out to be wrong. Keep talking. Don't smile.

"It all got away from you. When are you going to wake up to the fact that this a lousy plan?"

"You're so full of shit," he murmurs, like it's actually news. He jerks us around in a circle, the knife slewing close to my eyes. He wants me to smack at his nose, but to do that I'd have to straighten the arm, and then he'll have a lock. It's what everyone says about fighting to the death in an abandoned seafront property—dislocation, dislocation, dislocation. Split second choice: go for it or don't, but if I don't he'll get the lock anyway if he just moves his weight right. He knows that's the option, and he knows I have to try. It's an endgame moment.

I don't go for it.

Instead, I squeeze the fist in front of him as hard as I can, and the tubes of superglue that I palmed from my pocket when I threw the wire-seeker rupture into his face and all over my hand. Matthew makes a kind of bark. This kind of adhesive stings like a fucker, but that's not his real problem. I don't want him thinking ahead, so I grab onto him and we swing around and around. The glue landed high and right; his left nostril is mostly clear, and a bit less than half of his mouth. He's still worrying about his eye because that's what hurts, and his training doesn't like him being all caught up with my body weight advantage. Priorities: get loose, get vision back. Not panicking, but not thinking it through. He blinks hard: once, twice, and then the third time the lid stays closed, glued shut. He lands a couple of punches. They hurt and I don't care. They're not strategic. He's trying to buy time.

File under: things Matthew Lidgate does not have.

I waggle the hand on his neck and feel skin stretch and follow, feel the tendons and blood vessels underneath. He feels it too, and now he's working on making some distance, but how? All the disengages they teach in combat classes tend to assume your opponent is gripping on. Matthew's only option here is to rip my hand away, which means pulling off a chunk of his own skin over some fairly big arteries. In pure physical terms it's hard to get the leverage, but deciding to do it when you've never imagined having to: even harder. Matthew spends his time thinking about winning. He has never asked what it would feel like to have his eyelid stuck to the surface of his eye, or how to tear his own skin off on purpose, because no one does that.

He wants to puke, but with his nose sealed, if he does that there's a good chance he'll choke. He clamps down and swallows: vagus nerve reset. I squeeze again, spill the rest of the adhesive onto the floor between us. Fancy footwork is about to get much harder. We're not dancing now, we're not clever. This is about weight and power and who's a bigger bastard, and he's outclassed in all three.

Matthew weaves the knife back and forth, trying to punch it into me, trying to slice at my face, but I keep jamming him at the elbow and I've got the reach. I have to hand it to him, he's in terrific cardiovascular health. Maybe sixty percent airflow at best and he's still upright, still fighting. Better do something about that.

"You're done," I tell him. "I won, you lost. Let's talk."

He tries to gut me. It's pretty much what I'd expect. I've pissed him off, he's at a disadvantage, but hardly helpless, and his ego is bruised. He wants a quick score to set me back, so he drives the knife straight at me, low and fast to make a hole in the weave. I twist, feel the point snag in my shirt, punch through and scrape a shallow line across my skin. If I'd got that wrong, the blade would be in my abdominal muscles, opening them the way you open an envelope. But my body's not where he wants it to be. Athena will be angry with me for getting cut, and it hurts, but being a Titan I'm developing a strange relationship with injury: if it doesn't kill me I can just put it right back the way it was. I don't even have to have scars if I don't want them. What's pain if it doesn't mean anything?

And he's made another mistake. I pull on the hand that's still glued to his neck and drive my forehead into his face, then again, and one more time. My bones are twenty percent thicker than a baseline human's. T7 doesn't just make you big, it makes you solid. Plus I'm getting the left side of his face, his mouth and nose. He sucks air through the mess, and doesn't get enough. He tries again, and then again, and I see him get it.

I'm not knocking him down. I'm choking him out.

Matthew Lidgate goes wild. Slapping, slashing, punching, and all of it weak and off-target and a waste of oxygen.

File under: things Matthew Lidgate does not have.

He comes at me again, slow like a drunkard at the end of the night, like Bill Tracey just before Iverson pulled the trigger.

I think about Simon Mirador and the video; the kid with the fever in his face. I think about twenty years ago, sitting on the couch with Athena and watching the worst thing I'd ever seen play out on TV. I think about hitting him the way that makes me want to, a big hero haymaker for the knockdown.

Then he falls over on his hands and knees. He says something indistinct and tries to get up.

Here's how I see it, and what I need Matthew Lidgate to confirm for me: I think Mary Ann Grey worked for him from day one. I think she hated her lying, violent father and his pious bullshit so much she went all in with the other side, and if you blame her for that then maybe you've got more in common with Dina and less with Tony. Mary Ann Grey wasn't protected by the people who owed it to her, and she chose her own path. It was a lousy choice, but it was the only thing she ever had that no one could take from her. Until Torrance.

One way and another that path ended with the last of the Lidgate Company, and with the man who called himself Matthew Jimson, after the weed. When Bail Erskine went looking for money that wanted a bath, he found a willing supplier in a dead felon looking for a new face, and thought himself clever. Lidgate repaid him by sending Mary Ann Grey off on her travels, playing the same old game he did before: stir up the appearance of revolution so that the bosses get scared and buy in to the Lidgate way. Get that money out of escrow and put Jimson on the board, and little by little it wouldn't be the Erskine Company any more, it'd be the new shell for Matthew Lidgate, and praise the Lord of riot, for he shall rise again. Every step she took before Shearwater was to confirm her legend: angry working firebrand. The bomb in the blue container was always supposed to be found, and I played right into his hands when I showed up at Erskine Hill and said Martha was the target.

All that is the easy part, just another dumb corporate scam. Maybe Matthew Lidgate is more dangerous to the people around him than Bail or Martha, maybe not. He's a monster, but maybe that just means they have better impulse control, or better janitorial.

I look down at the monster on the floor, and I wish that hadn't been so easy. I get the disposable pen from my pocket and flick the ink tube out onto the floor, then put the empty shell between his teeth so he doesn't suffocate while we wait.

Sporty Jasmine arrives an hour or so later, courtesy of New Rafiq. She lets herself in to the lighthouse and looks around. "This isn't what I was expecting."

"What were you expecting?"

"More moose heads and gold leaf, less chic maritime. This is practically cosy."

"Bad guys like comfort, too."

She checks Lidgate's head and frowns at me. "You didn't clear his airways properly."

"I didn't want him all frisky and awake."

She tugs at the superglue in Lidgate's nose, but it's stuck fast. "Oh, shit, Sounder, did you do that?"

"Hey, it's just like eosin."

"It's really not."

She hunts around and finds a pair of small scissors, cuts through the plug so Lidgate can breathe easier. Then she washes his face with warm water and soap until his lips open. Figure that's not a comfortable process, but it seems like luxury travel to me, for a guy like him. We don't do the eye because according to the instructions on the adhesive packaging that's strictly an ER procedure at this point and Sporty Jasmine has standards. We prop him up in a chair so we can talk.

Finally, his good eye opens.

"Why did you kill Mary Ann Grey?" I ask him.

"I didn't," Lidgate says, and he won't move from that, no matter how many times I ask. I keep asking anyway.

"Can I get a drink?"

"You've got a drink."

"It's water with a straw."

"Hydration is important in your situation."

"I mean a real drink, Sounder."

"Don't make like we're friendly, Matthew."

"Did you meet Kathleen Walker?"

"Yeah."

"Did you like her?"

"No."

"Then we got something in common."

"Mary Ann Grey."

"I didn't—"

"I beat you, Matthew. I won."

And deep down, Matthew believes that when you win, you get

prizes. Or maybe he's just scared. I'll work with either. He tells the Mary Ann Grey story from the beginning: bad dad, dying mom, no place to call her own. A liquid ton of anger and the desire to belong somewhere, all bouncing around in a sarong and deck shoes.

"I walked her through a dozen jobs, man, and she made a mark on all of them. Iverson would have gone back along her history, found all that, the container. Perfect 1848 bullshit. I paid her with Bail's money, that was the best part. Discretionary security budget, keeping the Erskine Company safe from whatever the fuck, doing industrial espionage, taking care of the family. I told him not to ask what it was for and he practically doubled it. His fucking mouth was watering. You give a guy like that sight of dirty tricks, they get hard so fast it's shocking. Like if you're doing bad things, you must be real important."

"Who were the men in the container?"

"What men? Jesus, there were no men. Just three pairs of shoes, Sounder, and a spitball. I rolled the barrels in myself, put the bomb parts together, Mary did the pamphlets. She said they were her dad's from the basement. I thought they were awful, man, but they were authentic. Did you not know all this?"

Yes. "No." Because now he's talking, I want him to keep feeling smart. I want the truth, or lies I can pick open.

"I really hope you had some of it, because I'd hate to think you just lucked out."

"It had too many moving parts, Matthew. You only had to be unlucky the once."

"Oh, I was unlucky more than once."

"Bill Tracey."

"I didn't kill him either, you know."

"Worked him over pretty good."

"That was different. I was drinking, okay? Just . . . I just wanted to go someplace where people drink and don't look one another in the eye. Where you can sit in the fucking corner and hate yourself for an hour and . . . everyone else is doing the same. So I picked a bar at random and went in. Suddenly this guy's in my face, all 'I know you, you bastard you bastard, I recognise you!' Like, come on! Alton Lidgate is dead. Everyone knows that. There's not even pictures of my dad when he was this age, not like that. How the fuck does Tracey know it's me? But he knows, and he will not let go. 'Bastard bastard bastard.' So." He shrugs. "I just got pissed off."

"You've got a temper."

"Everyone's got a temper. Mine is just fine. I'm a bit more effective about expressing it when I lose my shit is all. But look, see? All of them alive."

"But he recognised you."

"Not properly. He thought I was my dad. And he woke up embarrassed in the morning because Alton Lidgate is dead. Come on, you never met someone who looks like someone? He came and found me, we had a laugh about it. Parted as friends, I swear."

"Like Mary Ann Grey. You parted as friends too."

"That was nuts. Mary—who's, like, the hardest hardass—Mary meets some kid in a cabana on the beach and suddenly it's all different. Everything's changed. It's true fucking love and she doesn't know whether she can do this any more. I just didn't know where to put my face."

"So you killed her." Tell me you did, so I can go home.

"Again, not me. I offered her the sweetest bribe: stay with the programme, you and Torrance get out from under Bail, and you share the centuries. She was all for it. I'm— I was going to say reformed, but actually I'm the same asshole, I just learned something."

"You've been on a journey."

"Yeah." He looks down. "Tilehurst ... we did bad things, Sounder. Real bad. But ... the most of it was Kathleen Walker. She loves the blood. Just ... loves knowing people died."

"Bullshit."

"Yeah, fair enough. We killed a city. Still blows my mind, you know?"

"You said it was Kathleen."

"It absolutely was, but I didn't say I wasn't there. Are you going to ask me about my pets now?"

"Sure, tell me about your pets."

"I had a puppy, my dad shot it. I think that's why he bought it in the first place."

"Is that true?"

"Yes. Mary Ann Grey. That's what we were talking about. So, then the next thing I know she's dead on the beach."

"How did you pitch it to her?"

"What?"

"How did you pitch your deal? Stick with me, displace Bail, blah blah. Did you take her out to lunch? Walk along the beach? Or go someplace secluded?"

"Walk along the beach? Sounder, is that how you think this shit gets done? Have you ever even read a spy novel? You don't walk down the beach with your handler. Jesus. We didn't meet the whole damn year after I brought her in. She had a one-time pad—do you know what that is?"

"Code book. Random numbers."

"That. Exactly. She wrote to me, we had a system, I wrote back. No fucking covert lunch dates. It was a tight operation, is what I'm saying. Then . . . this. She gets strangled. That's a rage move, right?"

"Most times. Or a pro wanting it to look like one."

"I wouldn't go there myself. You know why?"

"Because you get a shitshow like this."

"Because you get a shitshow like this. Some flatfoot like you shows up and now here we are. Fuck. Can I get that drink? There's a bunch of old Scotch in the cabinet."

I turn to the cabinet and he's up, out of the chair so fast I barely have time to blink. He's not after me, he wants Sporty Jasmine, and the thing in his hand is that razor blade, palmed from his belt. He's reaching out for her, uncoiling, and I'm too far out to stop him.

I see the back of his head break and fly away before I hear the shot.

Matthew Lidgate hits the ground slowly, and makes a sound like pudding.

Mini Denton puts the gun back under her arm.

"Asshole," she murmurs.

"Yeah, he was," I say.

"I'm not talking about him, Sounder. Did you tie him up with fucking taffy? What the fuck is wrong with you?" She lunges at me and beats my shoulder, and I put my arms around her because I don't know what else to do. It seems to work. She stops hitting me and goes still, just standing inside the circle, head lightly touching my chest.

It occurs to me that she's never killed anyone before.

So now, at last, I call Iverson.

There's a part of me that wants to stall, work out the angles, and there's another part that says I should give Martha Erskine the heads-up.

But Iverson is right here, and he's a friend.

He and Iqaluq come in together and we let them go upstairs, and the incident guys in their moonsuits go up a while later. I tell Iverson I was driving by and saw a light. He asks why I hadn't told him about this place, and I ask Mini if she called it in like I said. When she says the tip line sent her a confirmation, he looks sidewise at me like I'm gonna hear about it later, but not now. The razor in Lidgate's hand says a lot, but it's who he is that shuts down any urge anyone has to ask hard questions. Sure, they'll test our story, because that's the law, but not so hard as they might. There's the red sailing jacket right there, and the terminal. There'll be more, I'm sure.

"That's quite the collar, Cal," Iverson says.

"It's not really a collar when they're dead, I guess."

"Call it a solve, then. Hey, you got there before I did."

"I'm sure you would have done it if I hadn't."

"You tell your client yet?"

"Yeah. I still need to tie up a few loose ends. Bail's in it up to his ass, so it has to be right."

"Take your time, Cal. Let me know if you need anything. Files, backstory. I've got the financial team in Laedecker running the numbers."

"I'll send over what I have."

"I didn't get your money guy's name. He does good work—I might want to use him."

I think of Orhan working for the legitimate law, and laugh. "I'll send over what I have."

"Oh, sure, you just want to keep on making me look bad in my own town."

"That's actually why I came. The money's nice and everything, and of course who doesn't love solving murders and getting blown up, but it's the opportunity to fuck up your day that really closes the deal."

"Har dee har."

"Tim?" Iqaluq calls out.

"Here," Iverson says.

"Main bedroom," she calls again. "I found something."

When we get there, Iqaluq isn't touching it, and one of the technicians is taking photographs. Coiled up on the base of the bedside lamp is a thin line of gold chain, with stupid pendant tags hanging off: a rabbit, a four-leafed clover, a bikini and a heart.

"I have to think that's Mary Ann Grey's bracelet," Iqaluq says. "Fallon will be able to tell us for sure."

I look down at the little thing on the nightstand, and think of Matthew Lidgate just now lunging for Mini Denton, and Alton Lidgate twenty years ago, off the hook in Tilehurst.

"Damn," Iverson says. "Good spot. I missed it."

"Yes," I agree. "Great spot."

And there it is: Lidgate was my guy, all along. I can go tell Martha, take my fee and go home. I really want to, but like I told Iverson: loose ends. Mary Ann didn't go to the lighthouse the night she died, so why are her things here, just waiting for us to find them? If Matthew Lidgate killed his own agent, why did he do it so badly? What was he so angry about that he got hot under the collar and dumb for that long night?

Sporty Jasmine books into the room one floor down at Celia's and instantly complains she can hear me stomping around up above, so Miles moves her to just along the hall; a smaller space, but it has a floor-to-ceiling picture window. We camp out in front of the view and eat Chinese food from cardboard boxes, and I watch to make sure she actually has something. Her appetite seems okay. I'm looking for flashbacks, combat stress. It can happen to anyone, but by the same token it can just not. Maybe she'll be fine.

I get her to tell me what it was like being young Sporty Jasmine, before Mac Denton, before meeting me. She says she liked it okay, but it was boring, and her love life was a revolving door of also-rans.

"And now?"

"Now it's a fucking desert, Sounder, but it's all mine. Every last cactus and tumbleweed and scorpion is mine."

After a while she falls asleep, and I carry her to the bed and lay a blanket over her. I tell Miles I'm going out for a walk and to call me if she wakes and needs anything.

I quite like Shearwater, I realise, in the hot salt lunchtime of a summer afternoon, with Mary Ann Grey's murderer cooling next to her in Fallon's work room. I buy an ice cream at Dansen's, one of the ones I used to hanker after when I was nine years old, before I ever knew what mortality was, or heard of T7; before Alton Lidgate was even a thing in the world. Not that nothing bad ever happened back then, just I didn't have to deal with it. I get two more ice creams for Ricky and his sister and carry them down to the Sleeper beach fast, before they melt.

When I get there it's not how I remember. Dijkstra, the fisherman turned cop, is arguing with two big guys in flannel workshirts, telling them to get lost, but behind him there's a hive of people coming and going with bottled water and food and clothes, and the parking spaces the beach traders use are all filled with big, sturdy RVs.

All along the sand there are ordinary people just sitting down and talking to the Sleepers, and not all of them are still staring into space. Ricky's mom is standing at the edge of the water with her hands held to her face and a trim, muscular woman propping her up as she heaves tears and vomit into the shallows. When they turn, I see Tony, and her eyes bright over a warrior's grin. She waves: "Cal!"

"Hi, Tony."

Dijkstra breaks off and steps around the flannel shirt guys, and I realise who they'll be before they turn: both Costanza brothers, running interference while the Lacarte Community Union expands the definition of that middle word to include the wretched of the Shearwater strand.

"Jesus fuck, Sounder, is this you? Some fucking Titan intervention, is that it?" Dijkstra scowling over his notebook.

"Watch your mouth," Marto says. "Titan, my ass. Do I look like a Titan to you?"

Marto Costanza is a natural 190 centimetres. The correct answer isn't going to help anyone. I put my hands up.

"It's not me, Dijkstra. This is real-people stuff. Look at it, man. Just . . . stop for a second and look."

Dijkstra does. A narrow clerical man four metres away turns slightly on his lounger and looks him dead in the eye. "Water, please," the guy says.

Dijkstra stares for a moment, and then a smile lights up his pug face. He looks around and finds an urban communist with a box of cassava plastic bulbs full of water. He's in a hurry now, like he's the thirsty one, like he's been waiting all along for this moment.

"You mind?"

The woman shakes her head, and Dijkstra grabs a handful and kneels down in the dry black sand, passing them one by one into the meagre, emaciated hands. "Fuck are you waiting for?" Dijkstra says to all the bemused communists. "Get the fuck on with it. Help these people. That's why you came, isn't it?"

Marto looks thunderous, but Matias laughs and claps him on the shoulder. "Another convert," he says.

"Bullshit," Dijkstra tells him. But he's still smiling, still looks like he just left a decade by the side of the road.

I look around and find Ricky a few paces off, and I hand him the melting ice cream. The girl appears from nowhere.

"I never got your name," I tell her, handing over the other.

"Hannah," she says.

We sit and look out at the waves.

"Your mom looks better," I suggest, and Ricky nods.

"Everyone is," he says.

"Oh, good," Hannah says, around the edges of the ice cream. "You found her other friend."

I nod and say yes, telling myself I don't know what she means, kids say things that don't make sense, and then I feel his hand on my shoulder and I see the relief in his smile.

"Wow, it's a good day, Cal," Tim Iverson says.

"Yeah, Tim. It's a good day."

We're all sitting in Martha's water room celebrating. This must be the strangest group of people I've ever seen under one roof, although it's not really a roof now, rolled back to let in the air, and the great glass panels are folded away so that we're in a kind of deck garden that washes into the sea.

On a swing set under a fern is Zoegar, wearing a summer suit that must still be way too hot, representing Nugent Holdings, and unofficially checking Bail Erskine's statement for bullshit at Martha's request. In the loose shadow of the same trees are the Costanza brothers, because Martha very much approves of what's happening with the Sleepers, and the latest addition to my top ten things I never expected to witness was her splashing in the shallows with half a dozen kids and their newly awoken parents, talking schools and scholarships and jobs, and arguing the pros and cons of Ujamaa with a bewildered Matias, who is now in danger of being the best-funded socialist bar owner in the world.

Watching Bail make his apologies to Martha was midway between someone falling on their sword and a schoolkid getting raked over the coals for a poor attendance record. All the hard edge and bluster in Bail dealing with people lower on the ladder evaporated as he faced his own boss with cap in hand. Martha brought in Rudi Basu and told him to Bail's face he could have everything in his latest set of proposals, made Bail nod it through right there, then after Basu sashayed out she told Bail he was paying the difference personally. That could last for ever, if she decides to keep him alive through multiple doses. It depends on how Martha calculates interest.

Dixie stands alone by a bookcase, her eyes occasionally flicking to Iverson like there's something she wants to say. He's already noticed, and he's smiling more than I've ever seen. Torrance is here too, sitting in the corner with Ashley, scared and confused and for the first time looking like a kid becoming a man. I stare at him until he makes eye contact, and try to will him to stand up and say something, anything, to make Martha take notice. Maybe it works, because he does, and then for a moment I think he's got nothing else.

"I'd like to apologise," Torrance pronounces after a moment. "I haven't been much of anything up to now. I feel stupid, because I fell in love with a woman I barely knew and she turned out to be a liar, but Cal says she was trying to be something else, because of me. Or, I guess because of us. Cal says that part wasn't a lie. So I'd like to be something else, too, and I'm open to suggestions as to how. I don't mean to interrupt, I know there's more important stuff going on, but I won't get a chance again soon to say this to this many people who might be able to tell me where to start, and I didn't want to miss the moment."

He sits back down, and everyone exhales, because it may have been too earnest and too much, but it was a solid thing, and worth the time it took. Even Martha takes a second or two to glance at the boy and see him for the first time, and whatever she sees is interesting enough that she gives him a little nod.

So now it's all coming to a close, happy endings, and then I have to do my thing.

Seraphine can tell something's off. She keeps checking on me, obviously concerned that I've got something bad in my pocket. Mini Denton knows too, and she's pissed because I won't tell her. She thinks it's some big, splashy nonsense that'll make some kind of statement, but all I have is regret, and a feeling of having stood in the path of the obvious until it ran me down.

Iverson, with Dixie watching, gets up to round it all off, take the detective's bow. He is the police captain, after all. He told me he has to live here. So I let him explain to the great and the good how Matthew Lidgate was running Mary Ann Grey as an agent, how she wanted to quit, and he killed her; how Bill Tracey recognised him, and then realised what had happened and was going to tell the cops.

And now I can't sit still any longer.

"That's my problem, Tim," I say. "Matthew Lidgate didn't kill Mary Ann Grey."

I get to my feet as Iverson turns towards me, and he looks so damn tired, just like I feel. "It's a good case, Cal."

"It isn't bad."

"It's good." He's asking me a favour, friend to friend: please, believe. "It's all there. Alton Lidgate's youngest, twenty years on, running the old game on Bail Erskine. He killed Mary Ann for being in love with Torrance and Tracey for knowing who he was. It's a real good case."

"Naw. It's just not bad. Matthew said it before he died: what kind of superspy takes their agent for a walk on the beach? That's amateur hour. They had all those dead drops and clever cut-outs, shell companies and fake ID. The Sleeper kids saw her with a man. Not Torrance, and not Matthew. Martha actually told me who it was, I just wasn't listening hard enough."

Now he looks me in the eye, and he's just as broken up as I am.

"Shit, Sounder."

"You said it, Tim."

I stare out at the sea, out beyond Martha's deck. There's no horizon line, just a perfect elision from water to sky. Some kind of ship at anchor is hovering next to a white cloud.

"See, I was slow on the uptake. It's because no one really understands age any more. The kids saw you with her and they thought you were her other boyfriend. Not old but not young, they said. I figured that for the handler, so I thought Lidgate. Then Martha said Mary Ann Grey was with someone here at the party that night. She said Mary Ann had a fight with one of the beautiful children and I thought Torrance, why wouldn't I? Hell, Tim, you're a hundred years old. But to Martha? We're all the same. Just kids."

"Yes, we are," Iverson says. He's still looking out at the impossible ship. There's just the two of us now, in all the world, surrounded by people and all alone.

"See, that's the thing. She's not wrong. We are kind of the same. I just got this way and I'm still learning how. Athena's thought about it a lot, and I wasn't sure she was right, but she is. All the weight of time . . . no one can carry that alone, and you can't ask but one person to carry all of it for you. You need family and partners and lovers and friends. But you . . . You're just Iverson, the police captain, day in and day out, for however long you live. In twenty years you'll be young again, and still dancing the same dance with Dixie, or not dancing at all. Until you met Mary Ann Grey. That is what happened, isn't it? You just got to talking on the beach one evening, and again, and again. And suddenly there it was. Friends."

He doesn't say anything, and for a moment I wonder if I've got this wrong, if somehow he's like Martha, walking and dreaming at the same time. Everyone else is very quiet, staring. I don't know if they think I've gone crazy or they're looking at Iverson and seeing what I see. I don't take my eyes off him, and no one speaks.

"Cal?"

"Yes, Tim."

"We weren't lovers."

"I know."

"She was my friend, you're right. The first I've made in . . . oh, such a long, long time. Until just this week when you came along. Two in a few months. I must be learning something, right?"

"I guess you are." Though honest to god, I have no idea what.

"She was funny, did you know that?"

"No. I never met her."

He brushes that aside, like, of course I didn't, he'd killed her by then, but that's not the important thing. "She was so funny. Like funny bones funny, the way some comics can't say anything without making you laugh. It comes from anger, I get that, and pain and life. All that life in such a short time. That was Mary. She was that kind of funny."

I picture Iverson laughing, then double it: Iverson convulsed, tears running down his face, unable to stop, and Mary Ann Grey leaning on him, trying to catch her breath. Sitting somewhere on the grey shingle between the Grand Erskine and the Sleeper beach, alive and talking about nothing, having the best time.

"She was my friend," Iverson says again, and this time I can hear the horror in it, how much he hates every part of himself now, and always will.

"She liked you too."

"Yes."

"You and Torrance, both at the same time. You both changed her mind about things. Love with him, and—I have to imagine you were kind of like a dad, Tim. I don't want to put you in a box. I don't think she even knew that's what it was, because . . . how would she?"

"I wondered about that. I even asked her. You're right, she didn't know. Said she didn't want to. Friends, she said, and I said: of course. She told me all about Torrance. How he was sweet and dumb and pretty, but deep underground there was something real in him, and she couldn't see how it got there, how growing up in that world could possibly have let him find the real one. She was serious about him. She wanted to do it all right, live differently. Afterwards."

His voice is breaking, and I don't think he knows it yet, but he's about to cry. When that happens I won't get anything more from him.

"She tried to read you in, didn't she? To what she and Matthew were doing."

He nods.

"I can see how she might. Here's you, you're a shirt-tail Erskine and a real law man in a corporate town. She was young and smart and just naive enough to think you'd be sympathetic to the proposition: put Bail down, raise up Matthew, and get a chair at the table. 'Come on, Tim, they don't value you, they don't know you like I do. You and me together, we can take on the world.' Like that. Hell of a plan, when you look at it. Hell of a redemption story for everyone. The son of Alton Lidgate takes control of a Titan family concern with the daughter of Aloysius Grey. The sheer brass. Stefan would have eaten it up. He loves winners and turnarounds."

Iverson nods again, raises his hands like a little child standing over a broken vase, half-curled into fists: *I didn't mean to, I broke it because I was angry, it's not my fault.*

"She lied to me," he says.

"She lied to everyone, Tim. She wasn't really trying to. She just needed to be someone new. She and Torrance had that. She wanted the same feeling for you. New day, old sorrows and hurts washed away. She thought you'd want that too. And maybe you would have, but it was all such a damn shock, I guess."

Money. Ideology. Compromise. Ego. Every damn one of them at the same damn time. The wrong pitch, perfectly wrong, to Iverson, who has found his place, the perfect fit for who he is, with the one gap in his armour: that dawning awareness of being a man alone, compressed into a space that's ever more too small. And first she shows him a way to be more, the same way Athena sees: friends and new worlds not over the top of what you are, but growing out and out into the new. And then she says: I am not what I told you. I want to tear down what you have. Join me on the other side of the looking glass.

"I was so angry." Out loud now, and the hands again, up and down at his sides. "I went from being a man with one friend in the world to being alone again. I couldn't see. I couldn't breathe. When I could . . . "

When he could, she was out cold, and he thought she was dead. He put her in the boat and sank her, still alive. Down past dreaming Martha, into the dark.

"If you'd known she was still alive, would you still have put her in the water?"

Iverson takes one long look at the missing horizon and then down to somewhere else. "Yes," he says.

"And Bill Tracey?"

He nods: details. "Oh, him. The frame, for Lidgate, of course. Tracey would have told you who he was if you'd just talked to him. I kept pushing you together and you wouldn't go. In a proper investigation, Tracey would have led you to Lidgate and the name would have given you the lighthouse, with Mary Ann's stuff all over it. Done, and done. And he knew I knew her, anyway. Torrance must have told him. So . . . "

He shrugs, then turns around, and I think for a moment he's going to swing at me. Maybe he'll barge past all of us and go on the run, a gangster in an old movie laughing at the world. Behind and to my left, I can feel Seraphine moving ever so slightly, and I wonder how fast he'll die. I realise I don't want him to. He was my friend. The man I thought I knew never existed, and perhaps I don't much like this new one, but that doesn't mean he has to be erased. Turns out that's where we differ.

"Come on, Tim." Come where? Do what? I have no idea. Go to jail, be a bad example, a fallen hero. But that's what time is for: to pass on out of impossible situations into new ones.

He shakes his head. "I have to go now," he says.

"Go where? You can't just leave, Tim. You understand that, right?"

"Yes, Cal. I can."

He turns, slowly, and walks down to the water, to the sea.

"Tim—"

I reach out after him but I feel something warm and inevitable take my arm, big, gentle fingers strong like the hoops on a barrel. Martha is holding me in place, her huge head looking down at me and her expression absolute: No.

And I realise I don't control what's happening here.

Iverson slips into the sea and I think he's smiling, maybe at me, maybe Martha, maybe Dixie. He turns away and steps down. He doesn't start to swim, just drops, using that density of bone, falling the way Mary Ann Grey fell, down into Martha's depths. I can see him land on the bottom in the clear water before he walks a few more steps and drops again into the endless dark. Part of me hopes he'll struggle before he disappears, even if it's just the body refusing to go quiet. If that happens then I can dive in and get him back. If he shows the slightest sign of changing his mind, maybe Martha will let me go.

But he never does.

ACKNOWLEDGEMENTS

Thanks are due, to—

Clare, of course, without whom just none of it is possible.

Clemency and Thomas, who make the world anew for me each day.

My brothers, Stephen and Simon, who continue to teach me things by magnificent example.

Patrick, who always believes and always knows what to say.

Olivia, who patiently but enthusiastically makes it all real.

And all our respective collaborators, teams, fellow conspirators and partners in crime.

Thank you.